PENGUIN TWENTIETH-CENTURY CLASSICS

# THE PRUSSIAN OFFICER AND OTHER STORIES

David Herbert Lawrence was born into a miner's family in Eastwood, Nottinghamshire, in 1885, the fourth of five children. He attended Beauvale Board School and Nottingham High School, and trained as an elementary schoolteacher at Nottingham University College. He taught in Croydon from 1908. His first novel, *The White Peacock*, was published in 1911, just a few weeks after the death of his mother, to whom he had been extraordinarily close. His career as a schoolteacher was ended by serious illness at the end of 1911.

In 1912 Lawrence went to Germany with Frieda Weekley, the German wife of the Professor of Modern Languages at the University College of Nottingham. They were married on their return to England in 1914. Lawrence had published *Sons and Lovers* in 1913; but *The Rainbow*, completed in 1915, was suppressed, and for three years he could not find a publisher for *Women in Love*, completed in 1917.

After the war Lawrence lived abroad, and sought a more fulfilling mode of life than he had so far experienced. With Frieda, he lived in Sicily, Sri Lanka, Australia, New Mexico and Mexico. They returned to Europe in 1925. His last novel, *Lady Chatterley's Lover*, was published in 1928 but was banned in England and America. In 1930 he died in Vence, in the south of France, at the age of forty-four.

Lawrence's life may have been short, but he lived it intensely. He also produced an amazing body of work: novels, stories, poems, plays, essays, travel books, translations, paintings and letters (over five thousand of which survive). After his death Frieda wrote, 'What he had seen and felt and known he gave in his writing to his fellow men, the splendour of living, the hope of more and more life . . . a heroic and immeasurable gift.'

Brian Finney took his first degree at Reading University, studying under Professor Frank Kermode, and his PhD on D. H. Lawrence's shorter fiction at Birkbeck College, London. After twenty-three years at London University Centre for Extra-Mural Studies, where he became a senior lecturer in literature, he moved to Southern California in 1987, where he has been an adjunct professor at UCLA, UC Riverside, USC and Cal State University, Long Beach. He is the author of *Since How It Is: Samuel Beckett's Later Fiction*, *The Inner I: British Literary Autobiography of the Twentieth Century* and a Penguin Critical Study of *Sons and Lovers*.

John Worthen is advisory editor for the works of D. H. Lawrence in Penguin Twentieth-Century Classics. Currently Professor of D. H. Lawrence Studies at the University of Nottingham, he has published widely on Lawrence; his acclaimed biography, *D. H. Lawrence: The Early Years, 1885–1912*, was published in 1991. He has also edited a number of volumes in the authoritative Cambridge Lawrence Edition whose texts Penguin Twentieth-Century Classics are reproducing.

D. H. LAWRENCE

# THE PRUSSIAN OFFICER
# AND OTHER STORIES

EDITED BY JOHN WORTHEN
WITH AN INTRODUCTION AND NOTES
BY BRIAN FINNEY

PENGUIN BOOKS

PENGUIN BOOKS

Published by the Penguin Group
Penguin Books Ltd, 27 Wrights Lane, London w8 5tz, England
Penguin Books USA Inc., 375 Hudson Street, New York, New York 10014, USA
Penguin Books Australia Ltd, Ringwood, Victoria, Australia
Penguin Books Canada Ltd, 10 Alcorn Avenue, Toronto, Ontario, Canada m4v 3b2
Penguin Books (NZ) Ltd, 182–190 Wairau Road, Auckland 10, New Zealand

Penguin Books Ltd, Registered Offices: Harmondsworth, Middlesex, England

First published by Cambridge University Press 1983
Published in Penguin Books 1995
1 3 5 7 9 10 8 6 4 2

Filmset by Datix International Limited, Bungay, Suffolk
Printed in England by Clays Ltd, St Ives plc

# Contents

## Note on the Penguin Lawrence Edition

D. H. Lawrence stands in the very front rank of English writers this century; unlike some other famous writers, however, he has always appealed to a large popular audience as well as to students of literature, and his work still arouses passionate loyalties and fervent disagreements. The available texts of his books have nevertheless been notoriously inaccurate. The Penguin Lawrence Edition uses the authoritative texts of Lawrence's work established by an international team of scholars engaged on the *Cambridge Edition of the Works of D. H. Lawrence* under its General Editors, Professor James T. Boulton and Professor Warren Roberts. Through rigorous study of surviving manuscripts, typescripts, proofs and early printings the Cambridge editors have provided texts as close as possible to those which Lawrence himself would have expected to see printed. Deletions deliberately made by printers, publishers or their editors, accidentally by typists and printers – at times removing whole pages of text – have been restored; while house-styling introduced by printers is removed as far as is possible. The Penguin Lawrence Edition thus offers both general readers and students the only texts of Lawrence which have any claim to be the authentic productions of his genius.

# Chronology

1885     David Herbert Richards Lawrence (hereafter DHL) born in Eastwood, Nottinghamshire, the fourth child of Arthur John Lawrence, collier, and Lydia, née Beardsall, daughter of a pensioned-off engine fitter.

1891–8     Attends Beauvale Board School.

1898–     Becomes first boy from Eastwood to win a County Council
1901     scholarship to Nottingham High School, which he attends until July 1901.

1901     Works three months as a clerk at Haywood's surgical appliances factory in Nottingham; severe attack of pneumonia.

1902     Begins frequent visits to the Chambers family at Haggs Farm, Underwood, and starts his friendship with Jessie Chambers.

1902–5     Pupil-teacher at the British School, Eastwood; sits the King's Scholarship exam in December 1904 and is placed in the first division of the first class.

1905–6     Works as uncertificated teacher at the British School; writes his first poems and starts his first novel *Laetitia* (later *The White Peacock*, 1911).

1906–8     Student at Nottingham University College following the normal course leading to a teacher's certificate; qualifies in July 1908. Wins *Nottinghamshire Guardian* Christmas 1907 short-story competition with 'A Prelude' (submitted under name of Jessie Chambers); writes second version of *Laetitia*.

1908–11     Elementary teacher at Davidson Road School, Croydon.

1909     Meets Ford Madox Hueffer (later Ford), who begins to publish his poems and stories in the *English Review* and recommends rewritten version of *The White Peacock* to William Heinemann; DHL writes *A Collier's Friday Night* (1934) and first version of 'Odour of Chrysanthemums' (1911); friendship with Agnes Holt.

s *The Saga of Siegmund* (first version of *The Tres-
ser*, 1912), based on the experiences of his friend, the
Croydon teacher Helen Corke; starts affair with Jessie
Chambers; writes first version of *The Widowing of Mrs.
Holroyd* (1914); ends affair with Jessie Chambers but
continues friendship; starts to write *Paul Morel* (later *Sons
and Lovers*, 1913); death of Lydia Lawrence in December;
gets engaged to his old friend Louie Burrows.

1911     Fails to finish *Paul Morel*; strongly attracted to Helen
Corke; starts affair with Alice Dax, wife of an Eastwood
chemist; meets Edward Garnett, publisher's reader for
Duckworth, who advises him on writing and publication.
In November falls seriously ill with pneumonia and has to
give up school-teaching; *The Saga* accepted by Duckworth; DHL commences its revision as *The Trespasser*.

1912     Convalesces in Bournemouth; breaks off engagement to
Louie; returns to Eastwood; works on *Paul Morel*; in
March meets Frieda Weekley, wife of Ernest, Professor at
Nottingham University College; ends affair with Alice
Dax; goes to Germany on a visit to his relations on 3 May;
travels, however, with Frieda to Metz. After many vicissi-
tudes, some memorialized in *Look! We Have Come
Through!* (1917), Frieda gives up her marriage and her
children for DHL; in August they journey over the Alps
to Italy and settle at Gargnano, where DHL writes the
final version of *Sons and Lovers*.

1913     *Love Poems* published; writes *The Daughter-in-Law* (1965)
and 200 pp. of *The Insurrection of Miss Houghton* (aban-
doned); begins *The Sisters*, eventually to be split into *The
Rainbow* (1915) and *Women in Love* (1920). DHL and
Frieda spend some days at San Gaudenzio, then stay at
Irschenhausen in Bavaria; DHL writes first versions of
'The Prussian Officer' and 'The Thorn in the Flesh'
(1914); *Sons and Lovers* published in May. DHL and
Frieda return to England in June, meet John Middleton
Murry and Katherine Mansfield. They return to Italy
(Fiascherino, near Spezia) in September; DHL revises *The
Widowing of Mrs. Holroyd*; resumes work on *The Sisters*.

1914     Rewrites *The Sisters* (now called *The Wedding Ring*) yet
again; agrees for Methuen to publish it; takes J. B. Pinker

as agent. DHL and Frieda return to England in June, marry on 13 July. DHL meets Catherine Carswell and S. S. Koteliansky; compiles short-story collection *The Prussian Officer* (1914). Outbreak of war prevents DHL and Frieda returning to Italy; at Chesham he first writes *Study of Thomas Hardy* (1936) and then begins *The Rainbow*; starts important friendships with Ottoline Morrell, Cynthia Asquith, Bertrand Russell and E. M. Forster; grows increasingly desperate and angry about the war.

1915    Finishes *The Rainbow* in Greatham in March; plans lecture course with Russell; they quarrel in June. DHL and Frieda move to Hampstead in August; he and Murry bring out *The Signature* (magazine, three issues only). *The Rainbow* published by Methuen in September, suppressed at the end of October, prosecuted and banned in November. DHL meets painters Dorothy Brett and Mark Gertler; he and Frieda plan to leave England for Florida; decide to move to Cornwall instead.

1916    Writes *Women in Love* between April and October; publishes *Twilight in Italy* and *Amores*.

1917    *Women in Love* rejected by publishers; DHL continues to revise it. Makes unsuccessful attempts to go to America. Begins *Studies in Classic American Literature* (1923); publishes *Look! We Have Come Through!*. In October he and Frieda evicted from Cornwall on suspicion of spying; in London he begins *Aaron's Rod* (1922).

1918    DHL and Frieda move to Hermitage, Berkshire, then to Middleton-by-Wirksworth; he publishes *New Poems*; writes *Movements in European History* (1921), *Touch and Go* (1920), and the first version of 'The Fox' (1920).

1919    Seriously ill with influenza; moves back to Hermitage; publishes *Bay*. In the autumn, Frieda goes to Germany and then joins DHL in Florence; they visit Picinisco and settle in Capri.

1920    Writes *Psychoanalysis and the Unconscious* (1921). He and Frieda move to Taormina, Sicily; DHL writes *The Lost Girl* (1920), *Mr Noon* (1984), continues with *Aaron's Rod*; on summer visit to Florence has affair with Rosalind Baynes; writes many poems from *Birds, Beasts and Flowers* (1923). *Women in Love* published.

1921    DHL and Frieda visit Sardinia and he writes *Sea and Sardinia* (1921); meets Earl and Achsah Brewster; finishes *Aaron's Rod* in the summer and writes *Fantasia of the Unconscious* (1922) and 'The Captain's Doll' (1923); plans to leave Europe and visit USA; puts together collection of stories *England, My England* (1922) and group of short novels *The Ladybird*, *The Fox* and *The Captain's Doll* (1923).

1922    DHL and Frieda leave for Ceylon, stay with Brewsters, then travel to Australia; he translates Verga. In Western Australia meets Mollie Skinner; at Thirroul, near Sydney, he writes *Kangaroo* (1923) in six weeks. Between August and September, he and Frieda travel to California via South Sea islands, and meet Witter Bynner and Willard Johnson; settle in Taos, New Mexico, at invitation of Mabel Dodge (later Luhan). In December, move up to Del Monte ranch, near Taos; DHL rewrites *Studies in Classic American Literature* (1923).

1923    Finishes *Birds, Beasts and Flowers*. He and Frieda spend summer at Chapala in Mexico where he writes *Quetzalcoatl* (first version of *The Plumed Serpent*, 1926). Frieda returns to Europe in August after serious quarrel with DHL; he journeys in USA and Mexico, rewrites Mollie Skinner's *The House of Ellis* as *The Boy in the Bush* (1924); arrives back in England in December.

1924    At dinner in Café Royal, DHL invites his friends to come to New Mexico; Dorothy Brett accepts and accompanies him and Frieda in March. Mabel Luhan gives Lobo (later renamed Kiowa Ranch to Frieda; DHL gives her *Sons and Lovers* manuscript in return. During summer on ranch he writes *St. Mawr* (1925), 'The Woman Who Rode Away' (1925) and 'The Princess' (1925); in August, suffers his first bronchial haemorrhage. His father dies in September; in October, he, Frieda and Brett move to Oaxaca, Mexico, where he starts *The Plumed Serpent* and writes most of *Mornings in Mexico* (1927).

1925    Finishes *The Plumed Serpent*, falls ill and almost dies of typhoid and pneumonia in February; in March diagnosed as suffering from tuberculosis. Recuperates at Kiowa Ranch, writes *David* (1926) and compiles *Reflections on the*

*Death of a Porcupine* (1925). He and Frieda return to Europe in September, spend a month in England and settle at Spotorno, Italy; DHL writes first version of *Sun* (1926); Frieda meets Angelo Ravagli.

1926    Writes *The Virgin and the Gypsy* (1930); serious quarrel with Frieda during visit from DHL's sister Ada. DHL visits Brewsters and Brett; has affair with Brett. Reconciled, DHL and Frieda move to Villa Mirenda, near Florence, in May and visit England (his last visit) in late summer. On return to Italy in October, he writes first version of *Lady Chatterley's Lover* (1944); starts second version in November. Friendship with Aldous and Maria Huxley; DHL starts to paint.

1927    Finishes second version of *Lady Chatterley's Lover* (1972); visits Etruscan sites with Earl Brewster; writes *Sketches of Etruscan Places* (1932) and the first part of *The Escaped Cock* (1928). In November, after meetings with Michael Arlen and Norman Douglas, works out scheme for private publication with Pino Orioli, and starts final version of *Lady Chatterley's Lover* (1928).

1928    Finishes *Lady Chatterley's Lover* and arranges for its printing and publication in Florence; fights many battles to ensure its despatch to subscribers in Britain and USA. In June writes second part of *The Escaped Cock* (1929). He and Frieda travel to Switzerland (Gsteig) and the island of Port Cros, then settle in Bandol, in the south of France. He writes many of the poems in *Pansies* (1929); *Lady Chatterley's Lover* pirated in Europe and USA.

1929    Visits Paris to arrange for cheap edition of *Lady Chatterley's Lover* (1929); unexpurgated typescript of *Pansies* seized by police; exhibition of his paintings in London raided by police. He and Frieda visit Majorca, France and Bavaria, returning to Bandol for the winter. He writes *Nettles* (1930), *Apocalypse* (1931) and *Last Poems* (1932); sees much of Brewsters and Huxleys.

1930    Goes into Ad Astra sanatorium in Vence at start of February; discharges himself on 1 March; dies at Villa Robermond, Vence, on Sunday 2 March; buried on 4 March.

1935    Frieda sends Angelo Ravagli (now living with her at Kiowa Ranch – they marry in 1950) to Vence to have DHL exhumed, cremated, and his ashes brought back to the ranch.

1956    Frieda dies and is buried at Kiowa Ranch.

John Worthen, 1994

# Introduction

The twelve stories printed in this collection were written between 1907 and 1914. They constitute Lawrence's first published collection of short stories and were chosen by him from a much larger number written by 1914. During these seven years Lawrence made astonishing advances in his handling of narrative fiction. It is impossible to see the full extent of those advances from the stories as printed because Lawrence repeatedly revised and rewrote the stories as his ideas about the nature of fiction rapidly evolved over this period.[1] Nevertheless, a reader of this volume can reach a pretty good idea of the revolutionary changes that Lawrence effected in his short fiction during these crucial seven early years. Within that span of time he transformed himself from an imitative late Victorian writer to a leading member of the emergent modernist movement.

Two of the earliest stories (the original versions of 'A Fragment of Stained Glass' and 'The White Stocking') were written for a competition in the *Nottinghamshire Guardian* in the autumn of 1907. At this time Lawrence was a 22-year-old student at Nottingham University College who the year before had started writing his first novel, *The White Peacock*. As Janice Harris has shown, all Lawrence's early stories (including the first version of 'The Shadow in the Rose Garden') set his fiction alongside that of his late Victorian English predecessors.[2] The stories tend to be either fantastic or anecdotal, while stylistically they suffer from the same tendency to overwrite that Lawrence subsequently discerned in *The White Peacock*, which he dismissed in the autumn of 1910 as a 'florid prose poem'.[3]

The next phase of Lawrence's fictional writing is attributable to the influence of the newly published *English Review*, which he first read in December 1908. There he found the writings of such early modernists as Henry James and Conrad, what he called 'the exciting new school of realism'.[4] It has been argued that the stories written between 1909 and 1912 abandon the fantastic for the familiar, and represent a brief realist phase in his career.[5] It seems clear that Ford Madox Hueffer (later Ford), the editor of the *English Review* at this time, encouraged Lawrence in 1909 to turn to working-class life for his subjects.[6] The stories parallel the composition of *Sons and Lovers*, a novel that Lawrence wrote in reaction against his first two novels, *The White Peacock* and *The Trespasser* (which he disparaged as 'a decorated idyll').[7] In the early versions of stories such as 'Odour of Chrysanthemums' and 'Daughters of the Vicar' he drew on his family's working-class life to introduce English readers to a world they knew little about.

In 1912 Lawrence first used an ironic voice to describe the lives of Midlands working people in 'A Miner at Home' and 'The Christening' (as well as in 'Her Turn', 'Strike Pay', not published in this volume, and 'A Sick Collier'). Lawrence was to develop this comic–satiric vein in his later fiction. Then in 1913 he began work on the first version of *The Rainbow*, a novel that would thrust Lawrence into the avant-garde of British modernism. The same year he wrote the first versions of 'The Prussian Officer' and 'The Thorn in the Flesh'. This third phase is the product of a fusion of personal experience and a newly evolved outlook, or 'metaphysic' as Lawrence termed it.

He had first attempted to express this metaphysic in the Foreword to *Sons and Lovers* he had written in January 1913 – before, that is, the *Prussian Officer* stories were transformed in the summer of 1913 and the summer and autumn of 1914 into their final published form. Between 'forging them up' in July 1914, as he described it,[8] and his last minute additions (some highly significant) to the page proofs in October 1914 Lawrence began to work out the first major expression of his metaphysic in his 'Study of Thomas Hardy', which remained unpublished during his lifetime. The 'Study' sets out to describe 'the structural skeleton of some theory of being' that Lawrence considered was needed by any work of fiction.[9] It offers a dualistic vision of human life in which man and woman, Love and Law, the Will-to-Motion and the Will-to-Inertia strive to reach a dynamic equilibrium that results in an evolutionary leap forward into the unknown. It is imbalance, the domination of one over the other, he argues, that causes human disasters such as the outbreak of the First World War in August 1914. Lawrence also holds it responsible for the failure in relationships between the sexes such as occurs in the case of Mary's bodiless marriage to Massey in 'Daughters of the Vicar'.

The newly worked out metaphysic enabled Lawrence to give his stories a representative quality that the early versions lacked. *Sons and Lovers*, which he wrote in November 1912, is no simple fictionalization of his own early life. 'It's the tragedy of thousands of young men in England'.[10] His aim now was 'the setting behind the small actions of his protagonists the terrific action of unfathomed nature'.[11] This led him to conceive character in a totally different way to his predecessors. In June 1914 Lawrence defended his new novel, *The Rainbow*, to Edward Garnett, his literary mentor, who represented just those older aesthetic values that Lawrence was rebelling against in his novel and short stories: 'that which is physic – non-human, in humanity, is more interesting to me than the old-fashioned human element – which causes one to conceive a character in a certain moral scheme and make him consistent.'[12] The divergence between the two men's poetics is illustrated by the way in which Garnett retitled both 'Honour and Arms' and the book in which it appeared with its current title, 'The Prussian Officer', presumably to give it contemporary relevance once Britain declared war on Germany in August 1914. For Lawrence the real war was the war within the human psyche. Subsequently Lawrence took violent exception to this externalization of the warring within men effected by Garnett's arbitrary title change: 'Garnett was a devil to call my book of stories *The Prussian Officer* – what Prussian Officer?'[13]

Lawrence's new attitude to fiction finds its first embodiment not in *The Rainbow*, but in such stories as 'The White Stocking' where Elsie, when she dances with Sam Adams, 'felt herself slipping away from herself', or in 'The Prussian Officer' where both captain and orderly succumb to a violence that is impersonal and operates at the level of the unconscious. All three characters show the amoral workings of psychic forces that disrupt any unitary concept of personality. Repeatedly one can see in the characters that people the *Prussian Officer* stories that 'glimpse of the eternal and the unchangeable' that Lawrence discerned in everyone at this time.[14] What distinguishes this phase of his writing is an ability to fuse 'the struggle, the stream, the change' of everyday life with 'the great impersonal . . . out of which all change comes', which is one of the central insights of his metaphysic.[15] He sees it as the function of his art to reveal behind the fights, triumphs and defeats of his fictionalized individuals the permanent forces of nature exercising their timeless sway. As the orderly in 'The Prussian Officer' lies dying of thirst he gazes at the distant unmoving mountains that represent everything he lacks. 'He stared till his eyes went black, and the mountains as they stood in their beauty, so clean and cool, seemed to have it, that which was lost in him' (20:27–30). In that one sentence Lawrence has fused the immediacy of human experience with the immutability of a nature to which the orderly belongs and to which he is returned only through his death at the end of the story.

Anyone truly interested in following Lawrence's development as a short-story writer during these seven years can trace the development of 'Odour of Chrysanthemums' from its inception in 1909 (see Appendix I), through its revised state in 1910 and further amendments and additions in 1911,[16] to its first periodical appearance in the *English Review*,[17] to its much altered state in *The Prussian Officer*, the product of two revisions in July and October 1914. The earliest version shows Lawrence overwhelmed by an unconscious identification with the mother figure. This leads him to end the story with a sentimental rendering of Elizabeth Bates's highly egotistical feeling of pity for her dead husband, pity which she can afford to indulge now that he is 'more helpless than a baby' (205:22). But had he returned alive (and drunk) 'her anger and scorn would rise like fire' (205:18). It took Lawrence four rewritings over a period of four years to uncover the essential imbalance that Elizabeth had created in the relationship and to have her reach the conclusion that she 'had denied him what he was' (198:22). In the final version of 'Odour of Chrysanthemums' Lawrence achieved an equipoise that he confessed later he had failed to find in *Sons and Lovers*.[18] Both husband and wife are at fault in failing to allow one another the space that every individual needs in a satisfactory relationship. It is more difficult for Elizabeth to recognize her own complicity in the breakdown in their marriage than her husband's contribution. But Lawrence finally metes out equal justice in her realization that both of them 'had denied each other in life' (198:40).[19]

The same radical changes have been effected in virtually all the stories contained in this collection, which is why it is difficult to illustrate the distance Lawrence had travelled between 1907 and 1914 from the stories as published in 1914. However, one or two stories still show traces of their origins. Both 'A Fragment of Stained Glass' and 'Goose Fair' still reveal a reliance on the strange and exotic that characterized Lawrence's first phase of story writing. 'Goose Fair' began life as a story written by Lawrence's fiancée,

Louie Burrows, in 1909. Lawrence, after revising it, called it 'your, my, story',[20] and after further revision sent it under his name to the *English Review* which published it in February 1910. In 1914 he substantially revised the magazine version for its book publication. Even by 1910 Lawrence must have considered the story his, rather than a joint production. But it sits uneasily among the more mature stories collected in *The Prussian Officer*. It shows a nineteenth-century reliance on plot reversal that turns on a question of social morality for its denouement. Set in a year of industrial crisis (1871), it features a priggish female protagonist and a spoiled boor of a young man in a love–hate relationship that is the only feature to bear traces of Lawrence's growing interest in the importance of hetero-sexual relations. The story also shows the damaging effect of class antagonism on English society, but again this is given crude and over-simplified narrative expression. Overall this story gives the reader the best idea in this collection of how different and unsubtle many of the stories in it were before receiving revision or complete rewritings in the two years prior to publication.

'A Fragment of Stained Glass' also bears traces of its origins as 'Legend' in 1907. But in this case Lawrence has revised the story so extensively in 1911 for its appearance in the *English Review* in September, and in 1914 for its publication in book form, that it stands as a transition piece. Its reliance on the exotic and the supernatural of medieval times and its frame narrator places it firmly in the tradition of Kipling and Stevenson. But its description of the turbulent relations between the escaped serf and Martha, his sweet-heart, reminds one more of the Lawrence of *The Rainbow* than of the author of *The White Peacock*. The story pits society against individual passion. What is distinctive about it is the way the violence that characterizes the relations between serf and master (killing a horse in anger, flogging, burning down the house) resurfaces in the liberating sexual relationship between serf and Martha. He kisses her with his bleeding mouth, combining pain and pleasure.

After they have escaped to the woods and he has torn off a fragment of stained red glass, the stakes are raised. The ambivalent conjunction of desire and danger is embodied in the glass. To her it is 'magic', it is 'red and shining', and she wants it even if 'it shines like . . . the eye of a wolf in the doorway' (96:25–32). To him it is his 'bloodstone' or 'life-stone' (96:33–40). 'It will hurt us,' he warns her, 'we shall die in blood' (96:34–5). When he gives it to her she yields her presumably virgin body to him, itself a rite of passion, blood and pain. But the full consequences of their indulging in private passion and flouting public order come in the form of the approaching wolves as the evening draws on. Deprived of social safeguards passion is literally all-consuming. Lawrence is to become the defender of individual passion against the encroachment of public morality and class decorum. But here he maintains an ambivalent attitude to the liberating and annihilating act of sex that brings the internal narration to a modern ending without full closure. The frame narration ends on a more clumsily handled note of ambiguity which foregrounds the fictional nature of the entire story. A happy ending such as the vicar (who acts as a stand-in for the writer of the 1907 story) attempts to impose is no longer acceptable to the modern frame narrator. In Roland Barthes's terminology, Lawrence replaces the readerly text of 1907 with the writerly text of 1914.[21] In the latter the reader is allowed to participate with the writer in the pleasure of constructing meaning.

Two more of the stories first written in 1912 and revised in 1913 and 1914 stand a little apart from the body of this collection. 'A Sick Collier' and 'The Christening' show the influence of Chekhov in their inconsequentiality, their focus on the nuances of behaviour, and their suggestion of the presence of heavily repressed feelings and motives operating on characters at the level of the unconscious. 'A Sick Collier' opens with a portrait of a successful marriage between Willy, a young collier of limited intelligence and immense physical well-being, and Lucy, brighter than him but attracted by his masculine presence. Two years after getting married Willy has a mining accident which confines him to bed for six weeks. In the climactic incident he watches his fellow miners on strike setting off for a football match and when Lucy restrains him from joining them he turns temporarily mad, attempting to kill her because, he shouts, '"it's 'er fault as th' pain comes on"' (170:15). What brings on the unprecedented attack on a wife he loves? Is it that his limited intelligence makes him ill equipped to cope with the pain he suffers from incessantly? Is he a victim of his confinement to the life of the senses alone? Is it that his diminished physical and economic status creates an imbalance in the relationship that, as Kingsley Widmer argues, deprives him of his manhood and destroys the marriage?[22] Or is Lawrence once more revealing the violence underlying all intense passion? The story withholds any overt judgement. It is equally for the reader to decide what the significance is of Lucy's concern about the possible loss of Willy's strike pay, should news of his mad fit reach his employer. She too has been displaced from their earlier paradisal state of innocence.

'The Christening' combines the ambivalence that characterizes 'A Fragment of Stained Glass' and 'A Sick Collier' with a new comic–ironic note that Lawrence develops further in stories he wrote towards the end of his life, stories like 'Jimmy and the Desperate Woman', 'Things' and 'Mother and Daughter'. The story focuses primarily on the ageing father of a family of four, the youngest daughter of which has had a bastard son by the local baker's man. The father is a Victorian tyrant, an Old Testament patriarch whose vitality, despite his physical deterioration, dominates the household. Read as a religious analogy, the authority of the Old Testament prophet negates the 'vague tenderness' (175:36) of the New Testament vicar come to christen the innocent bastard child. The numerous biblical echoes in the story have led critics to assert that 'The Christening' describes a perverse baptism from which there can be no rebirth.[23] Those who read the story in this light maintain that it portrays a father whose demanding ego cripples the growth of his children. Even the father's prayer to be forgiven for having 'done 'em mischief' and his admission that it 'would ha' been better if they'd never known no father' (178:35–6) is ironically negated by his insistence on having his illegitimate grandson christened Joseph William after him. Yet it has been argued that even if his authoritarian aspect is condemned by the narrator (180:10) his vitality is meant to be admired. In dishonouring the father, the argument goes, the children diminish themselves.[24] Irony is a two-edged weapon, and Lawrence appears to be exploiting its ambiguous nature right up to the closing tableau of the father rejoicing in a natural world that he has simultaneously rendered hateful to his own offspring. Even the natural rebellious behaviour of his youngest daughter proves a source of shame to every member of the family except the ebullient father.

By devoting a chapter of *D. H. Lawrence: Novelist* called 'Lawrence and Class' to 'Daughters of the Vicar', F. R. Leavis focused subsequent interpretations of this long short story on the central place which class occupies in it. The part that class distinctions 'play in the given tale is a sinister one,' he wrote, 'and the theme is their defeat – the triumph over them of life.'[25] Keith Cushman has shown how in the earlier versions called 'Two Marriages' (see Appendix II) Lawrence had not yet reached this insight into the destructive nature of class.[26] Up to 1913 Alfred is described as 'straightforward in his mind, if not very profound' (246:26 note in Cambridge edition). His ultimate role is to compensate for his social inferiority by serving Louisa for the rest of his life. The final version of the story eliminates this and other suggestions that class has any inherent psychological reality. It is a social construct that has been given additional life by the unusually fast progress of the industrial revolution in Britain. The opening section of the story describes how the class distinctions of an earlier agricultural society failed to synchronize with economic differences after the arrival of mining in the nineteenth century. Seen in Marxist terms the alienation of the miners caused by the industrial process left the class war in place after they had overtaken the earnings of much of the genteel middle class.

Yet even the first section of the story translates these governing socio-economic factors into individualized psychological insights. Mr Lindley's false sense of superiority ultimately negates his Christian vocation with 'his conscious hatred of the majority of his flock', and ends up with 'unconscious hatred of himself' (41:10). Mrs Lindley only controls her hatred of everyone around her by turning herself into a lifelong invalid. From the start, then, reliance on a sense of class superiority is seen to be self-destructive. With the arrival of Mr Massey, however, the story no longer targets social class as the principal enemy of life. Massey is Lawrence's grotesque embodiment of the rational mind and the moral will. The Lindleys are left to represent the deadly effects of social snobbery. Massey is employed to illustrate how the intellectual and moral life is equally cut off from the life of the senses. A reliance on class, rationality and abstract morality are all shown in the course of this story to deny the essential life of the body. As Lawrence wrote in January 1913: 'All I want is to answer to my blood, direct, without fribbling intervention of mind, or moral, or what not.'[27] Substitute 'class' for 'what not' and Lawrence could have been describing the major theme of 'Daughters of the Vicar'. Here he can be seen groping his way towards the formulation of his new metaphysic.

This newly evolving metaphysic is primarily responsible for the transformation of earlier versions of 'Daughters of the Vicar' into the finished story of 1914. This transformation affects more than the thematic content. It imposes on the chaotic material of 'Two Marriages' a sense of form that gives aesthetic shape and expression to the dichotomies underlying his philosophical outlook at this time – to Law and Love, the flesh and the mind, woman and man. 'Daughters of the Vicar' began as a story contrasting two very different marriages – one socially acceptable but physically and emotionally destructive, the other socially unacceptable but physically and emotionally fulfilling. The development of a metaphysic enabled Lawrence to extend this duality to almost every aspect of the story. The opposing dualities proliferate beyond those between the two daughters and their respective husbands. There are also the contrasting communities of workers and impoverished middle-class representatives, of the households of the Lindleys and the Durants, of the two mothers and of the two fathers, of the socially snobbish Mr Lindley and the intellectually snobbish Mr Massey, of the life of the flesh and the life of the mind. Every character and every incident now has a place in the overarching design of the metaphysic that enables Lawrence to handle his large cast and extensive narrative material with an effortless control missing from 'Two Marriages'.

In particular this embracing vision enabled Lawrence to draw a surprising parallel between the predicaments in which Mary and Alfred find themselves. Once she has married Massey, Mary discovers in him a surprisingly powerful will. This produces in her 'a deep craven fear of him, something slave-like' (56–7:2). In marrying him Mary 'was pure will acquiescing to him' (56:17). She has forced herself to resign the control of her life to another in the name of 'a higher freedom' (56:18). The result of abrogating control over her life is to produce in her a similar sense of self-murder as her father experienced and a similar urge to 'bring about death . . . by a general destruction' (57:12) as her mother felt before taking to her bed. What might be missed is how closely her actions approximate to Alfred's method of denying responsibility for his own life. Like Paul in *Sons and Lovers* (and Lawrence), Alfred is seen to be overly dependent on his mother. One consequence is that he becomes 'spiritually impotent' (67:39), which is itself a manifestation of a larger 'dumb humility before life, a fear of living' (67:14). Even his attempt to fly from his mother's hold takes the form of a different kind of service – military service. Like Mary he chooses to put himself in the hands of others, and in the process represses his innermost instinctual needs. He uses this sense of servitude to hold Louisa at a distance during his mother's terminal illness. He sees her as 'a wonderful distance' (75:12), and is 'glad to serve her, but keeping himself quite removed from her' (74:36). He reveres her for what he is not, as Mary does Massey.

However, in the climactic scene of the story Alfred and Louisa manage to break down this life-threatening sense of servitude that has already destroyed Mary. In this instance it is Louisa who takes on the role of waking Alfred, the Sleeping Prince, from his self-subjection. As they finally embrace a strange new sense of impersonality overtakes them. Both die out of the old life of willed consciousness and emerge into a new state of unconscious fatality in which each seems 'eternal' to the other. This is what Lawrence had in mind when talking about his new conception of character 'as representing some greater, inhuman will'.[28] Louisa and Alfred's semi-religious entry into an unknown area of experience simultaneously gives concrete expression to Lawrence's shift to a non-realist mode of narration. At the same time it offers a microcosmic instance of the evolution of Western civilization that Lawrence argued in his 'Study of Thomas Hardy' was inevitable some time in the near future. In the 'Study' he historicized the polarity between Law and Love. Law had governed our world until the advent of Christianity had replaced Law by Love. Drawing on what Frank Kermode has called Lawrence's habitual trinitarianism,[29] the 'Study' forecasts a new age which will unify male Love with female Law, when the man and woman become reconciled and usher in the era of the Holy Spirit.[30] The scene in which Louisa and Alfred overcome differences of class and morality to make love and enter the New World together, then, can also be seen as the dramatic enactment of this apocalyptic moment in Western history. The metaphysic has thrown the intimate relations between this one couple against the backdrop of the advance of Western civilization and given the story resonances that much of Lawrence's fiction, especially *The Rainbow*, assumes from this moment in his writing life onward.

In his celebrated essay, 'Art as Technique', Viktor Shklovsky asserted, 'Art is thinking in images', 'which means,' he went on, 'that art is the making of symbols.' His further suggestion that 'images belong to no one: they are "the Lord's" '[31] is echoed by Lawrence in a letter he wrote in December 1914:

> I think there is the dual way of looking at things: our way, which
> is to say '*I* am all. All things are but radiations out from me.' –
> The other way is to try to conceive the Whole, to build up a
> Whole by means of symbolism, because symbolism avoids the I
> and puts aside the egotist; and, in the Whole, to take our decent
> place.[32]

By 1914 symbolism meant for Lawrence not an aesthetic technique,
but a linguistic means of expressing his dualistic metaphysic in
concrete terms. At times he uses it sparingly to enhance or give
depth to a story. This is the case in 'Odour of Chrysanthemums'
where the chrysanthemums come to represent the failed potentiality
of the marriage. Beginning with the promise of a genuine blooming
of love when Walter gives Elizabeth chrysanthemums at their wedding, they start withering when he is first brought home drunk
(186:39–40) and are finally literally displaced by his corpse which
spells out the death of their joint hopes of reaching fruition together
in their relationship (194:1).

In 'The Shadow in the Rose Garden' flowers also come to
symbolize the initial failure of the married couple to emerge from
their budded state. Surrounded by an abundance of roses in full
bloom, the wife is exposed as 'no more than a rose, a rose that could
not quite come into blossom' (126:3). Both husband and wife remain
blind to one another, and blindness and (in)sight act as another set
of opposing images that help place the couple within the wider
metaphysic. He mistakenly assumes that he knows everything about
her. She remains oblivious to his presence in the boarding-house
garden, fixated on her previous lover. But when she meets this lover
from her past in the rose garden, he emerges from the vicarage the
windows of which are 'curtainless and dark' (125:5), and his eyes
'stared without seeing' (126:16). In their final confrontation over her
revelation of her earlier affair with the now mad vicar's son, husband
and wife are finally forced through their anger to confront one
another, to see each other as they really are for the first time. And
hatred produces the growth that false love had failed to foster. 'They
were both shocked so much, they were impersonal' (132:35). The
symbolic reversal from blindness to sight has put both of them in
touch with those impersonal forces of nature that Lawrence identified
with both the unknown reality of life and with the symbolic mode
itself. Although the story appears to end on an unresolved note, the
symbolic content points to a breakthrough in the final episode in

which the shadow of the past forces both husband and wife into a blossoming they have resisted until then.

'The Shades of Spring' also evokes the beauty of the natural landscape of Lawrence's youth as a symbolic norm amidst which his two major characters are set and against which they are judged. Syson, returning to the country and the sweetheart of his youth, attempts to identify with its beauty which he used to bring alive for Hilda during their courtship. About to enter the 'enduring vision' (98:34) of his past life, he finds his way barred by the new game-keeper, Hilda's new lover. As the story progresses Syson is forced to recognize that he has become no more than a trespasser in this former Garden of Eden. Leaving the gamekeeper, he finds in his bad temper the landscape turning to ashes (101:22). But Lawrence makes a point of assuring the reader that the beauty of the landscape remains unaltered. Hilda then reverses their former roles (and also those played out by their corresponding characters in *Sons and Lovers*) by showing Syson the wonders and secrets of the countryside. She remains a child of nature and uncovers to him a series of natural matings ending in her own fur-lined nest where she and the game-keeper now conduct their mating ritual. Where before she relied on him for her moments of communion with the spiritual in nature, now she is her own mistress: 'You could make things *wonderful*. I have found it out – it is true. But I have them all for myself now' (107:33–4). She even reproaches him for being unnaturally bodiless and failing to consummate their love affair sexually.

After they have parted, Syson continues through the marvels of the spring landscape. 'What a wonderful world it was – marvellous, for ever new. He felt as if it were underground, like the fields of monotone hell, notwithstanding' (110:27–9). Syson has become a modern Pluto, a figure of death, deprived of Persephone in the spring. What caused his separation from Hilda was his cultiva-tion of the mental life at the expense of the physical, and this deficiency is primarily exposed by his exclusion from the world of nature. In the final tableau he turns his back on the passionate embraces of the two natural lovers and returns to the fallen world of the city. The story reads as both an expulsion from the paradise of his youth and an evolution from the mis-recognition (or *méconnais-sance*, to use Jacques Lacan's term) of his past to a new understanding of the duality of life, to a realization that spring also has its shades. To continue the Lacanian parallel, one could argue that he has finally left the imaginary for the symbolic order in which he has to accept the perpetual postponement of real satisfaction and be content with the knowledge he has acquired in its place.[33]

In other stories such as 'Second Best' and 'The White Stocking' symbolism forms the dominant narrative mode. Ostensibly 'Second Best' is a story about two sisters, Frances and Anne. Frances has returned home after being rejected by Jimmy, her intellectual fiancé of five years' standing. By the end of the story she has chosen Tom, an unsophisticated country boy, as a second-best replacement for Jimmy. The title and various passages in the story seem explicitly to categorize her choice of Tom as a let-down and disappointment. 'If she could not have the best – Jimmy, whom she knew to be something of a snob – she would have the second best, Tom' (118:25–7). Yet Michael Black has questioned whether Frances 'isn't wiser in [choosing Tom] than she knows'.[34] One's understanding of the story depends on just how the symbolism of the mole is seen to function. And symbols, as Northrop Frye has argued, are invariably governed by 'the principle of manifold or "polysemous" meaning'.[35] A characteristic of symbols is their propensity to signify simultaneously in multiple ways.

The turning point in the story occurs when Anne first captures and subsequently kills a mole. What is it that the mole evokes? It is blind. It lives underground and it feels its way by touch. It is a natural part of the brilliant summer landscape: 'paddling, snuffing, touching things to discover them, running in blindness, delighted to ecstasy by the sunlight and the hot strange things that caressed its belly and its nose' (115:17–20). What is its corollary in humans? Clearly that which is most natural and sensuous in them. Also that which is sightless and lives in the dark – like the unconscious? In acquiescing to Anne's killing of the mole, Frances appears to be acquiescing to the killing of all that the mole represents within herself. Immediately the landscape goes dead for her: 'Something had died in her, so that things lost their poignancy' (117:26–7). After having deliberately sought out another mole and presented its corpse to Tom as a kind of propitiatory sacrifice, she agrees to his proposal that they start going out together: '"Yes," she replied, in a dead voice. But there was a thrill of pleasure in this death' (120:32–3). It is hard to agree with Michael Black that this represents a necessary death (such as Alfred and Louisa experience) prior to their awakening into a new world of love. Yet the ambiguity surrounding Lawrence's symbolic use of the mole does undercut any unitary application of its meaning to the main narrative. Had Jimmy and not Tom been the simple, physical type, one would have better understood how Frances's ritualistic renunciation of him might involve a loss of her more natural, instinctual side. As it stands the symbolism enriches but simultaneously complicates and even obfuscates this brief story. It is as if art and metaphysic are at war with each other in this case.

Yet both the mole in 'Second Best' and the dance (and physical contact in general) in 'The White Stocking' make that connection between the personal and the universal that Northrop Frye has detected in the use of symbols as archetypes and what he calls monads. In this last usage, he explains, 'nature becomes, not the container, but the thing contained'.[36] Nature, that is, the natural, is itself the product of a godlike imagination. In participating in the natural order humans enter the realm of the divine. But what is natural for human beings is complex. In Lawrence's dualistic vision we participate in the fecundity of the natural world and yet our form of blooming involves both blood and intellect. To deny either dooms us to exclusion from the divine in nature. In 'The White Stocking' touch is used to evoke the power of the blood and the unconscious forces that reach their most powerful expression in the sexual act. The forces of the intellect are represented by sight and voice. The sheer power of sexuality as a force in its own right is enacted in the flashback to the dance at which Elsie's boss, Adams, a roué, uses his skill at dancing to lure her into an unconscious state in which his body 'would fuse right through her, and she would be as liquid to him' (153:17–18). But in Lawrence's metaphysic fusion is a danger to be avoided if each individual is to retain a sense of inviolable self. A true relationship entails losing yourself in the other in order to find yourself again. Elsie's problem is that she wants to place responsibility for herself in first Adams's and then Whiston's, her husband's, hands. In the dance sequence Whiston with his distant surveillance does succeed in 'forcing her into consciousness' (155:13); yet he 'had not made himself real to her' (155:32–3). Reality has to embrace the physical and the unconscious as well as the conscious intellect. This conjunction occurs when Whiston drags her from the dance in a fury and they finally make up with kisses and an embrace.

But once married Elsie makes the same mistake as the wife in 'The Shadow in the Rose Garden', feeling that inside marriage she 'was rid of the responsibility of herself' (158:23–4). She accepts

Adams's Valentine's Day gift of stockings and jewellery. When Whiston discovers her secret she taunts him with a solo dance of defiance that forms a narrative parallel with her highly sexual dance with Adams two years earlier. Once again the physical imbalance that her wholly physical act produces can only be counteracted in Lawrence's terms by an equally physical act – the blow that Whiston delivers to her face. Love, sex and violence are yet again brought into intimate connection in this impersonal battle of psychic forces. It is as if nature were bent on reestablishing an equilibrium that Elsie had unconsciously disturbed by her failure to take responsibility for herself. That is what Lawrence meant by his doctrine of impersonality. The petty actions of the ego are subsumed in the larger forces of nature before which husband and wife are swept along helpless. One could argue from a feminist viewpoint that in this final episode Lawrence is intent on forcing representative woman back into a subordinate status. But this is to ignore the way the symbolic use of touch supersedes either party's egotistical demands and invites a reading of the story that makes it one episode in what Lawrence called the 'great attempt at formulating the whole history of the Soul of Man'.[37]

The last stories to be written in this collection were the two military tales, 'The Thorn in the Flesh' and 'The Prussian Officer'. Lawrence had first come into contact with the German military at the garrison town of Metz (where Frieda's home was) in 1912. There he was mistaken for an English officer spying on the fortifications. This incident led to his only meeting with Baron von Richthofen, his future father-in-law, who had been retired from active service in the Prussian army after being injured in the war of 1870–71 against the French.[38] After leaving Metz Lawrence wrote four articles about fortified Germany. The subject of German militarism found a fictional outlet the following year in the first versions of the two stories. Both invite comparison with *The Rainbow*. While 'The Prussian Officer' is a story about the cruelty and mutual destruction that also characterizes the relationship between Ursula and Skrebensky in the novel, 'The Thorn in the Flesh' is a story of resurrection in the flesh that has similarities to that between Tom Brangwen and Lydia Lensky.

Both Bachmann, a soldier, and Emilie, a servant in a household modelled on that of Frieda's father, the baron, share a debilitating defect. Each has chosen to place responsibility for him- or herself in the hands of a higher authority. Bachmann 'found satisfaction in delivering himself to his duty' (23:1–2). Emilie's 'desire was to serve' the baron and his wife (31:37). Like Alfred in 'Daughters of the Vicar', each suffers from the imbalance this choice produces in their psyche. Bachmann finds himself forced to climb the heights of the fortifications despite his wholly instinctual fear of heights. Humiliated by his sergeant, he knocks him off the ramparts. This reflex action is skilfully represented as a wholly unconscious physical response to a physical threat (16:14). Bachmann finds himself outside the protective embrace of the military, a fugitive. His response is to attempt to place himself in the hands of yet another external force in the shape of his sweetheart, Emilie.

Emilie, however, has her own problems. She is fiercely virginal: 'a wild instinct made her shrink away from any hands which might be laid on her' (31:5–6). This is precisely how Bachmann felt about the encroachment of the sergeant. It is interesting that it is Emilie who breaks the invisible barrier holding the two lovers apart, although once again Lawrence renders their love-making more in terms of magnetic fields of force finding an equilibrium than in individual psychological terms. Michael Black has suggested that each episode evokes a New Testament parallel – Bachmann on the ramparts hints at a form of Crucifixion; Emilie's early attitudes are similar to those of the Virgin; and their sexual consummation is described in terms of the Resurrection.[39] Established by linguistic association, these parallels point to Lawrence's conviction by 1914 that his task as a modern writer is to place the actions of his particular characters within the larger theatre of the natural and supernatural world. This is what accounts for the lack of concern that both lovers show to Bachmann's arrest in the finale. The petty doings of the social world have little impact on them now that '[t]hey were themselves' (38:33). They have become part of the larger natural forces of this world, part of the divine scheme of things, leaving only the shells of their bodies at the disposal of the smaller human world.

After first writing it in June 1913, Lawrence called 'Honour and Arms' (as he titled 'The Prussian Officer') the best short story he had ever done.[40] It manages to condense all the fictional innovations that he had been working out during the previous six years. It is the story in this collection at the greatest remove from realism. Jack Stewart has traced its roots to the Expressionist movement and cites

Frederick Levine's definition: 'The ultimate goal of Expressionism was literally to "lose its own mind", to seek an identification with forms of precognitive existence as a manifestation of its collective desire to re-enter the world of "unconscious consciousness" . . .'[41] The concept of 'unconscious consciousness' is as complex and obscure as is this story. Almost every critic to comment on it has offered a different interpretation. F. R. Leavis dismissed it as 'sultrily overcharged' and immature.[42] Kingsley Widmer sees it as one of Lawrence's 'Parables of Annihilation'.[43] Janice Harris calls it a 'transposed resurrection tale'.[44]

What is most striking about it is the way it doesn't simply relate humans to the landscape through which they move. It fuses the two in such a way that it is impossible to read about the landscape without reading qualities pertaining to it as belonging equally to one of the two main characters. But which qualities attach to which character is a matter of contention. Keith Cushman, for instance, associates the valley with the orderly and the mountains with the captain – 'heat and cold, life and death'.[45] Janice Harris denies this association, pointing out that the orderly's girlfriend comes from the mountains, which are at any rate described in the story as 'half earth, half heaven' (1:20–21). She claims that 'the mountains represent an ideal of integration that points out what is missing in both of these trapped soldiers'.[46] One of the external pieces of evidence that has clouded this debate is Lawrence's famous letter to Ernest Collings of 17 January 1913: 'My great religion is a belief in the blood, the flesh, as being wiser than the intellect. We can go wrong in our minds. But what our blood feels and believes and says, is always true.'[47] But Lawrence was writing to someone whom he charges in the same letter as being 'too onesided'. This is not a considered statement of his dualistic metaphysic, but an application of part of it to one individual. Yet this feeling that Lawrence was prejudiced in favour of one side of the duality has been responsible for interpretations such as that offered by Cushman.

What has to be appreciated is that each of the two protagonists is deficient in different ways. Each lacks what the other has. The orderly has an 'instinctive sureness of movement of an unhampered young animal that irritated the officer' (3:19–20) because the captain is 'a man that fights with life' (2:18–19). The captain has 'light blue eyes that were always flashing with cold fire' (2:19-20), and it is through his eyes that he comes to dominate his orderly. By contrast the orderly has 'dark, expressionless eyes, that seemed never to have thought, only to have received life directly through the senses, and acted straight from instinct' (2:40–3:2). Eyes in Lawrence's mature fiction act as indicators of intelligence. The orderly is clearly too much of a pure animal. He lacks the necessary mental power to defend himself against the captain's abuse of his authority. Equally the captain is unequipped to understand the feeling that is driving him into physical contact with his orderly. Lawrence makes it obvious to the reader that the captain is attracted in a sadistic way to his servant, as the kicks he gives him on the buttocks make clear.

This dualism extends into and is fused with different aspects of the landscape. Lawrence's dualistic metaphysic achieves artistic expression through his symbolic treatment of humans and the natural scenery through which they move. Both protagonists show opposing deficiencies in their natural make-up. Nature takes revenge on the unnatural pair and the human order reverts to its natural equilibrium. The actions of the two men are described in an impersonal, physically heightened manner as the barriers between self and external world dissolve. Rather than discerning the dualism of Lawrence's metaphysic in the contrast between the mountains and the hot valley, one might concentrate on the contrast between sunlight and darkness. In the hot sunny fields the orderly is as much tormented by the heat of the brilliant sun as he is by the gaze of the captain's steely eyes on him. The orderly 'wanted to stay in shadow, not to be forced into consciousness' (11:8–9). Eyesight and sunlight become one with the conscious self. But once inside the shade of the wood the 'captain was less real than himself' (13:29–30). His killing of the officer is described in curiously impersonal terms, almost as if it were inevitable. The underlying dualism reasserts itself with the picture of the blood running from the captain's nostrils into his eyes. Blood, representing the life of the body that the captain has denied, blinds the eyesight of the mind.

This leaves the orderly alone without the intellectual resources possessed by the man he has just murdered. He finds himself isolated from the sunlit world beyond the wood, confined to a phantasmagorical world of shadows and darkness. Lawrence brilliantly describes the inverted values of this world that the orderly inhabits, in which lightning at night exposes a 'half-revealed world', (19:36) a 'ghostly shadow, thrown for a moment upon the pure darkness, which returned ever whole and complete' (19:39–40). The orderly can only exist now in the dark, and it is wholly appropriate that he should die of sunstroke. The cause of death is equally physical and metaphysical or symbolic. The story ends with two images, both of which reconcile the polarization that characterized the two men. The orderly's last sight before his death is of the mountains that 'seemed to have it, that which was lost in him' (20:30). The other image is of the two corpses lying side by side which together make up the same whole that the mountains have come to represent. One could argue that within the story Lawrence has deconstructed his own polarities. Having first reversed the normal prioritization of mental over instinctual, he then reinscribes the former within the latter in his final images. But deconstruction can be an endless process, so that one could go on to argue that Lawrence's positives are undermined by the story's fascination with negativity, cruelty and death. However one understands this story, it represents one of the highlights of Lawrence's fictional *œuvre* and demonstrates the success of his innovatory achievements before *The Rainbow*, the novel that finally established his reputation as a major modernist.

## NOTES ON THE INTRODUCTION

1. Anyone interested in tracing the growth of Lawrence's command of the genre over this time should consult Keith Cushman, *D. H. Lawrence at Work. The Emergence of the* Prussian Officer *Stories* (University Press of Virginia, 1978).

2. Janice Hubbard Harris, *The Short Fiction of D. H. Lawrence* (Rutgers University Press, 1984).

3. James T. Boulton, ed., *The Letters of D. H. Lawrence*, vol. I (Cambridge University Press, 1979), p. 184. (Hereafter referred to as *Letters*, i.)

4. *Letters*, i. 139.

5. Harris, *The Short Fiction*, p. 5.

6. John Worthen, *D. H. Lawrence: The Early Years, 1885–1912* (Cambridge University Press, 1991), pp. 216–18.

7. *Letters*, i. 184.

8. George J. Zytaruk and James T. Boulton, eds., *The Letters of D. H. Lawrence*, vol. II (Cambridge University Press, 1982), p. 198. (Hereafter referred to as *Letters*, ii.)

9. D. H. Lawrence, *Study of Thomas Hardy and Other Essays*, ed. Bruce Steele (Cambridge University Press, 1985), p. 91.

10. *Letters*, i. 477.

11. *Study of Thomas Hardy*, p. 29.
12. *Letters*, ii. 182.
13. *Letters*, ii. 241.
14. *Letters*, ii. 138.
15. *Letters*, ii. 138.
16. See James T. Boulton, 'D. H. Lawrence's *Odour of Chrysanthemums*: An Early Version', *Renaissance and Modern Studies*, xiii (1969), 4–48.
17. *English Review*, viii (June 1911), 415–33.
18. Frieda Lawrence, *Not I, But the Wind* . . . (Heinemann, 1935), p. 74.
19. Cf. Mara Kalnins, 'D. H. Lawrence's "Odour of Chrysanthemums": The Three Endings', *Studies in Short Fiction*, xiii, 4 (Fall 1976), 471–9.
20. *Letters*, i. 137.
21. Cf. Roland Barthes, *S/Z* (Seuil, 1970), trans. Richard Miller (Hill & Wang/Macmillan, 1975). *Le Plaisir du texte* (Seuil, 1973). *The Pleasure of the Text*, trans. Richard Miller (Hill & Wang, 1975/Jonathan Cape, 1976).
22. Kingsley Widmer, *The Art of Perversity. D. H. Lawrence's Shorter Fictions* (University of Washington Press, 1962), p. 150.
23. Ibid., p. 28. Cf. Cushman, *D. H. Lawrence at Work*, p. 222.
24. Harris, *The Short Fiction*, p. 77.
25. F. R. Leavis, *D. H. Lawrence: Novelist* (Penguin, 1964), p. 75.
26. Cushman, *D. H. Lawrence at Work*, pp. 84–92.
27. *Letters*, i. 503.
28. *Letters*, ii. 183.
29. Frank Kermode, *Lawrence* (Fontana/Collins, 1973), p. 40.
30. D. H. Lawrence, *Phoenix: The Posthumous Papers of D. H. Lawrence*, ed. Edward D. McDonald (Viking, 1936), pp. 515–16.
31. Lee T. Lemon and Marion J. Reis, trans., *Russian Formalist Criticism. Four Essays* (University of Nebraska Press, 1965), p. 7.
32. *Letters*, ii. 248.
33. See Jacques Lacan, *Écrits. A Selection*, trans. Alan Sheridan, especially chapters 1 and 5 (Tavistock Publications, 1977).
34. Michael Black, *D. H. Lawrence: The Early Fiction. A Commentary* (Macmillan, 1986), p. 142.
35. Northrop Frye, *Anatomy of Criticism. Four Essays* (Princeton University Press, 1957), p. 72.
36. Frye, *Anatomy of Criticism*, p. 119.
37. *Letters*, ii. 248.
38. Worthen, *The Early Years*, p. 398.
39. Black, *The Early Fiction*, p. 230.
40. *Letters*, ii. 21.
41. Jack F. Stewart, 'Expressionism in "The Prussian Officer"', *D. H.*

*Lawrence Review*, xviii (Summer 1986), 276. Cf. Frederick S. Levine, *The Apocalyptic Vision: The Art of Franz Mark as German Expressionism* (Harper, 1979), p. 3.

42. Leavis, *D. H. Lawrence: Novelist*, p. 257.
43. Widmer, *The Art of Perversity*, p. 3.
44. Harris, *The Short Fiction*, p. 94.
45. Cushman, *D. H. Lawrence at Work*, p. 170.
46. Harris, *The Short Fiction*, pp. 95–6.
47. *Letters*, i. 503.

# Note on the Texts

Following the Cambridge edition of the *The Prussian Officer and Other Stories*, edited by John Worthen, 1983, the base texts for all the stories in this edition, with the exception of 'A Sick Collier', are the first edition of *The Prussian Officer and Other Stories*, published on 26 November 1914 by Duckworth & Co. In the case of 'A Sick Collier' the base text is the autograph manuscript in the collection of Mr George Lazarus.

Because Lawrence's copyists, typists, copy editors and printers saw fit to alter his punctuation, spelling and word-use at their own discretion, the base text of the Duckworth first edition has invariably been emended where necessary by reference to the duplicate page proofs that Lawrence retained and which have survived and are located in Nottinghamshire County Library, and by reference to the original autograph manuscript where this has survived and still bears a direct relation to the final text. The original punctuation has to be restored if the meaning is not to change significantly in some cases. For example, in 'Odour of Chrysanthemums' DHL originally wrote: 'the children played subduedly, intent, fertile of invention,' (187:12–13). This was printed, however, in the first edition as: 'the children played, subduedly intent, fertile of invention,' where 'subduedly' relates to the adjective 'intent' instead of the verb 'played', with a corresponding change in meaning.

Five of the typescripts that played a part in the transmission of the texts of the *Prussian Officer* volume were typed by Douglas Clayton. In the case of 'The Shades of Spring' both the 1911 manuscript Clayton used and the typescript he produced from it in early 1912 have survived. The twenty-six typed pages contain ninety-five alterations from Lawrence's manuscript. For example, Clayton altered Lawrence's 'in' to 'on in' (98:6), 'Willeywater' to 'Willey-water' (99:23), 'pippin' to 'pipkin' (102:7), 'in' to 'into' (103:29), 'round' to 'the round' (104:11), 'called' to 'called him' (104:30), 'I'd' to 'I had' (105:15), 'you' to 'and you' (108:31), and 'you'll' to 'you will' (111:25). All of these unauthorized alterations, which found their way into the first edition, have been eliminated in this edition.

Another interesting example of the extent to which a modern editor is able to re-establish Lawrence's text occurs in 'Odour of Chrysanthemums'. Lawrence wrote the first version (a surviving six-page fragment of which is reprinted in Appendix I) in 1909. He revised the 1910 *English Review* page proofs twice in 1910, then again in 1911. He sent these heavily altered proofs to Louie Burrows to make a fair copy for the *English Review* printers. In copying the proof corrections she altered the text on more than 200 occasions, changing punctuation, making twenty-two cuts, many intentionally, and changing Lawrence's wording on twenty-seven other occasions. Lawrence did not check her fair copy against his original when correcting the magazine proofs, and so most of her emendations were incorporated into the *English Review* text of 1911. Lawrence used this printed text of 1911 to revise the story in July 1914 for the Duckworth first edition, and made additional extensive corrections and rewrites to the page proofs in October 1914. Where Louie Burrows made a cut and the sentence survived in its cut form unaltered the Cambridge editor, John Worthen, has felt free to restore Lawrence's original uncut sentence. An example of such a restored cut is 'only his movement seemed visible' (184:8–9). But take the text's 'glancing at the litter' (189:33). Lawrence originally wrote 'glancing again over the litter'. Louie Burrows omitted 'again'. When he received the magazine proofs which read 'glancing over the litter' Lawrence corrected this to read 'glancing at the litter'. Although he might not have felt the need to make this correction had Louie Burrows not omitted his original 'again', the fact that Lawrence did make the later alteration has prevented the editor from in this instance restoring the original wording.

Other instances of the modern editor's ability to restore the text in small but significant ways can be found in 'The Prussian Officer'. Where DHL wrote in the autograph manuscript of how the valley in which the story is set 'glistered with heat' (1:7), the *English Review* substituted the less archaic but also non-dialect 'glittered'. On the other hand when DHL wrote in the manuscript of the Captain's 'dithering smile' (7:37) he was anticipating the first recorded usage in the *OED* of this word meaning 'confusing, making nervous'. The periodical version substituted the clichéd and inappropriate 'withering'. The manuscript version is equally superior to that of the periodical in the case of the highly impressionistic vision of the forest that the delirious orderly has – of 'trees, and glitter of greenery, and reddish bright, still pieces of sunshine on the floor' (17:12). To substitute 'litter' for 'glitter', as the *English Review* did, is to ignore the chain of highly visual images that DHL is accumulating here for a special effect.

In the case of 'A Sick Collier' the original autograph manuscript has been used as the base text because Lawrence reverted to the duplicate typescript made from his original manuscript when preparing copy for the Duckworth first edition in 1914. Clearly his manuscript is more trustworthy than Clayton's typescript. But emendations he made to the *New Statesman* galley proofs in 1913, to the duplicate typescript in July 1914 and to the Duckworth page proofs in October 1914 have been incorporated where authentic.

## Advisory Editor's Note

I would like to thank Professor James T. Boulton and Professor Warren Roberts, General Editors of the *Cambridge Edition of the Works of D. H. Lawrence*, for their advice and planning in the preparation of this edition.

John Worthen, 1994

*Facsimile of the title page of the first English edition.*

# THE
# PRUSSIAN OFFICER

## AND OTHER STORIES

BY

## D. H. LAWRENCE

LONDON
DUCKWORTH & CO.
3 HENRIETTA STREET, COVENT GARDEN

# The Prussian Officer
## [*Honour and Arms*]

### I.

They had marched more than thirty kilometres since dawn, along the white, hot road, where occasional thickets of trees threw a moment of shade, then out into the glare again. On either hand, the valley, wide and shallow, glistered with heat; dark green patches of rye, pale young corn, fallow and meadow and black pine-woods spread in a dull, hot diagram under a glistening sky. But right in front the mountains ranged across, pale blue and very still, the snow gleaming gently out of the deep atmosphere. And towards the mountains, on and on, the regiment marched between the rye-fields and the meadows, between the scraggy fruit-trees set regularly on either side the highroad. The burnished, dark green rye threw off a suffocating heat, the mountains drew gradually nearer and more distinct. While the feet of the soldiers grew hotter, sweat ran through their hair under their helmets, and their knapsacks could burn no more in contact with their shoulders, but seemed instead to give off a cold, prickly sensation.

He walked on and on in silence, staring at the mountains ahead, that rose sheer out of the land, and stood fold behind fold, half earth, half heaven, the heaven, the barrier with slits of soft snow in the pale, bluish peaks.

He could now walk almost without pain. At the start, he had determined not to limp. It had made him sick to take the first steps, and during the first mile or so, he had compressed his breath, and the cold drops of sweat had stood on his forehead. But he had walked it off. What were they after all but bruises! He had looked at them, as he was getting up: deep bruises on the backs of his thighs. And since he had made his first step in the morning, he had been conscious of them, till now he had a tight, hot place in his chest, with suppressing the pain, and holding himself in. There seemed no air when he breathed. But he walked almost lightly.

The captain's hand had trembled in taking his coffee at dawn: his orderly saw it again. And he saw the fine figure of the captain wheeling on horseback at the farm-house ahead, a handsome figure in pale blue uniform with facings of scarlet, and the metal gleaming on the black helmet and the sword scabbard, and dark streaks of sweat coming on the silky bay horse. The orderly felt he was connected with that figure moving so suddenly on horseback: he followed it like a shadow, mute and inevitable and damned by it. And the officer was always aware of the tramp of the company behind, the march of his orderly among the men.

The captain was a tall man of about forty, grey at the temples. He had a handsome, finely-knit figure, and was one of the best horsemen in the West. His orderly, having to rub him down, admired the amazing riding-muscles of his loins.

For the rest, the orderly scarcely noticed the officer any more than he noticed himself. It was rarely he saw his master's face: he did not look at it. The captain had reddish-brown, stiff hair, that he wore short upon his skull. His moustache also was cut short and bristly over a full, brutal mouth. His face was rather rugged, the cheeks thin. Perhaps the man was the more handsome for the deep lines in his face, the irritable tension of his brow, which gave him the look of a man who fights with life. His fair eyebrows stood bushy over light blue eyes that were always flashing with cold fire.

He was a Prussian aristocrat, haughty and overbearing. But his mother had been a Polish Countess. Having made too many gambling debts when he was young, he had ruined his prospects in the army, and remained an infantry captain. He had never married: his position did not allow it, and no woman had ever moved him to it. His time he spent riding—occasionally he rode one of his own horses at the races—and at the officers' club. Now and then he took himself a mistress. But after such an event, he returned to duty with his brow still more tense, his eyes still more hostile and irritable. With the men, however, he was merely impersonal, though a devil when roused, so that on the whole they feared him but had no great aversion from him. They accepted him as the inevitable.

To his orderly he was at first cold and just and indifferent: he did not fuss over trifles. So that his servant knew practically nothing about him, except just what orders he would give, and how he wanted them obeyed. That was quite simple. Then the change gradually came.

The orderly was a youth of about twenty-two, of medium height, and well-built. He had strong, heavy limbs, was swarthy, with a soft, black, young moustache. There was something altogether warm and young about him. He had firmly marked eyebrows over dark,

2

expressionless eyes, that seemed never to have thought, only to have received life direct through his senses, and acted straight from instinct.

Gradually the officer had become aware of his servant's young, vigorous, unconscious presence about him. He could not get away from the sense of the youth's person, while he was in attendance. It was like a warm flame upon the older man's tense, rigid body, that had become almost unliving, fixed. There was something so free and self-contained about him, and something in the young fellow's movement, that made the officer aware of him. And this irritated the Prussian. He did not choose to be touched into life by his servant. He might easily have changed his man, but he did not. He now very rarely looked direct at his orderly, but kept his face averted, as if to avoid seeing him. And yet as the young soldier moved unthinking about the apartment, the elder watched him, and would notice the movement of his strong young shoulders under the blue cloth, the bend of his neck. And it irritated him. To see the soldier's young, brown, shapely peasants' hands grasp the loaf or the wine-bottle sent a flash of hate or of anger through the elder man's blood. It was not that the youth was clumsy: it was rather the blind, instinctive sureness of movement of an unhampered young animal that irritated the officer to such a degree.

Once, when a bottle of wine had gone over, and the red gushed out onto the table-cloth, the officer had started up with an oath, and his eyes, bluey like fire, had held those of the confused youth for a moment. It was a shock for the young soldier. He felt something sink deeper, deeper into his soul, where nothing had ever gone before. It left him rather blank and wondering. Some of his natural completeness in himself was gone, a little uneasiness took its place. And from that time an undiscovered feeling had held between the two men.

Henceforward the orderly was afraid of really meeting his master. His subconsciousness remembered those steely blue eyes and the harsh brows, and did not intend to meet them again. So he always stared past his master, and avoided him. Also, in a little anxiety, he waited for the three months to have gone, when his time would be up. He began to feel a constraint in the captain's presence, and the soldier even more than the officer wanted to be left alone in his neutrality as servant.

He had served the captain for more than a year, and knew his duty. This he performed easily, as if it were natural to him. The officer and his commands he took for granted, as he took the sun and the rain, and he served as a matter of course. It did not implicate him personally.

But now if he were going to be forced into a personal interchange with his master, he would be like a wild thing caught, he felt he must get away.

But the influence of the young soldier's being had penetrated through the officer's stiffened discipline, and perturbed the man in him. He, however, was a gentleman, with long fine hands and cultivated movements, and was not going to allow such a thing as the stirring of his innate self. He was a man of passionate temper, who had always kept himself suppressed. Occasionally there had been a duel, an outburst before the soldiers. He knew himself to be always on the point of breaking out. But he kept himself hard to the idea of the Service. Whereas the young soldier seemed to live out his warm, full nature, to give it off in his very movements, which had a certain zest, such as wild animals have in free movement. And this irritated the officer more and more.

In spite of himself, the captain could not regain his neutrality of feeling towards his orderly. Nor could he leave the man alone. In spite of himself, he watched him, gave him sharp orders, tried to take up as much of his time as possible. Sometimes he flew into a rage with the young soldier, and bullied him. Then the orderly shut himself off, as it were out of earshot, and waited with sullen, flushed face, for the end of the noise. The words never pierced to his intelligence, he made himself, protectively, impervious to the feelings of his master.

He had a scar on his left thumb, a deep seam going across the knuckle. The officer had long suffered from it, and wanted to do something to it. Still it was there, ugly and brutal on the young, brown hand. At last the captain's reserve gave way. One day, as the orderly was smoothing out the table-cloth, the officer pinned down his thumb with a pencil, asking:

"How did you come by that?"

The young man winced and drew back at attention.

"A wood-axe, Herr Hauptmann," he answered.

The officer waited for further explanation. None came. The orderly went about his duties. The elder man was sullenly angry. His servant avoided him. And the next day he had to use all his will-power to avoid seeing the scarred thumb. He wanted to get hold of it and—. A hot flame ran in his blood.

He knew his servant would soon be free, and would be glad. As yet, the soldier had held himself off from the elder man. The captain grew madly irritable. He could not rest when the soldier was away, and when

4

he was present, he glared at him with tormented eyes. He hated those fine black brows over the unmeaning dark eyes, he was infuriated by the free movement of the handsome limbs, which no military discipline could make stiff. And he became harsh and cruelly bullying, using contempt and satire. The young soldier only grew more mute and expressionless.

"What cattle were you bred by, that you can't keep straight eyes. Look me in the eyes when I speak to you."

And the soldier turned his dark eyes to the other's face, but there was no sight in them: he stared with the slightest possible cast, holding back his sight, perceiving the blue of his master's eyes, but receiving no look from them. And the elder man went pale, and his reddish eyebrows twitched. He gave his order, barrenly.

Once he flung a heavy military glove into the young soldier's face. Then he had the satisfaction of seeing the black eyes flare up into his own, like a blaze when straw is thrown on a fire. And he had laughed with a little tremor and a sneer.

But there were only two months more. The youth instinctively tried to keep himself intact: he tried to serve the officer as if the latter were an abstract authority, and not a man. All his instinct was to avoid personal contact, even definite hate. But in spite of himself the hate grew, responsive to the officer's passion. However, he put it in the background. When he had left the army he could dare acknowledge it. By nature he was active, and had many friends. He thought what amazing good fellows they were. But, without knowing it, he was alone. Now this solitariness was intensified. It would carry him through his term. But the officer seemed to be going irritably insane, and the youth was deeply frightened.

The soldier had a sweetheart, a girl from the mountains, independent and primitive. The two walked together, rather silently. He went with her, not to talk, but to have his arm round her, and for the physical contact. This eased him, made it easier for him to ignore the captain; for he could rest with her held fast against his chest. And she, in some unspoken fashion, was there for him. They loved each other.

The captain perceived it, and was mad with irritation. He kept the young man engaged all the evenings long, and took pleasure in the dark look that came on his face. Occasionally, the eyes of the two men met, those of the younger sullen and dark, doggedly unalterable, those of the elder sneering with restless contempt.

The officer tried hard not to admit the passion that had got hold of him. He would not know that his feeling for his orderly was anything but that of a man incensed by his stupid, *perverse* servant. So, keeping quite justified and conventional in his consciousness, he let the other thing run on. His nerves, however, were suffering. At last he slung the end of a belt in his servant's face. When he saw the youth start back, the pain-tears in his eyes and the blood on his mouth, he had felt at once a thrill of deep pleasure, and of shame.

But this, he acknowledged to himself was a thing he had never done before. The fellow was too exasperating. His own nerves must be going to pieces. He went away for some days with a woman.

It was a mockery of pleasure. He simply did not want the woman. But he stayed on for his time. At the end of it, he came back in an agony of irritation, torment, and misery. He rode all the evening, then came straight in to supper. His orderly was out. The officer sat with his long, fine hands lying on the table, perfectly still, and all his blood seemed to be corroding.

At last his servant entered. He watched the strong, easy young figure, the fine eyebrows, the thick black hair. In a week's time the youth had got back his old well-being. The hands of the officer twitched, and seemed to be full of mad flame. The young man stood at attention, unmoving, shut off.

The meal went in silence. But the orderly seemed eager. He made a clatter with the dishes.

"Are you in a hurry?" asked the officer, watching the intent, warm face of his servant. The other did not reply.

"Will you answer my question?" said the captain.

"Yes Sir," replied the orderly, standing with his pile of deep army-plates. The captain waited, looked at him, then asked again:

"Are you in a hurry?"

"Yes Sir," came the answer, that sent a flash through the listener.

"For what?"

"I was going out Sir."

"I want you this evening."

There was a moment's hesitation. The officer had a curious stiffness of countenance.

"Yes Sir," replied the servant, in his throat.

"I want you tomorrow evening also—in fact you may consider your evenings occupied, unless I give you leave."

The mouth with the young moustache set close.

"Yes Sir," answered the orderly, loosening his lips for a moment.

He again turned to the door.

"And why have you a piece of pencil in your ear?"

The orderly hesitated, then continued on his way without answering. He set the plates in a pile outside the door, took the stump of pencil from his ear, and put it in his pocket. He had been copying a verse for his sweetheart's birthday-card. He returned to finish clearing the table. The officer's eyes were dancing, he had a little, eager smile.

"Why have you a piece of pencil in your ear?" he asked.

The orderly took his hands full of dishes. His master was standing near the great green stove, a little smile on his face, his chin thrust forward. When the young soldier saw him his heart suddenly ran hot. He felt blind. Instead of answering, he turned dazedly to the door. As he was crouching to set down the dishes, he was pitched forward by a kick from behind. The pots went in a stream down the stairs, he clung to the pillar of the banisters. And as he was rising he was kicked heavily again, and again, so that he clung sickly to the post for some moments. His master had gone swiftly into the room and closed the door. The maid-servant downstairs looked up the staircase and made a mocking face at the crockery disaster.

The officer's heart was plunging. He poured himself a glass of wine, part of which he spilled on the floor, and gulped the remainder, leaning against the cool, green stove. He heard his man collecting the dishes from the stairs. Pale, as if intoxicated, he waited. The servant entered again. The captain's heart gave a pang, as of pleasure, seeing the young fellow bewildered and uncertain on his feet, with pain.

"Schöner!" he said.

The soldier was a little slower in coming to attention.

"Yes Sir!"

The youth stood before him, with pathetic young moustache, and fine eyebrows very distinct on his forehead of dark marble.

"I asked you a question."

"Yes Sir."

The officer's tone bit like acid.

"Why had you a pencil in your ear?"

Again the servant's heart ran hot, and he could not breathe. With dark, strained eyes, he looked at the officer, as if fascinated. And he stood there sturdily planted, unconscious. The dithering smile came into the captain's eyes, and he lifted his foot.

"I—I forgot it—Sir," panted the soldier, his dark eyes fixed on the other man's dancing blue ones.

"What was it doing there?"

He saw the young man's breast heaving as he made an effort for words.

"I had been writing."

"Writing what?"

Again the soldier looked him up and down. The officer could hear him panting. The smile came into the blue eyes. The soldier worked his dry throat, but could not speak. Suddenly the smile lit like a flame on the officer's face, and a kick came heavily against the orderly's thigh. The youth moved a pace sideways. His face went dead, with two black, staring eyes.

"Well?" said the officer.

The orderly's mouth had gone dry, and his tongue rubbed in it as on dry brown paper. He worked his throat. The officer raised his foot. The servant went stiff.

"Some poetry, Sir," came the crackling, unrecognisable sound of his voice.

"Poetry, what poetry?" asked the captain, with a sickly smile.

Again there was the working in the throat. The captain's heart had suddenly gone down heavily, and he stood sick and tired.

"For my girl, Sir," he heard the dry, inhuman sound.

"Oh!" he said, turning away. "Clear the table."

'Click!'—went the soldier's throat; then again, 'click!'; and then the half articulate:

"Yes Sir."

The young soldier was gone, looking old, and walking heavily. The officer, left alone, held himself rigid, to prevent himself from thinking. His instinct warned him that he must not think. Deep inside him was the intense gratification of his passion, still working powerfully. Then there was a counteraction, a horrible breaking down of something inside him, a whole agony of reaction. He stood there for an hour motionless, a chaos of sensations, but rigid with a will to keep blank his consciousness, to prevent his mind grasping. And he held himself so until the worst of the stress had passed, when he began to drink, drank himself to an intoxication, till he slept obliterated. When he woke in the morning he was shaken to the base of his nature. But he had fought off the realisation of what he had done. He had prevented his mind from taking it in, had suppressed it along with his instincts, and the conscious man had nothing to do with it. He felt only as after a bout of intoxication, weak, but the affair itself all dim and not to be

8

recovered. Of the drunkenness of his passion he successfully refused remembrance. And when his orderly appeared with coffee, the officer assumed the same self he had had the morning before. He refused the event of the past night—denied it had ever been—and was successful in his denial. He had not done any such thing—not he himself. Whatever there might be lay at the door of a stupid, insubordinate servant.

The orderly had gone about in a stupor all the evening. He drank some beer because he was parched, but not much, the alcohol made his feeling come back, and he could not bear it. He was dulled, as if nine-tenths of the ordinary man in him were inert. He crawled about disfigured. Still, when he thought of the kicks, he went sick, and when he thought of the threats of more kicking, in the room afterwards, his heart went hot and faint, and he panted, remembering the one that had come. He had been forced to say 'For my girl'. He was much too done even to want to cry. His mouth hung slightly open, like an idiot's. He felt vacant, and wasted. So, he wandered at his work, painfully, and very slowly and clumsily, fumbling blindly with the brushes, and finding it difficult, when he sat down, to summon the energy to move again. His limbs, his jaw were slack and nerveless. But he was very tired. He got to bed at last and slept inert, relaxed, in a sleep that was rather stupor than slumber, a dead night of stupefaction shot through with gleams of anguish.

In the morning were the manœuvres. But he woke even before the bugle sounded. The painful ache in his chest, the dryness of his throat, the awful steady feeling of misery made his eyes come awake and dreary at once. He knew without thinking, what had happened. And he knew that the day had come again, when he must go on with his round. The last bit of darkness was being pushed out of the room. He would have to move his inert body and go on. He was so young, and had known so little trouble, that he was bewildered. He only wished it would stay night, so that he could lie still, covered up by the darkness. And yet nothing would prevent the day from coming, nothing would save him from having to get up, and saddle the captain's horse, and make the captain's coffee. It was there, inevitable. And then, he thought, it was impossible. Yet they would not leave him free. He must go and take the coffee to the captain. He was too stunned to understand it. He only knew it was inevitable—inevitable, however long he lay inert.

At last, after heaving at himself, for he seemed to be a mass of inertia, he got up. But he had to force every one of his movements from behind, with his will. He felt lost, and dazed, and helpless. Then he clutched hold of the bed, the pain was so keen. And looking at his thighs, he saw the darker bruises on his swarthy flesh and he knew that, if he pressed one of his fingers on one of the bruises, he should faint. But he did not want to faint—he did not want anybody to know. No one should ever know. It was between him and the captain. There were only the two people in the world now—himself and the captain.

Slowly, economically, he got dressed and forced himself to walk. Everything was obscure, except just what he had his hands on. But he managed to get through his work. The very pain revived his dulled senses. The worst remained yet. He took the tray and went up to the captain's room. The officer, pale and heavy, sat at the table. The orderly, as he saluted, felt himself put out of existence. He stood still for a moment submitting to his own nullification—then he gathered himself, seemed to regain himself, and then the captain began to grow vague, unreal, and the younger soldier's heart beat up. He clung to this sensation—that the captain did not exist, so that he himself might live. But when he saw his officer's hand tremble as he took the coffee, he felt everything falling shattered. And he went away, feeling as if he himself were coming to pieces, disintegrated. And when the captain was there on horseback, giving orders, while he himself stood, with rifle and knapsack, sick with pain, he felt as if he must shut his eyes—as if he must shut his eyes on everything. It was only the long agony of marching with a parched throat that filled him with one single, sleep-heavy intention: to save himself.

## 2.

He was getting used even to his parched throat. That the snowy peaks were radiant among the sky, that the whitey-green glacier river twisted through its pale shoals, in the valley below, seemed almost supernatural. But he was going mad with fever and thirst. He plodded on, uncomplaining. He did not want to speak, not to anybody. There were two gulls, like flakes of water and snow, over the river. The scent of green rye soaked in sunshine came like a sickness. And the march continued, monotonously, almost like a bad sleep.

At the next farm-house, which stood low and broad near the highroad, tubs of water had been put out. The soldiers clustered round to drink. They took off their helmets, and the steam mounted from their wet hair. The captain sat on horseback, watching. He needed to see his orderly. His helmet threw a dark shadow over his light, fierce eyes, but his moustache and mouth and chin were distinct in the sunshine. The orderly must move under the presence of the figure of the horseman. It was not that he was afraid, or cowed. It was as if he were disembowelled, made empty, like an empty shell. He felt himself as nothing, a shadow creeping under the sunshine. And, thirsty as he was, he could scarcely drink, feeling the captain near him. He would not take off his helmet to wipe his wet hair. He wanted to stay in shadow, not to be forced into consciousness. Starting, he saw the light heel of the officer prick the belly of the horse; the captain cantered away, and he himself could relapse into vacancy.

Nothing, however, could give him back his living place in the hot, bright morning. He felt like a gap among it all. Whereas the captain was prouder, overriding. A hot flash went through the young servant's body. The captain was firmer and prouder with life, he himself was empty as a shadow. Again the flash went through him, dazing him out. But his heart ran a little firmer.

The company turned up the hill, to make a loop for the return. Below, from among the trees, the farm-bell clanged. He saw the laborers mowing barefoot at the thick grass leave off their work and go downhill, their scythes hanging over their shoulders, like long, bright claws curving down behind them. They seemed like dream-people, as if they had no relation to himself. He felt as in a blackish dream: as if all the other things were there and had form, but he himself was only a consciousness, a gap that could think and perceive.

The soldiers were tramping silently up the glaring hillside. Gradually his head began to revolve slowly, rhythmically. Sometimes it was dark before his eyes, as if he saw this world through a smoked glass, frail shadows and unreal. It gave him a pain in his head to walk.

The air was too scented, it gave no breath. All the lush green-stuff seemed to be issuing its sap, till the air was deathly, sickly with the smell of greenness. There was the perfume of clover, like pure honey and bees. Then there grew a faint acrid tang—they were near the beeches; and then a queer clattering noise, and a suffocating, hideous smell: they were passing a flock of sheep, a shepherd in a black smock, holding his hook. Why should the sheep huddle together under this fierce sun? He felt that the shepherd could not see him, though he could see the shepherd.

At last there was the halt. They stacked rifles in a conical stack, put down their kit in a scattered circle around it, and dispersed a little, sitting on a small knoll high on the hillside. The chatter began. The soldiers were steaming with heat, but were lively. He sat still, seeing the blue mountains rise upon the land, twenty kilometres away. There was a blue fold in the ranges, then out of that, at the foot, the broad pale bed of the river, stretches of whitey-green water between pinkish-grey shoals among the dark pine-woods. There it was, spread out a long way off. And it seemed to come downhill, the river. There was a raft being steered, a mile away. It was a strange country. Nearer, a red-roofed, broad farm with white base and square dots of windows crouched beside the wall of beech-foliage on the wood's edge. There were long strips of rye and clover and pale green corn. And just at his feet, below the knoll, was a darkish bog, where globe flowers stood breathless still on their slim stalks. And some of the pale gold bubbles were burst, and a broken fragment hung in the air. He thought he was going to sleep.

Suddenly something moved into this coloured mirage before his eyes. The captain, a small, light blue and scarlet figure, was trotting evenly between the strips of corn, along the level brow of the hill. And the man making flag-signals was coming on.—Proud and sure moved the horseman figure, the quick, bright thing in which was concentrated all the light of this morning, which for the rest lay a fragile, shining shadow. Submissive, apathetic, the young soldier sat and stared. But as the horse slowed to a walk, coming up the last steep path, the great flash flared over the body and soul of the orderly. He sat waiting. The back of his head felt as if it were weighted with a heavy piece of fire. He did not want to eat. His hands trembled slightly as he moved them. Meanwhile the officer on horseback was approaching slowly and proudly. The tension grew in the orderly's soul. Then again, seeing the captain ease himself on the saddle, the flash blazed through him.

The captain looked at the patch of light blue and scarlet, and dark heads, scattered closely on the hillside. It pleased him. The command pleased him. And he was feeling proud. His orderly was among them in common subjection. The officer rose a little on his stirrups to look. The young soldier sat with averted, dumb face. The captain relaxed on his seat. His slim legged, beautiful horse, brown as a beech nut, walked proudly uphill. The captain passed into the zone of the company's atmosphere: a hot smell of men, of sweat, of leather. He knew it very well. After a word with the lieutenant, he went a few paces higher, and sat there, a dominant figure, his sweat-marked horse swishing its tail, while he looked down on his men, on his orderly, a nonentity among the crowd.

The young soldier's heart was like fire in his chest, and he breathed with difficulty. The officer, looking downhill, saw three of the young soldiers, two pails of water between them, staggering across a sunny green field. A table had been set up under a tree, and there the slim lieutenant stood importantly busy. Then the captain summoned himself to an act of courage. He called his orderly.

The flame leapt into the young soldier's throat as he heard the command, and he rose blindly, stifled. He saluted, standing below the officer. He did not look up. But there was the flicker in the captain's voice.

"Go to the inn and fetch me— —"—the officer gave his commands. "Quick!" he added.

At the last word, the heart of the servant leapt with a flash, and he felt the strength come over his body. But he turned in mechanical obedience, and set off at a heavy run downhill, looking almost like a bear, his trousers bagging over his military boots. And the officer watched this blind, plunging run all the way.

But it was only the outside of the orderly's body that was obeying so humbly and mechanically. Inside had gradually accumulated a core into which all the energy of that young life was compact and concentrated. He executed his commission, and plodded quickly back uphill. There was a pain in his head, as he walked, that made him twist his features unknowingly. But hard there in the centre of his chest was himself, himself, firm, and not to be plucked to pieces.

The captain had gone up into the wood.—The orderly plodded through the hot, powerfully smelling zone of the company's atmosphere. He had a curious mass of energy inside him now. The captain was less real than himself. He approached the green entrance to the wood. There, in the half-shade, he saw the horse standing, the sunshine and the flickering shadow of leaves dancing over his brown body. There was a clearing where timber had lately been felled. Here, in the gold-green shade beside the brilliant cup of sunshine, stood two figures, blue and pink, the bits of pink showing out plainly. The captain was talking to his lieutenant.

The orderly stood on the edge of the bright clearing, where great trunks of trees, stripped and glistening, lay stretched like naked, brown-skinned bodies. Chips of wood littered the trampled floor, like splashed light, and the bases of the felled trees stood here and there, with their raw, level tops. Beyond was the brilliant, sunlit green of a beech.

"Then I will ride forward," the orderly heard his captain say. The lieutenant saluted and strode away. He himself went forward. A hot flash passed through his belly, as he tramped towards his officer.

The captain watched the rather heavy figure of the young soldier stumble forward, and his veins too ran hot. This was to be man to man between them. He yielded before the solid, stumbling figure with bent head. The orderly stooped and put the food on a level-sawn tree-base. The captain watched the glistening, sun-inflamed, naked hands. He wanted to speak to the young soldier, but could not. The servant propped a bottle against his thigh, pressed open the cork, and poured out the beer into the mug. He kept his head bent. The captain accepted the mug.

"Hot!" he said, as if amiably.

The flame sprang out of the orderly's heart, nearly suffocating him.

"Yes Sir," he replied, between shut teeth.

And he heard the sound of the captain's drinking, and he clenched his fists, such a strong torment came into his wrists. Then came the faint clang of the closing of the pot-lid. He looked up. The captain was watching him. He glanced swiftly away. Then he saw the officer stoop and take a piece of bread from the tree-base. Again the flash of flame went through the young soldier, seeing the stiff body stoop beneath him, and his hands jerked. He looked away. He could feel the officer was nervous. The bread fell as it was being broken. The officer ate the other piece. The two men stood tense and still, the master laboriously chewing his bread, the servant staring with averted face, his fists clenched.

Then the young soldier started. The officer had pressed open the lid of the mug again. The orderly watched the lid of the mug, and the white hand that clenched the handle, as if he were fascinated. It was raised. The youth followed it with his eyes. And then he saw the thin, strong throat of the elder man moving up and down as he drank, the strong jaw working. And the instinct which had been jerking at the young man's wrists suddenly jerked free. He jumped, feeling as if he were rent in two by a strong flame.

The spur of the officer caught in a tree-root, he went down backwards with a crash, the middle of his back thudding sickeningly against the sharp-edged tree-base, the pot flying away. And in a second the orderly, with serious, earnest young face, and underlip between his teeth, had got his knee in the officer's chest and was pressing the chin backward over the farther edge of the tree-stump, pressing, with all his heart behind in a passion of relief, the tension of his wrists exquisite with relief. And with the base of his palms he shoved at the chin, with all his might. And it was pleasant too to have that chin, that hard jaw already slightly rough with beard, in his hands. He did not relax one hair's-breadth but, all the force of all his blood exulting in his thrust, he shoved back the head of the other man, till there was a little 'cluck' and a crunching sensation. Then he felt as if his heart went to vapour. Heavy convulsions shook the body of the officer, frightening and horrifying the young soldier. Yet it pleased him too to repress them. It pleased him to keep his hands pressing back the chin, to feel the chest of the other man yield in expiration to the weight of his strong young knee, to feel the hard twitchings of the prostrate body jerking his own whole frame, which was pressed down on it.

But it went still. He could look into the nostrils of the other man, the eyes he could scarcely see. How curiously the mouth was pushed out, exaggerating the full lips, and the moustache bristling up from them. Then, with a start, he noticed the nostrils gradually filled with blood. The red brimmed, hesitated, ran over, and went in a thin trickle down the face to the eyes.

It shocked and distressed him. Slowly, he got up. The body twitched and sprawled there inert. He stood and looked at it in silence. It was a pity *it* was broken. It represented more than the thing which had kicked and bullied him. He was afraid to look at the eyes. They were hideous now, only the whites showing, and the blood running to them. The face of the orderly was drawn with horror at the sight. Well, it was so. In his heart he was satisfied. He had hated the face of the captain. It was extinguished now. There was a heavy relief in the orderly's soul. That was as it should be. But he could not bear to see the long, military body lying broken over the tree-base, the fine fingers crisped. He wanted to hide it away.

Quickly, busily, he gathered it up and pushed it under the felled tree-trunks, which rested their beautiful smooth length either end on logs. The face was horrible with blood. He covered it with the helmet. Then he pushed the limbs straight and decent, and brushed the dead leaves off the fine cloth of the uniform. So, it lay quite still in the shadow under there. A little strip of sunshine ran along the breast, from a chink between the logs. The orderly sat by it for a few moments. Here his own life also ended.

Then, through his daze, he heard the lieutenant, in a loud voice, explaining to the men outside the wood that they were to suppose the bridge on the river below was held by the enemy. Now they were to march to the attack in such and such a manner. The lieutenant had no gift of expression. The orderly, listening from habit, got muddled. And when the lieutenant began it all again, he ceased to hear.

He knew he must go. He stood up. It surprised him that the leaves were glittering in the sun, and the chips of wood reflecting white from the ground. For him a change had come over the world. But for the rest it had not—all seemed the same. Only he had left it. And he could not go back.—It was his duty to return with the beer-pot and the bottle. He could not. He had left all that. The lieutenant was still hoarsely explaining. He must go, or they would overtake him. And he could not bear contact with anyone now.

He drew his fingers over his eyes, trying to find out where he was. Then he turned away. He saw the horse standing in the path. He went up to it and mounted. It hurt him to sit in the saddle. The pain of keeping his seat occupied him as they cantered through the wood. He would not have minded anything, but he could not get away from the sense of being divided from the others. The path led out of the trees. On the edge of the wood he pulled up and stood watching. There in the spacious sunshine of the valley soldiers were moving in a little swarm. Every now and then, a man harrowing on a strip of fallow shouted to his oxen, at the turn. The village and the white-towered church was small in the sunshine. And he no longer belonged to it—he sat there, beyond, like a man outside in the dark. He had gone out from everyday life into the unknown, and he could not, he even did not want to go back.

Turning from the sun-blazing valley, he rode deep into the wood. Tree-trunks, like people standing grey and still, took no notice as he went. A doe, herself a moving bit of sunshine and shadow, went running through the flecked shade. There were bright green rents in the foliage. Then it was all pine-wood, dark and cool. And he was sick with pain, he had an intolerable great pulse in his head, and he was sick. He had never been ill in his life. He felt lost, quite dazed with all this.

Trying to get down from the horse, he fell, astonished at the pain and his lack of balance. The horse shifted uneasily. He jerked its bridle and sent it cantering jerkily away. It was his last connection with the rest of things.

But he only wanted to lie down and not be disturbed. Stumbling through the trees, he came on a quiet place where beeches and pine trees grew on a slope. Immediately he had lain down and closed his eyes, his consciousness went racing on without him. A big pulse of sickness beat in him as if it throbbed through the whole earth. He was burning with dry heat. But he was too busy, too tearingly active in the incoherent race of delirium, to observe.

### 3.

He came to with a start. His mouth was dry and hard, his heart beat heavily, but he had not the energy to get up. His heart beat heavily. Where was he?—the barracks,—at home? There was something knocking. And, making an effort, he looked round—trees, and glitter of greenery, and reddish bright, still pieces of sunshine on the floor. He did not believe he was himself, he did not believe what he saw. Something was knocking. He made a struggle towards consciousness, but relapsed. Then he struggled again. And gradually his surroundings fell into relationship with himself. He knew, and a great pang of fear went through his heart. Somebody was knocking. He could see the heavy, black rags of a fir-tree overhead. Then everything went black. Yet he did not believe he had closed his eyes. He had not. Out of the blackness sight slowly emerged again. And someone was knocking. Quickly, he saw the blood-disfigured face of his captain, which he hated. And he held himself still with horror. Yet, deep inside him, he knew that it was so, the captain should be dead. But the physical delirium got hold of him. Someone was knocking. He lay perfectly still, as if dead, with fear. And he went unconscious.

When he opened his eyes again, he started, seeing something creeping swiftly up a tree-trunk. It was a little bird. And a bird was whistling overhead. Tap-tap-tap—it was the small, quick bird rapping the tree-trunk with its beak, as if its head were a little round hammer. He watched it curiously. It shifted sharply, in its creeping fashion. Then, like a mouse, it slid down the bare trunk. Its swift creeping sent a flash of revulsion through him. He raised his head. It felt a great weight. Then, the little bird ran out of the shadow across a still patch of sunshine, its little head bobbing swiftly, its white legs twinkling brightly for a moment. How neat it was in its build, so compact, with pieces of white on its wings. There were several of them. They were so pretty—but they crept like swift, erratic mice, running here and there among the beech-mast.

He lay down again exhausted, and his consciousness lapsed. He had a horror of the little creeping birds. All his blood seemed to be darting and creeping in his head. And yet he could not move.

He came to with a further ache of exhaustion. There was the pain in his head, and the horrible sickness, and his inability to move. He had never been ill in his life. He did not know where he was or what he was. Probably he had got sunstroke. Or what else?—he had silenced the captain for ever—some time ago—oh, a long time ago. There had been blood on his face, and his eyes had turned upwards. It was all right, somehow. It was peace. But now he had got beyond himself. He had never been here before. Was it life, or not-life? He was by himself. They were in a big, bright place, those others, and he was outside. The town, all the country, a big bright place of light: and he was outside, here, in the darkened open beyond, where each thing existed alone. But they would all have to come out there sometime, those others. Little, and left behind him, they all were. There had been father and mother and sweetheart. What did they all matter. This was the open land.

He sat up. Something scuffled. It was a little brown squirrel running in lovely, undulating bounds over the floor, its red tail completing the undulation of its body—and then, as it sat up, furling and unfurling. He watched it, pleased. It ran on again, friskily, enjoying itself. It flew wildly at another squirrel, and they were chasing each other, and making little scolding, chattering noises. The soldier wanted to speak to them. But only a hoarse sound came out of his throat. The squirrels burst away—they flew up the trees. And then he saw the one peeping round at him, half way up a tree-trunk. A start of fear went through him, though, in so far as he was conscious, he was amused. It still stayed, its little keen face staring at him half way up the tree-trunk, its little ears pricked up, its clawey little hands clinging to the bark, its white breast reared. He started from it in panic.

Struggling to his feet, he lurched away. He went on walking, walking, looking for something—for a drink. His brain felt hot and inflamed for want of water. He stumbled on. Then he did not know anything. He went unconscious as he walked. Yet he stumbled on, his mouth open.

When, to his dumb wonder, he opened his eyes on the world again, he no longer tried to remember what it was. There was thick, golden light behind golden-green glitterings, and tall, grey-purple shafts, and darknesses further off, surrounding him, growing deeper. He was conscious of a sense of arrival. He was amid the reality, on the real, dark bottom. But there was the thirst burning in his brain. He felt lighter, not so heavy. He supposed it was newness. The air was muttering with thunder. He thought he was walking wonderfully swiftly and was coming straight to relief—or was it to water?

Suddenly he stood still with fear. There was a tremendous flare of gold, immense—just a few dark trunks like bars between him and it. All the young level wheat was burnished, gold glaring on its silky green. A woman, full-skirted, a black cloth on her head for head dress, was passing like a block of shadow through the glistering green corn, into the full glare. There was a farm, too, pale blue in shadow, and the timber black. And there was a church spire nearly fused away in the gold. The woman moved on, away from him. He had no language with which to speak to her. She was the bright, solid unreality. She would make a noise of words that would confuse him, and her eyes would look at him without seeing him. She was crossing there to the other side. He stood against a tree.

When at last he turned, looking down the long, bare groove whose flat bed was already filling dark, he saw the mountains in a wonder-light, not far away, and radiant. Behind the soft, grey ridge of the nearest range the further mountains stood golden and pale grey, the snow all radiant like pure, soft gold. So still, gleaming in the sky, fashioned pure out of the ore of the sky, they shone in their silence. He stood and looked at them, his face illuminated. And like the golden, lustrous gleaming of the snow he felt his own thirst bright in him. He stood and gazed, leaning against a tree. And then everything slid away into space.

During the night the lightning fluttered perpetually, making the whole sky white. He must have walked again. The world hung livid around him for moments, fields a level sheen of grey-green light, trees in dark bulk, and a range of clouds black across a white sky. Then the darkness fell like a shutter, and the night was whole. A faint flutter of a half-revealed world, that could not quite leap out of the darkness!—Then there again stood a sweep of pallor for the land, dark shapes looming, a range of clouds hanging overhead. The world was a ghostly shadow, thrown for a moment upon the pure darkness, which returned ever whole and complete.

And the mere delirium of sickness and fever went on inside him—his brain opening and shutting like the night—then sometimes convulsions of terror from something with great eyes that stared round a tree—then the long agony of the march, and the sun decomposing his blood—then the pang of hate for the captain, followed by a pang of tenderness and ease. But everything was distorted, born of an ache and resolving into an ache.

In the morning he came definitely awake. Then his brain flamed with the sole horror of thirstiness. The sun was on his face, the dew was steaming from his wet clothes. Like one possessed, he got up. There, straight in front of him, blue and cool and tender, the mountains ranged across the pale edge of the morning sky. He wanted them—he wanted them alone—he wanted to leave himself and be identified with them. They did not move, they were still and soft, with white, gentle markings of snow. He stood still, mad with suffering, his hands crisping and clutching. Then he was twisting in a paroxysm on the grass.

He lay still, in a kind of dream of anguish. His thirst seemed to have separated itself from him, and to stand apart, a single demand. Then the pain he felt was another single self. Then there was the clog of his body, another separate thing. He was divided among all kinds of separate beings. There was some strange, agonised connection between them, but they were drawing further apart. Then they would all split. The sun, drilling down on him, was drilling through the bond. Then they would all fall, fall through the everlasting lapse of space.

Then again his consciousness reasserted itself. He roused onto his elbow and stared at the gleaming mountains. There they ranked, all still and wonderful between earth and heaven. He stared till his eyes went black, and the mountains as they stood in their beauty, so clean and cool, seemed to have it, that which was lost in him.

4.

When the soldiers found him, three hours later, he was lying with his face over his arm, his black hair giving off heat under the sun. But he was still alive. Seeing the open, black mouth the young soldiers dropped him in horror.

He died in the hospital at night, without having seen again.

The doctors saw the bruises on his legs, behind, and were silent.

The bodies of the two men lay together, side by side, in the mortuary, the one white and slender, but laid rigidly at rest, the other looking as if every moment it must rouse into life again, so young and unused, from a slumber.

# The Thorn in the Flesh

A wind was running, so that occasionally the poplars whitened as if a flame flew up them. The sky was broken and blue among moving clouds. Patches of sunshine lay on the level fields, and shadows on the rye and the vineyards. In the distance, very blue, the cathedral bristled against the sky, and the houses of the city of Metz clustered vaguely below, like a hill.

Among the fields by the lime trees stood the barracks, upon bare, dry ground, a collection of round-roofed huts of corrugated iron, where the soldiers' nasturtiums climbed brilliantly. There was a tract of vegetable garden at the side, with the soldiers' yellowish lettuces in rows, and at the back the big, hard drilling-yard surrounded by a wire fence.

At this time in the afternoon, the huts were deserted, all the beds pushed up, the soldiers were lounging about under the lime trees waiting for the call to drill. Bachmann sat on a bench in the shade that smelled sickly with blossom. Pale green, wrecked lime flowers were scattered on the ground. He was writing his weekly post-card to his mother. He was a fair, long, limber youth, good looking. He sat very still indeed, trying to write his post-card. His blue uniform, sagging on him as he sat bent over the card, disfigured his youthful shape. His sunburnt hand waited motionless for the words to come. "Dear mother"—was all he had written. Then he scribbled mechanically: "Many thanks for your letter with what you sent. Everything is all right with me. We are just off to drill on the fortifications——" Here he broke off and sat suspended, oblivious of everything, held in some definite suspense. He looked again at the card. But he could write no more. Out of the knot of his consciousness no word would come. He signed himself, and looked up, as a man looks to see if anyone has noticed him in his privacy.

There was a self-conscious strain in his blue eyes, and a pallor about his mouth, where the young, fair moustache glistened. He was almost girlish in his good looks and his grace. But he had something of military consciousness, as if he believed in the discipline for himself, and found satisfaction in delivering himself to his duty. There was also a trace of youthful swagger and dare-devilry about his mouth and his limber body, but this was in suppression now.

He put the post-card in the pocket of his tunic, and went to join a group of his comrades who were lounging in the shade, laughing and talking grossly. To-day he was out of it. He only stood near to them for the warmth of the association. In his own consciousness something held him down.

Presently they were summoned to ranks. The sergeant came out to take command. He was a strongly built, rather heavy man of forty. His head was thrust forward, sunk a little between his powerful shoulders, and the strong jaw was pushed out aggressively. But the eyes were smouldering, the face hung slack and sodden with drink.

He gave his orders in brutal, barking shouts, and the little company moved forward, out of the wire-fenced yard to the open road, marching rhythmically, raising the dust. Bachmann, one of the inner file of four deep, marched in the airless ranks, half suffocated with heat and dust and enclosure. Through the moving of his comrades' bodies, he could see the small vines dusty by the road-side, the poppies among the tares fluttering and blown to pieces, the distant spaces of sky and fields all free with air and sunshine. But he was bound in a very dark enclosure of anxiety within himself.

He marched with his usual ease, being healthy and well adjusted. But his body went on by itself. His spirit was clenched apart. And ever the few soldiers drew nearer and nearer to the town, ever the consciousness of the youth became more gripped and separate, his body worked by a kind of mechanical intelligence, a mere presence of mind.

They diverged from the high road and passed in single file down a path among trees. All was silent and green and mysterious, with shadow of foliage and long, green, undisturbed grass. Then they came out in the sunshine on a moat of water, which wound silently between the long, flowery grass, at the foot of the earthworks, that rose in front in terraces walled smooth on the face, but all soft with long grass at the top. Marguerite daisies and lady's-slipper glimmered white and gold in the lush grass, preserved here in the intense peace of the fortifications. Thickets of trees stood round about. Occasionally a puff of mysterious wind made the flowers and the long grass that crested the earthworks above bow and shake as with signals of oncoming alarm.

The group of soldiers stood at the end of the moat, in their light blue and scarlet uniforms, very bright. The sergeant was giving them instructions, and his shout came sharp and alarming in the intense, untouched stillness of the place. They listened, finding it difficult to make the effort of understanding.

Then it was over, and the men were moving to make preparations. On the other side of the moat the ramparts rose smooth and clear in the sun, sloping slightly back. Along the summit grass grew and tall daisies stood ledged high, like magic, against the dark green of the tree-tops behind. The noise of the town, the running of tram-cars, was heard distinctly, but it seemed not to penetrate this still place.

The water of the moat was motionless. In silence the practice began. One of the soldiers took a scaling ladder, and passing along the narrow ledge at the foot of the earthworks, with the water of the moat just behind him, tried to get a fixture on the slightly sloping wall-face. There he stood, small and isolated, at the foot of the wall, trying to get his ladder settled. At last it held, and the clumsy, groping figure in the baggy blue uniform began to clamber up. The rest of the soldiers stood and watched. Occasionally the sergeant barked a command. Slowly the clumsy blue figure clambered higher up the wall-face. Bachmann stood with his bowels turned to water. The figure of the climbing soldier scrambled out on to the terrace up above, and moved, blue and distinct, among the bright green grass. The officer shouted from below. The soldier tramped along, fixed the ladder in another spot, and carefully lowered himself on to the rungs. Bachmann watched the blind foot groping in space for the ladder, and he felt the world fall away beneath him. The figure of the soldier clung cringing against the face of the wall, cleaving, groping downwards like some unsure insect working its way lower and lower, fearing every movement. At last, sweating and with a strained face, the figure had landed safely and turned to the group of soldiers. But still it had a stiffness and a blank, mechanical look, was something less than human.

Bachmann stood there heavy and condemned, waiting for his own turn and betrayal. Some of the men went up easily enough, and without fear. That only showed it could be done lightly, and made Bachmann's case more bitter. If only he could do it lightly, like that.

His turn came. He knew intuitively that nobody knew his condition. The officer just saw him as a mechanical thing. He tried to keep it up, to carry it through on the face of things. His inside gripped tight, as yet under control, he took the ladder and went along under the wall.

He placed his ladder with quick success, and wild, quivering hope possessed him. Then blindly he began to climb. But the ladder was not very firm, and at every hitch a great, sick, melting feeling took hold of him. He clung on fast. If only he could keep that grip on himself, he would get through. He knew this, in agony. What he could not understand was the blind gush of white-hot fear, that came with great force whenever the ladder swerved, and which almost melted his belly and all his joints, and left him powerless. If once it melted all his joints and his belly, he was done. He clung desperately to himself. He knew the fear, he knew what it did when it came, he knew he had only to keep a firm hold. He knew all this. Yet, when the ladder swerved, and his foot missed, there was the great blast of fear blowing on his heart and bowels, and he was melting weaker and weaker, in a horror of fear and lack of control, melting to fall.

Yet he groped slowly higher and higher, always staring upwards with desperate face, and always conscious of the space below. But all of him, body and soul, was growing hot to fusion point. He would have to let go for very relief's sake. Suddenly his heart began to lurch. It gave a great, sickly swoop, rose, and again plunged in a swoop of horror. He lay against the wall inert as if dead, inert, at peace, save for one deep core of anxiety, which knew that it was *not* all over, that he was still high in space against the wall. But the chief effort of will was gone.

There came into his consciousness a small, foreign sensation. He woke up a little. What was it? Then slowly it penetrated him. His water had run down his leg. He lay there, clinging, still with shame, half conscious of the echo of the sergeant's voice thundering from below. He waited, in depths of shame beginning to recover himself. He had been shamed so deeply. Then he could go on, for his fear for himself was conquered. His shame was known and published. He must go on.

Slowly he began to grope for the rung above, when a great shock shook through him. His wrists were grasped from above, he was being hauled out of himself up, up to the safe ground. Like a sack he was dragged over the edge of the earthworks by the large hands, and landed there on his knees, grovelling in the grass to recover command of himself, to rise up on his feet.

Shame, blind, deep shame and ignominy overthrew his spirit and left it writhing. He stood there shrunk over himself, trying to obliterate himself.

Then the presence of the officer who had hauled him up made itself felt upon him. He heard the panting of the elder man, and then the voice came down on his veins like a fierce whip. He shrank in tension of shame.

"Put up your head—eyes front," shouted the enraged sergeant, and mechanically the soldier obeyed the command, forced to look into the eyes of the sergeant. The brutal, hanging face of the officer violated the youth. He hardened himself with all his might from seeing it. The tearing noise of the sergeant's voice continued to lacerate his body.

Suddenly he set back his head, rigid, and his heart leapt to burst. The face had suddenly thrust itself close, all distorted and showing the teeth, the eyes smouldering into him. The breath of the barking words was on his nose and mouth. He stepped aside in revulsion. With a scream the face was upon him again. He raised his arm, involuntarily, in self-defence. A shock of horror went through him, as he felt his forearm hit the face of the officer a brutal blow. The latter staggered, swerved back, and with a curious cry, reeled backwards over the ramparts, his hands clutching the air. There was a second of silence, then a crash of water.

Bachmann, rigid, looked out of his inner silence upon the scene. Soldiers were running.

"You'd better clear," said one young, excited voice to him. And with immediate instinctive decision he started to walk away from the spot. He went down the tree-hidden path to the high road where the trams ran to and from the town. In his heart was a sense of vindication, of escape. He was leaving it all, the military world, the shame. He was walking away from it.

Officers on horseback rode sauntering down the street, soldiers passed along the pavement. Coming to the bridge, Bachmann crossed over to the town that heaped before him, rising from the flat, picturesque French houses down below at the water's edge, up a jumble of roofs and chasms of streets, to the lovely dark cathedral with its myriad pinnacles making points at the sky.

He felt for the moment quite at peace, relieved from a great strain. So he turned along by the river to the public gardens. Beautiful were the heaped, purple lilac trees upon the green grass, and wonderful the walls of the horse-chestnut trees, lighted like an altar with white flowers on every ledge. Officers went by, elegant and all coloured, women and girls sauntered in the chequered shade. Beautiful it was, he walked in a vision, free.

## II

But where was he going? He began to come out of his trance of delight and liberty. Deep within him he felt the steady burning of shame in the flesh. As yet he could not bear to think of it. But there it was, submerged beneath his attention, the raw, steady-burning shame.

It behoved him to be intelligent. As yet he dared not remember what he had done. He only knew the need to get away, away from everything he had been in contact with.

But how? A great pang of fear went through him. He could not bear his shamed flesh to be put again between the hands of authority. Already the hands had been laid upon him, brutally upon his nakedness, ripping open his shame and making him maimed, crippled in his own control.

Fear became an anguish. Almost blindly he was turning in the direction of the barracks. He could not take the responsibility of himself. He must give himself up to someone. Then his heart, obstinate in hope, became obsessed with the idea of his sweetheart. He would make himself her responsibility.

Blenching as he took courage, he mounted the small, quick-hurrying tram that ran out of the town in the direction of the barracks. He sat motionless and composed, static.

He got out at the terminus and went down the road. A wind was still running. He could hear the faint whisper of the rye, and the stronger swish as a sudden gust was upon it. No one was about. Feeling detached and impersonal, he went down a field-path between the low vines. Many little vine trees rose up in spires, holding out tender pink shoots, waving their tendrils. He saw them distinctly, and wondered over them. In a field a little way off, men and women were taking up the hay. The bullock-waggon stood by on the path, the men in their blue shirts, the women with white cloths over their heads carried hay in their arms to the cart, all brilliant and distinct upon the shorn, glowing green acres. He felt himself looking out of darkness on to the glamorous, brilliant beauty of the world around him, outside him.

The Baron's house, where Emilie was maidservant, stood square and mellow among trees and garden and fields. It was an old French grange. The barracks was quite near. Bachmann walked, drawn by a single purpose, towards the courtyard. He entered the spacious, shadowy, sun-swept place. The dog, seeing a soldier, only jumped and whined for greeting. The pump stood peacefully in a corner, under a lime tree, in the shade.

The kitchen door was open. He hesitated, then walked in, speaking shyly and smiling involuntarily. The two women started, but with pleasure. Emilie was preparing the tray for afternoon coffee. She stood beyond the table, drawn up, startled, and challenging, and glad. She had the proud, timid eyes of some wild animal, some proud animal. Her black hair was closely banded, her grey eyes watched steadily. She wore a peasant dress of blue cotton sprigged with little red roses, that buttoned tight over her strong maiden breasts.

At the table sat another young woman, the nursery governess, who was picking cherries from a huge heap, and dropping them into a bowl. She was young, pretty, freckled.

"Good day!" she said pleasantly. "The unexpected."

Emilie did not speak. The flush came in her dark cheek. She still stood watching, between fear and a desire to escape, and on the other hand joy that kept her in his presence.

"Yes," he said, bashful and strained, while the eyes of the two women were upon him. "I've got myself in a mess this time."

"What?" asked the nursery governess, dropping her hands in her lap. Emilie stood rigid.

Bachmann could not raise his head. He looked sideways at the glistening, ruddy cherries. He could not recover the normal world.

"I knocked Sergeant Huber over the fortifications down into the moat," he said. "It was accident—but——"

And he grasped at the cherries, and began to eat them, unknowing, hearing only Emilie's little exclamation.

"You knocked him over the fortifications!" echoed Fräulein Hesse. in horror. "How?"

Spitting the cherry-stones into his hand, mechanically, absorbedly, he told them.

"Ach!" exclaimed Emilie sharply.

"And how did you get here?" asked Fräulein Hesse.

"I ran off," he said.

There was a dead silence. He stood, putting himself at the mercy of the women. There came a hissing from the stove, and a stronger smell of coffee. Emilie turned swiftly away. He saw her flat, straight back and her strong loins, as she bent over the stove.

"But what are you going to do?" said Fräulein Hesse, aghast.

"I don't know." he said, grasping at more cherries. He had come to an end.

"You'd better go to the barracks," she said. "We'll get the Herr Baron to come and see about it."

Emilie was swiftly and quietly preparing the tray. She picked it up, and stood with the glittering china and silver before her, impassive, waiting for his reply. Bachmann remained with his head dropped, pale and obstinate. He could not bear to go back.

"I'm going to try to get into France," he said.

"Yes, but they'll catch you," said Fräulein Hesse.

Emilie watched with steady, watchful grey eyes.

"I can have a try, if I could hide till to-night," he said.

Both women knew what he wanted. And they all knew it was no good. Emilie picked up the tray, and went out. Bachmann stood with his head dropped. Within himself he felt the dross of shame and incapacity.

"You'd never get away," said the governess.

"I can try," he said.

To-day he could not put himself between the hands of the military. Let them do as they liked with him to-morrow, if he escaped to-day.

They were silent. He ate cherries. The colour flushed bright into the cheek of the young governess.

Emilie returned to prepare another tray.

"He could hide in your room," the governess said to her.

The girl drew herself away. She could not bear the intrusion.

"That is all I can think of that is safe from the children," said Fräulein Hesse.

Emilie gave no answer. Bachmann stood waiting for the two women. Emilie did not want the close contact with him.

"You could sleep with me," Fräulein Hesse said to her.

Emilie lifted her eyes and looked at the young man, direct, clear, reserving herself.

"Do you want that?" she asked, her strong virginity proof against him.

"Yes—yes——" he said uncertainly, destroyed by shame.

She put back her head.

"Yes," she murmured to herself.

Quickly she filled the tray, and went out.

"But you can't walk over the frontier in a night," said Fräulein Hesse.

"I can cycle," he said.

Emilie returned, a restraint, a neutrality in her bearing.

"I'll see if it's all right," said the governess.

In a moment or two Bachmann was following Emilie through the square hall, where hung large maps on the walls. He noticed a child's blue coat with brass buttons on the peg, and it reminded him of Emilie walking holding the hand of the youngest child, whilst he watched, sitting under the lime tree. Already this was a long way off. That was a sort of freedom he had lost, changed for a new, immediate anxiety.

They went quickly, fearfully up the stairs and down a long corridor. Emilie opened her door, and he entered, ashamed, into her room.

"I must go down," she murmured, and she departed, closing the door softly.

It was a small, bare, neat room. There was a little dish for holy water, a picture of the Sacred Heart, a crucifix, and a *prie-Dieu*. The small bed lay white and untouched, the wash-hand bowl of red earth stood on a bare table, there was a little mirror and a small chest of drawers. That was all.

Feeling safe, in sanctuary, he went to the window, looking over the courtyard at the shimmering, afternoon country. He was going to leave this land, this life. Already he was in the unknown.

He drew away into the room. The curious simplicity and severity of the little Roman Catholic bedroom was foreign but restoring to him. He looked at the crucifix. It was a long, lean, peasant Christ carved by a peasant in the Black Forest. For the first time in his life, Bachmann saw the figure as a human thing. It represented a man hanging there in helpless torture. He stared at it, closely, as if for new knowledge.

Within his own flesh burned and smouldered the restless shame. He could not gather himself together. There was a gap in his soul. The shame within him seemed to displace his strength and his manhood.

He sat down on his chair. The shame, the roused feeling of exposure acted on his brain, made him heavy, unutterably heavy.

Mechanically, his wits all gone, he took off his boots, his belt, his tunic, put them aside, and lay down, heavy, and fell into a kind of drugged sleep.

Emilie came in a little while, and looked at him. But he was sunk in sleep. She saw him lying there inert, and terribly still, and she was afraid. His shirt was unfastened at the throat. She saw his pure white flesh, very clean and beautiful. And he slept inert. His legs, in the blue uniform trousers, his feet in the coarse stockings, lay foreign on her bed. She went away.

### III

She was uneasy, perturbed to her last fibre. She wanted to remain clear, with no touch on her. A wild instinct made her shrink away from any hands which might be laid on her.

She was a foundling, probably of some gipsy race, brought up in a Roman Catholic Rescue Home. A naïve, paganly religious being, she was attached to the Baroness, with whom she had served for seven years, since she was fourteen.

She came into contact with no one, unless it were with Ida Hesse, the governess. Ida was a calculating, good-natured, not very straight-forward flirt. She was the daughter of a poor country doctor. Having gradually come into connection with Emilie, more an alliance than an attachment, she put no distinction of grade between the two of them. They worked together, sang together, walked together, and went together to the rooms of Franz Brand, Ida's sweetheart. There the three talked and laughed together, or the women listened to Franz, who was a forester, playing on his violin.

In all this alliance there was no personal intimacy between the young women. Emilie was naturally secluded in herself, of a reserved, native race. Ida used her as a kind of weight to balance her own flighty movement. But the quick, shifty governess, occupied always in her dealings with admirers, did all she could to move the violent nature of Emilie towards some connection with men.

But the dark girl, primitive yet sensitive to a high degree, was fiercely virgin. Her blood flamed with rage when the common soldiers made the long, sucking, kissing noise behind her as she passed. She hated them for their almost jeering offers. She was well protected by the Baroness.

And her contempt of the common men in general was ineffable. But she loved the Baroness, and she revered the Baron, and she was at her ease when she was doing something for the service of a gentleman. Her whole nature was at peace in the service of real masters or mistresses. For her, a gentleman had some mystic quality that left her free and proud in service. The common soldiers were brutes, merely nothing. Her desire was to serve.

She held herself aloof. When, on Sunday afternoon, she had looked through the windows of the Reichshalle in passing, and had seen the soldiers dancing with the common girls, a cold revulsion and anger had possessed her. She could not bear to see the soldiers taking off their belts and pulling open their tunics, dancing with their shirts showing through the open, sagging tunic, their movements gross, their faces transfigured and sweaty, their coarse hands holding their coarse girls under the arm-pits, drawing the female up to their breasts. She hated to see them clutched breast to breast, the legs of the men moving grossly in the dance.

At evening, when she had been in the garden, and heard on the other side of the hedge the sexual, inarticulate cries of the girls in the embraces of the soldiers, her anger had been too much for her, and she had cried, loud and cold:

"What are you doing there, in the hedge?"

She would have had them whipped.

But Bachmann was not quite a common soldier. Fräulein Hesse had found out about him, and had drawn him and Emilie together. For he was a handsome, blond youth, erect and walking with a kind of pride, unconscious yet clear. Moreover, he came of a rich farming stock, rich for many generations. His father was dead, his mother controlled the moneys for the time being. But if Bachmann wanted a hundred pounds at any moment, he could have them. By trade he, with one of his brothers, was a waggon-builder. The family had the farming, smithy, and waggon-building of their village. They worked because that was the form of life they knew. If they had chosen, they could have lived independent upon their means.

In this way, he was a gentleman in sensibility, though his intellect was not developed. He could afford to pay freely for things. He had, moreover, his native, fine breeding. Emilie wavered uncertainly before him. So he became her sweetheart, and she hungered after him. But she was virgin, and shy, and needed to be in subjection, because she was primitive and had no grasp on civilized forms of living, nor on civilized purposes.

IV

At six o'clock came the inquiry of the soldiers: Had anything been seen of Bachmann? Fräulein Hesse answered, pleased to be playing a rôle:

"No, I've not seen him since Sunday—have you, Emilie?"

"No, I haven't seen him," said Emilie, and her awkwardness was construed as bashfulness. Ida Hesse, stimulated, asked questions, and played her part.

"But it hasn't killed Sergeant Huber?" she cried in consternation.

"No. He fell into the water. But it gave him a bad shock, and smashed his foot on the side of the moat. He's in hospital. It's a bad look-out for Bachmann."

Emilie, implicated and captive, stood looking on. She was no longer free, working with all this regulated system which she could not understand and which was almost god-like to her. She was put out of her place. Bachmann was in her room, she was no longer the faithful in service serving with religious surety.

Her situation was intolerable to her. All evening long the burden was upon her, she could not live. The children must be fed and put to sleep. The Baron and Baroness were going out, she must give them light refreshment. The man-servant was coming in to supper after returning with the carriage. And all the while she had the insupportable feeling of being out of the order, self-responsible, bewildered. The control of her life should come from those above her, and she should move within that control. But now she was out of it, uncontrolled and troubled. More than that, the man, the lover, Bachmann, who was he, what was he? He alone of all men contained for her the unknown quantity which terrified her beyond her service. Oh, she had wanted him as a distant sweetheart, not close, like this, casting her out of her world.

When the Baron and Baroness had departed, and the young man-servant had gone out to enjoy himself, she went upstairs to Bachmann. He had wakened up, and sat dimly in the room. Out in the open he heard the soldiers, his comrades, singing the sentimental songs of the nightfall, the drone of the concertina rising in accompaniment.

"Wenn ich zu mei...nem Kinde geh'...
In seinem Au...g' die Mutter seh'...."

But he himself was removed from it now. Only the sentimental cry of young, unsatisfied desire in the soldiers' singing penetrated his blood and stirred him subtly. He let his head hang; he had become gradually roused: and he waited in concentration, in another world.

The moment she entered the room where the man sat alone, waiting intensely, the thrill passed through her, she died in terror, and after the death, a great flame gushed up, obliterating her. He sat in trousers and shirt on the side of the bed. He looked up as she came in, and she shrank from his face. She could not bear it. Yet she entered near to him.

33

"Do you want anything to eat?" she said.

"Yes," he answered, and as she stood in the twilight of the room with him, he could only hear his heart beat heavily. He saw her apron just level with his face. She stood silent, a little distance off, as if she would be there for ever. He suffered.

As if in a spell she waited, standing motionless and looming there, he sat rather crouching on the side of the bed. A second will in him was powerful and dominating. She drew gradually nearer to him, coming up slowly, as if unconscious. His heart beat up swiftly. He was going to move.

As she came quite close, almost invisibly he lifted his arms and put them round her waist, drawing her with his will and desire. He buried his face into her apron, into the terrible softness of her belly. And he was a flame of passion intense about her. He had forgotten. Shame and memory were gone in a whole, furious flame of passion.

She was quite helpless. Her hands leapt, fluttered, and closed over his head, pressing it deeper into her belly, vibrating as she did so. And his arms tightened on her, his hands spread over her loins, warm as flame on her loveliness. It was intense anguish of bliss for her, and she lost consciousness.

When she recovered, she lay translated in the peace of satisfaction.

It was what she had had no inkling of, never known could be. She was strong with eternal gratitude. And he was there with her. Instinctively, with an instinct of reverence and gratitude, her arms tightened in a little embrace upon him who held her thoroughly embraced.

And he was restored and completed, close to her. That little, twitching, momentary clasp of acknowledgement that she gave him in her satisfaction, roused his pride unconquerable. They loved each other, and all was whole. She loved him, he had taken her, she was given to him. It was right. He was given to her, and they were one, complete.

Warm, with a glow in their hearts and faces, they rose again, modest, but transfigured with happiness.

"I will get you something to eat," she said, and in joy and security of service again, she left him, making a curious little homage of departure. He sat on the side of the bed, escaped, liberated, wondering, and happy.

34

## V

Soon she came again with the tray, followed by Fräulein Hesse. The two women watched him eat, watched the pride and wonder of his being, as he sat there blond and naïf again. Emilie felt rich and complete. Ida was a lesser thing than herself.

"And what are you going to do?" asked Fräulein Hesse, jealous.

"I must get away," he said.

But words had no meaning for him. What did it matter? He had the inner satisfaction and liberty.

"But you'll want a bicycle," said Ida Hesse.

"Yes," he said.

Emilie sat silent, removed and yet with him, connected with him in passion. She looked from this talk of bicycles and escape.

They discussed plans. But in two of them was the one will, that Bachmann should stay with Emilie. Ida Hesse was an outsider.

It was arranged, however, that Ida's lover should put out his bicycle, leave it at the hut where he sometimes watched. Bachmann should fetch it in the night, and ride into France. The hearts of all three beat hot in suspense, driven to thought. They sat in a fire of agitation.

Then Bachmann would get away to America, and Emilie would come and join him. They would be in a fine land then. The tale burned up again.

Emilie and Ida had to go round to Franz Brand's lodging. They departed with slight leave-taking. Bachmann sat in the dark, hearing the bugle for retreat sound out of the night. Then he remembered his post-card to his mother. He slipped out after Emilie, gave it her to post. His manner was careless and victorious, hers shining and trustful. He slipped back to shelter.

There he sat on the side of the bed, thinking. Again he went over the events of the afternoon, remembering his own anguish of apprehension because he had known he could not climb the wall without fainting with fear. Still, a flush of shame came alight in him at the memory. But he said to himself: "What does it matter—I can't help it, well then I can't. If I go up a height, I get absolutely weak, and can't help myself." Again memory came over him, and a gush of shame, like fire. But he sat and endured it. It had to be endured, admitted, and accepted—"I'm not a coward, for all that," he continued. "I'm not afraid of danger. If I'm made that way, that heights melt me and make me let go my water"—it was torture for him to pluck at this truth—"if I'm made like that, I shall have to abide by it, that's all. It isn't all of me." He thought of Emilie, and was satisfied. "What I am, I am; and let it be enough," he thought.

Having accepted his own defect, he sat thinking, waiting for Emilie, to tell her. She came at length, saying that Franz could not arrange about his bicycle this night. It was broken. Bachmann would have to stay over another day.

They were both happy. Emilie, confused before Ida, who was excited and prurient, came again to the young man. She was stiff and dignified with an agony of unusedness. But he took her between his hands, and uncovered her, and enjoyed almost like madness her helpless, virgin body that suffered so strongly, and that took its joy so deeply. While the moisture of torment and modesty was still in her eyes, she clasped him closer, and closer, to the victory and the deep satisfaction of both of them. And they slept together, he in repose still satisfied and peaceful, and she lying close in her static reality.

## VI

In the morning, when the bugle sounded from the barracks they rose and looked out of the window. She loved his body that was proud and blond and able to take command. And he loved her body that was soft and eternal. They looked at the faint grey vapour of summer steaming off from the greenness and ripeness of the fields. There was no town anywhere, their look ended in the haze of the summer morning. Their bodies rested together, their minds tranquil. Then a little anxiety stirred in both of them from the sound of the bugle. She was called back to her old position, to realize the world of authority she did not understand but had wanted to serve. But this call died away again from her. She had all.

She went downstairs to her work, curiously changed. She was in a new world of her own, that she had never even imagined, and which was the land of promise for all that. In this she moved and had her being. And she extended it to her duties. She was curiously happy and absorbed. She had not to strive out of herself to do her work. The doing came from within her without call or command. It was a delicious outflow, like sunshine, the activity that flowed from her and put her tasks to rights.

Bachmann sat busily thinking. He would have to get all his plans ready. He must write to his mother, and she must send him money to Paris. He would go to Paris, and from thence, quickly, to America. It had to be done. He must make all preparations. The dangerous part was the getting into France. He thrilled in anticipation. During the day he would need a time-table of the trains going to Paris—he would need to think. It gave him delicious pleasure, using all his wits. It seemed such an adventure.

This one day, and he would escape then into freedom. What an agony of need he had for absolute, imperious freedom. He had won to his own being, in himself and Emilie, he had drawn the stigma from his shame, he was beginning to be himself. And now he wanted madly to be free to go on. A home, his work, and absolute freedom to move and to be, in her, with her, this was his passionate desire. He thought in a kind of ecstasy, living an hour of painful intensity.

Suddenly he heard voices, and a tramping of feet. His heart gave a great leap, then went still. He was taken. He had known all along. A complete silence filled his body and soul, a silence like death, a suspension of life and sound. He stood motionless in the bedroom, in perfect suspension.

Emilie was busy passing swiftly about the kitchen preparing the children's breakfasts when she heard the tramp of feet and the voice of the Baron. The latter had come in from the garden, and was wearing an old green linen suit. He was a man of middle stature, quick, finely made, and of whimsical charm. His right hand had been shot in the Franco-Prussian war, and now, as always when he was much agitated, he shook it down at his side, as if it hurt. He was talking rapidly to a young, stiff Ober-leutnant. Two private soliders stood bearishly in the doorway.

Emilie, shocked out of herself, stood pale and erect, recoiling.

"Yes, if you think so, we can look," the Baron was hastily and irascibly saying.

"Emilie," he said, turning to the girl, "did you put a post-card to the mother of this Bachmann in the box last evening?"

Emilie stood erect and did not answer.

"Yes?" said the Baron sharply.

"Yes, Herr Baron," replied Emilie, neutral.

The Baron's wounded hand shook rapidly in exasperation. The lieutenant drew himself up still more stiffly. He was right.

"And do you know anything of the fellow?" asked the Baron, looking at her with his blazing, greyish-golden eyes. The girl looked back at him steadily, dumb, but her whole soul naked before him. For two seconds he looked at her in silence. Then in silence, ashamed and furious, he turned away.

"Go up!" he said, with his fierce, peremptory command, to the young officer.

The lieutenant gave his order, in military cold confidence, to the soldiers. They all tramped across the hall. Emilie stood motionless, her life suspended.

The Baron marched swiftly upstairs and down the corridor, the lieutenant and the common soldiers followed. The Baron flung open the door of Emilie's room, and looked at Bachmann, who stood watching, standing in shirt and trousers beside the bed, fronting the door. He was perfectly still. His eyes met the furious, blazing look of the Baron. The latter shook his wounded hand, and then went still. He looked into the eyes of the soldier, steadily. He saw the same naked soul exposed, as if he looked really into the *man*. And the man was helpless, the more helpless for his singular nakedness.

"Ha!" he exclaimed impatiently, turning to the approaching lieutenant.

The latter appeared in the doorway. Quickly his eyes travelled over the bare footed youth. He recognized him as his object. He gave the brief command to dress.

Bachmann turned round for his clothes. He was very still, silent in himself. He was in an abstract, motionless world. That the two gentlemen and the two soldiers stood watching him, he scarcely realized. They could not see him.

Soon he was ready. He stood at attention. But only the shell of his body was at attention. A curious silence, a blankness, like something eternal, possessed him. He remained true to himself.

The lieutenant gave the order to march. The little procession went down the stairs with careful, respectful tread, and passed through the hall to the kitchen. There Emilie stood with her face uplifted, motionless and expressionless. Bachmann did not look at her. They knew each other. They were themselves. Then the little file of men passed out into the courtyard.

The Baron stood in the doorway watching the four figures in uniform pass through the chequered shadow under the lime trees. Bachmann was walking neutralized, as if he were not there. The lieutenant went brittle and long, the two soldiers lumbered beside. They passed out into the sunny morning, growing smaller, going towards the barracks.

The Baron turned into the kitchen. Emilie was cutting bread.

"So he stayed the night here?" he said.

The girl looked at him, scarcely seeing. She was too much herself. The Baron saw the dark, naked soul of her body in her unseeing eyes.

"What were you going to do?" he asked.

"He was going to America," she replied, in a still voice.

"Pah! You should have sent him straight back," fired the Baron.

Emilie stood at his bidding, untouched.

"He's done for now," he said.

But he could not bear the dark, deep nakedness of her eyes, that scarcely changed under this suffering.

"Nothing but a fool," he repeated, going away in agitation, and preparing himself for what he could do.

# Daughters of the Vicar

## 1.

Mr Lindley was first vicar of Aldecross. The cottages of this tiny hamlet had nestled in peace since their beginning, and the country folk had crossed the lanes and farm-lands, two or three miles, to the parish church at Greymeed, on the bright Sunday mornings.

But when the pits were sunk, blank rows of dwellings started up beside the high-roads, and a new population, skimmed from the floating scum of workmen, was filled in, the cottages and the country people almost obliterated.

To suit the convenience of these new collier-inhabitants, a church must be built at Aldecross. There was not too much money. And so the little building crouched like a humped stone-and-mortar mouse, with two little turrets at the west corners for ears, in the fields near the cottages and the apple-trees, as far as possible from the dwellings down the high road. It had an uncertain, timid look about it. And so they planted big-leaved ivy, to hide its shrinking newness. So that now the little church stands buried in its greenery, stranded and sleeping among the fields, while the brick houses elbow nearer and nearer, threatening to crush it down. It is already obsolete.

The Reverend Ernest Lindley, aged twenty-seven, and newly married, came from his curacy in Suffolk to take charge of his church. He was just an ordinary young man, who had been to Cambridge and taken orders. His wife was a self-assured young woman, daughter of a Cambridgeshire rector. Her father had spent the whole of his thousand a year, so that Mrs Lindley had nothing of her own. Thus, the young married people came to Aldecross to live on a stipend of about a hundred and twenty pounds, and to keep up a superior position.

They were not very well received by the new, raw, disaffected population of colliers. Being accustomed to farm labourers, Mr Lindley had considered himself as belonging indisputably to the upper or ordering classes. He had to be humble to the county families, but still, he was of their kind, whilst the common people were something different. He had no doubts of himself.

He found, however, that the collier population refused to accept this arrangement. They had no use for him in their lives, and they told him so, callously. The women merely said, "they were throng," or else, "Oh, it's no good you coming here, we're chapel." The men were quite good-humoured so long as he did not touch them too nigh, they were cheerfully contemptuous of him, with a preconceived contempt he was powerless against.

At last, passing from indignation to silent resentment, even, if he dared have acknowledged it, to conscious hatred of the majority of his flock, and unconscious hatred of himself, he confined his activities to a narrow round of cottages, and he had to submit. He had no particular character, having always depended on his position in society to give him position among men. Now he was so poor, he had no social standing even among the common vulgar tradespeople of the district, and he had not the nature nor the wish to make his society agreeable to them, nor the strength to impose himself where he would have liked to be recognized. He dragged on, pale and miserable and neutral.

At first his wife raged with mortification. She took on airs and used a high hand. But her income was too small, the wrestling with tradesmen's bills was too pitiful, she only met with general, callous ridicule when she tried to be impressive.

Wounded to the quick of her pride, she found herself isolated in an indifferent, callous population. She raged indoors and out. But soon she learned that she must pay too heavily for her outdoor rages, and then she only raged within the walls of the rectory. There her feeling was so strong, that she frightened herself. She saw herself hating her husband, and she knew that, unless she were careful, she would smash her form of life and bring catastrophe upon him and upon herself. So in very fear, she went quiet. She hid, bitter and beaten by fear, behind the only shelter she had in the world, her gloomy, poor parsonage.

Children were born one every year; almost mechanically, she continued to perform her maternal duty, which was forced upon her. Gradually, broken by the suppressing of her violent anger and misery and disgust, she became an invalid and took to her couch.

The children grew up healthy, but unwarmed and rather rigid. Their father and mother educated them at home, made them very proud and very genteel, put them definitely and cruelly in the upper classes, apart from the vulgar around them. So they lived quite isolated. They were good-looking, and had that curiously clean, semi-transparent look of the genteel, isolated poor.

Gradually Mr and Mrs Lindley lost all hold on life, and spent their hours, weeks and years merely haggling to make ends meet, and bitterly repressing and pruning their children into gentility, urging them to ambition, weighting them with duty. On Sunday morning the whole family, except the mother, went down the lane to church, the long-legged girls in skimpy frocks, the boys in black coats and long, grey, unfitting trousers. They passed by their father's parishioners with mute clear faces, childish mouths closed in pride that was like a doom to them, and childish eyes already unseeing. Miss Mary, the eldest, was the leader. She was a long, slim thing with a fine profile and a proud, pure look of submission to a high fate. Miss Louisa, the second, was short and plump and obstinate looking. She had more enemies than ideals. She looked after the lesser children, Miss Mary after the elder. The collier children watched this pale, distinguished procession of the vicar's family pass mutely by, and they were impressed by the air of gentility and distance, they made mock of the trousers of the small sons, they felt inferior in themselves, and hate stirred their hearts.

In her time, Miss Mary received as governess a few little daughters of tradesmen; Miss Louisa managed the house and went among her father's church-goers, giving lessons on the piano to the colliers' daughters at thirteen shillings for twenty-six lessons.

2

One winter morning, when his daughter Mary was about twenty years old, Mr Lindley, a thin unobtrusive figure in his black overcoat and his wideawake, went down into Aldecross with a packet of white papers under his arm. He was delivering the parish almanack.

A rather pale, neutral man of middle age, he waited while the train thumped over the level crossing, going up to the pit which rattled busily just along the line. A wooden-legged man hobbled to open the gate, Mr Lindley passed on. Just at his left hand, below the road and the railway, was the red roof of a cottage, showing through the bare twigs of apple trees. Mr Lindley passed round the low wall, and descended the worn steps that led from the highway down to the cottage which crouched darkly and quietly away below the rumble of passing trains and the clank of coal carts, in a quiet little under-world of its own. Snowdrops with tight-shut buds were hanging very still under the bare currant bushes.

42

The clergyman was just going to knock when he heard a clinking noise, and turning saw through the open door of a black shed just behind him an elderly woman in a black lace cap stooping among reddish big cans, pouring a very bright liquid into a tundish. There was a smell of paraffin. The woman put down her can, took the tundish and laid it on a shelf, then rose with a tin bottle. Her eyes met those of the clergyman.

"Oh is it you, Mr Lin'ley!" she said, in a complaining tone. "Go in."

The minister entered the house. In the hot kitchen sat a big elderly man with a great grey beard, taking snuff. He grunted in a deep, muttering voice, telling the minister to sit down, and then took no more notice of him, but stared vacantly into the fire. Mr Lindley waited.

The woman came in, the ribbons of her black lace cap, or bonnet, hanging on her shawl. She was of medium stature, everything about her was tidy. She went up a step out of the kitchen, carrying the paraffin tin. Feet were heard entering the room up the step. It was a little haberdashery shop, with parcels on the shelves of the walls, a big, old-fashioned sewing-machine with tailor's work lying round it, in the open space. The woman went behind the counter, gave the child, who had entered, the paraffin bottle, and took from her a jug.

"My mother says shall yer put it down," said the child, and she was gone. The woman wrote in a book, then came into the kitchen with her jug. The husband, a very large man, rose and brought more coal to the already hot fire. He moved slowly and sluggishly. Already he was going dead; being a tailor, his large form had become an encumbrance to him. In his youth he had been a great dancer and boxer. Now he was taciturn, and inert. The minister had nothing to say, so he sought for his phrases. But John Durant took no notice, existing silent and dull.

Mrs Durant spread the cloth. Her husband poured himself beer into a mug, and began to smoke and drink.

"Shall you have some?" he growled through his beard at the clergyman, looking slowly from the man to the jug, capable of this one idea.

"No, thank you," replied Mr Lindley, though he would have liked some beer. He must set the example in a drinking parish.

"We need a drop to keep us going," said Mrs Durant.

She had rather a complaining manner. The clergyman sat on uncomfortably while she laid the table for the half-past ten lunch. Her husband drew up to eat. She remained in her little round arm-chair by the fire.

She was a woman who would have liked to be easy in her life, but to whose lot had fallen a rough and turbulent family, and a slothful husband who did not care what became of himself or anybody. So, her rather good-looking square face was peevish, she had that air of having been compelled all her life to serve unwillingly, and to control where she did not want to control. There was about her too that masterful *aplomb* of a woman who has brought up and ruled her sons: but even them she had ruled unwillingly. She had enjoyed managing her little haberdashery shop, riding in the carrier's cart to Nottingham, going through the big warehouses to buy her goods. But the fret of managing her sons she did not like. Only she loved her youngest boy, because he was her last, and she saw herself free.

This was one of the houses the clergyman visited occasionally. Mrs Durant, as part of her regulation, had brought up all her sons in the church. Not that she had any religion. Only, it was what she was used to. Mr Durant was without religion. He read the fervently evangelical *Life* of John Wesley with a curious pleasure, getting from it a satisfaction as from the warmth of the fire, or a glass of brandy. But he cared no more about John Wesley, in fact, than about John Milton, of whom he had never heard.

Mrs Durant took her chair to the table.

"I don't feel like eating," she sighed.

"Why—aren't you well?" asked the clergyman, patronising.

"It isn't that," she sighed. She sat with shut, straight mouth. "I don't know what's going to become of us."

But the clergyman had ground himself down so long, that he could not easily sympathise.

"Have you any trouble?" he asked.

"Ay, have I any trouble!" cried the elderly woman. "I shall end my days in the workhouse."

The minister waited unmoved. What could she know of poverty, in her little house of plenty.

"I hope not," he said.

"And the one lad as I wanted to keep by me—" she lamented.

The minister listened without sympathy, quite neutral.

"And the lad as would have been a support to my old age. What is going to become of us?" she said.

The clergyman, justly, did not believe in the cry of poverty, but wondered what had become of the son.

"Has anything happened to Alfred?" he asked.

"We've got word he's gone for a Queen's sailor," she said sharply.

"He has joined the navy!" exclaimed Mr Lindley. "I think he could scarcely have done better—to serve his Queen and country on the sea— —"

"He is wanted to serve *me*," she cried. "And I wanted my lad at home."

Alfred was her baby, her last, whom she had allowed herself the luxury of spoiling.

"You will miss him," said Mr Lindley, "that is certain. But this is no regrettable step for him to have taken—on the contrary."

"That's easy for you to say, Mr Lindley," she replied tartly. "Do you think I want my lad climbing ropes at another man's bidding, like a monkey—"

"There is no *dishonour*, surely, in serving in the navy?"

"Dishonour this dishonour that," cried the angry old woman. "He goes and makes a slave of himself, and he'll rue it."

Her angry, scornful impatience nettled the clergyman, and silenced him for some moments.

"I do not see," he retorted at last, white at the gills and inadequate, "that the Queen's service is any more to be called slavery than working in a mine."

"At home he was at home, and his own master. *I* know he'll find a difference."

"It may be the making of him," said the clergyman. "It will take him away from bad companionship and drink."

Some of the Durants' sons were notorious drinkers, and Alfred was not quite steady.

"And why indeed shouldn't he have his glass," cried the mother. "He picks no man's pocket to pay for it."

The clergyman stiffened at what he thought was an allusion to his own profession, and his unpaid bills.

"With all due consideration, I am glad to hear he has joined the navy," he said.

"Me with my old age coming on, and his father working very little. I'd thank you to be glad about something else besides that, Mr Lindley.—"

The woman began to cry. Her husband, quite impassive, finished his lunch of meat pie, and drank some beer. Then he turned to the fire, as if there were no-one in the room but himself.

"I shall respect all men who serve God and their Country on the sea, Mrs Durant," said the clergyman, stubbornly.

"That is very well, when they are not your sons who are doing the dirty work.—It makes a difference," she replied tartly.

"I should be proud if one of my sons were to enter the navy."

"Ay—well—we're not all of us made alike——"

The minister rose. He put down a large folded paper.

"I've brought the almanack," he said.

Mrs Durant unfolded it.

"I do like a bit of colour in things," she said, petulantly.

The clergyman did not reply.

"There's that envelope for the organist's fund—" said the old woman, and rising, she took the thing from the mantelpiece, went into the shop, and returned sealing it up.

"Which is all I can afford," she said.

Mr Lindley took his departure, in his pocket the envelope containing Mrs Durant's offering for Miss Louisa's services. He went from door to door delivering the almanacks, in dull routine. Jaded with the monotony of the business, and with the repeated effort of greeting half-known people, he felt barren and rather irritable. At last he returned home.

In the dining room was a small fire. Mrs Lindley, grown very stout, lay on her couch. The vicar carved the cold mutton, Miss Louisa, short and plump and rather flushed, came in from the kitchen, Miss Mary, dark, with a beautiful white brow and grey eyes, served the vegetables, the children chattered a little, but not exuberantly. The very air seemed starved.

"I went to the Durants," said the vicar, as he served out the small portions of mutton. "It appears Alfred has run away to join the navy."

"Do him good," came the rough voice of the invalid. Miss Louisa, attending to the youngest child, looked up in protest.

"Why has he done that?" asked Mary's low, musical voice.

"He wanted some excitement, I suppose," said the vicar. "Shall we say grace?"

The children were arranged, all bent their heads, grace was pronounced. At the last word every face was being raised, to go on with the interesting subject.

"He's just done the right thing, for once," came the rather deep voice of the mother. "Save him from becoming a drunken sot, like the rest of them."

"They're not *all* drunken, mama," said Miss Louisa, stubbornly.

"It's no fault of their upbringing if they're not. Walter Durant is a standing disgrace."

"As I told Mrs Durant," said the vicar, eating hungrily, "it is the best thing he could have done. It will take him away from temptation during the most dangerous years of his life—how old is he—nineteen—?"

"Twenty," said Miss Louisa.

"Twenty!" repeated the vicar. "It will give him wholesome discipline and set before him some sort of standard of duty and honour—nothing could have been better for him. But—"

"We shall miss him from the choir," cried Miss Louisa, as if taking opposite sides to her parents.

"That is as it may be," said the vicar. "I prefer to know he is safe in the navy, than running the risk of getting into bad ways here."

"Was he getting into bad ways?" asked the stubborn Miss Louisa.

"You know, Louisa, he wasn't quite what he used to be," said Miss Mary gently and steadily. Miss Louisa shut her rather heavy jaw sulkily. She wanted to deny it, but she knew it was true.

For her he had been a laughing, warm lad, with something kindly and something rich about him. It had made her feel warm. It seemed the days would be colder since he had gone.

"Quite the best thing he could do," said the mother with emphasis.

"I think so," said the vicar. "But his mother was almost abusive because I suggested it."

He spoke in an injured tone.

"What does *she* care for her children's welfare," said the invalid. "Their wages is all her concern."

"I suppose she wanted him at home with her," said Miss Louisa.

"Yes, she did—at the expense of his learning to be a drunkard like the rest of them," retorted her mother.

"George Durant doesn't drink," defended her daughter.

"Because he got burned so badly when he was nineteen—in the pit—and that frightened him. The navy is a better remedy than that, at least."

"Certainly," said the vicar. "Certainly."

And to this Miss Louisa agreed. Yet she could not but feel angry that he had gone away for so many years. She herself was only nineteen.

### 3

It happened when Miss Mary was twenty three years old, Mr Lindley was very ill. The family was exceedingly poor at the time, such a lot of money was needed, so little was forthcoming. Neither Miss Mary nor Miss Louisa had suitors. What chance had they? They met no eligible young men in Aldecross. And what they earned was a mere drop in a void. The girls' hearts were chilled and hardened with fear of this perpetual cold penury, this narrow struggle, this horrible nothingness of their lives.

A clergyman had to be found for the church work. It so happened the son of an old friend of Mr Lindley's was waiting three months before taking up his duties. He would come and officiate, for nothing. The young clergyman was keenly expected. He was not more than twenty seven, a Master of Arts of Oxford, had written his thesis on Roman Law. He came of an old Cambridgeshire family, had some private means, was going to take a church in Northamptonshire with a good stipend, and was not married. Mrs Lindley incurred new debts, and scarcely regretted her husband's illness.

But when Mr Massey came, there was a shock of disappointment in the house. They had expected a young man with a pipe and a deep voice, but with better manners than Sidney, the eldest of the Lindleys. There arrived instead a small, chétif man, scarcely larger than a boy of twelve, spectacled, timid in the extreme, without a word to utter at first; yet with a certain inhuman self-sureness.

"What a little abortion!" was Mrs Lindley's exclamation to herself on first seeing him, in his buttoned-up clerical coat. And for the first time for many days, she was profoundly thankful to God: that all her children were decent specimens.

He had not normal powers of perception. They soon saw that he lacked the full range of human feelings, had rather a strong, philosophical mind, from which he lived. His body was almost unthinkable, in intellect he was something definite. The conversation at once took a balanced, abstract tone when he participated. There was no spontaneous exclamation, no violent assertion or expression of personal conviction, but all cold, reasonable assertion. This was very hard on Mrs Lindley. The little man would look at her, after one of her pronouncements, and then give, in his thin voice, his own calculated version, so that she felt as if she were tumbling into thin air through a hole in the flimsy floor on which their conversation stood. It was she who felt a fool. Soon she was reduced to a hardy silence.

Still, at the back of her mind, she remembered that he was an unattached gentleman, who would shortly have an income altogether of six or seven hundred a year. What did the man matter, if there were pecuniary ease! The man was a trifle thrown in. After twenty two years her sentimentality was ground away, and only the millstone of poverty mattered to her. So she supported the little man as a representative of a decent income.

His most irritating habit was that of a sneering little giggle, all on his own, which came when he perceived or related some illogical absurdity on the part of another person. It was the only form of humour he had. Stupidity in thinking seemed to him exquisitely funny. But any novel was unintelligibly meaningless and dull, and to an Irish sort of humour he listened curiously, examining it like mathematics, or else simply not hearing. In normal human relationship he was not there. Quite unable to take part in simple everyday talk, he padded silently round the house, or sat in the dining room looking nervously from side to side, always apart in a cold, rarefied little world of his own. Sometimes he made an ironic remark, that did not seem humanly relevant, or he gave his little laugh, like a sneer. He had to defend himself and his own insufficiency. And he answered questions grudgingly, with a yes or no, because he did not see their import, and was nervous. It seemed to Miss Louisa he scarcely distinguished one person from another, but that he liked to be near to her, or to Mary, for some sort of contact which stimulated him unknown.

Apart from all this, he was the most admirable workman. He was unremittingly shy, but perfect in his sense of duty: as far as he could conceive Christianity, he was a perfect Christian. Nothing that he realised he could do for anyone did he leave undone, although he was so incapable of coming into contact with another being, that he could not proffer help. Now he attended assiduously to the sick man, investigated all the affairs of the parish or the church which Mr Lindley had in control, straightened out accounts, made lists of the sick and needy, padded round with help and to see what he could do. He heard of Mrs Lindley's anxiety about her sons, and began to investigate means of sending them to Cambridge. His kindness almost frightened Miss Mary. She honoured it so, and yet she shrank from it. For in

49

it all Mr Massey seemed to have no sense of any person, any human being whom he was helping: he only realised a kind of mathematical working out, solving of given situations, a calculated well-doing. And it was as if he had accepted the Christian tenets as axioms. His religion consisted in what his scrupulous, abstract mind approved of.

Seeing his acts, Miss Mary must respect and honour him. In consequence she must serve him. To this she had to force herself, shuddering and yet desirous, but he did not perceive it. She accompanied him on his visiting in the parish, and whilst she was cold with admiration for him, often she was touched with pity for the little padding figure with bent shoulders, buttoned up to the chin in his overcoat. She was a handsome, calm girl, tall, with a beautiful repose. Her clothes were poor, and she wore a black silk scarf, having no furs. But she was a lady. As the people saw her walking down Aldecross beside Mr Massey, they said:

"My word, Miss Mary's got a catch. Did ever you see such a measley little shrimp!"

She knew they were talking so, and it made her heart grow hot against them, and she drew herself as it were protectively towards the little man beside her. At any rate, she could see and give honour to his genuine goodness.

He could not walk fast, or far.

"You have not been well?" she asked, in her dignified way.

"I have an internal trouble."

He was not aware of her slight shudder. There was silence, whilst she bowed to recover her composure, to resume her gentle manner towards him.

He was fond of Miss Mary. She had made it a rule of hospitality that he should always be escorted by herself or by her sister on his visits in the parish, which were not many. But some mornings she was engaged. Then Miss Louisa took her place. It was no good Miss Louisa's trying to adopt to Mr Massey an attitude of queenly service. She was unable to regard him save with aversion. When she saw him from behind, thin and bentshouldered, looking like a sickly lad of thirteen, she disliked him exceedingly, and felt a desire to put him out of existence. And yet a deeper justice in Mary made Louisa humble before her sister.

They were going to see Mr Durant, who was paralysed and not expected to live. Miss Louisa was crudely ashamed at being admitted to the cottage in company with the little clergyman.

Mrs Durant was, however, much quieter in the face of her real trouble.

"How is Mr Durant?" asked Louisa.

"He is no different—and we don't expect him to be," was the reply. The little clergyman stood looking on.

They went upstairs. The three stood for some time looking at the bed, at the grey head of the old man on the pillow, the grey beard over the sheet. Miss Louisa was shocked and afraid.

"It is so dreadful," she said, with a shudder.

"It is how I always thought it would be," replied Mrs Durant.

Then Miss Louisa was afraid of her. The two women were uneasy, waiting for Mr Massey to say something. He stood, small and bent, too nervous to speak.

"Has he any understanding?" he asked at length.

"Maybe," said Mrs Durant. "Can you hear, John?" she asked loudly. The dull blue eye of the inert man looked at her feebly.

"Yes, he understands," said Mrs Durant to Mr Massey. Except for the dull look in his eyes, the sick man lay as if dead. The three stood in silence. Miss Louisa was obstinate but heavy-hearted under the load of unlivingness. It was Mr Massey who kept her there in discipline. His non-human will dominated them all.

Then they heard a sound below, a man's footsteps, and a man's voice called subduedly:

"Are you upstairs mother?"

Mrs Durant started and moved to the door. But already a quick firm step was running up the stairs.

"I'm a bit early, mother," a troubled voice said, and on the landing they saw the form of the sailor. His mother came and clung to him. She was suddenly aware that she needed something to hold on to. He put his arms round her, and bent over her, kissing her.

"He's not gone, mother?" he asked anxiously, struggling to control his voice.

Miss Louisa looked away from the mother and son who stood together in the gloom on the landing. She could not bear it that she and Mr Massey should be there. The latter stood nervously, as if ill at ease before the emotion that was running. He was a witness, nervous, unwilling, but dispassionate. To Miss Louisa's hot heart it seemed all, all wrong that they should be there.

Mrs Durant entered the bedroom, her face wet.

"There's Miss Louisa and the vicar," she said, out of voice and quavering.

Her son, red faced and slender, drew himself up to salute. But Miss Louisa held out her hand. Then she saw his hazel eyes recognise her for a moment, and his small, white teeth showed in a glimpse of the greeting she used to love. She was covered with confusion. He went round to the bed; his boots clicked on the plaster floor, he bowed his head with dignity.

"How are you, Dad?" he said, laying his hand on the sheet, faltering. But the old man stared fixedly and unseeing. The son stood perfectly still for a few moments, then slowly recoiled. Miss Louisa saw the fine outline of his breast, under the blue sailor's blouse, as his chest began to heave.

"He doesn't know me," he said, turning to his mother. He gradually went white.

"No my boy!" cried the mother, pitiful, lifting her face. And suddenly she put her face against his shoulder, he was stooping down to her, holding her against him, and she cried aloud for a moment or two. Miss Louisa saw his sides heaving, and heard the sharp hiss of his breath. She turned away, tears streaming down her face. The father lay inert upon the white bed. Mr Massey looked queer and obliterated, so little now that the sailor with his sun-burned skin was in the room. He stood waiting. Miss Louisa wanted to die, she wanted to have done. She dared not turn round again to look.

"Shall I offer a prayer?" came the frail voice of the clergyman, and all kneeled down.

Miss Louisa was frightened of the inert man upon the bed. Then she felt a flash of fear of Mr Massey, hearing his thin, detached voice. And then, calmed, she looked up. On the far side of the bed were the heads of the mother and son, the one in the black lace cap, with the small white nape of the neck beneath, the other, with brown, sun scorched hair too close and wiry to allow of a parting, and neck tanned firm, bowed as if unwillingly. The great grey beard of the old man did not move, the prayer continued. Mr Massey prayed with a pure lucidity, that they all might conform to the higher will. He was like something that dominated the bowed heads, something dispassionate that governed them inexorably. Miss Louisa was afraid of him. And she was bound, during the course of the prayer, to have a little reverence for him. It was like a foretaste of inexorable, cold death, a taste of pure justice.

That evening she talked to Mary of the visit. Her heart, her veins were possessed by the thought of Alfred Durant as he held his mother in his arms; then the break in his voice, as she remembered it again and again, was like a flame through her; and she wanted to see his face more distinctly in her mind, ruddy with the sun, and his golden-brown eyes, kind and careless, strained now with a natural fear, the fine nose tanned hard by the sun, the mouth that could not help smiling at her. And it went through her with pride, to think of his figure, a straight, fine jet of life.

"He is a handsome lad," she said to Miss Mary, as if he had not been a year older than herself. Underneath was the deeper dread, almost hatred, of the inhuman being of Mr Massey. She felt she must protect herself and Alfred from him.

"When I felt Mr Massey there," she said, "I almost hated him. What right had he to be there!"

"Surely he has all right," said Miss Mary after a pause. "He is *really* a Christian."

"He seems to me nearly an imbecile," said Miss Louisa.

Miss Mary, quiet and beautiful, was silent for a moment.

"Oh no," she said. "Not *imbecile*—"

"Well then—he reminds me of a six months child—or a five months child—as if he didn't have time to get developed enough before he was born."

"Yes," said Miss Mary slowly. "There is something lacking. But there is something wonderful in him: and he is really *good*—"

"Yes," said Miss Louisa. "It doesn't seem right that he should be. What right has *that* to be called goodness!"

"But it *is* goodness," persisted Mary. Then she added, with a laugh: "And come, you wouldn't deny that as well."

There was a doggedness in her voice. She went about very quietly. In her soul, she knew what was going to happen. She knew that Mr Massey was stronger than she, and that she must submit to what he was. Her physical self was prouder, stronger than he, her physical self disliked and despised him. But she was in the grip of his moral, mental being. And she felt the days allotted out to her. And her family watched.

## 4

A few days after, old Mr Durant died. Miss Louisa saw Alfred once more, but he was stiff before her now, treating her not like a person, but as if she were some sort of will in command and he a separate, distinct will waiting in front of her. She had never felt such utter steel-plate separation from anyone. It puzzled her and frightened her. What had become of him? And she hated the military discipline—she was antagonistic to it. Now he was not himself. He was the will which obeys set over against the will which commands. She hesitated over accepting this. He had put himself out of her range. He had ranked himself inferior, subordinate to her. And that was how he would get away from her, that was how he would avoid all connection with her: by fronting her impersonally from the opposite camp, by taking up the abstract position of an inferior.

She went brooding steadily and sullenly over this, brooding and brooding. Her fierce, obstinate heart could not give way. It clung to its own rights. Sometimes she dismissed him. Why should he, her inferior, trouble her?

Then she relapsed to him, and almost hated him. It was his way of getting out of it. She felt the cowardice of it, his calmly placing her in a superior class, and placing himself inaccessibly apart, in an inferior, as if she, the sensient woman who was fond of him, did not count. But she was not going to submit. Dogged in her heart she held on to him.

## 5

In six months' time Miss Mary had married Mr Massey. There had been no love-making, nobody had made any remark. But everybody was tense and callous with expectation. When one day Mr Massey asked for Mary's hand, Mr Lindley started and trembled from the thin, abstract voice of the little man. Mr Massey was very nervous, but so curiously absolute.

"I shall be very glad," said the vicar, "but of course the decision lies with Mary herself." And his still feeble hand shook as he moved a Bible on his desk.

The small man, keeping fixedly to his idea, padded out of the room to find Miss Mary. He sat a long time by her, while she made some conversation, before he had readiness to speak. She was afraid of what was coming, and sat stiff in apprehension. She felt as if her body would rise and fling him aside. But her spirit quivered and waited. Almost in expectation she waited, almost wanting him. And then she knew he would speak.

"I have already asked Mr Lindley," said the clergyman, while suddenly she looked with aversion at his little knees, "if he would consent to my proposal." He was aware of his own disadvantage, but his will was set.

She went cold as she sat, and impervious, almost as if she had become stone. He waited a moment nervously. He would not persuade her. He himself never even heard persuasion, but pursued his own course. He looked at her, sure of himself, unsure of her, and said:

"Will you become my wife, Mary?"

Still her heart was hard and cold. She sat proudly.

"I should like to speak to Mama first," she said.

"Very well," replied Mr Massey.

And in a moment he padded away.

Mary went to her mother. She was cold and reserved.

"Mr Massey has asked me to marry him, Mama," she said. Mrs Lindley went on staring at her book. She was cramped in her feeling.

"Well, and what did you say?"

They were both keeping calm and cold.

"I said I would speak to you before answering him."

This was equivalent to a question. Mrs Lindley did not want to reply to it. She shifted her heavy form irritably on the couch. Miss Mary sat calm and straight, with closed mouth.

"Your father thinks it would not be a bad match," said the mother, as if casually.

Nothing more was said. Everybody remained cold and shut-off. Miss Mary did not speak to Miss Louisa, the Reverend Ernest Lindley kept out of sight.

At evening Miss Mary accepted Mr Massey.

"Yes, I will marry you," she said, with even a little movement of tenderness towards him. He was embarrassed, but satisfied. She could see him making some movement towards her, could feel the male in him, something cold and triumphant, asserting itself. She sat rigid, and waited.

When Miss Louisa knew, she was silent with bitter anger against everybody, even against Mary. She felt her faith wounded. Did the real things to her not matter after all? She wanted to get away. She thought of Mr Massey. He had some curious power, some unanswerable right. He was a will that they could not controvert.—Suddenly a flush started in her. If he had come to her she would have flipped him out of the room. He was never going to touch *her*. And she was glad. She was glad that her blood would rise and exterminate the little man, if he came too near to her, no matter how her judgment was paralysed by him, no matter how he moved in abstract goodness. She thought she was perverse to be glad, but glad she was. "I would just flip him out of the room," she said, and she derived great satisfaction from the open statement. Nevertheless, perhaps she ought still to feel that Mary, on her plane, was a higher being than herself. But then Mary was Mary, and she was Louisa, and that also was inalterable.

Mary, in marrying him, tried to become a pure reason such as he was, without feeling or impulse. She shut herself up, she shut herself rigid against the agonies of shame and the terror of violation which came at first. She *would* not feel, and she *would* not feel. She was a pure will acquiescing to him. She elected a certain kind of fate. She would be good and purely just, she would live in a higher freedom than she had ever known, she would be free of mundane care, she was a pure will towards right. She had sold herself, but had a new freedom. She had got rid of her body. She had sold a lower thing, her body, for a higher thing, her freedom from material things. She considered that she paid for all she got from her husband. So, in a kind of independence, she moved proud and free. She had paid with her body: that was henceforward out of consideration. She was glad to be rid of it. She had bought her position in the world—that henceforth was taken for granted. There remained only the direction of her activity towards charity and high-minded living.

She could scarcely bear other people to be present with her and her husband. Her private life was her shame. But then, she could keep it hidden. She lived almost isolated in the rectory of the tiny village miles from the railway. She suffered as if it were an insult to her own flesh, seeing the repulsion which some people felt for her husband, or the special manner they had of treating him, as if he were a 'case'. But most people were uneasy before him, which restored her pride.

If she had let herself, she would have hated him, hated his padding round the house, his thin voice devoid of human-understanding, his bent little shoulders and rather incomplete face that reminded her of an abortion. But rigorously she kept to her position. She took care of him and was just to him. There was also a deep, craven fear of him, something slave-like.

There was not much fault to be found with his behaviour. He was scrupulously just and kind according to his lights. But the male in him was cold and self-complete, and utterly domineering. Weak, insufficient little thing as he was, she had not expected this of him. It was something in the bargain she had not understood. It made her hold her head, to keep still. She knew, vaguely, that she was murdering herself. After all, her body was not quite so easy to get rid of. And this manner of disposing of it—ah, sometimes she felt she must rise and bring about death, lift her hand for utter denial of everything, by a general destruction.

He was almost unaware of the conditions about him. He did not fuss in the domestic way, she did as she liked in the house. Indeed, she was a great deal free of him. He would sit obliterated for hours. He was kind, and almost anxiously considerate. But when he considered he was right, his will was just blindly male, like a cold machine. And on most points he was logically right, or he had with him the right of the creed they both accepted. It was so. There was nothing for her to go against.

Then she found herself with child, and felt for the first time horror, afraid before God and man. This also she had to go through—it was the right. When the child arrived, it was a bonny, healthy lad. Her heart hurt in her body, as she took the baby between her hands. The flesh that was trampled and silent in her must speak again in the boy. After all, she had to live—it was not so simple after all. Nothing was finished completely. She looked and looked at the baby, and almost hated it, and suffered an anguish of love for it. She hated it because it made her live again in the flesh, when she *could* not live in the flesh, she could not. She wanted to trample her flesh down, down, extinct, to live in the mind. And now there was this child. It was too cruel, too racking. For she must love the child. Her purpose was broken in two again. She had to become amorphous, purposeless, without real being. As a mother, she was a fragmentary, ignoble thing.

Mr Massey, blind to everything else in the way of human feeling, became obsessed by the idea of his child. When it arrived, suddenly it filled the whole world of feeling for him. It was his obsession, his terror was for its safety and well-being. It was something new, as if he himself had been born a naked infant, conscious of his own exposure, and full of apprehension. He who had never been aware of any-one else, all his life, now was aware of nothing but the child. Not that he ever played with it, or kissed it, or tended it. He did nothing for it. But it dominated him, it filled, and at the same time emptied his mind. The world was all baby for him.

This his wife must also bear, his question: "What is the reason that he cries?"—his reminder, at the first sound: "Mary, that is the child,"—his restlessness if the feeding time were five minutes past. She had bargained for this—now she must stand by her bargain.


6


Miss Louisa, at home in the dingy vicarage, had suffered a great deal over her sister's wedding. Having once begun to cry out against it, during the engagement, she had been silenced by Mary's quiet: "I don't agree with you about him, Louisa, I *want* to marry him." Then Miss Louisa had been angry deep in her heart, and therefore silent. This dangerous state started the change in her. Her own revulsion made her recoil from the hitherto undoubted Mary.

"I'd beg the streets barefoot first," said Miss Louisa, thinking of Mr Massey.

But evidently Mary could perform a different heroism. So she, Louisa the practical, suddenly felt that Mary, her ideal, was questionable after all. How could she be pure—one cannot be dirty in act and spiritual in being. Louisa distrusted Mary's high spirituality. It was no longer genuine for her. And if Mary were spiritual and misguided, why did not her father protect her? Because of the money. He disliked the whole affair, but he backed away, because of the money. And the mother frankly did not care: her daughters could do as they liked. Her mother's pronouncement:

"Whatever happens to *him*, Mary is safe for life,"—so evidently and shallowly a calculation, incensed Louisa.

"I'd rather be safe in the workhouse," she cried.

"Your father will see to that," replied her mother brutally. This speech, in its indirectness, so injured Miss Louisa that she hated her mother deep, deep in her heart, and almost hated herself. It was a long time resolving itself out, this hate. But it worked and worked, and at last the young woman said:

"They are wrong—they are all wrong. They have ground out their souls for what isn't worth anything, and there isn't a grain of love in them anywhere. And I *will* have love. They want us to deny it. They've never found it, so they want to say it doesn't exist. But I *will* have it. I *will* love—it is my birthright. I will love the man I marry—that is all I care about."

So Miss Louisa stood isolated from everybody. She and Mary had parted over Mr Massey. In Louisa's eyes, Mary was degraded, married to Mr Massey. She could not bear to think of her lofty, spiritual sister degraded in the body like this. Mary was wrong, wrong, wrong: she was not superior, she was flawed, incomplete. The two sisters stood apart. They still loved each other, they would love each other as long as they lived. But they had parted ways. A new solitariness came over the obstinate Louisa, and her heavy jaw set stubbornly. She was going on her own way. But which way? She was quite alone, with a blank world before her? How could she be said to have any way. Yet she had her fixed will to love, to have the man she loved.

7

When her boy was three years old, Mary had another baby, a girl. The three years had gone by monotonously. They might have been an eternity, they might have been brief as a sleep. She did not know. Only, there was always a weight on top of her, something that pressed down her life. The only thing that had happened was that Mr Massey had had an operation. He was always exceedingly fragile. His wife had soon learned to attend to him mechanically, as part of her duty.

But this third year, after the baby girl had been born, Mary felt oppressed and depressed. Christmas drew near: the gloomy, un-leavened Christmas of the rectory, where all the days were of the same dark fabric. And Mary was afraid. It was as if the darkness were coming upon her.

"Edward, I should like to go home for Christmas," she said, and a certain terror filled her as she spoke.

"But you can't leave baby," said her husband, blinking.

"We can all go."

He thought, and stared in his collective fashion.

"Why do you wish to go?" he asked.

"Because I need a change. A change would do me good, and it would be good for the milk."

He heard the will in his wife's voice, and was at a loss. Her language was unintelligible to him. But somehow he felt that Mary was set upon it. And while she was breeding, either about to have a child, or nursing, he regarded her as a special sort of being.

"Wouldn't it hurt baby to take her by the train?" he said.

"No," replied the mother, "why should it."

They went. When they were in the train, it began to snow. From the window of his first-class carriage the little clergyman watched the big flakes sweep by, like a blind drawn across the country. He was obsessed by thought of the baby, and afraid of the draughts of the carriage.

"Sit right in the corner," he said to his wife, "and hold baby close back."

She moved at his bidding, and stared out of the window. His eternal presence was like an iron weight on her brain. But she was going partially to escape for a few days.

"Sit on the other side, Jack," said the father. "It is less draughty. Come to this window."

He watched the boy in anxiety. But his children were the only beings in the world who took not the slightest notice of him.

"Look, mother, look!" cried the boy. "They fly right at my face"—he meant the snowflakes.

"Come into this corner," repeated his father, out of another world.

"He's jumped on this one's back, mother, an' they're riding to the bottom!" cried the boy, jumping with glee.

"Tell him to come on this side," the little man bade his wife.

"Jack, kneel on this cushion," said the mother, putting her white hand on the place.

The boy slid over in silence to the place she indicated, waited still for a moment, then almost deliberately, stridently cried:

"Look at all those in the corner, mother, making a heap," and he pointed to the cluster of snowflakes with finger pressed dramatically on the pane, and he turned to his mother a bit ostentatiously.

"All in a heap!" she said.

He had seen her face, and had her response, and he was somewhat assured. Vaguely uneasy, he was reassured if he could win her attention.

They arrived at the vicarage at half-past two, not having had lunch.

"How are you, Edward?" said Mr Lindley, trying on his side to be fatherly. But he was always in a false position with his son-in-law, frustrated before him, therefore, as much as possible, he shut his eyes and ears to him. The vicar was looking thin and pale and ill-nourished.

He had gone quite grey. He was, however, still haughty, but, since the growing-up of his children, it was a brittle haughtiness, that might break at any moment and leave the vicar only an impoverished, pitiable figure. Mrs Lindley took all the notice of her daughter, and of the children. She ignored her son-in-law. Miss Louisa was clucking and laughing and rejoicing over the baby. Mr Massey stood aside, a bent, persistent little figure.

"Oh a pretty!—a little pretty!—oh a cold little pretty come in a railway-train!" Miss Louisa was cooing to the infant, crouching on the hearthrug opening the white woollen wraps and exposing the child to the fireglow.

"Mary," said the little clergyman. "I think it would be better to give baby a warm bath. She may take a cold."

"I think it is not necessary," said the mother, coming and closing her hand judiciously over the rosy feet and hands of the mite. "She is not chilly."

"Not a bit," cried Miss Louisa. "She's not caught cold."

"I'll go and bring her flannels," said Mr Massey, with one idea.

"I can bath her in the kitchen then," said Mary, in an altered, cold tone.

"You can't, the girl is scrubbing there," said Miss Louisa. "Besides, she doesn't want a bath at this time of day."

"She'd better have one," said Mary, quietly, out of submission. Miss Louisa's gorge rose, and she was silent. When the little man padded down with the flannels on his arm, Mrs Lindley asked:

"Hadn't *you* better take a hot bath Edward?"

But the sarcasm was lost on the little clergyman. He was absorbed in the preparations round the baby.

The room was dull and threadbare, and the snow outside seemed fairy-land by comparison, so white on the lawn and tufted on the bushes. Indoors the heavy pictures hung obscurely on the walls, everything was dingy with gloom.

Except in the fireglow, where they had laid the bath on the hearth! Mrs Massey, her black hair always smoothly coiled and queenly, kneeled by the bath, wearing a rubber apron, and holding the kicking child. Her husband stood holding the towels and the flannels to warm. Louisa, too cross to share in the joy of the baby's bath, was laying the table. The boy was hanging on the door-knob, wrestling with it to get out. His father looked round.

"Come away from the door, Jack" he said, ineffectually. Jack tugged harder at the knob as if he did not hear. Mr Massey blinked at him.

"He must come away from the door, Mary," he said. "There will be a draught if it is opened."

"Jack, come away from the door, dear," said the mother, dexterously turning the shiny wet baby onto her towelled knee, then glancing round, "Go and tell Auntie Louisa about the train."

Louisa, also afraid to open the door, was watching the scene on the hearth. Mr Massey stood holding the baby's flannel, as if assisting at some ceremonial. If everybody had not been subduedly angry, it would have been ridiculous.

"I want to see out of the window," Jack cried. His father turned hastily.

"Do *you* mind lifting him onto a chair, Louisa," said Mary hastily. The father was too delicate.

When the baby was flannelled, Mr Massey went upstairs and returned with four pillows, which he set in the fender to warm. Then he stood watching the mother feed her child, obsessed by the idea of his infant.

Louisa went on with her preparations for the meal. She could not have told why she was so sullenly angry. Mrs Lindley, as usual, lay silently watching.

Mary carried her child upstairs, followed by her husband with the pillows. After a while he came down again.

"What is Mary doing? Why doesn't she come down to eat?" asked Mrs Lindley.

"She is staying with baby. The room is rather cold. I will ask the girl to put in a fire."

He was going absorbedly to the door.

"But Mary has had nothing to eat. It is *she* who will catch cold," said the mother, exasperated.

Mr Massey seemed as if he did not hear. Yet he looked at his mother-in-law, and answered:

"I will take her something."

He went out. Mrs Lindley shifted on her couch with anger. Miss Louisa glowered. But no one said anything, because of the money that came to the vicarage from Mr Massey.

Louisa went upstairs. Her sister was sitting by the bed, reading a scrap of paper.

"Won't you come down and eat?" the younger asked.

"In a moment or two," Mary replied, in a quiet, reserved voice, that forbade anyone to approach her.

It was this that made Miss Louisa most furious. She went downstairs, and announced to her mother:

"I am going out. I may not be home to tea."

## 8

No one remarked on her exit. She put on her fur hat, that the village people knew so well, and the old norfolk jacket. Louisa was short and plump and plain. She had her mother's heavy jaw, her father's proud brow, and her own grey, brooding eyes that were very beautiful when she smiled. It was true, as the people said, that she looked sulky. Her chief attraction was her glistening, heavy, deep-blonde hair, which shone and gleamed with a richness that was not entirely foreign to her.

"Where am I going?" she said to herself, when she got outside in the snow. She did not hesitate, however, but, by mechanical walking, found herself descending the hill towards Old Aldecross. In the valley that was black with trees, the colliery breathed in stertorous pants, sending out high conical columns of steam that remained upright, whiter than the snow on the hills, yet shadowy, in the dead air. Louisa would not acknowledge to herself whither she was making her way, till she came to the railway crossing. Then the bunches of snow in the twigs of the apple tree that leaned towards the fence told her she must go and see Mrs Durant. The tree was in Mrs Durant's garden.

Alfred was now at home again, living with his mother in the cottage below the road. From the highway hedge, by the railroad crossing, the snowy garden sheered down steeply, like the side of a hole, then dropped straight in a wall. In this depth the house was snug, its chimney just level with the road. Miss Louisa descended the stone stairs, and stood below in the little back yard, in the dimness and the semi-secrecy. A big tree leaned overhead, above the paraffin hut. Louisa felt secure from all the world down there. She knocked at the open door, then looked round. The tongue of garden narrowing in from the quarry bed was white with snow: she thought of the thick fringes of snowdrops it would show beneath the currant bushes in a month's time. The ragged fringe of pinks hanging over from the garden brim behind her was whitened now with snow-flakes, that in summer held white blossom to Louisa's face. It was pleasant, she thought, to gather flowers that stooped to one's face from above.

She knocked again. Peeping in, she saw the scarlet glow of the kitchen, red firelight falling on the brick floor and on the bright chintz cushions. It was alive and bright as a peepshow. She crossed the scullery, where still an almanack hung. There was no one about. "Mrs Durant," called Louisa softly. "Mrs Durant!"

She went up the brick step into the front room, that still had its little shop counter and its bundles of goods, and she called from the stairfoot. Then she knew Mrs Durant was out.

She went into the yard, to follow the old woman's footsteps up the garden path.

She emerged from the bushes and raspberry canes. There was the whole quarry bed, a wide garden white and dimmed, brindled with dark bushes, lying half submerged. On the left, overhead, the little colliery train rumbled. Right away at the back was a mass of trees.

Louisa followed the open path, looking from right to left, and then she gave a cry of concern. The old woman was sitting rocking slightly among the ragged snowy cabbages. Louisa ran to her, found her whimpering with little, involuntary cries.

"Whatever have you done?" cried Louisa, kneeling in the snow.

"I've—I've—I was pulling a brussel-sprout stalk—and—Oh—h! —something tore inside me, I've had a pain—" the old woman wept from shock and suffering, gasping between her whimpers—"I've had a pain there—a long time—and now—Oh—Oh!" She panted, pressed her hand on her side, leaned as if she would faint, looking yellow against the snow. Louisa supported her.

"Do you think you could walk now," she asked.

"Yes," gasped the old woman.

Louisa helped her to her feet.

"Get the cabbage—I want it for Alfred's dinner," panted Mrs Durant. Louisa picked up the stalk of brussel-sprouts, and with difficulty got the old woman indoors. She gave her brandy, laid her on the couch, saying:

"I'm going to send for a doctor—wait just a minute."

The young woman ran up the steps to the public house a few yards away. The landlady was astonished to see Miss Louisa.

"Will you send for the doctor at once to Mrs Durant," she said, with some of her father in her commanding tone.

"Is somethink the matter—?" fluttered the landlady in concern. Louisa, glancing out up the road, saw the grocer's cart driving to Eastwood. She ran and stopped the man, and told him.

Mrs Durant lay on the sofa, her face turned away, when the young woman came back.

"Let me put you to bed," Louisa said. Mrs Durant did not resist.

Louisa knew the ways of the working people. In the bottom drawer of the dresser she found dusters and flannels. With the old pitflannel she snatched out the oven shelves, wrapped them up, and put them in the bed. From the son's bed she took a blanket, and, running down, set it before the fire. Having undressed the little old woman, Louisa carried her upstairs.

"You'll drop me, you'll drop me," cried Mrs Durant.

Louisa did not answer, but bore her burden quickly. She could not light a fire, because there was no fireplace in the bedroom. And the floor was plaster. So she fetched the lamp, and stood it lighted in one corner.

"It will air the room," she said.

"Yes," moaned the old woman.

Louisa ran with more hot flannels, replacing those from the oven shelves. Then she made a bran bag, and laid it on the woman's side. There was a big lump on the side of the abdomen.

"I've felt it coming a long time," moaned the old lady, when the pain was easier, "but I've not said anything; I didn't want to upset our Alfred."

Louisa did not see why "our Alfred" should be spared.

"What time is it?" came the plaintive voice.

"A quarter to four."

"Oh!" wailed the old lady, "he'll be here in half an hour, and no dinner ready for him."

"Let me do it?" said Louisa, gently.

"There's that cabbage—and you'll find the meat in the pantry—and there's an apple pie you can hot up. But *don't you* do it—!"

"Who will, then?" asked Louisa.

"I don't know," moaned the sick woman, unable to consider. Louisa did it.

The doctor came and gave serious examination. He looked very grave.

"What is it doctor?" asked the old lady, looking up at him with old, pathetic eyes in which already hope was dead.

"I think you've torn the skin in which a tumour hangs," he replied.

"Ay!" she murmured, and she turned away.

"You see, she may die any minute—and it *may* be swaled away," said the old doctor to Louisa.

The young woman went upstairs again.

"He says the lump may be swaled away, and you may get quite well again," she said.

"Ay!" murmured the old lady. It did not deceive her. Presently she asked:

"Is there a good fire?"

"I think so," answered Louisa.

"He'll want a good fire," the mother said. Louisa attended to it.

Since the death of Durant, the widow had come to church occasionally, and Louisa had been friendly to her. In the girl's heart the purpose was fixed. No man had affected her as Alfred Durant had done, and to that she kept. In her heart, she adhered to him. A natural sympathy existed between her and his rather hard, materialistic mother.

Alfred was the most lovable of the old woman's sons. He had grown up like the rest, however, headstrong and blind to everything but his own will. Like the other boys, he had insisted on going into the pit as soon as he left school, because that was the only way speedily to become a man, level with all the other men. This was a great chagrin to his mother, who would have liked to have this last of her sons a gentleman.

But still he remained constant to her. His feeling for her was deep and unexpressed. He noticed when she was tired, or when she had a new cap. And he bought little things for her occasionally. She was not wise enough to see how much he lived by her.

At the bottom he did not satisfy her, he did not seem manly enough. He liked to read books occasionally, and better still he liked to play the piccolo. It amused her to see his head nod over the instrument as he made an effort to get the right note. It made her fond of him, with tenderness, almost pity, but not with respect. She wanted a man to be fixed, going his own way without knowledge of women. Whereas she knew Alfred depended on her. He sang in the choir because he liked singing. In the summer he worked in the garden, attended to the fowls and pigs. He kept pigeons. He played on Saturdays in the cricket or football team. But to her he did not seem the man, the independent man her other boys had been. He was her baby—and whilst she loved him for it, she was a little bit contemptuous of him.

There grew up a little hostility between them. Then he began to drink, as the others had done; but not in their blind, oblivious way. He was a little self-conscious over it. She saw this, and she pitied it in him. She loved him most, but she was not satisfied with him because he was not free of her. He could not quite go his own way.

Then at twenty he ran away and served his time in the navy. This had made a man of him. He had hated it bitterly, the service, the subordination. For years he fought with himself under the military discipline, for his own self-respect, struggling through blind anger and shame and a cramping sense of inferiority. Out of humiliation and self-hatred, he rose into a sort of inner freedom. And his love for his mother, whom he idealised, remained the fact of hope and of belief.

He came home again, nearly thirty years old but naïve and inexperienced as a boy, only with a silence about him that was new: a sort of dumb humility before life, a fear of living. He was almost quite chaste. A strong sensitiveness had kept him from women. Sexual talk was all very well among men, but somehow it had no application to living women. There were two things for him, the *idea* of women, with which he sometimes debauched himself, and real women, before whom he felt a deep uneasiness, and a need to draw away. He shrank and defended himself from the approach of any woman. And then he felt ashamed. In his innermost soul he felt he was not a man, he was less than the normal man. In Genoa he went with an under officer to a drinking house where the cheaper sort of girl came in to look for lovers. He sat there with his glass, the girls looked at him, but they never came to him. He knew that if they did come he could only pay for food and drink for them, because he felt a pity for them, and was anxious lest they lacked good necessities. He could not have gone with one of them: he knew it, and was ashamed, looking with curious envy at the swaggering, easy-passionate Italian whose body went to a woman by instinctive impersonal attraction. They were men, he was not a man. He sat feeling short, feeling like a leper. And he went away imagining sexual scenes between himself and a woman, walking wrapt in this indulgence. But when the ready woman presented herself, the very fact that she was a palpable woman made it impossible for him to touch her. And this incapacity was like a core of rottenness in him.

So several times he went, drunk, with his companions, to the licensed prostitute houses abroad. But the sordid insignificance of the experience appalled him. It had not been anything really: it meant nothing. He felt as if he were, not physically, but spiritually impotent: not actually impotent, but intrinsically so.

67

He came home with this secret, never changing burden of his unknown, unbestowed self torturing him. His navy training left him in perfect physical condition. He was sensible of, and proud of his body. He bathed and used dumb-bells, and kept himself fit. He played cricket and football. He read books and began to hold fixed ideas which he got from the Fabians. He played his piccolo, and was considered an expert. But at the bottom of his soul was always this canker of shame and incompleteness: he was miserable beneath all his healthy cheerfulness, he was uneasy and felt despicable among all his confidence and superiority of ideas. He would have changed with any mere brute, just to be free of himself, to be free of this shame of self-consciousness. He saw some collier lurching straight forward without misgiving, pursuing his own satisfactions, and he envied him. Anything, he would have given anything for this spontaneity and this blind stupidity which went to its own satisfaction direct.

9

He was not unhappy in the pit. He was admired by the men, and well enough liked. It was only he himself who felt the difference between himself and the others. He seemed to hide his own stigma. But he was never sure that the others did not really despise him for a ninny, as being less a man than they were. Only he pretended to be more manly, and was surprised by the ease with which they were deceived. And, being naturally cheerful, he was happy at work. He was sure of himself there. Naked to the waist, hot and grimy with labour, they squatted on their heels for a few minutes and talked, seeing each other dimly by the light of the safety lamps, while the black coal rose jutting round them, and the props of wood stood like little pillars in the low, black, very dark temple. Then the pony came, and the gang-lad with a message from Number 7, or a bottle of water from the horse-trough or some news of the world above. The day passed pleasantly enough. There was an ease, a go-as-you-please about the day underground, a delightful camaraderie of men shut off alone from the rest of the world, in a dangerous place, and a variety of labour, holing, loading, timbering, and a glamour of mystery and adventure in the atmosphere, that made the pit not unattractive to him when he had again got over his anguish of desire for the open air and the sea.

This day there was much to do and Durant was not in humour to talk. He went on working in silence through the afternoon.

"Loose-all" came, and they tramped to the bottom. The white-washed underground-office shone brightly. Men were putting out their lamps. They sat in dozens round the bottom of the shaft, down which black, heavy drops of water fell continuously into the sumph. The electric lights shone away down the main underground road.

"Is it raining?" asked Durant.

"Snowing," said an old man, and the younger was pleased. He liked to go up when it was snowing.

"It'll just come right for Christmas?" said the old man.

"Ay," replied Durant.

"A green Christmas, a fat churchyard," said the other sententiously.

Durant laughed, showing his small, rather pointed teeth.

The cage came down, a dozen men lined on. Durant noticed tufts of snow on the perforated, arched roof of the chair, and he was pleased. He wondered how it liked its excursion underground. But already it was getting soppy with black water.

He liked things about him. There was a little smile on his face. But underlying it was the curious consciousness he felt in himself.

The upper world came almost with a flash, because of the glimmer of snow. Hurrying along the bank, giving up his lamp at the office, he smiled to feel the open about him again, all glimmering round him with snow. The hills on either hand were pale blue in the dusk, and the hedges looked savage and dark. The snow was trampled between the railway lines, but far ahead, beyond the black figures of miners moving home, it became smooth again, spreading right up to the dark wall of the coppice.

To the west there was a pinkness, and a big star hovered half revealed. Below, the lights of the pit came out crisp and yellow among the darkness of the buildings, and the lights of Old Aldecross twinkled in rows down the bluish twilight.

Durant walked glad with life among the miners, who were all talking animatedly because of the snow. He liked their company, he liked the white dusky world. It gave him a little thrill to stop at the garden gate, and see the light of home down below, shining on the silent blue snow.

## 10

By the big gate of the railway, in the fence, was a little latch gate, that he kept locked. As he unfastened it, he watched the kitchen light that shone onto the bushes and the snow outside. It was a candle burning till night set in, he thought to himself. He slid down the steep path to the level below. He liked making the first marks in the smooth snow. Then he came through the bushes to the house. The two women heard his heavy boots ring outside on the scraper, and his voice as he opened the door:

"How much worth of oil do you reckon to save by that candle, mother?" He liked a good light from the lamp.

He had just put down his bottle and snap-bag and was hanging his coat behind the scullery door, when Miss Louisa came upon him. He was startled, but he smiled.

His eyes began to laugh—then his face went suddenly straight, and he was afraid.

"Your mother's had an accident," she said.

"How!" he exclaimed.

"In the garden," she answered. He hesitated with his coat in his hands. Then he hung it up and turned to the kitchen.

"Is she in bed?" he asked.

"Yes," said Miss Louisa, who found it hard to deceive him. He was silent. He went into the kitchen, sat down heavily in his father's old chair, and began to pull off his boots. His head was small, rather finely shapen. His brown hair, close and crisp, would look jolly whatever happened. He wore heavy, moleskin trousers that gave off the stale, exhausted scent of the pit. Having put on his slippers, he carried his boots into the scullery.

"What is it?" he asked, afraid.

"Something internal," she replied.

He went upstairs. His mother kept herself calm for his coming. Louisa felt his tread shake the plaster floor of the bedroom above.

"What have you done?" he asked.

"It's nothing, my lad," said the old woman, rather hard. "It's nothing. You needn't fret, my boy, it's nothing more the matter with me than I had yesterday, or last week. The doctor said I'd done nothing serious."

"What were you doing?" asked her son.

"I was pulling up a cabbage, and I suppose I pulled too hard; for, oh—there was such a pain—"

Her son looked at her quickly. She hardened herself.

"But who doesn't have a sudden pain sometimes, my boy. We all do."

"And what's it done?"

"I don't know," she said, "but I don't suppose it's anything."

The big lamp in the corner was screened with a dark green screen, so that he could scarcely see her face. He was strung tight with apprehension, and many emotions. Then his brow knitted.

"What did you go pulling your inside out at cabbages for!" he asked, "and the ground frozen? You'd go on dragging and dragging, if you killed yourself."

"Somebody's got to get them," she said.

"You needn't do yourself harm."

But they had reached futility.

Miss Louisa could hear plainly downstairs. Her heart sank. It seemed so hopeless between them.

"Are you sure it's nothing much, mother?" he asked, appealing, after a little silence.

"Ay, it's nothing," said the old woman, rather bitter.

"I don't want you to—to—to be badly—you know."

"Go an' get your dinner," she said. She knew she was going to die: moreover the pain was torture just then. "They're only cosseting me up a bit because I'm an old woman. Miss Louisa's *very* good—and she'll have got your dinner ready, so you'd better go and eat it."

He felt stupid and ashamed. His mother put him off. He had to turn away. The pain burned in his bowels. He went downstairs. The mother was glad he was gone, so that she could moan with pain.

He had resumed the old habit of eating before he washed himself. Miss Louisa served his dinner. It was strange and exciting to her. She was strung up tense, trying to understand him and his mother. She watched him as he sat. He was turned away from his food, looking in the fire. Her soul watched him, trying to see what he was. His black face and arms were uncouth, he was foreign. His face was masked black with coal-dust. She could not see him, she could not know him. The brown eyebrows, the steady eyes, the coarse, small moustache above the closed mouth—these were the only familiar indications. What was he, as he sat there in his pit dirt? She could not see him, and it hurt her.

She ran upstairs, presently coming down with the flannels and the bran bag, to heat them, because the pain was on again.

He was half way through his dinner. He put down the fork, suddenly nauseated.

"They will soothe the wrench," she said. He watched, useless and left out.

"Is she bad?" he asked.

"I think she is," she answered.

It was useless for him to stir or comment. Louisa was busy. She went upstairs. The poor old woman was in a white, cold sweat of pain. Louisa's face was sullen with suffering as she went about to relieve her. Then she sat and waited. The pain passed gradually, the old woman sank into a state of coma. Louisa still sat silent by the bed. She heard the sound of water downstairs. Then came the voice of the old mother, faint but unrelaxing:

"Alfred's washing himself—he'll want his back washing."

Louisa listened anxiously, wondering what the sick woman wanted.

"He can't bear if his back isn't washed—" the old woman persisted, in a cruel attention to his needs. Louisa rose and wiped the sweat from the yellowish brow.

"I will go down," she said soothingly.

"If you would," murmured the sick woman.

Louisa waited a moment. Mrs Durant closed her eyes, having discharged her duty. The young woman went downstairs. Herself, or the man, what did they matter? Only the suffering woman must be considered.

Alfred was kneeling on the hearthrug, stripped to the waist, washing himself in a large panchion of earthenware. He did so every evening, when he had eaten his dinner; his brothers had done so before him. But Miss Louisa was strange in the house.

He was mechanically rubbing the white lather on his head, with a repeated, unconscious movement, his hand every now and then passing over his neck. Louisa watched. She had to brace herself to this also. He bent his head into the water, washed it free of soap, and pressed the water out of his eyes.

"Your mother said you would want your back washing," she said.

Curious how it hurt her to take part in their fixed routine of life! Louisa felt the almost repulsive intimacy being forced upon her. It was all so common, so like herding. She lost her own distinctness.

He ducked his face round, looking up at her in what was a very comical way. She had to harden herself.

"How funny he looks with his face upside down," she thought. After all, there was a difference between her and the common people. The water in which his arms were plunged was quite black, the soap-froth was darkish. She could scarcely conceive him as human. Mechanically, under the influence of habit, he groped in the black water, fished out the soap and flannel, and handed them backwards to Louisa. Then he remained rigid and submissive, his two arms thrust straight in the panchion, supporting the weight of his shoulders. His skin was beautifully white and unblemished, of an opaque, solid whiteness. Gradually Louisa saw it: this also was what he was. It fascinated her. Her feeling of separateness passed away: she ceased to draw back from contact with him and his mother. There was this living centre. Her heart ran hot. She had reached some goal in this beautiful, clear, male body. She loved him in a white, impersonal heat. But the sun-burnt, reddish neck and ears: they were more personal, more curious. A tenderness rose in her, she loved even his queer ears. A person—an intimate being he was to her. She put down the towel and went upstairs again, troubled in her heart. She had only seen one human being in her life—and that was Mary. All the rest were strangers. Now her soul was going to open, she was going to see another. She felt strange and pregnant.

"He'll be more comfortable," murmured the sick woman abstract- edly, as Louisa entered the room. The latter did not answer. Her own heart was heavy with its own responsibility. Mrs Durant lay silent awhile, then she murmured plaintively:

"You mustn't mind, Miss Louisa."

"Why should I?" replied Louisa, deeply moved.

"It's what we're used to," said the old woman.

And Louisa felt herself excluded again from their life. She sat in pain, with the tears of disappointment distilling in her heart. Was that all?

Alfred came upstairs. He was clean, and in his shirt sleeves. He looked a workman now. Louisa felt that she and he were foreigners, moving in different lives. It dulled her again. Oh, if she could only find some fixed relations, something sure and abiding.

"How do you feel?" he said to his mother.

"It's a bit better," she replied wearily, impersonally. This strange putting herself aside, this abstracting herself and answering him only what she thought good for him to hear, made the relations between mother and son poignant and cramping to Miss Louisa. It made the man so ineffectual, so nothing. Louisa groped as if she had lost him. The mother was real and positive—he was not very actual. It puzzled and chilled the young woman.

"I'd better fetch Mrs Harrison?" he said, waiting for his mother to decide.

"I suppose we shall have to have somebody," she replied.

Miss Louisa stood by, afraid to interfere in their business. They did not include her in their lives, they felt she had nothing to do with them, except as a help from outside. She was quite external to them. She felt hurt and powerless against this unconscious difference. But something patient and unyielding in her made her say:

"I will stay and do the nursing: you can't be left."

The other two were shy, and at a loss for an answer.

"Wes'll manage to get somebody," said the old woman wearily. She did not care very much what happened, now.

"I will stay until tomorrow, in any case," said Louisa. "Then we can see."

"I'm sure you've no right to trouble yourself," moaned the old woman. But she must leave herself in any hands.

Miss Louisa felt glad that she was admitted, even in an official capacity. She wanted to share their lives. At home they would need her, now Mary had come. But they must manage without her.

"I must write a note to the vicarage," she said.

Alfred Durant looked at her inquiringly, for her service. He had always that intelligent readiness to serve, since he had been in the navy. But there was a simple independence in his willingness, which she loved. She felt nevertheless it was hard to get at him. He was so deferential, quick to take the slightest suggestion of an order from her, implicitly, that she could not get at the man in him.

He looked at her very keenly. She noticed his eyes were golden brown, with a very small pupil, the kind of eyes that can see a long way off. He stood alert, at military attention. His face was still rather weather-reddened.

"Do you want pen and paper?" he asked, with deferential suggestion to a superior, which was more difficult for her than reserve.

"Yes, please," she said.

He turned and went downstairs. He seemed to her so self-contained, so utterly sure in his movement. How was she to approach him? For he would take not one step towards her. He would only put himself entirely and impersonally at her service, glad to serve her, but keeping himself quite removed from her. She could see he felt real joy in doing anything for her, but any recognition would confuse him and hurt him. Strange, it was to her, to have a man going about the house in his shirt sleeves, his waistcoat unbuttoned, his throat bare, waiting on her. He moved well, as if he had plenty of life to spare. She was attracted by his completeness. And yet, when all was ready, and there was nothing more for him to do, she quivered, meeting his questioning look.

As she sat writing, he placed another candle near her. The rather dense light fell in two places on the overfoldings of her hair till it glistened heavy and bright, like a dense golden plumage folded up. Then the nape of her neck was very white, with fine down and pointed wisps of gold. He watched it as it were a vision, losing himself. She was all that was beyond him, of revelation and exquisiteness. All that was ideal and beyond him, she was that—and he was lost to himself in looking at her. She had no connection with him. He did not approach her. She was there like a wonderful distance. But it was a treat, having her in the house. Even with this anguish for his mother tightening about him, he was sensible of the wonder of living this evening. The candles glistened on her hair, and seemed to fascinate him. He felt a little awe of her, and a sense of uplifting, that he and she and his mother should be together for a time, in the strange, unknown atmosphere. And, when he got out of the house, he was afraid. He saw the stars above ringing with fine brightness, the snow beneath just visible, and a new night was gathering round him. He was afraid almost with obliteration. What was this new night ringing about him, and what was he? He could not recognise himself nor any of his surroundings. He was afraid to think of his mother. And yet his chest was conscious of her, and of what was happening to her. He could not escape from her, she carried him with her into an unformed, unknown chaos.

II

He went up the road in an agony, not knowing what it was all about, but feeling as if red hot iron were gripped round his chest. Without thinking, he shook two or three tears onto the snow. Yet in his mind he did not believe his mother would die. He was in the grip of some greater consciousness. As he sat in the hall of the Vicarage, waiting whilst Mary put things for Louisa into a bag, he wondered why he had been so upset. He felt abashed and humbled by the big house, he felt again as if he were one of the rank and file. When Miss Mary spoke to him, he almost saluted.

"An honest man," thought Mary. And the patronage was applied as salve to her own sickness. She had station, so she could patronise:

75

it was almost all that was left to her. But she could not have lived without having a certain position. She could never have trusted herself outside of a definite place, nor respected herself except as a woman of superior class.

As Alfred came to the latch gate, he felt the grief at his heart again, and saw the new heavens. He stood a moment looking northward to the Plough clambering up the night, and at the far glimmer of snow in distant fields. Then his grief came on like physical pain. He held tight to the gate, biting his mouth, whispering 'Mother!' It was a fierce, cutting, physical pain of grief, that came on in bouts, as his mother's pain came on in bouts, and was so acute he could scarcely keep erect. He did not know where it came from, the pain, nor why. It had nothing to do with his thoughts. Almost it had nothing to do with him. Only it gripped him and he must submit. The whole tide of his soul, gathering in its unknown towards this expansion into death, carried him with it helplessly, all the fritter of his thought and consciousness caught up as nothing, the heave passing on towards its breaking, taking him further than he had ever been. When the young man had regained himself, he went indoors, and there he was almost gay. It seemed to excite him. He felt in high spirits: he made whimsical fun of things. He sat on one side of his mother's bed, Louisa on the other, and a certain gaiety seized them all. But the night and the dread was coming on.

Alfred kissed his mother and went to bed. When he was half undressed, the knowledge of his mother came upon him, and the suffering seized him in its grip like two hands, in agony. He lay on the bed screwed up tight. It lasted so long, and exhausted him so much, that he fell asleep, without having the energy to get up and finish undressing. He awoke after midnight to find himself stone cold. He undressed and got into bed, and was soon asleep again.

At a quarter to six he woke, and instantly remembered. Having pulled on his trousers and lighted a candle, he went into his mother's room. He put his hand before the candle flame so that no light fell on the bed.

"Mother!" he whispered.

"Yes," was the reply.

There was a hesitation.

"Should I go to work?"

He waited, his heart was beating heavily.

"I think I'd go, my lad."

76

His heart went down in a kind of despair.

"You want me to?"

He let his hand down from the candle flame. The light fell on the bed. There he saw Louisa lying looking up at him. Her eyes were upon him. She quickly shut her eyes and half buried her face in the pillow, her back turned to him. He saw the rough hair like bright vapour about her round head, and the two plaits flung coiled among the bedclothes. It gave him a shock. He stood almost himself, determined. Louisa cowered down. He looked, and met his mother's eyes. Then he gave way again, and ceased to be sure, ceased to be himself.

"Yes, go to work, my boy," said the mother.

"All right," replied he, kissing her. His heart was down at despair, and bitter. He went away.

"Alfred!" cried his mother faintly.

He came back with beating heart.

"What mother?"

"You'll always do what's right, Alfred?" the mother asked, beside herself in terror now he was leaving her. He was too terrified and bewildered to know what she meant.

"Yes," he said.

She turned her cheek to him. He kissed her, then went away, in bitter despair. He went to work.

12

By mid day his mother was dead. The word met him at the pit-mouth. As he had known, inwardly, it was not a shock to him, and yet he trembled. He went home calmly, feeling only heavy in his breathing.

Miss Louisa was still at the house. She had seen to everything possible. Very succinctly, she informed him of what he needed to know. But there was one point of anxiety for her.

"You *did* half expect it—it's not come as a blow to you?" she asked, looking up at him. Her eyes were dark and calm and searching. She too felt lost. He was so dark and inchoate.

"I suppose—yes," he said stupidly.

He looked aside, unable to endure her eyes on him.

"I could not bear to think—you might not have guessed," she said. He did not answer.

He felt it a great strain to have her near him at this time. He wanted to be alone. As soon as the relatives began to arrive, Louisa departed, and came no more. While everything was arranging, and a crowd was in the house, whilst he had business to settle, he went well enough, with only those uncontrollable paroxysms of grief. Before the rest, he was superficial. By himself, he endured the fierce, almost insane bursts of grief which passed again and left him calm, almost clear, just wondering. He had not known before that everything could break down, that he himself could break down, and all be a great chaos, very vast and wonderful. It seemed as if life in him had burst its bounds, and he was lost in a great, bewildering flood, immense and unpeopled. He himself was broken and spilled out amid it all. He could only breathe panting in silence. Then the anguish came on again.

When all the people had gone from the Quarry Cottage, leaving the young man alone with an elderly housekeeper, then the long trial began. The snow had thawed and frozen, a fresh fall had whitened the grey, this then began to thaw. The world was a place of loose grey slosh. Alfred had nothing to do in the evenings. He was a man whose life had been filled up with small activities. Without knowing it, he had been centralised, polarised in his mother. It was she who had kept him. Even now, when the old housekeeper had left him, he might still have gone on in his old way. But the force and balance of his life was lacking. He sat pretending to read, all the time holding his fists clenched and holding himself in, enduring he did not know what. He walked the black and soddened miles of field paths, till he was tired out: but all this was only running away from whence he must return. At work he was all right: if it had been summer he might have escaped by working in the garden till bed-time. But now, there was no escape, no relief, no help. He, perhaps, was made for action rather than for understanding; for doing rather than for being. He was shocked out of his activities, like a swimmer who forgets to swim.

For a week, he had the force to endure this suffocation and struggle, then he began to get exhausted, and knew he must come out. The instinct of self preservation became strongest. But then was the question: where was he to go? The public-house really meant nothing to him, it was no good going there. He began to think of emigration. In another country he would be all right. He wrote to the emigration offices.

On the Sunday after the funeral, when all the Durant people had attended church, Alfred had seen Miss Louisa, impassive and reserved, sitting with Miss Mary, who was proud and very distant, and with the other Lindleys, who were people removed. Alfred saw them as people remote. He did not think about it. They had nothing to do with his life. After service Louisa had come to him and shaken hands.

"My sister would like you to come to supper one evening, if you would be so good."

He looked at Miss Mary, who bowed. Out of kindness, Mary had proposed this to Louisa, disapproving of herself even as she did so. But she did not examine herself closely.

"Yes," said Durant awkwardly. "I'll come if you want me." But he vaguely felt that it was misplaced.

"You'll come tomorrow evening, then, about half-past six." He went. Miss Louisa was very kind to him. There could be no music, because of the babies. He sat with his fists clenched on his thighs, very quiet and unmoved, lapsing, among all those people, into a kind of muse or daze. There was nothing between him and them. They knew it as well as he. But he remained very steady in himself, and the evening passed slowly. Mrs Lindley called him 'young man.'

"Will you sit here, young man?"

He sat there. One name was as good as another. What had they to do with him?

Mr Lindley kept a special tone for him, kind, indulgent, but patronising. Durant took it all without criticism or offence, just submitting. But he did not want to eat—that troubled him, to have to eat in their presence. He knew he was out of place. But it was his duty to stay yet awhile. He answered precisely, in monosyllables.

When he left he winced with confusion. He was glad it was finished. He got away as quickly as possible. And he wanted still more intensely to go right away, to Canada.

Miss Louisa suffered in her soul, indignant with all of them, with him too, but quite unable to say why she was indignant.

## 13

Two evenings after, Louisa tapped at the door of the Quarry Cottage at half-past six. He had finished dinner, the woman had washed up and gone away, but still he sat in his pit dirt. He was going later to the New Inn. He had begun to go there because he must go somewhere. The mere contact with other men was necessary to him, the noise, the warmth, the forgetful flight of the hours. But still he did not move. He sat alone in the empty house till it began to grow on him like something unnatural.

He was in his pit dirt when he opened the door.

"I have been wanting to call—I thought I would," she said, and she went to the sofa. He wondered why she wouldn't use his mother's round arm-chair. Yet something stirred in him, like anger, when the housekeeper placed herself in it.

"I ought to have been washed by now," he said, glancing at the clock, which was adorned with butterflies and cherries, and the name of "T. Brooks, Mansfield." He laid his black hands along his mottled dirty arms. Louisa looked at him. There was the reserve, and the simple neutrality towards her, which she dreaded in him. It made it impossible for her to approach him.

"I'm afraid," she said, "that I wasn't kind in asking you to supper."

"I'm not used to it," he said, smiling with his mouth, showing the interspaced white teeth. His eyes, however, were steady and unseeing.

"It's not *that*," she said hastily. Her repose was exquisite, and her dark grey eyes rich with understanding. He felt afraid of her as she sat there, as he began to grow conscious of her.

"How do you get on alone?" she asked.

He glanced away to the fire.

"Oh—" he answered, shifting uneasily, not finishing his answer.

Her face settled heavily.

"How close it is in this room. You have such immense fires. I will take off my coat," she said.

He watched her take off her hat and coat. She wore a cream cashmere blouse embroidered with gold silk. It seemed to him a very fine garment, fitting her throat and wrists close. It gave him a feeling of pleasure and cleanness and relief from himself.

"What were you thinking about that you didn't get washed?" she asked, half intimately. He laughed, turning aside his head. The whites of his eyes showed very distinct in his black face.

"Oh," he said, "I couldn't tell you."

There was a pause.

"Are you going to keep this house on?" she asked.

He stirred in his chair, under the question.

"I hardly know," he said. "I'm very likely going to Canada."

Her spirit became very quiet and attentive.

"What for?" she asked.

Again he shifted restlessly on his seat.

"Well"—he said slowly—"to try the life."

"But which life?"

"There's various things—farming or lumbering or mining. I don't mind much what it is."

"And is that what you want?"

He did not think in these times, so he could not answer.

"I don't know," he said, "till I've tried."

She saw him drawing away from her for ever.

"Aren't you sorry to leave this house and garden?" she asked.

"I don't know," he answered reluctantly. "I suppose our Fred would come in—that's what he's wanting."

"You don't want to settle down?" she asked.

He was leaning forward on the arms of his chair. He turned to her. Her face was pale and set. It looked heavy and impassive, her hair shone richer as she grew white. She was to him something steady and immovable and eternal presented to him. His heart was hot in an anguish of suspense. Sharp twitches of fear and pain were in his limbs. He turned his whole body away from her. The silence was unendurable. He could not bear her to sit there any more. It made his heart go hot and stifled in his breast.

"Were you going out tonight?" she asked.

"Only to the New Inn," he said.

Again there was silence.

She reached for her hat. Nothing else was suggested to her. She *had* to go. He sat waiting for her to be gone, for relief. And she knew that if she went out of that house as she was, she went out a failure. Yet she continued to pin on her hat; in a moment she would have to go. Something was carrying her.

Then suddenly a sharp pang, like lightning, seared her from head to foot, and she was beyond herself.

"Do you want me to go?" she asked, controlled, yet speaking out of a fiery anguish, as if the words were spoken from her without her intervention.

He went white under his dirt.

"Why?" he asked, turning to her in fear, compelled.

"Do you want me to go?" she repeated.

"Why?" he asked again.

"Because I wanted to stay with you," she said, suffocated, with her lungs full of fire.

His face worked, he hung forward a little, suspended, staring straight into her eyes, in torment, in an agony of chaos, unable to collect himself. And as if turned to stone, she looked back into his eyes.

Their souls were exposed bare for a few moments. It was agony. They could not bear it. He dropped his head, whilst his body jerked with little sharp twitchings.

She turned away for her coat. Her soul had gone dead in her. Her hands trembled, but she could not feel any more. She drew on her coat. There was a cruel suspense in the room. The moment had come for her to go. He lifted his head. His eyes were like agate, expressionless, save for the black points of torture. They held her, she had no will, no life any more. She felt broken.

"Don't you want me?" she said helplessly.

A spasm of torture crossed his eyes, which held her fixed.

"I—I——" he began, but he could not speak. Something drew him from his chair to her. She stood motionless, spellbound, like a creature given up as prey. He put his hand tentatively, uncertainly, on her arm. The expression of his face was strange and inhuman. She stood utterly motionless. Then clumsily he put his arms round her, and took her, cruelly, blindly, straining her till she nearly lost consciousness, till he himself had almost fallen.

Then, gradually, as he held her gripped, and his brain reeled round, and he felt himself falling, falling from himself, and whilst she, yielded up, swooned to a kind of death of herself, a moment of utter darkness came over him, and they began to wake up again as if from a long sleep. He was himself.

After a while his arms slackened, she loosened herself a little, and put her arms round him, as he held her. So they held each other close, and hid each against the other for assurance, helpless in speech. And it was ever her hands that trembled more closely upon him, drawing him nearer into her, with love.

And at last she drew back her face and looked up at him, her eyes wet, and shining with light. His heart, which saw, was silent with fear. He was with her. She saw his face all sombre and inscrutable, and he seemed eternal to her. And all the echo of pain came back into the rarity of bliss, and all her tears came up.

"I love you," she said, her lips drawn to sobbing. He put down his head against her, unable to hear her, unable to bear the sudden coming of the peace and passion that almost broke his heart. They stood together in silence whilst the thing moved away a little.

At last she wanted to see him. She looked up. His eyes were strange and glowing, with a tiny black pupil. Strange, they were, and powerful over her. And his mouth came to hers, and slowly her eyelids closed, as his mouth sought hers closer and closer, and took possession of her.

They were silent for a long time, too much mixed up with passion and grief and death to do anything but hold each other in pain and kiss with long, hurting kisses wherein fear was transfused into desire. At last she disengaged herself. He felt as if his heart were hurt, but glad, and he scarcely dared look at her.

"I'm glad," she said also.

He held her hands in passionate gratitude and desire. He had not yet the presence of mind to say anything. He was dazed with relief.

"I ought to go," she said.

He looked at her. He could not grasp the thought of her going, he knew he could never be separated from her any more. Yet he dared not assert himself. He held her hands tight.

"Your face is black," she said.

He laughed.

"Yours is a bit smudged," he said.

They were afraid of each other, afraid to talk. He could only keep her near to him. After a while she wanted to wash her face. He brought her some warm water, standing by and watching her. There was something he wanted to say, that he dared not. He watched her wiping her face, and making tidy her hair.

"They'll see your blouse is dirty," he said.

She looked at her sleeves and laughed for joy.

He was sharp with pride.

"What shall you do?" he asked.

"How?" she said.

He was awkward at a reply.

"About me," he said.

"What do you want me to do?" she laughed.

He put his hand out slowly to her. What did it matter!

"But make yourself clean," she said.


14

As they went up the hill, the night seemed dense with the unknown. They kept close together, feeling as if the darkness were alive and full of knowledge, all around them. In silence they walked up the hill. At first the street lamps went their way. Several people passed them. He was more shy than she, and would have let her go had she loosened in the least. But she held firm.

Then they came into the true darkness, between the fields. They did not want to speak, feeling closer together in silence. So they arrived at the Vicarage gate. They stood under the naked horse chestnut tree.

"I wish you didn't have to go," he said.

She laughed a quick little laugh.

"Come tomorrow," she said, in a low tone, "and ask father."

She felt his hand close on hers.

She gave the same sorrowful little laugh of sympathy. Then she kissed him, sending him home.

At home, the old grief came on in another paroxysm, obliterating Louisa, obliterating even his mother for whom the stress was, raging like a burst of fever in a wound. But something was sound in his heart.

### 15

The next evening he dressed to go to the Vicarage, feeling it was to be done, not imagining what it would be like. He would not take this seriously. He was sure of Louisa, and this marriage was like fate to him. It filled him also with a blessed feeling of fatality. He was not responsible, neither had her people anything really to do with it.

They ushered him into the little study, which was fireless. By and by the vicar came in. His voice was cold and hostile as he said:

"What can I do for you, young man?"

He knew already, without asking.

Durant looked up at him, again like a sailor before a superior. He had the subordinate manner. Yet his spirit was clear.

"I wanted, Mr Lindley——" he began respectfully, then all the colour suddenly left his face. It seemed now a violation to say what he had to say. What was he doing there? But he stood on, because it had to be done. He held firmly to his own independence and self-respect. He must not be indecisive. He must put himself aside: the matter was bigger than just his personal self. He must not feel. This was his highest duty.

"You wanted——" said the vicar.

Durant's mouth was dry, but he answered with steadiness:

"Miss Louisa—Louisa—promised to marry me——"

"You asked Miss Louisa if she would marry you—yes—," corrected the vicar. Durant reflected he hadn't asked her this:

"If she would marry me, sir. I hope you—don't mind."

He smiled. He was a good-looking man, and the vicar could not help seeing it.

"And my daughter was willing to marry you?" said Mr Lindley.

"Yes," said Durant seriously. It was pain to him, nevertheless. He felt the natural hostility between himself and the elder man.

"Will you come this way," said the vicar. He led into the dining room, where were Mary, Louisa, and Mrs Lindley. Mr Massey sat in a corner with a lamp.

"This young man has come on your account, Louisa?" said Mr Lindley.

"Yes," said Louisa, her eyes on Durant, who stood erect, in discipline. He dared not look at her, but he was aware of her.

"You don't want to marry a collier, you little fool," cried Mrs Lindley harshly. She lay obese and helpless upon the couch, swathed in a loose, dove-grey gown.

"Oh, hush, mother," cried Mary, with quiet intensity and pride.

"What means have you to support a wife?" demanded the vicar's wife roughly.

"I!" Durant replied, starting. "I think I can earn enough."

"Well, and how much?" came the rough voice.

"Seven and six a day," replied the young man.

"And will it get to be any more?"

"I hope so."

"And are you going to live in that poky little house?"

"I think so," said Durant, "if it's all right."

He took small offence, only was upset, because they would not think him good enough. He knew that, in their sense, he was not.

"Then she's a fool, I tell you, if she marries you," cried the mother roughly, casting her decision.

"After all, mama, it is Louisa's affair," said Mary distinctly, "and we must remember——"

"As she makes her bed, she must lie—but she'll repent it," interrupted Mrs Lindley.

"And after all," said Mr Lindley, "Louisa cannot quite hold herself free to act entirely without consideration for her family."

"What do you want, papa?" asked Louisa sharply.

"I mean that if you marry this man, it will make my position very difficult for me, particularly if you stay in this parish. If you were moving quite away, it would be simpler. But living here in a collier's

85

cottage, under my nose, as it were—it would be almost unseemly. I have my position to maintain, and a position which may not be taken lightly."

"Come over here, young man," cried the mother, in her rough voice, "and let us look at you."

Durant, flushing, went over and stood—not quite at attention, so that he did not know what to do with his hands. Miss Louisa was angry to see him standing there, obedient and acquiescent. He ought to show himself a man.

"Can't you take her away and live out of sight," said the mother. "You'd both of you be better off."

"Yes, we can go away," he said.

"Do you want to?" asked Miss Mary clearly.

He faced round. Mary looked very stately and impressive. He flushed.

"I do if it's going to be a trouble to anybody," he said.

"For yourself, you would rather stay?" said Mary.

"It's my home," he said, "and that's the house I was born in."

"Then"—Mary turned clearly to her parents, "I really don't see how you can make the conditions, papa. He has his own rights, and if Louisa wants to marry him——"

"Louisa, Louisa!" cried the father impatiently. "I cannot understand why Louisa should not behave in the normal way. I cannot see why she should only think of herself, and leave her family out of count. The thing is enough in itself, and she ought to try to ameliorate it as much as possible. And if——"

"But I love the man, papa," said Louisa.

"And I hope you love your parents, and I hope you want to spare them as much of the—the loss of prestige, as possible."

"We *can* go away to live," said Louisa, her face breaking to tears. At last she was really hurt.

"Oh, yes, easily," Durant replied hastily, pale, distressed.

There was dead silence in the room.

"I think it would really be better," murmured the vicar, mollified.

"Very likely it would," said the rough-voiced invalid.

"Though I think we ought to apologise for asking such a thing," said Mary haughtily.

"No," said Durant. "It will be best all round." He was glad there was no more bother.

"And shall we put up the banns here or go to the registrar?" he asked clearly, like a challenge.

"We will go to the registrar," replied Louisa decidedly.

Again there was a dead silence in the room.

"Well, if you will have your own way, you must go your own way," said the mother emphatically.

All the time Mr Massey had sat obscure and unnoticed in a corner of the room. At this juncture he got up, saying:

"There is baby, Mary."

Mary rose and went out of the room, stately; her little husband padded after her. Durant watched the fragile, small man go, wondering.

"And where," asked the vicar, almost genial, "do you think you will go when you are married?"

Durant started.

"I was thinking of emigrating," he said.

"To Canada? or where?"

"I think to Canada."

"Yes, that would be very good."

Again there was a pause.

"We shan't see much of you then, as a son-in-law," said the mother, roughly but amicably.

"Not much," he said.

Then he took his leave. Louisa went with him to the gate. She stood before him in distress.

"You won't mind them, will you?" she said humbly.

"I don't mind them, if they don't mind me!" he said. Then he stooped and kissed her.

"Let us be married soon," she murmured, in tears.

"All right," he said. "I'll go tomorrow to Barford."

# A Fragment of Stained Glass

Beauvale is, or was, the largest parish in England. It is thinly populated, only just netting the stragglers from shoals of houses in three large mining villages. For the rest, it holds a great tract of woodland, fragment of old Sherwood, a few hills of pasture and arable land, three collieries, and, finally, the ruins of a Cistercian abbey. These ruins lie in a still rich meadow at the foot of the last fall of woodland, through whose oaks shines a blue of hyacinths, like water, in Maytime. Of the abbey, there remains only the east wall of the chancel standing, a wild thick mass of ivy weighting one shoulder, while pigeons perch in the tracery of the lofty window. This is the window in question.

The vicar of Beauvale is a bachelor of forty-two years. Quite early in life some illness caused a slight paralysis of his right side, so that he drags a little, and so that the right corner of his mouth is twisted up into his cheek with a constant grimace, unhidden by a heavy moustache. There is something pathetic about this twist on the vicar's countenance: his eyes are so shrewd and sad. It would be hard to get near to Mr Colbran. Indeed, now, his soul has some of the twist of his face, so that, when he is not ironical, he is satiric. Yet a man of more complete tolerance and generosity scarcely exists. Let the boors mock him, he merely smiles on the other side, and there is no malice in his eyes, only a quiet expression of waiting till they have finished. His people do not like him, yet none could bring forth an accusation against him, save that "you never can tell when he's having you."

I dined the other evening with the vicar in his study. The room scandalises the neighbourhood because of the statuary which adorns it: a Laocoön and other classic copies, with bronze and silver Italian Renascence works. For the rest, it is all dark and tawny.

Mr Colbran is an archæologist. He does not take himself seriously, however, in his hobby, so that nobody knows the worth of his opinions on the subject.

"Here you are," he said to me after dinner. "I've found another paragraph for my great work."

"What's that?" I asked.

"Haven't I told you I was compiling a Bible of the English people—the Bible of their hearts—their exclamations in presence of the unknown. I've found a fragment at home, a jump at God from Beauvale."

"Where?" I asked, startled.

The vicar closed his eyes whilst looking at me.

"Only on parchment," he said.

Then, slowly, he reached for a yellow book, and read, translating as he went:

"Then, while we chanted, came a crackling at the window, at the great east window where hung our Lord on the Cross. It was a malicious coveitous Devil wrathed by us, rended the lovely image of the glasse. We saw the iron clutches of the fiend pick the window, and a face flaming red like fire in a basket did glower down on us. Our hearts melted away, our legs broke, we thought to die. The breath of the wretch filled the chapel.

"But our dear Saint etc. etc.—came hastening down heaven to defend us. The fiend began to groan and bray— —he was daunted and beat off—

"When the sun uprose, and it was morning, some went out in dread upon the thin snow. There the figure of our Saint was broken and thrown down, whilst in the window was a wicked hole as from the Holy Wounds the Blessed Blood was run out at the touch of the Fiend, and on the snow was the Blood, sparkling like gold. Some gathered it up for the joy of this House— — —."

"Interesting," I said. "Where's it from?"

"Beauvale records—fifteenth century."

"Beauvale Abbey," I said; "they were only very few, the monks. What frightened them, I wonder."

"I wonder," he repeated.

"Somebody climbed up," I supposed, "and attempted to get in."

"What—!" he exclaimed, smiling.

"Well, what do you think?"

"Pretty much the same," he replied. "I glossed it out for my book."

"Your great work? Tell me."

He put a shade over the lamp, so that the room was almost in darkness.

"Am I more than a voice?" he asked.

"I can see your hand," I replied. He moved entirely from the circle of light. Then his voice began, sing-song, sardonic:

"I was a serf at Rollestoun's, Newthorpe Manor, master of the stables I was. One day a horse bit me as I was grooming him. He was an old enemy of mine. I fetched him a blow across the nose. Then, when he got a chance, he lashed out at me and caught me a gash over the mouth. I snatched at a hatchet and cut his head. He yelled, fiend as he was, and strained for me with all his teeth bare. I brought him down.

"For killing him they flogged me till they thought I was dead. I was sturdy, because we house serfs got plenty to eat. I was sturdy, but they flogged me till I did not move. The next night I set fire to the stables, and the stables set fire to the house. I watched and saw the red flame rise and look out of the window, I saw the folk running, each for himself, master no more than one of a frightened party. It was freezing, but the heat made me sweat. I saw them all turn again to watch, all rimmed with red. They cried, all of them when the roof went in, when the sparks splashed up at rebound. They cried then like dogs at the bagpipes howling. Master cursed me, till I laughed as I lay under a bush quite near.

"As the fire went down I got frightened. I ran for the woods, with fire blazing in my eyes and crackling in my ears. For hours I was all fire. Then I went to sleep under the bracken. When I woke it was evening. I had no mantle, was frozen stiff. I was afraid to move, lest all the sores of my back should be broken like thin ice. I lay still until I could bear my hunger no longer. I moved then to get used to the pain of movement, when I began to hunt for food. There was nothing to be found but hips.

"After wandering about till I was faint I dropped again in the bracken. The boughs above me creaked with frost. I started and looked round. The branches were like hair among the starlight. My heart stood still. Again there was a creak, creak, and suddenly a whoop, that whistled in fading. I fell down in the bracken like dead wood. Yet, by the peculiar whistling sound at the end, I knew it was only the ice bending or tightening in the frost. I was in the woods above the lake, only two miles from the Manor. And yet, when the lake whooped hollowly again, I clutched the frozen soil, every one of my muscles as stiff as the stiff earth. So all the night long I dare not move my face, but pressed it flat down, and taut I lay as if pegged down and braced.

"When morning came still I did not move, I lay still in a dream. By afternoon my ache was such it enlivened me. I cried, rocking my breath in the ache of moving. Then again I became fierce. I beat my hands on the rough bark to hurt them, so that I should not ache so much. In such a rage I was, I swung my limbs to torture, till I fell sick with pain. Yet I fought the hurt, fought it and fought by twisting and flinging myself, until it was overcome. Then the evening began to draw on. All day the sun had not loosened the frost. I felt the sky chill again towards afternoon. Then I knew the night was coming, and, remembering the great space I had just come through, horrible so that it seemed to have made me another man, I fled across the wood.

"But in my running I came upon the oak where hanged five bodies. There they must hang, bar-stiff, night after night. It was a terror worse than any. Turning, blundering through the forest, I came out where the trees thinned, where only hawthorns, ragged and shaggy, went down to the lake's edge.

"The sky across was red, the ice on the water glistened as if it were warm. A few wild geese sat out like stones on the sheet of ice. I thought of Martha. She was the daughter of the miller at the upper end of the lake. Her hair was red like beech leaves in a wind. When I had gone often to the mill with the horses she had brought me food.

"'I thought,' said I to her, ''twas a squirrel sat on your shoulder. 'Tis your hair fallen loose.'

"'They call me the fox,' she said.

"'Would I were your dog,' said I.

"She would bring me bacon and good bread, when I called at the mill with the horses. The thought of cakes of bread and of bacon made me reel as if drunk. I had torn at the rabbit holes, I had chewed wood all day. In such a dimness was my head that I felt neither the soreness of my wounds, nor the cuts of thorns on my knees, but stumbled towards the mill, almost past fear of man and death, panting with fear of the darkness that crept behind me from trunk to trunk.

"Coming to the gap in the wood, below which lay the pond, I heard no sound. Always I knew the place filled with the buzz of water, but now it was silent. In fear of this stillness I ran forward, forgetting myself, forgetting the frost. The wood seemed to pursue me. I fell, just in time, down by a shed wherein were housed the few wintry pigs. The miller came riding in on his horse, and the barking of dogs was for him. I heard him curse the day, curse his servant, curse me, whom he had been out to hunt, in his rage of wasted labor, curse all. As I lay I heard inside the shed a sucking. Then I knew that the sow was there, and that the most of her sucking pigs would be already killed for tomorrow's Christmas. The miller, from forethought to have young at that time, made profit by his sucking pigs that were sold for the mid-winter feast.

"When for a moment all was silent in the dusk, I broke the bar and came into the shed. The sow grunted, but did not come forth to discover me. By and by I crept in towards her warmth. She had but three young left, which now angered her, she being too full of milk. Every now and again she slashed at them and they squealed. Busy as she was with them, I in the darkness advanced toward her. I trembled so that scarce dared I trust myself near her, for long dared not put my naked face towards her. Shuddering with hunger and fear, I at last fed of her, guarding my face with my arm. Her own full young tumbled squealing against me, but she, feeling her ease, lay grunting. At last, I, too, lay drunk, swooning.

"I was roused by the shouting of the miller. He, angered by his daughter who wept, abused her, driving her from the house to feed the swine. She came, bowing under a yoke, to the door of the shed. Finding the pin broken she stood afraid, then, as the sow grunted, she came cautiously in. I took her with my arm, my hand over her mouth. As she struggled against my breast, my heart began to beat loudly. At last she knew it was I. I clasped her. She hung in my arms, turning away her face, so that I kissed her throat. The tears blinded my eyes, I know not why, unless it were the hurt of my mouth, wounded by the horse, was keen.

"'They will kill you,' she whispered.

"'No,' I answered.

"And she wept softly. She took my head in her arms, and kissed me, wetting me with her tears, brushing me with her keen hair, warming me through.

"'I will not go away from here,' I said. 'Bring me a knife, and I will defend myself.'

"'No,' she wept. 'Ah no!'

"When she went, I lay down, pressing my chest, where she had rested, on the earth, lest being alone were worse emptiness than hunger.

"Later she came again. I saw her bend in the doorway, a lanthorn hanging in front. As she peered under the redness of her falling hair, I was afraid of her. But she came with food. We sat together in the dull light. Sometimes still I shivered and my throat would not swallow.

"'If,' said I, 'I eat all this you have brought me, I shall sleep till somebody finds me.'

"Then she took away the rest of the meat.

"'Why,' said I, 'should I not eat?' She looked at me in tears of fear.

"'What?' I said, but still she had no answer. I kissed her, and the hurt of my wounded mouth angered me.

"'Now there is my blood,' said I, 'on your mouth.'

"Wiping her smooth hand over her lips, she looked thereat, then at me.

"'Leave me,' I said, 'I am tired.' She rose to leave me.

"'But bring a knife,' I said. Then she held the lanthorn near my face, looking as at a picture.

"'You look to me,' she said, 'like a stirk that is roped for the axe. Your eyes are dark, but they are wide open.'

"'Then I will sleep,' said I, 'but will not wake too late.'

"'Do not stay here,' she said.

"'I will not sleep in the wood,' I answered, and it was my heart that spoke, 'for I am afraid. I had better be afraid of the voice of man and dogs, than the sounds in the woods. Bring me a knife, and in the morning I will go. Alone will I not go now.'

"'The searchers will take you,' she said.

"'Bring me a knife,' I answered.

"'Ah, go,' she wept.

"'Not now—I will not—'

"With that she lifted the lanthorn, lit up her own face and mine. Her blue eyes dried of tears. Then I took her to myself, knowing she was mine.

"'I will come again,' she said.

"She went, and I folded my arms, lay down and slept.

"When I woke, she was rocking me wildly to rouse me.

"'I dreamed,' said I, 'that a great heap, as if it were a hill, lay on me and above me.'

"She put a cloak over me, gave me a hunting knife and a wallet of food, and other things I did not note. Then under her own cloak she hid the lanthorn.

"'Let us go,' she said, and blindly I followed her.

"When I came out into the cold someone touched my face and my hair.

"'Ha!' I cried. 'Who now—'—then she swiftly clung to me, hushed me.

"'Someone has touched me,' I said aloud, still dazed with sleep.

"'Oh hush!' she wept. ''Tis snowing.' The dogs within the house began to bark. She fled forward, I after her. Coming to the ford of the stream she ran swiftly over, but I broke through the ice. Then I knew where I was. Snowflakes, fine and rapid, were biting at my face. In the wood there was no wind nor snow.

"'Listen,' said I to her, 'listen, for I am locked up with sleep.'

"'I hear roaring overhead,' she answered. 'I hear in the trees like great bats squeaking.'

"'Give me your hand,' said I.

"We heard many noises as we passed. Once as there uprose a whiteness before us, she cried aloud.

"'Nay,' said I, 'do not untie thy hand from mine,' and soon we were crossing fallen snow. But ever and again she started back from fear.

"'When you draw back my arm,' I said, angry, 'you loosen a weal on my shoulder.'

"Thereafter she ran by my side like a fawn beside its mother.

"'We will cross the valley and gain the stream,' I said. 'That will lead us on its ice as on a path deep into the forest. There we can join the outlaws. The wolves are driven from this part. They have followed the driven deer.'

"We came directly on a large gleam that shaped itself up among flying grains of snow.

"'Ah!' she cried, and she stood amazed.

"Then I thought we had gone through the bounds into faery realm, and I was no more a man. How did I know what eyes were gleaming at me between the snow, what cunning spirits in the draughts of air? So I waited for what would happen, and I forgot her, that she was there. Only I could feel the spirits whirling and blowing about me.

"Whereupon she clung upon me, kissing me lavishly, and, were dogs or men or demons come upon us at that moment, she had let us be stricken down, nor heeded not. So we moved forward to the shadow that shone in colours upon the passing snow. We found ourselves under a door of light which shed its colours mixed with snow. This Martha had never seen, nor I, this door open for a red and brave issuing like fires. We wondered.

"'It is faery,' she said, and after a while, 'Could one catch such—Ah no!'

"Through the snow shone bunches of red and blue.

"'Could one have such a little light like a red flower?—only a little, like a rose-berry scarlet on one's breast!—then one were singled out as Our Lady.'

"I flung off my cloak and my burden to climb up the face of the shadow. Standing on rims of stone, then in pockets of snow, I reached upward. My hand was red and blue, but I could not take the stuff. Like colour of a moth's wing it was on my hand, it flew on the increasing snow. I stood higher on the head of a frozen man, reached higher my hand. Then I felt the bright stuff cold. I could not pluck it off. Down below she cried to me to come again to her. I felt a rib that yielded, I struck at it with my knife. There came a gap in the redness. Looking through, I saw below as it were white stunted angels, with sad faces lifted in fear: Two faces, they had each, and round rings of hair. I was afraid. I grasped the shining red, I pulled. Then the cold man under me sank, so I fell as if broken onto the snow.

"Soon I was risen again, and we were running downwards towards the stream. We felt ourselves eased when the smooth road of ice was beneath us. For a while it was resting, to travel thus evenly. But the wind blew round us, the snow hung upon us, we leaned us this way and that, towards the storm. I drew her along, for she came as a bird that stems lifting and swaying against the wind. By and by the snow came smaller, there was no wind in the wood. Then I felt nor labor, nor cold. Only I knew the darkness drifted by on either side, that overhead was a lane of paleness where a moon fled us before. Still, I can feel the moon fleeing from me, can feel the trees passing round me in slow dizzy reel, can feel the hurt of my shoulder and my straight arm torn with holding her. I was following the moon and the stream, for I knew, where the water peeped from its burrow in the ground, there were shelters of the outlaw. But she fell, without sound or sign.

"I gathered her up and climbed the bank. There all round me hissed the larchwood, dry beneath, and laced with its dry fretted cords. For a little way I carried her into the trees. Then I laid her down till I cut flat hairy boughs. I put her in my bosom on this dry bed, so we swooned together through the night. I laced her round and covered her with myself, so she lay like a nut within its shell.

"Again, when morning came, it was pain of cold that woke me. I groaned, but my heart was warm as I saw the heap of red hair in my arms. As I looked at her, her eyes opened into mine. She smiled—from out of her smile came fear. As if in a trap, she pressed back her head.

"'We have no flint,' said I.

"'Yes—in the wallet, flint and steel and tinder box,' she answered.

"'God yield you blessing,' I said.

"In a place a little open I kindled a fire of larch boughs. She was afraid of me, hovering near, yet never crossing a space.

"'Come,' said I, 'let us eat this food.'

"'Your face,' she said, 'is smeared with blood.'

"I opened out my cloak.

"'But come,' said I, 'you are frosted with cold.'

"I took a handful of snow in my hand, wiping my face with it, which then I dried on my cloak.

"'My face is no longer painted with blood, you are no longer afraid of me. Come here then, sit by me while we eat.'

"But as I cut the cold bread for her, she clasped me suddenly, kissing me. She fell before me, clasped my knees to her breast, weeping. She laid her face down to my feet, so that her hair spread like a fire before me. I wondered at the woman. 'Nay,' I cried. At that she lifted her face to me from below. 'Nay,' I cried, feeling my tears fall. With her head on my breast, my own tears rose from their source, wetting my cheek and her hair, which was wet with the rain of my eyes.

"Then I remembered and took from my bosom the coloured light of that night before. I saw it was black and rough.

"'Ah,' said I, 'this is magic.'

"'The black stone!' she wondered.

"'It is the red light of the night before,' I said.

"'It is magic,' she answered.

"'Shall I throw it,' said I, lifting the stone, 'shall I throw it away, for fear.'

"'It shines!' she cried, looking up, 'it shines like the eye of a creature at night, the eye of a wolf in the doorway.'

"''Tis magic,' I said, 'let me throw it from us.' But nay, she held my arm.

"'It is red and shining,' she cried.

"'It is a bloodstone,' I answered. 'It will hurt us, we shall die in blood.'

"'But give it to me,' she answered.

"'It is red of blood,' I said.

"'Ah give it to me,' she called.

"'It is my blood,' I said.

"'Give it,' she commanded, low.

"'It is my life-stone,' I said.

"'Give it me,' she pleaded.

"I gave it her. She held it up, she smiled, she smiled in my face, lifting her arms to me. I took her with my mouth, her mouth, her white throat. Nor she ever shrank, but trembled with happiness.

"What woke us, when the woods were filling again with shadow, when the fire was out, when we opened our eyes and looked up as if drowned, into the light which stood bright and thick on the tree-tops, what woke us was the sound of wolves— — —"

"Nay," said the vicar, suddenly rising, "they lived happily ever after."

"No," I said.

# The Shades of Spring

## I

It was a mile nearer through the wood. Mechanically, Syson turned up by the forge and lifted the field-gate. The blacksmith and his mate stood still, watching the trespasser. But Syson looked too much a gentleman to be accosted. They let him go in silence across the small field to the wood.

There was not the least difference between this morning and those of the bright springs, six or eight years back. White and sandy-gold fowls still scratched round the gate, littering the earth and the field with feathers and scratched-up rubbish. Between the two thick holly bushes in the wood-hedge, was the hidden gap whose fence one climbed to get into the wood; the bars were scored just the same by the keeper's boots. He was back in the eternal.

Syson was extraordinarily glad. Like an uneasy spirit he had returned to the country of his past, and he found it waiting for him, unaltered. The hazels still spread glad little hands downwards, the bluebells here were still wan and few, among the lush grass and in shade of the bushes.

The path through the wood, on the very brow of a slope, ran winding easily for a time. All around were twiggy oaks, just issuing their gold, and floor spaces diapered with woodruff, with patches of dog-mercury, and tufts of hyacinth. Two fallen trees still lay across the track. Syson jolted down a steep, rough slope, and came again upon the open land, this time looking north as through a great window in the wood. He stayed to gaze over the level fields of the hill top, at the village which strewed the bare upland as if it had tumbled off the passing waggons of industry, and been forsaken. There was a stiff, modern, grey little church, and blocks and rows of red dwellings lying at random; at the back, the twinkling headstocks of the pit, and the looming pit-hill. All was naked and out-of-doors, not a tree. It was quite unaltered.

Syson turned satisfied, to follow the path that sheered down-hill into the wood. He was curiously elated, feeling himself back in an enduring vision. He started. A keeper was standing a few yards in front, barring the way.

"Where might you be going this road, sir?" asked the man. The tone of his question had a challenging twang. Syson looked at the fellow with an impersonal, observant gaze. It was a young man of four or five and twenty, ruddy, and well favoured. His dark blue eyes now stared aggressively at the intruder. His black moustache, very thick, was cropped short over a small, rather soft mouth. In every other respect the fellow was manly and good-looking. He stood just above middle height; the strong forward thrust of his chest, and the perfect ease of his erect, self-sufficient body, gave one the feeling that he was taut with animal life, like the thick jet of a fountain balanced in itself. He stood with the butt of his gun on the ground, looking uncertainly and questioningly at Syson. The dark, restless eyes of the trespasser, examining the man and penetrating into him without heeding his office, troubled the keeper and made him flush.

"Where is Naylor? Have you got his job?" Syson asked.

"You're not from the House, are you?" inquired the keeper. It could not be, since everyone was away.

"No, I'm not from the House," the other replied. It seemed to amuse him.

"Then might I ask where you were making for?" said the keeper, nettled.

"Where I am making for?" Syson repeated. "I am going to Willeywater Farm."

"This isn't th' road."

"I think so. Down this path, past the well, and out by the white gate."

"But that's not the public road."

"I suppose not. I used to come so often, in Naylor's time, I had forgotten. Where is he, by the way?"

"Crippled with rheumatism," the keeper answered reluctantly.

"Is he?" Syson exclaimed in pain.

"And who might you be?" asked the keeper, with a new intonation.

"John Adderley Syson; I used to live in Cordy Lane."

"Used to court Hilda Millership?"

Syson's eyes opened with a pained smile. He nodded. There was an awkward silence.

"And you—who are you?" asked Syson.

"Arthur Pilbeam—Naylor's my uncle," said the other.

"You live here in Nuttall?"

"I'm lodgin' at my uncle's—at Naylor's."

"I see!"

"Did you say you was goin' down to Willeywater?" asked the keeper.

"Yes."

There was a pause of some moments, before the keeper blurted: "*I'm* courtin' Hilda Millership."

The young fellow looked at the intruder with a stubborn defiance, almost pathetic. Syson opened new eyes.

"Are you?" he said, astonished. The keeper flushed dark.

"She and me are keeping company," he said.

"I didn't know!" said Syson. The other man waited uncomfortably.

"What, is the thing settled?" asked the intruder.

"How, settled?" retorted the other sulkily.

"Are you going to get married soon, and all that?"

The keeper stared in silence for some moments, impotent.

"I suppose so," he said, full of resentment.

"Ah!" Syson watched closely.

"I'm married myself," he added, after a time.

"You are?" said the other incredulously.

Syson laughed in his brilliant, unhappy way.

"This last fifteen months," he said.

The keeper gazed at him with wide, wondering eyes, apparently thinking back, and trying to make things out.

"Why, didn't you know?" asked Syson.

"No, I didn't," said the other sulkily.

There was silence for a moment.

"Ah well!" said Syson, "I will go on. I suppose I may." The keeper stood in silent opposition. The two men hesitated in the open, grassy space, set round with small sheaves of sturdy bluebells; a little open platform on the brow of the hill. Syson took a few indecisive steps forward, then stopped.

"I say, how beautiful!" he cried.

He had come in full view of the downslope. The wide path ran from his feet like a river, and it was full of bluebells, save for a green winding thread down the centre, where the keeper walked. Like a stream, the path opened into azure shallows at the levels, and there were pools of bluebells, with still the green thread winding through, like a thin current of ice-water through blue lakes. And from under the twig-purple of the bushes swam the shadowed blue, as if the flowers lay in flood water over the woodland.

"Ah, isn't it lovely!" Syson exclaimed; this was his past, the country he had abandoned, and it hurt him to see it so beautiful. Wood pigeons cooed overhead, and the air was full of brightness of birds singing.

"If you're married, what do you keep writing to her for, and sending her poetry books and things?" asked the keeper. Syson stared at him, taken aback and humiliated. Then he began to smile.

"Well," he said, "I did not know about you— — —"

Again the keeper flushed darkly:

"But if you are married—" he charged.

"I am," answered the other cynically.

Then, looking down the blue, beautiful path, Syson felt his own humiliation. "What right *have* I to hang on to her?" he thought, bitterly self-contemptuous.

"She knows I'm married, and all that," he said.

"But you keep sending her books," challenged the keeper.

Syson, silenced, looked at the other man quizzically, half pitying. Then he turned.

"Good-day," he said, and was gone. Now, everything irritated him: the two sallows, one all gold and perfume and murmur, one silver-green and bristly, reminded him that here he had taught her about pollination. What a fool he was! What god-forsaken folly it all was!

"Ah well," he said to himself; "the poor devil seems to have a grudge against me. I'll do my best for him." He grinned to himself, in a very bad temper.

## II

The farm was less than a hundred yards from the wood's edge. The wall of trees formed the fourth side to the open quadrangle. The house faced the wood. With tangled emotions, Syson noted the plum blossom falling on the profuse, coloured primroses, which he himself had brought here and set. How they had increased! There were thick tufts of scarlet, and pink, and pale purple primroses, under the plum trees. He saw somebody glance at him through the kitchen window, heard men's voices.

The door opened suddenly: very womanly she had grown! He felt himself going pale.

"You—?—Addy!" she exclaimed, and stood motionless.

"Who?" called the farmer's voice. Men's low voices answered.

Those low voices, curious, and almost jeering, roused the tormented spirit in the visitor. Smiling brilliantly at her, he waited.

"Myself—why not?" he said.

The flush burned very deep on her cheek and throat.

"We are just finishing dinner," she said.

"Then I will stay outside." He made a motion to show that he would sit on the red earthenware pippin that stood near the door among the daffodils, and contained the drinking water.

"Oh no, come in," she said hurriedly. He followed her. In the doorway, he glanced swiftly over the family, and bowed. Everyone was confused. The farmer, his wife, and the four sons sat at the coarsely laid dinner-table, the men with arms bare to the elbows.

"I am sorry I come at lunch-time," said Syson.

"Hello, Addy!" said the farmer, assuming the old form of address, but his tone cold. "How are you?"

And he shook hands.

"Shall you have a bit?" he invited the young visitor, but taking for granted the offer would be refused. He assumed that Syson was become too refined to eat so roughly. The young man winced at the imputation.

"Have you had any dinner?" asked the daughter.

"No," replied Syson. "It is too early. I shall be back at half-past one."

"You call it lunch, don't you?" asked the eldest son, almost ironical. He had once been an intimate friend of this young man.

"We'll give Addy something when we've finished," said the mother, an invalid, deprecating.

"No—don't trouble. I don't want to give you any trouble," said Syson.

"You could allus live on fresh air an' scenery," laughed the youngest son, a lad of nineteen.

Syson went round the buildings, and into the orchard at the back of the house, where daffodils all along the hedge-row swung like yellow, ruffled birds on their perches. He loved the place extraordinarily, the hills ranging round, with bear-skin woods covering their giant shoulders, and small red farms like brooches clasping their garments; the blue streak of water in the valley, the bareness of the home pasture, the sound of myriad-threaded bird-singing, which went mostly unheard. To his last day, he would dream of this place, when he felt the sun on his face, or saw the small handfuls of snow between the winter-twigs, or smelt the coming of spring.

Hilda was very womanly. In her presence he felt constrained. She was twenty-nine, as he was, but she seemed to him much older. He felt foolish, almost unreal, beside her. She was so static. As he was fingering some shed plum blossom on a low bough, she came to the back door to shake the table cloth. Fowls raced from the stack yard, birds rustled from the trees. Her dark hair was gathered up in a coil like a crown on her head. She was very straight, distant in her bearing. As she folded the cloth, she looked away over the hills.

Presently Syson returned indoors. She had prepared eggs and curd cheese, stewed gooseberries and cream.

"Since you will dine tonight," she said, "I have only given you a light lunch."

"It is awfully nice," he said. "You keep a real idyllic atmosphere— your belt of straw and ivy buds."

Still they hurt each other.

He was uneasy before her. Her brief, sure speech, her distant bearing, were unfamiliar to him. He admired again her grey-black eyebrows, and her lashes. Their eyes met. He saw, in the beautiful grey and black of her glance, tears and a strange light, and at the back of all, calm acceptance of herself, and triumph over him.

He felt himself shrinking. With an effort, he kept up the ironic manner.

She sent him into the parlour while she washed the dishes. The long low room was re-furnished from the Abbey sale, with chairs upholstered in claret-coloured rep, many years old, and an oval table of polished walnut, and another piano, handsome, though still antique. In spite of the strangeness, he was pleased. Opening a high cupboard let in the thickness of the wall, he found it full of his books, his old lesson books, and volumes of verse he had sent her, English and German. The daffodils in the white window-bottoms shone across the room, he could almost feel their rays. The old glamour caught him again. His youthful water-colours on the wall no longer made him grin; he remembered how fervently he had tried to paint for her, twelve years before.

She entered, wiping a dish, and he saw again the bright, kernel-white beauty of her arms.

"You are quite splendid here," he said, and their eyes met.

"Do you like it?" she asked. It was the old low, husky tone of intimacy. He felt a quick change beginning in his blood. It was the old, delicious sublimation, the thinning, almost the vaporising of himself, as if his spirit were to be liberated.

"Ay," he nodded, smiling at her like a boy again. She bowed her head.

"This was the countess' chair," she said in low tones. "I found her scissors down here between the padding."

"Did you? Where are they?"

Quickly, with a lilt in her movement, she fetched her work-basket, and together they examined the long-shanked old scissors.

"What a ballad of dead ladies!" he said, laughing, as he fitted his fingers into round loops of the countess' scissors.

"I knew you could use them," she said, with certainty. He looked at his fingers, and at the scissors. She meant his fingers were fine enough for the small-looped scissors.

"That is something to be said for me," he laughed, putting the scissors aside. She turned to the window. He noticed the fine, fair down on her cheek and her upper lip, and her soft, white neck, like the throat of a nettle flower, and her fore-arms, bright as newly blanched kernels. He was looking at her with new eyes, and she was a different person to him. He did not know her. But he could regard her objectively now.

"Shall we go out awhile?" she asked.

"Yes!" he answered. But the predominant emotion, that troubled the excitement and perplexity of his heart, was fear, fear of that which he saw. There was about her the same manner, the same intonation in her voice, now as then, but she was not what he had known her to be. He knew quite well what she had been for him. And gradually he was realising that she was something quite other, and always had been.

She put no covering on her head, merely took off her apron, saying: "We will go by the larches." As they passed the old orchard, she called in to show him a blue-tit's nest in one of the apple trees, and a sycock's in the hedge. He rather wondered at her surety, at a certain hardness like arrogance hidden under her humility.

"Look at the apple buds," she said, and he then perceived myriads of little scarlet balls among the drooping boughs. Watching his face, her eyes went hard. She saw the scales were fallen from him, and at last he was going to see her as she was. It was the thing she had most dreaded in the past, and most needed, for her soul's sake. Now he was going to see her as she was. He would not love her, and he would know he never could have loved her. The old illusion gone, they were strangers, crude and entire. But he would give her her due—she would have her due from him.

She was brilliant as he had not known her. She showed him nests: a jenny wren's in a low bush.

"See this jinty's!" she exclaimed.

He was surprised to hear her use the local name. She reached carefully through the thorns, and put her finger in the nest's round door.

"Five!" she said. "Tiny little things."

She showed him nests of robins, and chaffinches, and linnets, and buntings; of a wag-tail beside the water:

"And if we go down, nearer the lake, I will show you a kingfisher's..."

"Among the young fir trees," she said, "there's a throstle's or a blackie's on nearly every bough, every ledge. The first day, when I'd seen them all, I felt as if I mustn't go in the wood. It seemed a city of birds: and in the morning, hearing them all, I thought of the noisy early markets. I was afraid to go in my own wood."

She was using the language they had both of them invented. Now it was all her own. He had done with it. She did not mind his silence, but was always dominant, letting him see her wood. As they came along a marshy path where forget-me-nots were opening in a rich blue drift:

"We know all the birds, but there are many flowers we can't find out," she said. It was half an appeal to him, who had known the names of things.

She looked dreamily across to the open fields that slept in the sun:

"I have a lover as well, you know," she said, with assurance, yet dropping again almost into the intimate tone.

This woke in him the spirit to fight her.

"I think I met him. He is good-looking—also in Arcady."

Without answering, she turned into a dark path that led uphill, where the trees and undergrowth were very thick.

"They did well," she said at length, "to have various altars to various gods, in old days."

"Ah yes!" he agreed. "To whom is the new one?"

"There are no old ones," she said. "I was always looking for this."

"And whose is it?" he asked.

"I don't know," she said, looking full at him.

"I'm very glad, for your sake," he said, "that you are satisfied."

"Ay—but the man doesn't matter so much," she said. There was a pause.

"No!" he exclaimed, astonished, yet recognising her as her real self.

"It is one's self that matters," she said. "Whether one is being one's own self and serving one's own God."

There was silence, during which he pondered. The path was almost flowerless, gloomy. At the side, his heels sank into soft clay.

### III

"I," she said, very slowly, "I was married the same night as you."

He looked at her.

"Not legally, of course," she replied. "But—actually."

"To the keeper?" he said, not knowing what else to say.

She turned to him.

"You thought I could not?" she said. But the flush was deep in her cheek and throat, for all her assurance.

Still he would not say anything.

"You see"—she was making an effort to explain—"*I* had to understand also."

"And what does it amount to, this *understanding*?" he asked.

"A very great deal—does it not to you?" she replied. "One is free."

"And you are not disappointed?"

"Far from it!" Her tone was deep and sincere.

"You love him?"

"Yes, I love him."

"Good!" he said.

This silenced her for a while.

"Here, among his things, I love him," she said.

His conceit would not let him be silent.

"It needs this setting?" he asked.

"It does," she cried. "You were always making me to be not myself."

He laughed shortly.

"But is it a matter of surroundings?" he said. He had considered her all spirit.

"I am like a plant," she replied. "I can only grow in my own soil."

They came to a place where the undergrowth shrank away, leaving a bare, brown space, pillared with the brick-red and purplish trunks of pine trees. On the fringe, hung the sombre green of elder trees, with flat flowers in bud, and below were bright, unfurling pennons of fern. In the midst of the bare space stood a keeper's log hut. Pheasant coops were lying about, some occupied by a clucking hen, some empty.

Hilda walked over the brown pine-needles to the hut, took a key from among the eaves, and opened the door. It was a bare wooden place with a carpenter's bench and form, carpenter's tools, an axe, snares, traps, some skins pegged down, everything in order. Hilda closed the door. Syson examined the weird flat coats of wild animals, that were pegged down to be cured. She turned some knotch in the side wall, and disclosed a second, small apartment.

"How romantic!" said Syson.

"Yes. He is very curious—he has some of a wild animal's cunning—in a nice sense—and he is inventive, and thoughtful—but not beyond a certain point."

She pulled back a dark green curtain. The apartment was occupied almost entirely by a large couch of heather and bracken, on which was spread an ample rabbit-skin rug. On the floor were patch-work rugs of cat-skin, and a red calf-skin, while hanging from the wall were other furs. Hilda took down one, which she put on. It was a cloak of rabbit-skin and of white fur, with a hood, apparently of the skins of stoats. She laughed at Syson from out of this barbaric mantle, saying:

"What do you think of it?"

"Ah—! I congratulate you on your man," he replied.

"And look!" she said.

In a little jar on a shelf were some sprays, frail and white, of the first honeysuckle.

"They will scent the place at night," she said.

He looked round curiously.

"Where does he come short, then?" he asked. She gazed at him for a few moments. Then, turning aside,

"The stars aren't the same with him," she said. "You could make them flash and quiver, and the forget-me-nots come up at me like phosphorescence. You could make things *wonderful*. I have found it out—it is true. But I have them all for myself, now."

He laughed, saying:

"After all, stars and forget-me-nots are only luxuries. You ought to make poetry."

"Ay," she assented. "But I have them all now."

Again he laughed bitterly at her.

She turned swiftly. He was leaning against the small window of the tiny obscure room, and was watching her, who stood in the doorway, still cloaked in her mantle. His cap was removed, so she saw his face and head distinctly in the dim room. His black, straight, glossy hair was brushed clean back from his brow. His black eyes were watching her, and his face, that was clear and cream, and perfectly smooth, was flickering.

"We are very different," she said bitterly.

Again he laughed.

"I see you disapprove of me," he said.

"I disapprove of what you have become," she said.

"You think we might"—he glanced at the hut—"have been like this—you and I?"

She shook her head.

"You! no; never! You plucked a thing and looked at it till you had found out all you wanted to know about it, then you threw it away," she said.

"Did I?" he asked. "And could your way never have been my way? I suppose not.",

"Why should it?" she said. "I am a separate being."

"But surely two people sometimes go the same way," he said.

"You took me away from myself," she said.

He knew he had mistaken her, had taken her for something she was not. That was his fault, not hers.

"And did you always know?" he asked.

"No—you never let me know. You bullied me. I couldn't help myself. I was glad when you left me, really."

"I know you were," he said. But his face went paler, almost deathly luminous.

"Yet," he said, "it was you who sent me the way I have gone."

"I!" she exclaimed, in pride.

"You *would* have me take the Grammar-school scholarship—you would have me foster poor little Botell's fervent attachment to me, till he couldn't live without me—and because Botell was rich and influential. You triumphed in the wine merchant's offer to send me to Cambridge, to befriend his only child. You wanted me to rise in the world. And all the time you were sending me away from you—every new success of mine put a separation between us, and more for you than for me. You never wanted to come with me: you wanted just to send me to see what it was like. I believe you even wanted me to marry a lady. You wanted to triumph over society in me."

"And I am responsible," she said, with sarcasm.

"I distinguished myself to satisfy you," he replied.

"Ah!" she cried, "you always wanted change, change, like a child."

"Very well! And I am a success, and I know it, and I do some good work. But—I thought you were different. What right have you to a man?"

"What do you want?" she said, looking at him with wide, fearful eyes.

He looked back at her, his eyes pointed, like weapons.

"Why, nothing," he laughed shortly.

There was a rattling at the outer latch, and the keeper entered. The woman glanced round, but remained standing, fur cloaked, in the inner doorway. Syson did not move.

The other man entered, saw, and turned away without speaking. The two also were silent.

Pilbeam attended to his skins.

"I must go," said Syson.

"Yes," she replied.

"Then I give you 'To our vast and varying fortunes'." He lifted his hand in pledge.

"'To our vast and varying fortunes'" she answered gravely, and speaking in cold tones.

"Arthur!" she said.

The keeper pretended not to hear. Syson, watching keenly, began to smile. The woman drew herself up.

"Arthur!" she said again, with a curious upward inflection, which warned the two men that her soul was trembling on a dangerous crisis.

The keeper slowly put down his tool and came to her.

"Yes," he said.

"I wanted to introduce you," she said, trembling.

"I've met him a'ready," said the keeper.

"Have you? It is Addy, Mr Syson, whom you know about.—This is Arthur, Mr Pilbeam," she added, turning to Syson. The latter held out his hand to the keeper, and they shook hands in silence.

"I'm glad to have met you," said Syson. "We drop our correspondence, Hilda?"

"Why need we?" she asked.

The two men stood at a loss.

"*Is* there no need?" said Syson.

Still she was silent.

"It is as you will," she said.

They went all three together down the gloomy path.

"'Qu'il était bleu, le ciel, et grand l'espoir',"  quoted Syston, not knowing what to say.

"What do you mean?" she said. "Besides, *we* can't walk in *our* wild oats—we never sowed any."

Syson looked at her. He was startled to see his young love, his nun, his Botticelli angel, so revealed. It was he who had been the fool. He and she were more separate than any two strangers could be. She only wanted to keep up a correspondence with him—and he, of course, wanted it kept up, so that he could write to her, like Dante to some Beatrice who had never existed save in the man's own brain.

At the bottom of the path she left him. He went along with the keeper, towards the open, towards the gate that closed on the wood. The two men walked almost like friends. They did not broach the subject of their thoughts.

————

Instead of going straight to the high-road gate, Syson went along the wood's-edge, where the brook spread out in a little bog, and under the alder trees, among the reeds, great yellow stools and bosses of marigolds shone. Threads of brown water trickled by, touched with gold from the flowers. Suddenly, there was a blue flash in the air, as a kingfisher passed.

Syson was extraordinarily moved. He climbed the bank to the gorse bushes, whose sparks of blossom had not yet gathered into a flame. Lying on the dry brown turf, he discovered sprigs of tiny purple milkwort and pink spots of lousewort. What a wonderful world it was—marvellous, for ever new. He felt as if it were underground, like the fields of monotone hell, notwithstanding. Inside his breast was a pain like a wound. He remembered the poem of William Morris, where in the Chapel of Lyonesse a knight lay wounded, with the truncheon of a spear deep in his breast, lying always as dead, yet did not die, while day after day the coloured sunlight dipped from the painted window across the chancel, and passed away. He knew now it never had been true, that which was between him and her, not for a moment. The truth had stood apart all the time.

Syson turned over. The air was full of the sound of larks, as if the sunshine above were condensing and falling in a shower. Amid this bright sound, voices sounded small and distinct.

"But if he's married, an' quite willing to drop it off, what has ter against it?" said the man's voice.

"I don't want to talk about it now. I want to be alone."

Syson looked through the bushes. Hilda was standing in the wood, near the gate. The man was in the field, loitering by the hedge, and playing with the bees as they settled on the white bramble flowers.

There was silence for a while, in which Syson imagined her will among the brightness of the larks. Suddenly the keeper exclaimed "Ah!"—and swore. He was gripping at the sleeve of his coat, near the shoulder. Then he pulled off his jacket, threw it on the ground, and absorbedly rolled up his shirt sleeve, right to the shoulder.

"Ah!" he said vindictively, as he picked out the bee and flung it away. He twisted his fine, bright arm, peering awkwardly over his shoulder.

"What is it?" asked Hilda.

"A bee—crawled up my sleeve," he answered.

"Come here to me," she said.

The keeper went to her, like a sulky boy. She took his arm in her hands.

"Here it is—and the sting left in—poor bee!"

She picked out the sting, put her mouth to his arm, and sucked away the drop of poison. As she looked at the red mark her mouth had made, and at his arm, she said, laughing:

"That is the reddest kiss you'll ever have."

When Syson next looked up, at the sound of voices, he saw in the shadow the keeper with his mouth on the throat of his beloved, whose head was thrown back, and whose hair had fallen, so that one rough rope of dark brown hair hung across his bare arm.

"No," the woman answered. "I am not upset because he's gone. You won't understand..."

Syson could not distinguish what the man said. Hilda replied, clear and distinct:

"You know I love you.—He has gone quite out of my life—don't trouble about him..." He kissed her, murmuring. She laughed hollowly.

"Yes," she said, indulgent. "We will be married, we will be married. But not just yet." He spoke to her again. Syson heard nothing for a time. Then she said:

"You must go home, now, dear—you will get no sleep."

Again was heard the murmur of the keeper's voice, troubled by fear and passion.

"But why should we be married at once?" she said. "What more would you have, by being married? It is most beautiful as it is."

At last he pulled on his coat and departed. She stood at the gate, not watching him, but looking over the sunny country.

When at last she had gone, Syson also departed, going back to town.

## Second-Best

"Oh, I'm tired!" Frances exclaimed petulantly, and in the same instant she dropped down on the turf near the hedge-bottom. Anne stood a moment surprised, then, accustomed to the vagaries of her beloved Frances, said:

"Well, and aren't you always likely to be tired, after travelling that blessed long way from Liverpool yesterday!" and she plumped down beside her sister. Anne was a wise young body of fourteen, very buxom, brimming with common-sense. Frances was much older, about twenty-three, and whimsical, spasmodic. She was the beauty and the clever child of the family. She plucked the goose-grass buttons from her dress in a nervous, desperate fashion. Her beautiful profile, looped above with black hair, warm with the dusky-and-scarlet complexion of a pear, was calm as a mask, her thin brown hand plucked nervously.

"It's not the journey," she said, objecting to Anne's obtuseness. Anne looked inquiringly at her darling. The young girl, in her self-confident, practical way, proceeded to reckon up this whimsical creature. But suddenly she found herself full in the eyes of Frances; felt two dark, hectic eyes flaring challenge at her, and she shrank away. Frances was peculiar for these great, exposed looks, which disconcerted people by their violence and their suddenness.

"What's a matter, poor old duck?" asked Anne, as she folded the slight, wilful form of her sister in her arms. Frances laughed shakily, and nestled down for comfort on the budding breasts of the strong girl.

"Oh, I'm only a bit tired," she murmured, on the point of tears.

"Well of course you are, what do you expect?" soothed Anne. It was a joke to Frances that Anne should play elder, almost mother to her. But then, Anne was in her unvexed teens; men were like big dogs to her: while Frances, at twenty-three, suffered a good deal.

The country was intensely morning-still. On the common everything shone beside its shadow, and the hillside gave off heat in silence. The brown turf seemed in a low state of combustion, the leaves of the oaks were scorched brown. Among the blackish foliage in the distance shone the small red and orange of the village.

The willows in the brook-course at the foot of the common suddenly shook with a dazzling effect like diamonds. It was a puff of wind. Anne resumed her normal position. She spread her knees, and put in her lap a handful of hazel nuts, whitey-green leafy things, whose one cheek was tanned between brown and pink. These she began to crack and eat. Frances, with bowed head, mused bitterly.

"Eh, you know Tom Smedley?" began the young girl, as she pulled a tight kernel out of its shell.

"I suppose so," replied Frances sarcastically.

"Well, he gave me a wild rabbit what he'd caught, to keep with my tame ones—and it's living."

"That's a good thing," said Frances, very detached and ironic.

"Well, it *is*! He reckoned he'd take me to Ollerton Feast, but he never did. Look here, he took a servant from the rectory, I saw him."

"So he ought," said Frances.

"No he oughtn't! And I told him so—and I told him I should tell you—an' I have done."

Click and snap went a nut between her teeth. She sorted out the kernel, and chewed complacently.

"It doesn't make much difference," said Frances.

"Well—'appen it doesn't—but I was mad with him all the same."

"Why?"

"Because I was: he's no right to go with a servant."

"He's a perfect right," persisted Frances, very just and cold.

"No he hasn't, when he'd said he'd take me."

Frances burst into a laugh of amusement and relief.

"Oh no, I'd forgot that," she said—adding: "And what did he say when you promised to tell me?"

"He laughed, and said 'She won't fret her fat over that.'"

"And she won't," sniffed Frances.

There was silence. The common, with its sere, blonde headed thistles, its heaps of silent bramble, its brown-husked gorse, in the glare of sunshine seemed visionary. Across the brook began the immense pattern of agriculture, white chequering of barley stubble, brown squares of wheat, khaki patches of pasture, red stripes of fallow, with the woodland and the tiny village dark like ornaments, leading away to the distance, right to the hills, where the check-pattern grew smaller and smaller, till in the blackish haze of heat, far-off, only the tiny white squares of barley stubble showed distinct.

"Eh, I say, here's a rabbit-hole!" cried Anne suddenly.

"Should we watch if one comes out? You won't have to fidget, you know."

The two girls sat perfectly still. Frances watched certain objects in her surroundings: they had a peculiar, unfriendly look about them: the weight of greenish elderberries on their purpling stalks; the twinkling of the yellowing crab-apples that clustered high up in the hedge, against the sky; the exhausted, limp leaves of the primroses lying flat in the hedge-bottom: all looked strange to her. Then her eyes caught a movement. A mole was moving silently over the warm, red soil, nosing, shuffling hither and thither, flat and dark as a shadow, shifting about, and as suddenly brisk, and as silent, like a very ghost of joie de vivre. Frances started, from habit was about to call on Anne to kill the little pest. But today her lethargy of unhappiness was too much for her. She watched the little brute paddling, snuffing, touching things to discover them, running in blindness, delighted to ecstasy by the sunlight and the hot strange things that caressed its belly and its nose.

She felt a keen pity for the little creature.

"Eh, our Fran, look there! It's a mole."

Anne was on her feet, standing watching the dark, unconscious beast. Frances frowned with anxiety.

"It doesn't run off, does it?" said the young girl softly. Then she stealthily approached the creature. The mole paddled fumblingly away. In an instant Anne put her foot upon it, not too heavily. Frances could see the struggling, swimming movement of the little pink hands of the brute, the twisting and twitching of its pointed nose, as it wrestled under the sole of the boot.

"It *does* wriggle!" said the bonny girl, knitting her brows in a frown at the eerie sensation. Then she bent down to look at her trap. Frances could now see, beyond the edge of the boot-sole, the heaving of the velvet shoulders, the pitiful turning of the sightless face, the frantic rowing of the flat, pink hands.

"Kill the thing," she said, turning away her face.

"Oo—I'm not," laughed Anne, shrinking. "You can if you like."

"I *don't* like," said Frances, with quiet intensity.

After several dabbing attempts, Anne succeeded in picking up the little animal by the scruff of its neck. It threw back its head, flung its long blind snout from side to side, the mouth open in a peculiar oblong, with tiny pinkish teeth at the edge. The blind, frantic mouth gaped and writhed. The body, heavy and clumsy, hung scarcely moving.

"Isn't it a snappy little thing," observed Anne, twisting to avoid the teeth.

"What are you going to do with it?" asked Frances sharply.

"It's got to be killed—look at the damage they do. I s'll take it home and let Dadda or somebody kill it. I'm not going to let it go."

She swaddled the creature clumsily in her pocket-handkerchief, and sat down beside her sister. There was an interval of silence, during which Anne combated the efforts of the mole.

"You've not had much to say about Jimmy this time. Did you see him often in Liverpool?" Anne asked suddenly.

"Once or twice," replied Frances, giving no sign of how the question troubled her.

"And aren't you sweet on him any more, then?"

"I should think I'm not, seeing that he's engaged."

"Engaged! Jimmy Barrass! Well of all things!! I never thought *he'd* get engaged."

"Why not, he's as much right as anybody else?" snapped Frances.

Anne was fumbling with the mole.

"'Appen so," she said at length. "But I never thought Jimmy would, though."

"Why not?" snapped Frances.

"*I* don't know.—This blessed mole, it'll not keep still!—Who's he got engaged to?"

"How should I know."

"I thought you'd ask him, you've known him long enough.—I s'd think he thought he'd get engaged now he's a Doctor of Chemistry."

Frances laughed in spite of herself.

"What's that got to do with it," she asked.

"I'm sure it's got a lot. He'll want to feel *somebody* now, so he's got engaged.—Hey, stop it, go in!"

But at this juncture the mole almost succeeded in wriggling clear. It wrestled and twisted frantically, waved its pointed blind head, its mouth standing open like a little shaft, its big wrinkled hands spread out.

"Go in with you!" urged Anne, poking the little creature with her forefinger, trying to get it back into the handkerchief. Suddenly the mouth turned like a spark on her finger.

"Oh!" she cried. "He's bit me."

She dropped him to the floor. Dazed, the blind creature fumbled round. Frances felt like shrieking: she expected him to dart away in a flash, like a mouse, and there he remained groping; she wanted to cry to him to be gone. Anne, in a sudden decision of wrath, caught up her sister's walking-cane. With one blow, the mole was dead. Frances was startled and shocked. One moment, the little wretch was fussing in the heat, and the next it lay like a little bag, inert and black: not a struggle, scarce a quiver.

"It is dead!" Frances said breathlessly.

Anne took her finger from her mouth, looked at the tiny pinpricks, and said:

"Yes he is, and I'm glad. They're vicious little nuisances, moles are."

With which her wrath vanished. She picked up the dead animal.

"Hasn't it got a beautiful skin," she mused, stroking the fur with her forefinger, then with her cheek.

"Mind," said Frances sharply. "You'll have the blood on your skirt!"

One ruby drop of blood hung on the small snout, ready to fall. Anne shook it off onto some harebells. Frances suddenly became calm; in that moment, grown-up.

"I suppose they *have* to be killed," she said, and a certain rather dreary indifference succeeded to her grief. The twinkling crab-apples, the glitter of brilliant willows now seemed to her trifling, scarcely worth the notice. Something had died in her, so that things lost their poignancy. She was calm, indifference overlying her quiet sadness. Rising, she walked down to the brook course.

"Here, wait for me," cried Anne, coming tumbling after. Frances stood on the bridge, looking at the red mud trodden into pockets by the feet of cattle. There was not a drain of water left, but everything smelled green, succulent. Why did she care so little for Anne, who was so fond of her, she asked herself. Why did she care so little for anyone. She did not know, but she felt a rather stubborn pride in her isolation and indifference.

They entered a field where stooks of barley stood in rows, the straight, blonde tresses of the corn streaming onto the ground. The stubble was bleached by the intense summer, so that the expanse glared white. The next field was sweet and soft with a second crop of seeds, thin, straggling clover whose little pink knobs rested prettily in the dark green. The scent was faint and sickly. The girls came up in single file, Frances leading.

Near the gate, a young man was mowing with the scythe some fodder for the afternoon feed of the cattle. As he saw the girls, he left off working and waited in an aimless kind of way. Frances was dressed in white muslin, and she walked with dignity, detached and forgetful. Her lack of agitation, her simple, unheeding advance made him nervous. She had loved the far-off Jimmy for five years, having had in return his half-measures. This man only affected her slightly.

Tom was of medium stature, energetic in build. His smooth, fair skinned face was burned red, not brown, by the sun, and this ruddiness enhanced his appearance of good-humour and easiness. Being a year older than Frances, he would have courted her long ago had she been so inclined. As it was, he had gone his uneventful way amiably, chatting with many a girl, but remaining unattached, free of trouble for the most part. Only he knew he wanted a woman. He hitched his trousers just a trifle self-consciously as the girls approached. Frances was a rare, delicate kind of being, whom he realised with a queer and delicious stimulation in his veins. She gave him a slight sense of suffocation: somehow, this morning, she affected him more than usual. She was dressed in white. He, however, being matter-of-fact in his mind, did not realise. His feeling had never become conscious, purposive.

Frances knew what she was about. Tom was ready to love her as soon as she would show him. Now that she could not have Jimmy, she did not poignantly care. Still, she would have something. If she could not have the best—Jimmy, whom she knew to be something of a snob—she would have the second best, Tom. She advanced rather indifferently.

"You are back, then!" said Tom. She marked the touch of uncertainty in his voice.

"No," she laughed, "I'm still in Liverpool," and the undertone of intimacy made him burn.

"This isn't you, then?" he asked.

Her heart leapt up in approval. She looked in his eyes, and for a second, was with him.

"Why, what do you think?" she laughed.

He lifted his hat from his head with a distracted little gesture.—She liked him, his quaint ways, his humour, his ignorance, and his slow masculinity.

"Here, look here Tom Smedley," broke in Anne.

"A moudiwarp!—Did you find it dead?" he asked.

"No, it bit me," said Anne.

"Oh, ay!—an' that got your rag out, did it?"

"No, it didn't!" Anne scolded sharply. "Such language!"

"Oh—what's up wi' it?"

"I can't bear you to talk broad."

"Can't you?"

He glanced at Frances.

"It isn't nice," Frances said. She did not care, really. The vulgar speech jarred on her as a rule; Jimmy was a gentleman. But Tom's manner of speech did not matter to her.

"I like you to talk *nicely*," she added.

"Do you," he replied, tilting his hat, stirred.

"And generally you *do*, you know," she smiled.

"I s'll have to have a try," he said, rather tensely gallant.

"What?" she asked brightly.

"To talk nice to you," he said. Frances coloured furiously, bent her head for a moment, then laughed gaily, as if she liked this clumsy hint.

"Eh now, you mind what you're saying," cried Anne, giving the young man an admonitory pat.

"You wouldn't have to give yon mole many knocks like *that*," he teased, relieved to get on safe ground, rubbing his arm.

"No indeed, it died in one blow," said Frances, with a flippancy that was hateful to her.

"You're not so good at knockin' 'em?" he said, turning to her.

"I don't know, if I'm cross," she said, decisively.

"No?" he replied, with alert attentiveness.

"I could," she added, harder, "if it was necessary."

He was slow to feel her difference.

"And don't you consider it *is* necessary?" he asked, with misgiving.

"We—ell—is it?" she said, looking at him steadily, coldly.

"I reckon it is," he replied, looking away, but standing stubborn. She laughed quickly.

"But it isn't necessary for *me*," she said, with slight contempt.

"Yes, that's quite true," he answered.

She laughed in a shaky fashion.

"*I know it is*," she said; and there was an awkward pause.

"Why, would you *like* me to kill moles then?" she asked, tentatively, after a while.

"They do do us a lot of damage," he said, standing firm on his ground, angered.

"Well, I'll see, the next time I come across one," she promised, defiantly. Their eyes met, and she sank before him, her pride troubled. He felt uneasy and triumphant and baffled, as if fate had gripped him. She smiled as she departed.

"Well," said Anne, as the sisters went through the wheat stubble. "I don't know what you two's been jawing about, I'm sure."

"Don't you," laughed Frances, significantly.

"No I don't. But at any rate, Tom Smedley's a good deal better to my thinking than Jimmy, so there—and nicer."

"Perhaps he is," said Frances coldly.

And the next day, after a secret, persistent hunt, she found another mole playing in the heat. She killed it, and in the evening, when Tom came to the gate to smoke his pipe after supper, she took him the dead creature.

"Here you are then!" she said.

"Did you catch it?" he replied, taking the velvet corpse into his fingers and examining it minutely. This was to hide his trepidation.

"Did you think I couldn't?" she asked, her face very near his.

"Nay, I didn't know."

She laughed in his face, a strange little laugh that caught her breath, all agitation and tears and recklessness of desire. He looked frightened and upset. She put her hand to his arm.

"Shall you go out wi' me?" he asked, in a difficult, troubled tone.

She turned her face away, with a shaky laugh. The blood came up in him, strong, overmastering. He resisted it. But it drove him down, and he was carried away. Seeing the winsome, frail nape of her neck, fierce love came upon him for her, and tenderness.

"We s'll 'ave to tell your mother," he said. And he stood, suffering, resisting his passion for her.

"Yes," she replied, in a dead voice. But there was a thrill of pleasure in this death.

# The Shadow in the Rose Garden

A rather small young man sat by the window of a pretty seaside cottage trying to persuade himself that he was reading the newspaper. It was about half-past eight in the morning. Outside, the glory roses hung in the morning sunshine like little bowls of fire tipped up. The young man looked at the table, then at the clock, then at his own big silver watch. An expression of stiff endurance came onto his face. Then he rose and reflected on the oil-paintings that hung on the walls of the room, giving careful but hostile attention to "The Stag at Bay." He tried the lid of the piano, and found it locked. He caught sight of his own face in a little mirror, pulled his brown moustache, and an alert interest sprang into his eyes. He was not ill-favoured. He twisted his moustache. His figure was rather small, but alert and vigorous. As he turned from the mirror a look of self-commiseration mingled with his appreciation of his own physiognomy.

In a state of self-suppression, he went through into the garden. His jacket, however, did not look dejected. It was new, and had a smart and self-confident air, sitting upon a confident body. He contemplated the Tree of Heaven that flourished by the lawn, then sauntered on to the next plant. There was more promise in a crooked apple tree covered with brown-red fruit. Glancing round, he broke off an apple and, with his back to the house, took a clean, sharp bite. To his surprise the fruit was sweet. He took another. Then again he turned to survey the bedroom windows overlooking the garden. He started, seeing a woman's figure; but it was only his wife. She was gazing across to the sea, apparently ignorant of him.

For a moment or two he looked at her, watching her. She was a good-looking woman, who seemed older than he, rather pale, but healthy, her face yearning. Her rich auburn hair was heaped in folds on her forehead. She looked apart from him and his world, gazing away to the sea. It irked her husband that she should continue abstracted and in ignorance of him; he pulled poppy fruits and threw them at the window. She started, glanced at him with a wild smile, and looked away again. Then almost immediately she left the window. He went indoors to meet her. She had a fine carriage, very proud, and wore a dress of soft white muslin.

"I've been waiting long enough," he said.

"For me or for breakfast?" she said lightly. "You know we said nine o'clock. I should have thought you could have slept after the journey."

"You know I'm always up at five, and I couldn't stop in bed after six. You might as well be in pit as in bed, on a morning like this."

"I shouldn't have thought the pit would occur to you, here."

She moved about examining the room, looking at the ornaments under glass covers. He, planted on the hearthrug, watched her rather uneasily, and grudgingly indulgent. She shrugged her shoulders at the apartment.

"Come," she said, taking his arm, "let us go into the garden till Mrs. Coates brings the tray."

"I hope she'll be quick," he said, pulling his moustache. She gave a short laugh, and leaned on his arm as they went. He had lighted a pipe.

Mrs. Coates entered the room as they went down the steps. The delightful, erect old lady hastened to the window for a good view of her visitors. Her china-blue eyes were bright as she watched the young couple go down the path, he walking in an easy, confident fashion, with his wife on his arm. The landlady began talking to herself in a soft, Yorkshire accent.

"Just of a height they are. She wouldn't ha' married a man less than herself in stature, I think, though he's not her equal otherwise." Here her granddaughter came in, setting a tray on the table. The girl went to the old woman's side.

"He's been eating the apples, gran'," she said.

"Has he, my pet? Well, if he's happy, why not?"

Outside, the young, well-favoured man listened with impatience to the chink of the teacups. At last, with a sigh of relief, the couple came in to breakfast. After he had eaten for some time, he rested a moment and said:

"Do you think it's any better place than Bridlington?"

"I do," she said, "infinitely! Besides, I am at home here—it's not like a strange seaside place to me."

"How long were you here?"

"Two years."

He ate reflectively.

"I should ha' thought you'd rather go to a fresh place," he said at length.

She sat very silent, and then, delicately, put out a feeler.

"Why?" she said. "Do you think I shan't enjoy myself?"

He laughed comfortably, putting the marmalade thick on his bread.

"I hope so," he said.

She again took no notice of him.

"But don't say anything about it in the village, Frank," she said casually. "Don't say who I am, or that I used to live here. There's nobody I want to meet, particularly, and we should never feel free if they knew me again."

"Why did you come, then?"

"'Why?' Can't you understand why?"

"Not if you don't want to know anybody."

"I came to see the place, not the people."

He did not say any more.

"Women," she said, "are different from men. I don't know why I wanted to come—but I did."

She helped him to another cup of coffee, solicitously.

"Only," she resumed, "don't talk about me in the village." She laughed shakily. "I don't want my past brought up against me, you know." And she moved the crumbs on the cloth with her finger tip.

He looked at her as he drank his coffee; he sucked his moustache, and putting down his cup, said phlegmatically:

"I'll bet you've had a lot of past."

She looked with a little guiltiness, that flattered him, down at the tablecloth.

"Well," she said, caressive, "you won't give me away, who I am, will you?"

"No," he said, comforting, laughing, "I won't give you away."

He was pleased.

She remained silent. After a moment or two she lifted her head, saying:

"I've got to arrange with Mrs. Coates, and do various things. So you'd better go out by yourself this morning—and we'll be in to dinner at one."

"But you can't be arranging with Mrs. Coates all morning," he said.

"Oh, well—then I've some letters to write, and I must get that mark out of my skirt. I've got plenty of little things to do this morning. You'd better go out by yourself."

He perceived that she wanted to be rid of him, so that when she went upstairs, he took his hat and lounged out onto the cliffs, suppressedly angry.

Presently she too came out. She wore a hat with roses, and a long lace scarf hung over her white dress. Rather nervously, she put up her sunshade, and her face was half-hidden in its coloured shadow. She went along the narrow track of flag-stones that were worn hollow by the feet of the fishermen. She seemed to be avoiding her surroundings, as if she remained safe in the little obscurity of her parasol.

She passed the church, and went down the lane till she came to a high wall by the wayside. Under this she went slowly, stopping at length by an open doorway, which shone like a picture of light in the dark wall. There in the magic beyond the doorway, patterns of shadow lay on the sunny court, on the blue and white sea-pebbles of its paving, while a green lawn glowed beyond, where a bay tree glittered at the edges. She tiptoed nervously into the court-yard, glancing at the house that stood in shadow. The uncurtained windows looked black and soulless, the kitchen door stood open. Irresolutely she took a step forward, and again forward, leaning, yearning, towards the garden beyond.

She had almost gained the corner of the house when a heavy step came crunching through the trees. A gardener appeared before her. He held a wicker tray on which were rolling great, dark red gooseberries, over ripe. He moved slowly.

"The garden isn't open to-day," he said quietly to the attractive woman, who was poised for retreat.

For a moment she was silent with surprise. How should it be public at all?

"When is it open?" she asked, quick-witted.

"The rector lets visitors in on Fridays and Tuesdays."

She stood still, reflecting. How strange to think of the rector opening his garden to the public!

"But everybody will be at church," she said coaxingly to the man. "There'll be nobody here, will there?"

He moved, and the big gooseberries rolled.

"The rector lives at the new rectory," he said.

The two stood still. He did not like to ask her to go. At last she turned to him with a winning smile.

"Might I have *one* peep at the roses?" she coaxed, with pretty wilfulness.

"I don't suppose it would matter," he said, moving aside; "you won't stop long——"

She went forward, forgetting the gardener in a moment. Her face became strained, her movements eager. Glancing round, she saw all the windows giving onto the lawn were curtainless and dark. The house had a sterile appearance, as if it were still used, but not inhabited. A shadow seemed to go over her. She went across the lawn towards the garden, through an arch of crimson ramblers, a gate of colour. There beyond lay the soft blue sea within the bay, misty with morning, and the furthest headland of black rock jutting dimly out between blue and blue of the sky and water. Her face began to shine, transfigured with pain and joy. At her feet the garden fell steeply, all a confusion of flowers, and away below was the darkness of tree-tops covering the beck.

She turned to the garden that shone with sunny flowers around her. She knew the little corner where was the seat beneath the yew tree. Then there was the terrace where a great host of flowers shone, and from this, two paths went down, one at each side of the garden. She closed her sunshade and walked slowly among the many flowers. All round were rose bushes, big banks of roses, then roses hanging and tumbling from pillars, or roses balanced on the standard bushes. By the open earth were many other flowers. If she lifted her head, the sea was upraised beyond, and the Cape.

Slowly she went down one path, lingering, like one who has gone back into the past. Suddenly she was touching some heavy crimson roses that were soft as velvet, touching them thoughtfully, without knowing, as a mother sometimes fondles the hand of her child. She leaned slightly forward to catch the scent. Then she wandered on in abstraction. Sometimes a flame-coloured, scentless rose would hold her arrested. She stood gazing at it as if she could not understand it. Again the same softness of intimacy came over her, as she stood before a tumbling heap of pink petals. Then she wondered over the white rose, that was greenish, like ice, in the centre. So, slowly, like a white, pathetic butterfly, she drifted down the path, coming at last to a tiny terrace all full of roses. They seemed to fill the place, a sunny, gay throng. She was shy of them, they were so many and so bright. They seemed to be conversing and laughing. She felt herself in a strange crowd. It exhilarated her, carried her out of herself. She flushed with excitement. The air was pure scent.

Hastily, she went to a little seat among the white roses, and sat down.

Her scarlet sunshade made a hard blot of colour. She sat quite still, feeling her own existence lapse. She was no more than a rose, a rose that could not quite come into blossom, but remained tense. A little fly dropped on her knee, on her white dress. She watched it, as if it had fallen on a rose. She was not herself.

Then she started cruelly as a shadow crossed her and a figure moved into her sight. It was a man who had come in slippers unheard. He wore a linen coat. The morning was shattered, the spell vanished away. She was only afraid of being questioned. He came forward. She rose. Then, seeing him, the strength went from her and she sank on the seat again.

He was a young man, military in appearance, growing slightly stout. His black hair was brushed smooth and bright, his moustache was waxed. But there was something rambling in his gait. She looked up, blanched to the lips, and saw his eyes. They were black, and stared without seeing. They were not a man's eyes. He was coming towards her.

He stared at her fixedly, made an unconscious salute, and sat down beside her on the seat. He moved on the bench, shifted his feet, saying, in a gentlemanly, military voice:

"I don't disturb you—do I?"

She was mute and helpless. He was scrupulously dressed in dark clothes and a linen coat. She could not move. Seeing his hands, with the ring she knew so well upon the little finger, she felt as if she were going dazed. The whole world was deranged. She sat unavailing. For his hands, her symbols of passionate love, filled her with horror as they rested now on his strong thighs.

"May I smoke?" he asked intimately, almost secretly, his hand going to his pocket.

She could not answer, but it did not matter, he was in another world. She wondered, craving, if he recognized her—if he could recognize her. She sat pale with anguish. But she had to go through it.

"I haven't got any tobacco," he said thoughtfully.

But she paid no heed to his words, only she attended to him. Could he recognize her, or was it all gone? She sat still in a frozen kind of suspense.

"I smoke John Cotton," he said, "and I must economize with it, it is expensive. You know, I'm not very well off while these law suits are going on."

"No," she said, and her heart was cold, her soul kept rigid.

He moved, made a loose salute, rose, and went away. She sat motionless. She could see his shape, the shape she had loved with all her passion: his compact, soldier's head, his fine figure now slackened. And it was not he. It only filled her with horror too difficult to know.

Suddenly he came again, his hand in his jacket pocket.

"Do you mind if I smoke?" he said. "Perhaps I shall be able to see things more clearly."

He sat down beside her again, filling a pipe. She watched his hands with the fine strong fingers. They had always inclined to tremble slightly. It had surprised her, long ago, in such a healthy man. Now they moved inaccurately, and the tobacco hung raggedly out of the pipe.

"I have legal business to attend to. Legal affairs are always so uncertain. I tell my solicitor exactly, precisely what I want, but I can never get it done."

She sat and heard him talking. But it was not he. Yet those were the hands she had kissed, there were the glistening, strange black eyes that she had loved. Yet it was not he. She sat motionless with horror and silence. He dropped his tobacco pouch, and groped for it on the ground. Yet she must wait to see if he would recognize her. Why could she not go!—In a moment he rose.

"I must go at once," he said. "The owl is coming." Then he added confidentially: "His name isn't really the owl, but I call him that. I must go and see if he has come."

She rose too. He stood before her, uncertain. He was a handsome, soldierly fellow, and a lunatic. Her eyes searched him, and searched him, to see if he would recognize her, if she could discover him.

"You don't know me?" she asked, from the terror of her soul, standing alone.

He looked back at her quizzically. She had to bear his eyes. They gleamed on her, but with no intelligence. He was drawing nearer to her.

"Yes, I do know you," he said, fixed, intent, but mad, drawing his face nearer hers. Her horror was too great. The powerful lunatic was coming too near to her.

A man approached, hastening.

"The garden isn't open this morning," he said.

The deranged man stopped and looked at him. The keeper went to the seat and picked up the tobacco pouch left lying there.

"Don't leave your tobacco, sir," he said, taking it to the gentleman in the linen coat.

"I was just asking this lady to stay to lunch," the latter said politely. "She is a friend of mine."

The woman turned and walked swiftly, blindly, between the sunny roses, out from the garden, passed the house with the blank, dark windows, through the sea-pebbled court-yard to the street. Hastening and blind, she went forward without hesitating, not knowing whither. Directly she came to the house she went upstairs, took off her hat, and sat down on the bed. It was as if some membrane had been torn in two in her, so that she was not an entity that could think and feel. She sat staring across at the window, where an ivy spray waved slowly up and down in the sea wind. There was some of the uncanny luminousness of the sunlit sea in the air. She sat perfectly still, without any being. She only felt she might be sick, and it might be blood that was loose in her torn entrails. She sat perfectly still and passive.

After a time she heard the hard tread of her husband on the floor below, and, without herself changing, she registered his movement. She heard his rather disconsolate footsteps go out again, then his voice speaking, answering, growing cheery, and his solid tread drawing near.

He entered, ruddy, rather pleased, an air of complacency about his alert, sturdy figure. She moved stiffly. He faltered in his approach.

"What's the matter?" he asked, a tinge of impatience in his voice. "Aren't you feeling well?"

This was torture to her.

"Quite," she replied.

His brown eyes became puzzled and angry.

"What is the matter?" he said.

"Nothing."

He took a few strides, and stood obstinately, looking out of the window.

"Have you run up against anybody?" he asked.

"Nobody who knows me," she said.

His hands began to twitch. It exasperated him, that she was no more sensible to him than if he did not exist. Turning on her at length, driven, he asked:

"Something has upset you, hasn't it?"

"No, why?" she said, neutral. He did not exist for her, except as an irritant.

His anger rose, filling the veins in his throat.

"It seems like it," he said, making an effort not to show his anger, because there seemed no reason for it. He went away downstairs. She sat still on the bed, and with the residue of feeling left to her, she disliked him because he tormented her. The time went by. She could smell the dinner being served, the smoke of her husband's pipe from the garden. But she could not move. She had no being. There was a tinkle of the bell. She heard him come indoors. And then he mounted the stairs again. At every step her heart grew tight in her. He opened the door.

"Dinner is on the table," he said.

It was difficult for her to endure his presence, for he would interfere with her. She could not recover her life. She rose stiffly and went down. She could neither eat nor talk during the meal. She sat absent, torn, without any being of her own. He tried to go on as if nothing were the matter. But at last he became silent with fury. As soon as it was possible, she went upstairs again, and locked the bedroom door. She must be alone. He went with his pipe into the garden. All his suppressed anger against her who held herself superior to him filled and blackened his heart. Though he had not known it, yet he had never really won her, she had never loved him. She had taken him on sufferance. This had foiled him. He was only a labouring electrician in the mine, she was superior to him. He had always given way to her. But all the while the injury and ignominy had been working in his soul because she did not hold him seriously. And now all his rage came up against her.

He turned and went indoors. The third time, she heard him mounting the stairs. Her heart stood still. He turned the catch and pushed the door—it was locked. He tried it again, harder. Her heart was standing still.

"Have you fastened the door?" he asked quietly, because of the landlady.

"Yes. Wait a minute."

She rose and turned the lock, afraid he would burst it. She felt hatred towards him, because he did not leave her free. He entered, his pipe between his teeth, and she returned to her old position on the bed. He closed the door and stood with his back to it.

"What's the matter?" he asked determinedly.

She was sick with him. She could not look at him.

"Can't you leave me alone?" she replied, averting her face from him.

He looked at her quickly, fully, wincing with ignominy. Then he seemed to consider for a moment.

"There's something up with you, isn't there?" he asked definitely.

"Yes," she said, "but that's no reason why you should torment me."

"I don't torment you. What's the matter?"

"Why should you know!" she cried, in hate and desperation.

Something snapped. He started and caught his pipe as it fell from his mouth. Then he pushed forward the bitten-off mouth-piece with his tongue, took it from off his lips, and looked at it. Then he put out his pipe, and brushed the ash from his waistcoat. After which he raised his head.

"I want to know," he said. His face was greyish pale, and set uglily.

Neither looked at the other. She knew he was fired now. His heart was pounding heavily. She hated him, but she could not withstand him. Suddenly she lifted her head and turned on him.

"What right have you to know?" she asked.

He looked at her. She felt a pang of surprise for his tortured eyes and his fixed face. But her heart hardened swiftly. She had never loved him. She did not love him now.

But suddenly she lifted her head again swiftly, like a thing that tries to get free. She wanted to be free of it. It was not him so much, but it, something she had put on herself, that bound her so horribly. And having put the bond on herself, it was hardest to take it off. But now she hated everything and felt destructive. He stood with his back to the door, fixed, as if he would oppose her eternally, till she was extinguished. She looked at him. Her eyes were cold and hostile. His workman's hands spread on the panels of the door behind him.

"You know I used to live here?" she began, in a hard voice, as if wilfully to wound him. He braced himself against her, and nodded.

"Well, I was companion to Miss Birch of Torril Hall—she and the rector were friends, and Archie was the rector's son." There was a pause. He listened without knowing what was happening. He stared at his wife. She was squatted in her white dress on the bed, carefully folding and refolding the hem of her skirt. Her voice was full of hostility.

"He was an officer—a sub-lieutenant—then he quarrelled with his colonel and came out of the army. At any rate"—she plucked at her skirt hem, her husband stood motionless, watching her movements which filled his veins with madness—"he was awfully fond of me, and I was of him—awfully."

"How old was he?" asked the husband.

"When?—when I first knew him? or when he went away?——"

"When you first knew him."

"When I first knew him, he was twenty-six—now—he's thirty-one—nearly thirty-two—because I'm twenty-nine, and he is nearly three years older——"

She lifted her head and looked at the opposite wall.

"And what then?" said her husband.

She hardened herself, and said callously:

"We were as good as engaged for nearly a year, though nobody knew—at least—they talked—but—it wasn't open. Then he went away——"

"He chucked you?" said the husband brutally, wanting to hurt her into contact with himself. Her heart rose wildly with rage. Then "Yes," she said, to anger him. He shifted from one foot to the other, giving a "Ph!" of rage. There was silence for a time.

"Then," she resumed, her pain giving a mocking note to her words, "he suddenly went out to fight in Africa, and almost the very day I first met you, I heard from Miss Birch he'd got sunstroke—and two months after, that he was dead——"

"That was before you took on with me?" said the husband.

There was no answer. Neither spoke for a time. He had not understood. His eyes were contracted uglily.

"So you've been looking at your old courting places!" he said. "That was what you wanted to go out by yourself for this morning."

Still she did not answer him anything. He went away from the door to the window. He stood with his hands behind him, his back to her. She looked at him. His hands seemed gross to her, the back of his head paltry.

At length, almost against his will, he turned round, asking:

"How long were you carrying on with him?"

"What do you mean?" she replied coldly.

"I mean how long were you carrying on with him?"

She lifted her head, averting her face from him. She refused to answer. Then she said:

"I don't know what you mean, by carrying on. I loved him from the first days I met him—two months after I went to stay with Miss Birch."

"And do you reckon he loved you?" he jeered.

"I know he did."

"How do you know, if he'd have no more to do with you?"

There was a long silence of hate and suffering.

"And how far did it go between you?" he asked at length, in a frightened, stiff voice.

"I hate your not-straightforward questions," she cried, beside herself with his baiting. "We loved each other, and we *were* lovers—we were. I don't care what *you* think: what have you got to do with it? We were lovers before ever I knew you——"

"Lovers—lovers," he said, white with fury. "You mean you had your fling with an army man, and then came to me to marry you when you'd done——"

She sat swallowing her bitterness. There was a long pause.

"Do you mean to say you used to go—the whole hogger?" he asked, still incredulous.

"Why, what else do you think I mean?" she cried brutally.

He shrank, and became white, impersonal. There was a long, paralysed silence. He seemed to have gone small.

"You never thought to tell me all this before I married you," he said, with bitter irony, at last.

"You never asked me," she replied.

"I never thought there was any need."

"Well, then, you *should* think."

He stood with expressionless, almost childlike set face, revolving many thoughts, whilst his heart was mad with anguish.

Suddenly she added:

"And I saw him to-day," she said. "He is not dead, he's mad."

Her husband looked at her, startled.

"Mad!" he said involuntarily.

"A lunatic," she said. It almost cost her her reason to utter the word. There was a pause.

"Did he know you?" asked the husband, in a small voice.

"No," she said.

He stood and looked at her. At last he had learned the width of the breach between them. She still squatted on the bed. He could not go near her. It would be violation to each of them to be brought into contact with the other. The thing must work itself out. They were both shocked so much, they were impersonal, and no longer hated each other. After some minutes he left her and went out.

# Goose Fair

## 1.

Through the gloom of evening, and the flare of torches of the night before the fair, through the still fogs of the succeeding dawn, came paddling the weary geese, lifting their poor feet that had been dipped in tar for shoes and trailing them, along the cobble stones into the town. Last of all, in the afternoon, a country girl drove in her dozen birds, disconsolate, because she was so late. She was a heavily built girl, fair, with regular features, and yet unprepossessing. She needed chiselling down, her contours were brutal. Perhaps it was weariness that hung her eyelids a little lower than was pleasant. When she spoke to her clumsily lagging birds it was in a snarling nasal tone. One of the silly things sat down in the gutter and refused to move. It looked very ridiculous, but also rather pitiful squat there with its head up, refusing to be urged on by the ungentle toe of the girl. The latter swore heavily, then picked up the great, complaining bird, and, fronting her road stubbornly, drove on the lamentable eleven.

No one had noticed her. This afternoon the women were not sitting chatting on their doorsteps, seaming up the cotton hose, or swiftly passing through their fingers the piled white lace; and in the high dark houses the song of the hosiery frames was hushed: "Shackety-boom, Shackety, shackety-boom, Z—zzz!" As she dragged up Hollow Stone, people returning from the fair chaffed her, and asked her what o'clock it was. She did not reply, her look was sullen. The Lace Market was quiet as the Sabbath: even the great brass plates on the doors were dull with neglect. There seemed an afternoon atmosphere of raw discontent. The girl stopped a moment before the dismal prospect of one of the great warehouses that had been gutted with fire. She looked at the lean, threatening walls, and watched her white flock waddling in reckless misery below, and she would have laughed out loud had the wall fallen flat upon them, and relieved her of them. But the wall did not fall, so she crossed the road, and walking on the safe side, hurried after her charge. Her look was even more sullen. She remembered the state of trade,—Trade, the invidious enemy; Trade, which thrust out its hand and shut the factory doors and pulled the stockingers off their seats, and left the web half finished on the frame; Trade, which mysteriously choked up the sources of the rivulets of wealth, and, blacker and more secret than a pestilence, starved the town. Through this morose atmosphere of bad trade, in the afternoon of the first day of the fair, the girl strode down to the Poultry with eleven sound geese and one lame one to sell.

The Frenchmen were at the bottom of it! So everybody said, though nobody quite knew how. At any rate, they had gone to war with the Prussians and got beaten, and trade was ruined in Nottingham!

A little fog rose up, and the twilight gathered around. Then they flared abroad their torches, in the fair, insulting the night. The girl still sat in the Poultry, and her weary geese unsold on the stones, illuminated by the hissing lamp of a man who sold rabbits and pigeons and suchlike assorted live-stock.

2.

In another part of the town, near Sneinton Church, another girl came to the door to look at the night. She was tall and slender, dressed with the severe accuracy which marks the girl of superior culture. Her hair was arranged with simplicity about the long, pale, cleanly cut face. She leaned forward very slightly to glance down the street, listening. She very carefully preserved the appearance of having come quite casually to the door, yet she lingered and lingered, and stood very still to listen when she heard a footstep, but when it proved to be only a common man, she drew herself up proudly, and looked with a small smile over his head. He hesitated to glance into the open hall, lighted so spaciously with a scarlet shaded lamp, and at the slim girl in brown silk lifted up before the light. But she, she looked over his head. He passed on.

Presently she started, and hung in suspense. Somebody was crossing the road. She ran down the steps in a pretty welcome, not effuse, saying, in quick, but accurately articulated words:

"Will!—I began to think you'd gone to the fair. I came out to listen to it. I felt almost sure you'd gone. You're coming in, aren't you?" She waited a moment anxiously. "We expect you to dinner, you know," she added wistfully.

The man, who had a short face and spoke with his lip curling up on one side, in a drawling speech with ironically exaggerated intonation, replied after a short hesitation:

"I'm awfully sorry, I am, straight, Lois. It's a shame: I've got to go round to the biz. Man proposes—the devil disposes." He turned aside with irony in the darkness.

"But surely, Will!" remonstrated the girl, keenly disappointed.

"Fact, Lois!—I feel wild about it myself. But I've got to go down to the works. They may be getting a bit warm down there, you know"—he jerked his head in the direction of the fair. "If the Lambs get frisky!—they're a bit off about the work, and they'd just be in their element if they could set a lighted match to something——"

"Will, you don't think—!" exclaimed the girl, laying her hand on his arm in the true fashion of Romance, and looking up at him earnestly.

"Dad's not sure," he replied, looking down at her with gravity. They remained in this attitude for a moment, then he said:

"I might stop a bit. It's all right for an hour, I should think."

She looked at him earnestly, then said in tones of deep disappointment and of fortitude:

"No Will, you must go. You'd better go——"

"It's a shame!" he murmured, standing a moment at a loose end. Then, glancing down the street to see he was alone, he put his arm round her waist and said in a difficult voice: "How goes it?"

She let him keep her for a moment, then he kissed her as if afraid of what he was doing. They were both uncomfortable.

"Well——!" he said at length.

"Good night!" she said, setting him free to go.

He hung a moment near her, as if ashamed. Then "Good night," he answered, and he broke away. She listened to his footsteps in the night, before composing herself to turn indoors.

"Helloa!" said her father glancing over his paper as she entered the dining room, "what's up, then?"

"Oh nothing," she replied, in her calm tones. "Will won't be here to dinner tonight."

"What, gone to the fair?"

"No."

"Oh!—What's got him then?"

Lois looked at her father, and answered:

"He's gone down to the factory. They are afraid of the hands."

Her father looked at her closely.

"Oh, ay!" he answered, undecided, and they sat down to dinner.

### 3.

Lois retired very early. She had a fire in her bedroom. She drew the curtains, and stood holding aside a heavy fold, looking out on the night. She could see only the nothingness of the fog: not even the glare of the fair was evident, though the noise clamoured small in the distance. In front of everything she could see her own faint image. She crossed to the dressing table, and there leaned her face to the mirror, and looked at herself. She looked a long time, then she rose, changed her dress for a dressing jacket, and took up *Sesame and Lilies*.

Late in the night she was roused from sleep by a bustle in the house. She sat up, and heard a hurrying to and fro, and the sound of anxious voices. She put on her dressing gown and went out to her mother's room. Seeing her mother at the head of the stairs, she said in her quick, clean voice:

"Mother, what is it?"

"Oh child, don't ask me! Go to bed dear, do! I shall surely be worried out of my life."

"Mother, what is it?"—Lois was sharp and emphatic.

"I hope your father won't go. Now I do hope your father won't go. He's got a cold as it is."

"Mother, tell me what it is"—Lois took her mother's arm.

"It's Selby's—I should have thought you would have heard the fire engine:—and Jack isn't in yet. I hope we're safe!" Lois returned to her bedroom and dressed. She coiled her plaited hair, and having put on a cloak, left the house.

She hurried along under the fog-dripping trees towards the meaner part of the town. When she got near, she saw a glare in the fog, and closed her lips tight. She hastened on till she was in the crowd. With peaked, noble face she watched the fire. Then she looked a little wildly over the fire-reddened faces in the crowd, and, catching sight of her father, hurried to him.

"Oh Daddy—is he safe? Is Will safe——?"

"Safe, ay, why not? You've no business here. Here, here's Sampson, he'll take you home. I've enough to bother me: there's my own place to watch. Go home now, I can't do with you here."

"Have you seen Will?" she asked.

"Go home—Sampson, just take Miss Lois home—now!"

"You don't really know where he is—Father!"

136

"Go home now—I don't want you here——" her father ordered peremptorily.

The tears sprang to Lois' eyes. She looked at the fire, and the tears were quickly dried by fear. The flames roared and struggled upward. The great wonder of the fire made her forget even her indignation at her father's light treatment of herself and of her lover. There was a crashing and bursting of timber as the first floor fell in a mass into the blazing gulf, splashing the fire in all directions, to the terror of the crowd. She saw the steel of the machines growing white-hot and twisting like flaming letters. Piece after piece of the flooring gave way, and the machines dropped in red ruin as the wooden framework burned out. The air became unbreathable; the fog was swallowed up: sparks went rushing up as if they would burn the dark heavens: sometimes burning cards of lace went whirling into the gulf of the sky, waving with wings of fire. It was dangerous to stand near this great cup of roaring destruction.

Sampson, the grey old manager of Saxton and Co's, led her away as soon as she would turn her face to listen to him. He was a stout, irritable man. He elbowed his way roughly through the crowd, and Lois followed him, her head high, her lips closed. He led her for some distance without speaking, then at last, unable to contain his garrulous irritability, he broke out:

"What do they expect—what can they expect! They can't expect to stand a bad time. They spring up like mushrooms as big as a house side, but there's no stability in 'em. I remember William Selby when he'd run on my errands. Yes, there's some as can make much out of little, and there's some as can make much out of nothing, but they find it won't last. William Selby's sprung up in a day, and he'll vanish in a night. You can't trust to luck alone. Maybe he thinks it's a lucky thing this fire has come when things are looking black. But you can't get out of it as easy as that. There's been a few too many of 'em. No, indeed, a fire's the last thing I should hope to come to—the very last!"

Lois hurried and hurried, so that she brought the old manager panting in distress up the steps of her home. She could not bear to hear him talking so. They could get no one to open the door for some time. When at last Lois ran upstairs she found her mother dressed, but all unbuttoned again, lying back in the chair in her daughter's room, suffering from palpitation of the heart, with *Sesame and Lilies* crushed beneath her. Lois administered brandy, and her decisive words and movements helped largely to bring the good lady to a state of recovery sufficient to allow of her returning to her own bedroom.

Then Lois locked the door. She glanced at her fire-darkened face, and taking the flattened Ruskin out of the chair, sat down and wept. After a while she calmed herself, rose, and sponged her face. Then once more on that fatal night she prepared for rest. Instead, however, of retiring, she pulled a silk quilt from her disordered bed, and wrapping it round her, sat miserably to think. It was two o'clock in the morning.

4.

The fire was sunk to cold ashes in the grate, and the grey morning was creeping through the half opened curtains like a thing ashamed when Lois awoke. It was painful to move her head: her neck was cramped. The girl awoke in full recollection. She sighed, roused herself, and pulled the quilt closer about her. For a little while she sat and mused. A pale, tragic resignation fixed her face like a mask. She remembered her father's irritable answer to her question concerning her lover's safety—"Safe, ay—why not?" She knew that he suspected the factory of having been purposely set on fire. But then, he had never liked Will. And yet—and yet—Lois' heart was heavy as lead. She felt her lover was guilty. And she felt she must hide her secret of his last communication to her. She saw herself being cross-examined—"When did you last see this man!" But she would hide what he had said about watching at the works. How dreary it was—and how dreadful. Her life was ruined now, and nothing mattered any more. She must only behave with dignity, and submit to her own obliteration. For even if Will were never accused, she knew in her heart he was guilty. She knew it was over between them.

It was dawn among the yellow fog outside, and Lois, as she moved mechanically about her toilet, vaguely felt that all her days would arrive slowly struggling through a bleak fog. She felt an intense longing at this uncanny hour to slough the body's trammelled weariness and to issue at once into the new bright warmth of the far Dawn, where a lover waited transfigured; it is so easy and pleasant in imagination to step out of the chill grey dampness of another terrestrial daybreak straight into the sunshine of the eternal morning.—And who can escape his hour? So Lois performed the meaningless routine of her toilet, which at last she made meaningful when she took her black dress, and fastened a black-jet brooch at her throat.

Then she went downstairs and found her father eating a mutton chop. She quickly approached and kissed him on the forehead. Then she retreated to the other end of the table. Her father looked tired, even haggard.

"You are early," he said, after a while. Lois did not reply. Her father continued to eat for a few moments, then he said:

"Have a chop—here's one! Ring for a hot plate. Eh!—what? Why not?"

Lois was insulted, but she gave no sign. She sat down and took a cup of coffee, making no pretence to eat. Her father was absorbed, and had forgotten her.

"Our Jack's not come home yet," he said at last.

Lois stirred faintly: "Hasn't he?" she said.

"No." There was silence for a time. Lois was frightened. Had something happened also to her brother? This fear was closer and more irksome.

"Selby's was cleaned out, gutted. We had a near shave of it——"

"You have no loss, Dadda?"

"Nothing to mention." After another silence, her father said:

"I'd rather be myself than William Selby. Of course it may merely be bad luck—you don't know. But whatever it was, I wouldn't like to add one to the list of fires just now. Selby was at the 'George' when it broke out—I don't know where the lad was——!"

"Father," broke in Lois, "why do you talk like that? Why do you talk as if Will had done it?" She ended suddenly. Her father looked at her pale, mute face.

"I don't talk as if Will had done it," he said. "I don't even think it."

Feeling she was going to cry, Lois rose and left the room. Her father sighed, and leaning his elbows on his knees, whistled faintly into the fire. He was not thinking about her.

Lois went down to the kitchen, and asked Lucy, the parlour-maid, to go out with her. She somehow shrank from going alone, lest people should stare at her overmuch: and she felt an overpowering impulse to go to the scene of the tragedy, to judge for herself.

The churches were chiming half past eight when the young lady and the maid set off down the street. Nearer the fair, swarthy, thin-legged men were pushing barrels of water towards the market place, and the gipsy women, with hard brows, and dressed in tight velvet bodices, hurried along the pavement with jugs of milk, and great brass water-ewers, and loaves and breakfast parcels. People were just getting up, and in the poorer streets was a continual splash of tea-leaves flung out onto the cobble stones. A teapot came crashing down from an upper storey just behind Lois, and she, starting round and looking up, thought that the trembling, drink-bleared man at the upper window, who was stupidly staring after his pot, had had designs on her life; and she went on her way shuddering at the grim tragedy of life.

In the dull October morning, the ruined factory was black and ghastly. The window-frames were all jagged, and the walls stood gaunt. Inside was a tangle of twisted debris, the iron, in parts red with bright rust, looking still hot; the charred wood was black and satiny; from dishevelled heaps, sodden with water, a faint smoke rose dimly. Lois stood and looked. If he had done that! He might even be dead there, burned to ash and lost for ever. It was almost soothing to feel so. He would be safe in the eternity which now she must hope in.

At her side the pretty, sympathetic maid chattered plaintively. Suddenly, from one of her lapses into silence, she exclaimed:

"Why, if there isn't Mr Jack!"

Lois turned suddenly and saw her brother and her lover approaching her. Both looked soiled, untidy, and wan. Will had a black eye, some ten hours old, well coloured. Lois turned very pale as they approached. They were looking gloomily at the factory, and for a moment did not notice the girls.

"I'll be jiggered if there ain't our Lois!" exclaimed Jack, the reprobate, swearing under his breath.

"Oh God!" exclaimed the other in disgust.

"Jack, where have you been?" said Lois sharply, in keen pain, not looking at her lover. Her sharp tone of suffering drove her brother to defend himself with an affectation of comic recklessness.

"In quod," he replied, smiling sicklily.

"Jack!" cried his sister very sharply.

"Fact."

Will Selby shuffled on his feet and smiled, trying to turn away his face so that she should not see his black eye. She glanced at him. He felt her boundless anger and contempt, and, with great courage, he looked straight at her, smiling ironically. Unfortunately his smile would not go over his swollen eye, which remained grave and lurid.

"Do I look pretty?" he inquired with a hateful twist of his lip.

"Very!" she replied.

"I thought I did," he replied. And he turned to look at his father's ruined works, and he felt miserable and stubborn. The girl standing there so clean and out of it all! Oh, God, he felt sick. He turned to go home.

The three went together, Lois silent in anger and resentment. Her brother was tired and overstrung, but not suppressed. He chattered on, blindly.

"It was a lark we had! We met Bob Osborne and Freddy Mannsell coming down Poultry. There was a girl with some geese. She looked a tanger sitting there, all like statues, her and the geese. It was Will who began it. He offered her threepence and asked her to begin the show. She called him a—she called him something, and then somebody poked an old gander to stir him up, and somebody squirted him in the eye. He upped and squawked an' started off with his neck out. Laugh! We nearly killed ourselves, keeping back those old birds with squirts an' teasers: Oh Lum! These old geese, oh scrimmy, they didn't know where to turn, they fairly went off their dots, coming at us right an' left, and such a row—it was fun, you never knew. Then the girl she got up and knocked somebody over the jaw, and we were right in for it. Well, in the end, Billy here got hold of her round the waist,—"

"Oh, dry it up!" exclaimed Will bitterly.

Jack looked at him, laughed mirthlessly, and continued: "An' we said we'd buy her birds. So we got hold of one goose apiece—an' they took some holding, I can tell you—and off we set round the fair, Billy leading with the girl. The bloomin' geese squawked an' pecked. Laugh—I thought I should a' died. Well, then we wanted the girl to have her birds back—and then she fired up. She got some other chaps on her side, and there was a proper old row. The girl went tooth and nail for Will there—she was dead set against him. She gave him a black eye, by gum, and we went at it, I can tell you. It was a free fight, a beauty, an' we got run in. I don't know what became of the girl—."

Lois surveyed the two men. There was no glimmer of a smile on her face, though the maid behind her was sniggering. Will was very bitter. He glanced at his sweetheart and at the ruined factory.

"How's Dad taken it?" he asked, in a biting, almost humble tone.

"I don't know," she replied coldly. "Father's in an awful way. I believe everybody thinks you set the place on fire."

Lois drew herself up. She had delivered her blow. She drew herself up in cold condemnation and for a moment enjoyed her complete revenge. He was despicable, abject in his dishevelled, disfigured, unwashed condition.

"Ay, well, they made a mistake for once," he replied, with a curl of the lip.

Curiously enough, they walked side by side as if they belonged to each other. She was his conscience-keeper. She was far from forgiving him, but she was still further from letting him go. And he walked at her side like a boy who has to be punished before he can be exonerated. He submitted. But there was a genuine bitter contempt in the curl of his lip.

# The White Stocking

"I'm getting up, Teddilinks," said Mrs. Whiston, and she sprang out of bed briskly.

"What the Hanover's got you?" asked Whiston.

"Nothing. Can't I get up?" she replied animatedly.

It was about seven o'clock, scarcely light yet in the cold bedroom. Whiston lay still and looked at his wife. She was a pretty little thing, with her fleecy, short black hair all tousled. He watched her as she dressed quickly, flicking her small, delightful limbs, throwing her clothes about her. Her slovenliness and untidiness did not trouble him. When she picked up the edge of her petticoat, ripped off a torn string of white lace, and flung it on the dressing-table, her careless abandon made his spirit glow. She stood before the mirror and roughly scrambled together her profuse little mane of hair. He watched the quickness and softness of her young shoulders, calmly, like a husband, and appreciatively.

"Rise up," she cried, turning to him with a quick wave of her arm—"and shine forth."

They had been married two years. But still, when she had gone out of the room, he felt as if all his light and warmth were taken away, he became aware of the raw, cold morning. So he rose himself, wondering casually what had roused her so early. Usually she lay in bed as late as she could.

Whiston fastened a belt round his loins and went downstairs in shirt and trousers. He heard her singing in her snatchy fashion. The stairs creaked under his weight. He passed down the narrow little passage, which she called a hall, of the seven and sixpenny house which was his first home.

He was a shapely young fellow of about twenty-eight, sleepy now and easy with well-being. He heard the water drumming into the kettle, and she began to whistle. He loved the quick way she dodged the supper cups under the tap to wash them for breakfast. She looked an untidy minx, but she was quick and handy enough.

"Teddilinks," she cried.

"What?"

"Light a fire, quick."

She wore an old, sack-like dressing-jacket of black silk pinned across her breast. But one of the sleeves, coming unfastened, showed some delightful pink upper-arm.

"Why don't you sew your sleeve up?" he said, suffering from the sight of the exposed soft flesh.

"Where?" she cried, peering round. "Nuisance," she said, seeing the gap, then with light fingers went on drying the cups.

The kitchen was of fair size, but gloomy. Whiston poked out the dead ashes.

Suddenly a thud was heard at the door down the passage.

"I'll go," cried Mrs. Whiston, and she was gone down the hall.

The postman was a ruddy-faced man who had been a soldier. He smiled broadly, handing her some packages.

"They've not forgot you," he said impudently.

"No—lucky for them," she said, with a toss of the head. But she was interested only in her envelopes this morning. The postman waited inquisitively, smiling in an ingratiating fashion. She slowly, abstractedly, as if she did not know anyone was there, closed the door in his face, continuing to look at the addresses on her letters.

She tore open the thin envelope. There was a long, hideous, cartoon valentine. She smiled briefly and dropped it on the floor. Struggling with the string of a packet, she opened a white cardboard box, and there lay a white silk handkerchief packed neatly under the paper lace of the box, and her initial, worked in heliotrope, fully displayed. She smiled pleasantly, and gently put the box aside. The third envelope contained another white packet—apparently a cotton handkerchief neatly folded. She shook it out. It was a long white stocking, but there was a little weight in the toe. Quickly, she thrust down her arm, wriggling her fingers into the toe of the stocking, and brought out a small box. She peeped inside the box, then hastily opened a door on her left hand, and went into the little, cold sitting-room. She had her lower lip caught earnestly between her teeth.

With a little flash of triumph, she lifted a pair of pearl ear-rings from the small box, and she went to the mirror. There, earnestly, she began to hook them through her ears, looking at herself sideways in the glass. Curiously concentrated and intent she seemed as she fingered the lobes of her ears, her head bent on one side.

Then the pearl ear-rings dangled under her rosy, small ears. She shook her head sharply, to see the swing of the drops. They went chill against her neck, in little, sharp touches. Then she stood still to look at herself, bridling her head in the dignified fashion. Then she simpered at herself. Catching her own eye, she could not help winking at herself and laughing.

She turned to look at the box. There was a scrap of paper with this posy:

> "Pearls may be fair, but thou art fairer.
> Wear these for me, and I'll love the wearer."

She made a grimace and a grin. But she was drawn to the mirror again, to look at her ear-rings.

Whiston had made the fire burn, so he came to look for her. When she heard him, she started round quickly, guiltily. She was watching him with intent blue eyes when he appeared.

He did not see much, in his morning-drowsy warmth. He gave her, as ever, a feeling of warmth and slowness. His eyes were very blue, very kind, his manner simple.

"What ha' you got?" he asked.

"Valentines," she said briskly, ostentatiously turning to show him the silk handkerchief. She thrust it under his nose. "Smell how good," she said.

"Who's that from?" he replied, without smelling.

"It's a valentine," she cried. "How do I know who it's from?"

"I'll bet you know," he said.

"Ted!—I don't!" she cried, beginning to shake her head, then stopping because of the ear-rings.

He stood still a moment, displeased.

"They've no right to send you valentines, now," he said.

"Ted!—Why not? You're not jealous, are you? I haven't the least idea who it's from. Look—there's my initial"—she pointed with an emphatic finger at the heliotrope embroidery—

> "E for Elsie,
> Nice little gelsie,"

she sang.

"Get out," he said. "You know who it's from."

"Truth, I don't," she cried.

He looked round, and saw the white stocking lying on a chair.

"Is this another?" he said.

"No, that's a sample," she said. "There's only a comic." And she fetched in the long cartoon.

He stretched it out and looked at it solemnly.

"Fools!" he said, and went out of the room.

She flew upstairs and took off the ear-rings. When she returned, he was crouched before the fire blowing the coals. The skin of his face was flushed, and slightly pitted, as if he had had small-pox. But his neck was white and smooth and goodly. She hung her arms round his neck as he crouched there, and clung to him. He balanced on his toes.

"This fire's a slow-coach," he said.

"And who else is a slow-coach?" she said.

"One of us two, I know," he said, and he rose carefully. She remained clinging round his neck, so that she was lifted off her feet.

"Ha!—swing me," she cried.

He lowered his head, and she hung in the air, swinging from his neck, laughing. Then she slipped off.

"The kettle is singing," she sang, flying for the teapot. He bent down again to blow the fire. The veins in his neck stood out, his shirt collar seemed too tight.

> "Doctor Wyer,
> Blow the fire,
> Puff! puff! puff!"

she sang, laughing.

He smiled at her.

She was so glad because of her pearl ear-rings.

Over the breakfast she grew serious. He did not notice. She became portentous in her gravity. Almost it penetrated through his steady good-humour to irritate him.

"Teddy!" she said at last.

"What?" he asked.

"I told you a lie," she said, humbly tragic.

His soul stirred uneasily.

"Oh ay?" he said casually.

She was not satisfied. He ought to be more moved.

"Yes," she said.

He cut a piece of bread.

"Was it a good one?" he asked.

She was piqued. Then she considered—*was* it a good one? Then she laughed.

"No," she said, "it wasn't up to much."

"Ah!" he said easily, but with a steady strength of fondness for her in his tone. "Get it out then."

It became a little more difficult.

"You know that white stocking," she said earnestly. "I told you a lie. It wasn't a sample. It was a valentine."

A little frown came on his brow.

"Then what did you invent it as a sample for?" he said. But he knew this weakness of hers. The touch of anger in his voice frightened her.

"I was afraid you'd be cross," she said pathetically.

"I'll bet you were vastly afraid," he said.

"I *was*, Teddy."

There was a pause. He was resolving one or two things in his mind.

"And who sent it?" he asked.

"I can guess," she said, "though there wasn't a word with it—except——"

She ran to the sitting-room and returned with a slip of paper.

> "Pearls may be fair, but thou art fairer.
> Wear these for me, and I'll love the wearer."

He read it twice, then a dull red flush came on his face.

"And *who* do you guess it is?" he asked, with a ringing of anger in his voice.

"I suspect it's Sam Adams," she said, with a little virtuous indignation.

Whiston was silent for a moment.

"Fool!" he said. "An' what's it got to do with pearls?—and how can he say 'wear these for me' when there's only one? He hasn't got the brain to invent a proper verse."

He screwed the slip of paper into a ball and flung it into the fire.

"I suppose he thinks it'll make a pair with the one last year," she said.

"Why, did he send one then?"

"Yes. I thought you'd be wild if you knew."

His jaw set rather sullenly.

Presently he rose, and went to wash himself, rolling back his sleeves and pulling open his shirt at the breast. It was as if his fine, clear-cut temples and steady eyes were degraded by the lower, rather brutal part of his face. But she loved it. As she whisked about, clearing the table, she loved the way in which he stood washing himself. He was such a man. She liked to see his neck glistening with water as he swilled it. It amused her and pleased her and thrilled her. He was so sure, so permanent, he had her so utterly in his power. It gave her a delightful, mischievous sense of liberty. Within his grasp, she could dart about excitingly.

He turned round to her, his face red from the cold water, his eyes fresh and very blue.

"You haven't been seeing anything of him, have you?" he asked roughly.

"Yes," she answered, after a moment, as if caught guilty. "He got into the tram with me, and he asked me to drink a coffee and a Benedictine in the Royal."

"You've got it off fine and glib," he said sullenly. "And did you?"

"Yes," she replied, with the air of a traitor before the rack.

The blood came up into his neck and face, he stood motionless, dangerous.

"It was cold, and it was such fun to go into the Royal," she said.

"You'd go off with a nigger for a packet of chocolate," he said, in anger and contempt, and some bitterness. Queer how he drew away from her, cut her off from him.

"Ted—how beastly!" she cried. "You know quite well——" She caught her lip, flushed, and the tears came to her eyes.

He turned away, to put on his necktie. She went about her work, making a queer pathetic little mouth, down which occasionally dripped a tear.

He was ready to go. With his hat jammed down on his head, and his overcoat buttoned up to his chin, he came to kiss her. He would be miserable all the day if he went without. She allowed herself to be kissed. Her cheek was wet under his lips, and his heart burned. She hurt him so deeply. And she felt aggrieved, and did not quite forgive him.

In a moment she went upstairs to her ear-rings. Sweet they looked nestling in the little drawer—sweet! She examined them with voluptuous pleasure, she threaded them in her ears, she looked at herself, she posed and postured and smiled, and looked sad and tragic and winning and appealing, all in turn before the mirror. And she was happy, and very pretty.

She wore her ear-rings all morning, in the house. She was self-conscious, and quite brilliantly winsome, when the baker came, wondering if he would notice. All the tradesmen left her door with a glow in them, feeling elated, and unconsciously favouring the delightful little creature, though there had been nothing to notice in her behaviour.

She was stimulated all the day. She did not think about her husband.
He was the permanent basis from which she took these giddy little
flights into nowhere. At night, like chickens and curses, she would
come home to him, to roost.

Meanwhile Whiston, a traveller and confidential support of a small
firm, hastened about his work, his heart all the while anxious for her,
yearning for surety, and kept tense by not getting it.

II

She had been a warehouse girl in Adams' lace factory before she was
married. Sam Adams was her employer. He was a bachelor of forty,
growing stout, a man well dressed and florid, with a large brown
moustache and thin hair. From the rest of his well-groomed, showy
appearance, it was evident his baldness was a chagrin to him. He had
a good presence, and some Irish blood in his veins.

His fondness for the girls, or the fondness of the girls for him, was
notorious. And Elsie, quick, pretty, almost witty little thing—she
*seemed* witty, although, when her sayings were repeated, they were
entirely trivial—she had a great attraction for him. He would come
into the warehouse dressed in a rather sporting reefer coat, of fawn
colour, and trousers of fine black-and-white check, a cap with a big
peak and a scarlet carnation in his button-hole, to impress her. She
was only half impressed. He was too loud for her good taste.
Instinctively perceiving this, he sobered down to navy blue. Then a
well-built man, florid, with large brown whiskers, smart navy blue suit,
fashionable boots, and manly hat, he was the irreproachable. Elsie was
impressed.

But meanwhile Whiston was courting her, and she made splendid
little gestures, before her bedroom mirror, of the constant-and-true
sort.                "True, true till death—"

That was her song. Whiston was made that way, so there was no need
to take thought for him.

Every Christmas Sam Adams gave a party at his house, to which
he invited his superior work-people—not factory hands and labourers,
but those above. He was a generous man in his way, with a real warm
feeling for giving pleasure.

Two years ago Elsie had attended this Christmas-party for the last
time. Whiston had accompanied her. At that time he worked for Sam
Adams.

She had been very proud of herself, in her close-fitting, full-skirted dress of blue silk. Whiston called for her. Then she tripped beside him, holding her large cashmere shawl across her breast. He strode with long strides, his trousers handsomely strapped under his boots, and her silk shoes bulging the pockets of his full-skirted overcoat.

They passed through the park gates, and her spirits rose. Above them the Castle Rock loomed grandly in the night, the naked trees stood still and dark in the frost, along the boulevard.

They were rather late. Agitated with anticipation, in the cloak-room she gave up her shawl, donned her silk shoes, and looked at herself in the mirror. The loose bunches of curls on either side her face danced prettily, her mouth smiled.

She hung a moment in the door of the brilliantly lighted room. Many people were moving within the blaze of lamps, under the crystal chandeliers, the full skirts of the women balancing and floating, the side-whiskers and white cravats of the men bowing above. Then she entered the light.

In an instant Sam Adams was coming forward, lifting both his arms in boisterous welcome. There was a constant red laugh on his face.

"Come late, would you," he shouted, "like royalty."

He seized her hands and led her forward. He opened his mouth wide when he spoke, and the effect of the warm, dark opening behind the brown whiskers was disturbing. But she was floating into the throng on his arm. He was very gallant.

"Now then," he said, taking her card to write down the dances, "I've got carte blanche, haven't I?"

"Mr. Whiston doesn't dance," she said.

"I am a lucky man!" he said, scribbling his initials. "I was born with an *amourette* in my mouth."

He wrote on, quietly. She blushed and laughed, not knowing what it meant.

"Why, what is that?" she said.

"It's you, even littler than you are, dressed in little wings," he said.

"I should have to be pretty small to get in your mouth," she said.

"You think you're too big, do you!" he said easily.

He handed her her card, with a bow.

"Now I'm set up, my darling, for this evening," he said.

Then, quick, always at his ease, he looked over the room. She waited in front of him. He was ready. Catching the eye of the band, he nodded. In a moment, the music began. He seemed to relax, giving himself up.

"Now then, Elsie," he said, with a curious caress in his voice that seemed to lap the outside of her body in a warm glow, delicious. She gave herself to it. She liked it.

He was an excellent dancer. He seemed to draw her close in to him by some male warmth of attraction, so that she became all soft and pliant to him, flowing to his form, whilst he united her with him and they lapsed along in one movement. She was just carried in a kind of strong, warm flood, her feet moved of themselves, and only the music threw her away from him, threw her back to him, to his clasp, in his strong form moving against her, rhythmically, deliciously.

When it was over, he was pleased and his eyes had a curious gleam which thrilled her and yet had nothing to do with her. Yet it held her. He did not speak to her. He only looked straight into her eyes with a curious, gleaming look that disturbed her fearfully and deliciously. But also there was in his look some of the automatic irony of the *roué*. It left her partly cold. She was not carried away.

She went, driven by an opposite, heavier impulse to Whiston. He stood looking gloomy, trying to admit that she had a perfect right to enjoy herself apart from him. He received her with rather grudging kindliness.

"Aren't you going to play whist?" she asked.

"Ay," he said. "Directly."

"I do wish you could dance."

"Well, I can't," he said. "So you enjoy yourself."

"But I should enjoy it better if I could dance with you."

"Nay, you're all right," he said. "I'm not made that way."

"Then you ought to be!" she cried.

"Well, it's my fault, not yours. You enjoy yourself," he bade her. Which she proceeded to do, a little bit irked.

She went with anticipation to the arms of Sam Adams, when the time came to dance with him. It *was* so gratifying, irrespective of the man. And she felt a little grudge against Whiston, soon forgotten when her host was holding her near to him, in a delicious embrace. And she watched his eyes, to meet the gleam in them, which gratified her.

She was getting warmed right through, the glow was penetrating into her, driving away everything else. Only in her heart was a little tightness, like conscience.

When she got a chance, she escaped from the dancing-room to the card-room. There, in a cloud of smoke, she found Whiston playing cribbage. Radiant, roused, animated, she came up to him and greeted him. She was too strong, too vibrant a note in the quiet room. He lifted his head, and a frown knitted his gloomy forehead.

"Are you playing cribbage? Is it exciting? How are you getting on?" she chattered.

He looked at her. None of these questions needed answering, and he did not feel in touch with her. She turned to the cribbage-board.

"Are you white or red?" she asked.

"He's red," replied the partner.

"Then you're losing," she said, still to Whiston. And she lifted the red peg from the board. "One—two—three—four—five—six—seven—eight——Right up there you ought to jump——"

"Now put it back in its right place," said Whiston.

"Where was it?" she asked gaily, knowing her transgression. He took the little red peg away from her and stuck it in its hole.

The cards were shuffled.

"What a shame you're losing!" said Elsie.

"You'd better cut for him," said the partner.

She did so, hastily. The cards were dealt. She put her hand on his shoulder, looking at his cards.

"It's good," she cried, "isn't it?"

He did not answer, but threw down two cards. It moved him more strongly than was comfortable, to have her hand on his shoulder, her curls dangling and touching his ears, whilst she was roused to another man. It made the blood flame over him.

At that moment Sam Adams appeared, florid and boisterous, intoxicated more with himself, with the dancing, than with wine. In his eye the curious, impersonal light gleamed.

"I thought I should find you here, Elsie," he cried boisterously, a disturbing, high note in his voice.

"What made you think so?" she replied, the mischief rousing in her.

The florid, well-built man narrowed his eyes to a smile.

"I should never look for you among the ladies," he said, with a kind of intimate, animal call to her. He laughed, bowed, and offered her his arm.

"Madam, the music waits."

She went almost helplessly, carried along with him, unwilling, yet delighted.

That dance was an intoxication to her. After the first few steps, she felt herself slipping away from herself. She almost knew she was going, she did not even want to go. Yet she must have chosen to go. She lay in the arm of the steady, close man with whom she was dancing, and she seemed to swim away out of contact with the room, into him. She had passed into another, denser element of him, an essential privacy. The room was all vague around her, like an atmosphere, like under sea, with a flow of ghostly, dumb movements. But she herself was held real against her partner, and it seemed she was connected with him, as if the movements of his body and limbs were her own movements, yet not her own movements—and oh, delicious! He also was given up, oblivious, concentrated, into the dance. His eye was unseeing. Only his large, voluptuous body gave off a subtle activity. His fingers seemed to search into her flesh. Every moment, and every moment, she felt she would give way utterly, and sink molten: the fusion point was coming when she would fuse down into perfect unconsciousness at his feet and knees. But he bore her round the room in the dance, and he seemed to sustain all her body with his limbs, his body, and his warmth seemed to come closer into her, nearer, till it would fuse right through her, and she would be as liquid to him, as an intoxication only.

It was exquisite. When it was over, she was dazed, and was scarcely breathing. She stood with him in the middle of the room as if she were alone in a remote place. He bent over her. She expected his lips on her bare shoulder, and waited. Yet they were not alone, they were not alone. It was cruel.

"'Twas good, wasn't it, my darling?" he said to her, low and delighted. There was a strange impersonality about his low, exultant call that appealed to her irresistibly. Yet why was she aware of some part shut off in her? She pressed his arm, and he led her towards the door.

She was not aware of what she was doing, only a little grain of resistant trouble was in her. The man, possessed, yet with a superficial presence of mind, made way to the dining-room, as if to give her refreshment, cunningly working to his own escape with her. He was molten hot, filmed over with presence of mind, and bottomed with cold disbelief.

In the dining-room was Whiston, carrying coffee to the plain, neglected ladies. Elsie saw him, but felt as if he could not see her. She was beyond his reach and ken. A sort of fusion existed between her and the large man at her side. She ate her custard, but an incomplete fusion all the while sustained and contained within the being of her employer.

But she was growing cooler. Whiston came up. She looked at him, and saw him with different eyes. She saw his slim, young man's figure real and enduring before her. That was he. But she was in the spell with the other man, fused with him, and she could not be taken away.

"Have you finished your cribbage?" she asked, with hasty evasion of him.

"Yes," he replied. "Aren't you getting tired of dancing?"

"Not a bit," she said.

"Not she," said Adams heartily. "No girl with any spirit gets tired of dancing.—Have something else, Elsie. Come—sherry. Have a glass of sherry with us, Whiston."

Whilst they sipped the wine, Adams watched Whiston almost cunningly, to find his advantage.

"We'd better be getting back—there's the music," he said. "See the women get something to eat, Whiston, will you, there's a good chap."

And he began to draw away. Elsie was drifting helplessly with him. But Whiston put himself beside them, and went along with them. In silence they passed through to the dancing-room. There Adams hesitated, and looked round the room. It was as if he could not see.

A man came hurrying forward, claiming Elsie, and Adams went to his other partner. Whiston stood watching during the dance. She was conscious of him standing there observant of her, like a ghost, or a judgment, or a guardian angel. She was also conscious, much more intimately and impersonally, of the body of the other man moving somewhere in the room. She still belonged to him, but a feeling of distraction possessed her, and helplessness. Adams danced on, adhering to Elsie, waiting his time, with the persistence of cynicism.

The dance was over. Adams was detained. Elsie found herself beside Whiston. There was something shapely about him as he sat, about his knees and his distinct figure, that she clung to. It was as if he had enduring form. She put her hand on his knee.

"Are you enjoying yourself?" he asked.

"*Ever* so," she replied, with a fervent, yet detached tone.

"It's going on for one o'clock," he said.

"Is it?" she answered. It meant nothing to her.

"Should we be going?" he said.

She was silent. For the first time for an hour or more an inkling of her normal consciousness returned. She resented it.

"What for?" she said.

"I thought you might have had enough," he said.

A slight soberness came over her, an irritation at being frustrated of her illusion.

"Why?" she said.

"We've been here since nine," he said.

That was no answer, no reason. It conveyed nothing to her. She sat detached from him. Across the room Sam Adams glanced at her. She sat there exposed for him.

"You don't want to be too free with Sam Adams," said Whiston cautiously, suffering. "You know what he is."

"How, free?" she asked.

"Why—you don't want to have too much to do with him."

She sat silent. He was forcing her into consciousness of her position. But he could not get hold of her feelings, to change them. She had a curious, perverse desire that he should not.

"I like him," she said.

"What do you find to like in him?" he said, with a hot heart.

"I don't know—but I like him," she said.

She was immutable. He sat feeling heavy and dulled with rage. He was not clear as to what he felt. He sat there unliving whilst she danced. And she, distracted, lost to herself between the opposing forces of the two men, drifted. Between the dances, Whiston kept near to her. She was scarcely conscious. She glanced repeatedly at her card, to see when she would dance again with Adams, half in desire, half in dread. Sometimes she met his steady, glaucous eye as she passed him in the dance. Sometimes she saw the steadiness of his flank as he danced. And it was always as if she rested on his arm, were borne along, upborne by him, away from herself. And always there was present the other's antagonism. She was divided.

The time came for her to dance with Adams. Oh, the delicious closing of contact with him, of his limbs touching her limbs, his arm supporting her. She seemed to resolve. Whiston had not made himself real to her. He was only a heavy place in her consciousness.

But she breathed heavily, beginning to suffer from the closeness of strain. She was nervous. Adams also was constrained. A tightness, a tension was coming over them all. And he was exasperated, feeling something counteracting physical magnetism, feeling a will stronger with her than his own intervening in what was becoming a vital necessity to him.

Elsie was almost lost to her own control. As she went forward with him to take her place at the dance, she stooped for her pocket-handkerchief. The music sounded for quadrilles. Everybody was ready. Adams stood with his body near her, exerting his attraction over her. He was tense and fighting. She stooped for her pocket-handkerchief, and shook it as she rose. It shook out and fell from her hand. With agony, she saw she had taken a white stocking instead of a handkerchief. For a second it lay on the floor, a twist of white stocking. Then, in an instant, Adams picked it up, with a little, surprised laugh of triumph.

"That'll do for me," he whispered—seeming to take possession of her. And he stuffed the stocking in his trousers pocket, and quickly offered her his handkerchief.

The dance began. She felt weak and faint, as if her will were turned to water. A heavy sense of loss came over her. She could not help herself any more. But it was peace.

When the dance was over, Adams yielded her up. Whiston came to her.

"What was it as you dropped?" Whiston asked.

"I thought it was my handkerchief—I'd taken a stocking by mistake," she said, detached and muted.

"And he's got it?"

"Yes."

"What does he mean by that?"

She lifted her shoulders.

"Are you going to let him keep it?" he asked.

"I don't let him."

There was a long pause.

"Am I to go and have it out with him?" he asked, his face flushed, his blue eyes going hard with opposition.

"No," she said, pale.

"Why?"

"No—I don't want you to say anything about it."

He sat exasperated and nonplussed.

"You'll let him keep it, then?" he asked.

She sat silent and made no form of answer.

"What do you mean by it?" he said, dark with fury. And he started up.

"No!" she cried. "Ted!" And she caught hold of him, sharply detaining him.

It made him black with rage.

"Why?" he said.

Then something about her mouth was pitiful to him. He did not understand, but he felt she must have her reasons.

"Then I'm not stopping here," he said. "Are you coming with me?"

She rose mutely, and they went out of the room. Adams had not noticed.

In a few moments they were in the street.

"What the hell do you mean?" he said, in a black fury.

She went at his side, in silence, neutral.

"That great hog, an' all," he added.

Then they went a long time in silence through the frozen, deserted darkness of the town. She felt she could not go indoors. They were drawing near her house.

"I don't want to go home," she suddenly cried in distress and anguish. "I don't want to go home."

He looked at her.

"Why don't you?" he said.

"I don't want to go home," was all she could sob.

He heard somebody coming.

"Well, we can walk a bit further," he said.

She was silent again. They passed out of the town into the fields. He held her by the arm—they could not speak.

"What's a-matter?" he asked at length, puzzled.

She began to cry again.

At last he took her in his arms, to soothe her. She sobbed by herself, almost unaware of him.

"Tell me what's a-matter, Elsie" he said. "Tell me what's a-matter—my dear—tell me, then——"

He kissed her wet face, and caressed her. She made no response. He was puzzled and tender and miserable.

At length she became quiet. Then he kissed her, and she put her arms round him, and clung to him very tight, as if for fear and anguish. He held her in his arms, wondering.

"Ted!" she whispered, frantic. "Ted!"

"What, my love?" he answered, becoming also afraid.

"Be good to me," she cried. "Don't be cruel to me."

"No, my pet," he said, amazed and grieved. "Why?"

"Oh, be good to me," she sobbed.

And he held her very safe, and his heart was white hot with love for her. His mind was amazed. He could only hold her against his chest that was white hot with love and belief in her. So she was restored at last.

### III

She refused to go to her work at Adams' any more. Her father had to submit and she sent in her notice—she was not well. Sam Adams was ironical. But he had a curious patience. He did not fight.

In a few weeks, she and Whiston were married. She loved him with passion and worship, a fierce little abandon of love that moved him to the depths of his being, and gave him a permanent surety and sense of realness in himself. He did not trouble about himself any more: he felt he was fulfilled and now he had only the many things in the world to busy himself about. Whatever troubled him, at the bottom was surety. He had found himself in this love.

They spoke once or twice of the white stocking.

"Ah!" Whiston exclaimed. "What does it matter?"

He was impatient and angry, and could not bear to consider the matter. So it was left unresolved.

She was quite happy at first, carried away by her adoration of her husband. Then gradually she got used to him. He always was the ground of her happiness, but she got used to him, as to the air she breathed. He never got used to her in the same way.

Inside of marriage she found her liberty. She was rid of the responsibility of herself. Her husband must look after that. She was free to get what she could out of her time.

So that, when, after some months, she met Sam Adams, she was not quite as unkind to him as she might have been. With a young wife's new and exciting knowledge of men, she perceived he was in love with her, she knew he had always kept an unsatisfied desire for her. And, sportive, she could not help playing a little with this, though she cared not one jot for the man himself.

When Valentine's day came, which was near the first anniversary of her wedding day, there arrived a white stocking with a little amethyst brooch. Luckily Whiston did not see it, so she said nothing of it to him. She had not the faintest intention of having anything to do with Sam Adams, but once a little brooch was in her possession, it was hers, and she did not trouble her head for a moment, how she had come by it. She kept it.

Now she had the pearl ear-rings. They were a more valuable and a more conspicuous present. She would have to ask her mother to give them to her, to explain their presence. She made a little plan in her head. And she was extraordinarily pleased. As for Sam Adams, even if he saw her wearing them, he would not give her away. What fun, if he saw her wearing his ear-rings! She would pretend she had inherited them from her grandmother, her mother's mother. She laughed to herself as she went down town in the afternoon, the pretty drops dangling in front of her curls. But she saw no one of importance.

Whiston came home tired and depressed. All day the male in him had been uneasy, and this had fatigued him. She was curiously against him, inclined, as she sometimes was nowadays, to make mock of him and jeer at him and cut him off. He did not understand this, and it angered him deeply. She was uneasy before him.

She knew he was in a state of suppressed irritation. The veins stood out on the backs of his hands, his brow was drawn stiffly. Yet she could not help goading him.

"What did you do wi' that white stocking?" he asked, out of a gloomy silence, his voice strong and brutal.

"I put it in a drawer—why?" she replied flippantly.

"Why didn't you put it on the fire back?" he said harshly. "What are you hoarding it up for?"

"I'm not hoarding it up," she said. "I've got a pair."

He relapsed into gloomy silence. She, unable to move him, ran away upstairs, leaving him smoking by the fire. Again she tried on the ear-rings. Then another little inspiration came to her. She drew on the white stockings, both of them.

Presently she came down in them. Her husband still sat immovable and glowering by the fire.

"Look!" she said. "They'll do beautifully."

And she picked up her skirts to her knees, and twisted round, looking at her pretty legs in the neat stockings.

He filled with unreasonable rage, and took the pipe from his mouth.

"Don't they look nice?" she said. "One from last year and one from this, they just do. Save you buying a pair."

And she looked over her shoulders at her pretty calves, and at the dangling frills of her knickers.

"Put your skirts down and don't make a fool of yourself," he said.

"Why a fool of myself?" she asked.

And she began to dance slowly round the room, kicking up her feet half reckless, half jeering, in a ballet-dancer's fashion. Almost fearfully, yet in defiance, she kicked up her legs at him, singing as she did so. She resented him.

"You little fool, ha' done with it," he said. "And you'll backfire them stockings, I'm telling you." He was angry. His face flushed dark, he kept his head bent. She ceased to dance.

"I shan't," she said. "They'll come in very useful."

He lifted his head and watched her, with lighted, dangerous eyes.

"You'll put 'em on the fire back, I tell you," he said.

It was a war now. She bent forward, in a ballet-dancer's fashion, and put her tongue between her teeth.

"I shan't backfire them stockings," she sang, repeating his words, "I shan't, I shan't, I shan't."

And she danced round the room doing a high kick to the tune of her words. There was a real biting indifference in her behaviour.

"We'll see whether you will or not," he said, "trollops! You'd like Sam Adams to know you was wearing 'em, wouldn't you? That's what would please you."

"Yes, I'd like him to see how nicely they fit me, he might give me some more then."

And she looked down at her pretty legs.

He knew somehow that she *would* like Sam Adams to see how pretty her legs looked in the white stockings. It made his anger go deep, almost to hatred.

"Yer nasty trolley," he cried. "Put yer petticoats down, and stop being so foul-minded."

"I'm not foul-minded," she said. "My legs are my own. And why shouldn't Sam Adams think they're nice!"

There was a pause. He watched her with eyes glittering to a point.

"Have you been havin' owt to do with him?" he asked.

"I've just spoken to him when I've seen him," she said. "He's not as bad as you would make out."

"Isn't he!" he cried, a certain wakefulness in his voice. "Them who has anything to do wi' him is too bad for me, I tell you."

"Why, what are you frightened of him for?" she mocked.

She was rousing all his uncontrollable anger. He sat glowering. Every one of her sentences stirred him up like a red-hot iron. Soon it would be too much. And she was afraid herself; but she was neither conquered nor convinced.

A curious little grin of hate came on his face. He had a long score against her.

"What am I frightened of him for?" he repeated automatically. "What am I frightened of him for? Why, for you, you stray-running little bitch."

She flushed. The insult went deep into her, right home.

"Well, if you're so dull——" she said, lowering her eyelids, and speaking coldly, haughtily.

"If I'm so dull I'll break your neck the first word you speak to him," he said, tense.

"Pf!" she sneered. "Do you think I'm frightened of you?" She spoke coldly, detached.

She was frightened, for all that, white round the mouth.

His heart was getting hotter.

"You *will* be frightened of me, the next time you have anything to do with him," he said.

"Do you think *you'd* ever be told—ha!"

Her jeering scorn made him go white hot, molten. He knew he was incoherent, scarcely responsible for what he might do. Slowly, unseeing, he rose and went out of doors, stifled, moved to kill her.

He stood leaning against the garden fence, unable either to see or hear. Below him, far off, fumed the lights of the town. He stood still, unconscious with a black storm of rage, his face lifted to the night.

Presently, still unconscious of what he was doing, he went indoors again. She stood, a small, stubborn figure with tight-pressed lips and big, sullen, childish eyes, watching him, white with fear. He went heavily across the floor and dropped into his chair.

There was a silence.

"*You're* not going to tell me everything I shall do, and everything I shan't," she broke out at last.

He lifted his head.

"I tell you *this*," he said, low and intense. "Have anything to do with Sam Adams, and I'll break your neck."

She laughed, shrill and false.

"How I hate your word 'break your neck'," she said, with a grimace of the mouth. "It sounds so common and beastly. Can't you say something else——"

There was a dead silence.

"And besides," she said, with a queer chirrup of mocking laughter, "what do you know about anything? He sent me an amethyst brooch and a pair of pearl ear-rings."

"He what?" said Whiston, in a suddenly normal voice. His eyes were fixed on her.

"Sent me a pair of pearl ear-rings, and an amethyst brooch," she repeated, mechanically, pale to the lips.

And her big, black, childish eyes watched him, fascinated, held in her spell.

He seemed to thrust his face and his eyes forward at her, as he rose slowly and came to her. She watched transfixed in terror. Her throat made a small sound, as she tried to scream.

Then, quick as lightning, the back of his hand struck her with a crash across the mouth, and she was flung back blinded against the wall. The shock shook a queer sound out of her. And then she saw him still coming on, his eyes holding her, his fist drawn back, advancing slowly. At any instant the blow might crash into her.

Mad with terror, she raised her hands with a queer clawing movement to cover her eyes and her temples, opening her mouth in a dumb shriek. There was no sound. But the sight of her slowly arrested him. He hung before her, looking at her fixedly, as she stood crouched against the wall with open, bleeding mouth, and wide-staring eyes, and two hands clawing over her temples. And his lust to see her bleed, to break her and destroy her, rose from an old source against her. It carried him. He wanted satisfaction.

But he had seen her standing there, a piteous, horrified thing, and he turned his face aside in shame and nausea. He went and sat heavily in his chair, and a curious ease, almost like sleep, came over his brain.

She walked away from the wall towards the fire, dizzy, white to the lips, mechanically wiping her small, bleeding mouth. He sat motionless. Then, gradually, her breath began to hiss, she shook, and was sobbing silently, in grief for herself. Without looking, he saw. It made his mad desire to destroy her come back.

At length he lifted his head. His eyes were glowing again, fixed on her.

"And what did he give them you for?" he asked, in a steady, unyielding voice.

Her crying dried up in a second. She also was tense.

"They came as valentines," she replied, still not subjugated, even if beaten.

"When, to-day?"

"The pearl ear-rings to-day——the amethyst brooch last year."

"You've had it a year?"

"Yes."

She felt that now nothing would prevent him if he rose to kill her. She could not prevent him any more. She was yielded up to him. They both trembled in the balance, unconscious.

"What have you had to do with him?" he asked, in a barren voice.

"I've not had anything to do with him," she quavered.

"You just kept 'em because they were jewellery?" he said.

A weariness came over him. What was the worth of speaking any more of it? He did not care any more. He was dreary and sick.

She began to cry again, but he took no notice. She kept wiping her mouth on her handkerchief. He could see it, the blood-mark. It made him only more sick and tired of the responsibility of it, the violence, the shame.

When she began to move about again, he raised his head once more from his dead, motionless position.

"Where are the things?" he said.

"They are upstairs," she quavered. She knew the passion had gone down in him.

"Bring them down," he said.

"I won't," she wept, with rage. "You're not going to bully me and hit me like that on the mouth."

And she sobbed again. He looked at her in contempt and compassion and in rising anger.

"Where are they?" he said.

"They're in the little drawer under the looking-glass," she sobbed.

He went slowly upstairs, struck a match, and found the trinkets. He brought them downstairs in his hand.

"These?" he said, looking at them as they lay in his palm.

She looked at them without answering. She was not interested in them any more.

He looked at the little jewels. They were pretty.

"It's none of their fault," he said to himself.

And he searched round slowly, persistently, for a box. He tied the things up and addressed them to Sam Adams. Then he went out in his slippers to post the little package.

When he came back she was still sitting crying.

"You'd better go to bed," he said.

She paid no attention. He sat by the fire. She still cried.

"I'm sleeping down here," he said. "Go you to bed."

In a few moments she lifted her tear-stained, swollen face and looked at him with eyes all forlorn and pathetic. A great flash of anguish went over his body. He went over, slowly, and very gently took her in his hands. She let herself be taken. Then as she lay against his shoulder, she sobbed aloud:

"I never meant——"

"My love—my little love——" he cried, in anguish of spirit, holding her in his arms.

# A Sick Collier

She was too good for him, everybody said. Yet still she did not regret marrying him. He had come courting her when he was only nineteen, and she twenty. He was in build what they call a tight little fellow: short, dark, with a warm colour, and that upright set of the head and chest, that flaunting way in movement recalling a mating bird, which denote a body taut and compact with life. Being a good worker, he had earned decent money in the mine, and, having a good home, had saved a little.

She was a cook at 'Uplands', a tall, fair girl, very quiet. Having seen her walk down the street, Horsepool had followed her from a distance. He was taken with her, he did not drink, and he was not lazy. So, although he seemed a bit simple, without much intelligence, but having a sort of physical brightness, she considered, and accepted him.

When they were married they went to live in Scargill Street, in a highly respectable six-roomed house which they had furnished between them. The street was built up the side of a long, steep hill. It was narrow and rather tunnel-like. Nevertheless, the back looked out over the adjoining pasture, across a wide valley of fields and woods, in the bottom of which the mine lay snugly.

He made himself gaffer in his own house. She was unacquainted with a collier's mode of life. They were married on a Saturday. On the Sunday night, he said:

"Set th' table for my breakfast, an' put my pit-things afront o' th' fire. I s'll be gettin' up at ha'ef pas' five. Tha nedna shift thy-sen not till when ter likes."

He showed her how to put a newspaper on the table for a cloth. When she demurred:

"I want none o' your white cloths i' th' mornin'. I like ter be able to slobber if I feel like it," he said.

He put before the fire his mole-skin trousers, a clean singlet, or sleeveless vest of thick flannel, a pair of stockings and his pit boots, arranging them all to be warm and ready for morning.

"Now tha sees. That wants doin' ivery night."

Punctually at half-past five, he left her, without any form of leave-taking, going down-stairs in his shirt.

When he arrived home at four o'clock in the afternoon, his dinner was ready to be dished up. She was startled when he came in, a short, sturdy figure, with a face indescribably black and streaked. She stood before the fire in her white blouse and white apron, a fair girl, the picture of beautiful cleanliness. He 'clommaxed' in, in his heavy boots.

"Well how 'as ter gone on?" he asked.

"I was ready for you to come home," she replied tenderly. In his black face, the whites of his brown eyes flashed at her.

"An' I wor ready for commin'," he said.

He planked his tin bottle and snap-bag on the dresser, took off his coat and scarf and waistcoat, dragged his arm-chair nearer the fire, and sat down.

"Let's ha'e a bit o' dinner, then—I'm about clammed," he said.

"Aren't you goin' to wash yourself first?"

"What am I to wesh my-sen for?"

"Well, you can't eat your dinner—"

"Oh, strike a daisy Missis! Dunna I eat my snap i' th' pit wi'out weshin'?—forced to."

She served the dinner, and sat opposite him. His small, bullet head was quite black, save for the whites of his eyes and his scarlet lips. It gave her a queer sensation to see him open his red mouth, and bare his white teeth, as he ate. His arms and hands were mottled black; his bare, strong neck got a little fairer as it settled towards his shoulders, reassuring her. There was the faint indescribable odour of the pit in the room, an odour of damp, exhausted air.

"Why is your vest so black on the shoulders?" she asked.

"My singlet? That's wi' th' watter droppin' on us from th' roof. This is a dry un as I put on afore I come up. They ha'e gre't clothes-'osses, an' as we change us things we put 'em on theer ter dry."

When he washed himself, kneeling on the hearth rug stripped to the waist, she felt afraid of him again. He was so muscular, he seemed so intent on what he was doing, so intensely himself, like a vigorous animal. And as he stood wiping himself, with his naked breast towards her, she felt rather sick, seeing his thick arms bulge their muscles.

They were nevertheless very happy. He was at a great pitch of pride because of her. The men in the pit might chaff him, they might try to entice him away, but nothing could reduce his self-assured pride because of her, nothing could unsettle his almost infantile satisfaction. In the evening he sat in his arm-chair chattering to her, or listening as she read the newspaper to him. When it was fine, he would go into the street, squat on his heels as colliers do, with his back against the wall of his parlour, and call to the passers by, in greeting, one after another. If no one were passing, he was content just to squat and smoke, having such a fund of sufficiency and satisfaction in his heart. He was well married.

They had not been wed a year when all Brent and Wellwood's men came out on strike. Willy was in the Union, so with a pinch they scrambled through. The furniture was not all paid for, and other debts were incurred. She worried and contrived, he left it to her. But he was a good husband; he gave her all he had.

The men were out fifteen weeks. They had been back just over a year when Willy had an accident in the mine, tearing his bladder. At the pit-head, the doctor talked of the hospital. Losing his head entirely, the young collier raved like a madman, what with pain and fear of hospital.

"Tha s'llt go whoam, Willy, tha s'llt go whoam," the deputy said.

A lad warned the wife to have the bed ready. Without speaking or hesitating, she prepared. But when the ambulance came, and she heard him shout with pain at being moved, she was afraid lest she should sink down. They carried him in.

"Yo' should 'a had a bed i' th' parlour, Missis," said the deputy, "then we shouldna ha' had to hawkse 'im upstairs, an' it 'ud 'a saved your legs."

But it was too late now. They got him upstairs.

"They let me lie, Lucy," he was crying, "they let me lie two mortal hours on th' sleck, afore they took me outer th' stall. Th' peen, Lucy, th' peen, Oh, Lucy, th' peen, th' peen!"

"I know th' pain's bad, Willy, I know. But you must try an' bear it a bit."

"Tha munna carry on in that form, lad, thy Missis 'll niver be able ter stan' it," said the deputy.

"I canna 'elp it, it's th' peen, it's th' peen," he cried again. He had never been ill in his life. When he had had a smashed finger, he could look at the wound. But this pain came from inside, and terrified him.

At last he was soothed and exhausted.

It was some time before she could undress him and wash him. He would let no other woman do for him, having that savage modesty usual in such men.

For six weeks he was in bed, suffering much pain. The doctors were not quite sure what was the matter with him, and scarcely knew what to do. He could eat, he did not lose flesh, nor strength, yet the pain continued, and he could hardly walk at all.

In the sixth week, the men came out in the national strike. He would get up quite early in the morning, and sit by the window. On Wednesday, the second week of the strike, he sat gazing out on the street as usual, a bullet headed young man, still vigorous looking, but with a peculiar expression of hunted fear in his face.

"Lucy," he called, "Lucy!"

She, pale and worn, ran upstairs at his bidding.

"Gi'e me a han'kercher," he said.

"Why, you've got one," she replied, coming near.

"Tha nedna touch me," he cried. Feeling in his pocket, he produced a white handkerchief.

"I non want a white un, gi'e me a red un," he said.

"An' if anybody comes to see you," she answered, giving him a red handkerchief.

"Besides," she continued, "you needn't ha' brought me upstairs for that."

"I b'lieve th' peen's commin' on again," he said, with a little horror in his voice.

"It isn't, you know it isn't," she replied. "The doctor says you imagine it's there when it isn't."

"Canna I feel what's inside me!" he shouted.

"There's a traction engine coming down-hill," she said. "That'll scatter them.—I'll just go an' finish your pudding."

She left him. The traction engine went by, shaking the houses. Then the street was quiet, save for the men. A gang of youths from fifteen to twenty-five years old were playing marbles in the middle of the road. Other little groups of men were playing on the pavement. The street was gloomy. Willy could hear the endless calling and shouting of men's voices.

"Tha 'rt skinchin'!"

"I arena!"

—"Come 'ere with that blood-alley."

"Swop us four for 't."

"Shonna, gie 's hold on 't."

He wanted to be out, he wanted to be playing marbles. The pain had weakened his mind, so that he hardly knew any self-control.

Presently, another gang of men lounged up the street. It was pay morning. The Union was paying the men in the Primitive Chapel. They were returning with their half sovereigns.

"Sorry!" bawled a voice, "Sorry!"

The word is a form of address, corruption probably of 'Sirrah.' Willy started almost out of his chair.

"Sorry!" again bawled a great voice. "Art goin' wi' me to see Notts play Villa?"

Many of the marble players started up.

"What time is it?—There's no treens, we s'll ha'e ter walk."

The street was alive with men.

"Who's goin' ter Nottingham ter see th' match?" shouted the same big voice. A very large, tipsy man, with his cap over his eye, was calling.

"Com' on—ay, com' on!" came many voices. The street was full of the shouting of men. They split up in excited cliques and groups.

"Play up Notts," the big man shouted.

"Plee up Notts!" shouted the youths and men. They were at kindling pitch. It only needed a shout to rouse them. Of this, the careful authorities were aware.

"I'm goin', I'm goin'!" shouted the sick man at his window.

Lucy came running upstairs.

"I'm goin' ter see Notts play Villa on th' Meadows ground," he declared.

"You—*you* can't go. There are no trains. You can't walk nine miles."

"I'm goin' ter see th' match," he declared, rising.

"You know you can't—Sit down now an' be quiet."

She put her hand on him. He shook it off.

"Leave me alone, leave me alone. It's thee as ma'es th' peen come, it's thee. I'm goin' ter Nottingham to see th' football match."

"Sit down—folks'll hear you, and what will they think."

"Come off'n me. Com' off. It's her, it's her as does it. Com' off."

He seized hold of her. His little head was bristling with madness, and he was strong as a lion.

"Oh Willy!" she cried.

"It's 'er, it's 'er. Kill her," he shouted, "Kill her."

"Willy, folks'll hear you."

"Th' peen's commin' on again, I tell yer. I'll kill her for it."

He was completely out of his mind. She struggled with him, to prevent his going to the stairs. When she escaped from him, who was shouting and raving, she beckoned to her neighbour, a girl of twenty four, who was cleaning the window across the road.

Ethel Mellor was the daughter of a well-to-do check-weighman. She ran across in fear to Mrs Horsepool. Hearing the man raving, people were running out in the street, and listening. Ethel hurried upstairs. Everything was clean and pretty in the young home.

Willy was staggering round the room, after the slowly retreating Lucy, shouting:

"Kill 'er! Kill 'er!"

"Mr Horsepool!" cried Ethel, leaning against the bed, white as the sheets, and trembling. "Whatever are you saying?"

"I tell yer it's 'er fault as th' pain comes on—I tell yer it is! Kill 'er—kill 'er."

"Kill Mrs Horsepool!" cried the trembling girl. "Why you're ever so fond of her, you know you are."

"The peen—I ha'e such a lot o' peen—I want to kill 'er."

He was subsiding. When he sat down, his wife collapsed in a chair, weeping noiselessly. The tears ran down Ethel's face. He sat staring out of the window; then the old, hurt look came on his face.

"What 'ave I been sayin'?" he asked, looking piteously at his wife.

"Why!" said Ethel. "You've been carrying on something awful, saying 'Kill her, kill her!'"

"Have I, Lucy?" he faltered.

"You didn't know what you was saying," said his young wife gently but coldly.

His face puckered up. He bit his lip, then broke into tears, sobbing uncontrollably, with his face to the window.

There was no sound in the room but of three people crying bitterly, breath caught in sobs.—Suddenly Lucy put away her tears, and went over to him.

"You didn't know what you was sayin', Willy, I know you didn't. I knew you didn't, all the time. It doesn't matter, Willy. Only don't do it again."

In a little while, when they were calmer, she went down-stairs with Ethel.

"See if anybody is looking in the street," she said.

Ethel went into the parlour and peeped through the curtains.

"Ay!" she said. "You may back your life Lena an' Mrs Severn 'll be out gorping, and that clat-fartin' Mrs Allsop."

"Oh, I hope they haven't heard anything! If it gets about as he's out of his mind, they'll stop his compensation, I know they will."

"They'd never stop his compensation for *that*," protested Ethel.

"Well, they *have* been stopping some——"

"It'll not get about. I s'll tell nobody."

"Oh, but if it does, whatever shall we do?—"

# The Christening

The mistress of the British School stepped down from her school-gate, and instead of turning to the left as usual, she turned to the right. Two women who were hastening home to scramble their husbands' dinners together—it was five minutes to four—stopped to look at her. They stood gazing after her for a moment; then they glanced at each other with a woman's little grimace.

To be sure, the retreating figure was ridiculous: small and thin, with a black straw hat, and a rusty cashmere dress hanging full all round the skirt. For so small and frail and rusty a creature to sail with slow deliberate stride was also absurd. Hilda Rowbotham was less than thirty, so it was not years that set the measure of her pace; she had heart disease. Keeping her face, that was small with sickness, but not uncomely, firmly lifted and fronting ahead, the young woman sailed on past the market place, like a black swan of mournful, disreputable plumage.

She turned into Berryman's, the baker's. The shop displayed bread, and cakes, sacks of flour and oatmeal, flitches of bacon, hams, lard and sausages. The combination of scents was not unpleasing. Hilda Rowbotham stood for some minutes nervously tapping and pushing a large knife that lay on the counter, and looking at the tall, glittering brass scales. At last a morose man with sandy whiskers came down the step from the houseplace:

"What is it?" he asked, not apologising for his delay.

"Will you give me six pennyworth of assorted cakes and pastries, and put in some macaroons please," she asked, in remarkably rapid and nervous speech. Her lips fluttered like two leaves in a wind, and her words crowded and rushed like a flock of sheep at a gate.

"We've got no macaroons," said the man churlishly. He had evidently caught that word. He stood waiting.

"Then I can't have any, Mr Berryman. Now I do feel disappointed. I like those macaroons, you know, and it's not often I treat myself. One gets so tired of trying to spoil oneself, don't you think? It's less

172

profitable even than trying to spoil somebody else"—she laughed a quick little nervous laugh, putting her hand to her face.

"Then what'll you have?" asked the man without the ghost of an answering smile. He evidently had not followed, so he looked more glum than ever.

"Oh, anything you've got," replied the schoolmistress, flushing slightly. The man moved slowly about, dropping the cakes from various dishes one by one into a paper bag.

"How's that sister o' yours getting on?" he asked, as if he were talking to the flour scoop.

"Whom do you mean?" snapped the schoolmistress.

"The youngest," answered the stooping, pale-faced man, with a note of sarcasm.

"Emma!—Oh, she's very well thank you!"—the schoolmistress was very red, but she spoke with sharp, ironical defiance. The man grunted. Then he handed her the bag, and watched her out of the shop, without bidding her "good-afternoon."

She had the whole length of the main street to traverse, a half mile of slow-stepping torture, with shame flushing over her neck. But she carried her white bag with an appearance of steadfast unconcern. When she turned into the field she seemed to droop a little. The wide valley opened out from her, with the far woods withdrawing into twilight, and away in the centre the great pit streaming its white smoke and chuffing as the men were being turned up. A full, rose-coloured moon, like a flamingo flying low under the far, dusky east, drew out of the mist. It was beautiful, and it made her irritable sadness soften, diffuse.

Across the field, and she was at home. It was a new, substantial cottage, built with unstinted hands, such a house as an old miner could build himself out of his savings. In the rather small kitchen a woman of dark, saturnine complexion sat nursing a baby in a long white gown; a young woman, of heavy, brutal cast, stood at the table cutting bread and butter. She had a downcast, humble mien that sat unnaturally on her, and which was strangely irritating. She did not look round when her sister entered. Hilda put down the bag of cakes and left the room, not having spoken to Emma, nor to the baby, nor to Mrs Carlin who had come in to help for the afternoon.

Almost immediately the father entered from the yard with a dustpan full of coals. He was a large man, but he was going to pieces. As he passed through, he gripped the door with his free hand to steady himself, but turning he lurched and swayed. He began putting the coals on the fire, piece by piece. One lump fell from his hand and smashed on the white hearth. Emma Rowbotham looked round, and began in a rough loud voice of anger: "Look at you—!"—then she consciously moderated her tones—"I'll sweep it up in a minute—don't you bother, you'll only be going head-first into the fire."

Her father bent down nevertheless to clear up the mess he had made, saying, articulating his words loosely and slavering in his speech: "The lousy bit of a thing, it slipped between my fingers like a fish."

As he spoke he went tilting towards the fire. The dark-browed woman cried out; he put his hand on the hot stove to save himself; Emma swung round and dragged him off.

"Didn't I tell you!" she cried roughly—"Now have you burnt yourself—?"

She held tight hold of the big man, and pushed him into his chair.

"What's the matter?" cried a sharp voice from the other room. The speaker appeared, a hard well-favoured woman of twenty-eight—"Emma, don't speak like that to father"—then, in a tone not so cold, but just as sharp: "Now, Father, what have you been doing?"

Emma withdrew to her table sullenly.

"It's nöwt," said the old man, vainly protesting. "It's nöwt at a'! Get on wi' what you're doin'."

"I'm afraid 'e 's burnt 'is 'and," said the black-browed woman, speaking of him with a kind of hard pity, as if he were a cumbersome child. Bertha took the old man's hand and looked at it, making a quick 'tut-tutting' noise of impatience:

"Emma, get that zinc ointment—and some white rag," she commanded sharply. The younger sister put down her loaf with the knife in it, and went. To a sensitive observer, this obedience was more intolerable than the most hateful discord. The dark woman bent over the baby, and made silent, gentle movements of motherliness to it. The little one smiled, and moved on her lap. It continued to move and twist.

"I believe this child's hungry," she said, "how long is it since he had anything?"

"Just afore dinner," said Emma dully.

"Good gracious!" exclaimed Bertha, "you needn't starve the child now you've got it. Once every two hours it ought to be fed, as I've told you, and now it's three. Take him, poor little mite—I'll cut the bread"—she bent and looked at the bonny baby. She could not help herself: she smiled, and pressed its cheek with her finger, and nodded to it, making little noises. Then she turned and took the loaf from her sister. The woman rose and gave the child to its mother. Emma bent over the little, sucking mite. She hated it when she looked at it, and saw it as a symbol, but when she felt it, her love was like fire in her blood.

"I should think 'e canna be comin'," said the father uneasily, looking up at the clock.

"Nonsense Father—the clock's fast! It is but half past four! Don't fidget!"—Bertha continued to cut the bread and butter.

"Open a tin of pears," she said to the woman, in a much milder tone. Then she went into the next room. As soon as she was gone, the old man said again:

"I should 'a thought he'd 'a bin 'ere by now, if he means comin'."

Emma, engrossed, did not answer. The father had ceased to consider her, since she had become humbled.

"'E'll come, 'e'll come!" assured the stranger.

A few minutes later Bertha hurried into the kitchen taking off her apron. The dog barked furiously. She opened the door, commanded the dog silence, and said: "He will be quiet now, Mr Kendal."

"Thank you!" said a sonorous voice, and there was the sound of a bicycle being propped against the wall.

A clergyman entered, a big-boned, thin, ugly man of nervous manner. He went straight to the father:

"Ah—how are you?" he asked, musically, peering down on the great frame of the miner, ruined by locomotor ataxy.

His voice was full of gentleness, but he seemed as if he could not see distinctly, could not get things clear.

"Have you hurt your hand!" he said comfortingly, seeing the white rag.

"It wor nöwt but a pestered bit o' coal as dropped, an' I put my hand on th' hub.—I thought tha worna commin'—"

The familiar 'tha', and the reproach, were unconscious retaliation on the old man's part. The minister smiled, half indulgence, half wistfully. He was full of vague tenderness. Then he turned to the young mother, who flushed sullenly because her dishonored breast was uncovered.

"How are *you*?" he asked, very soft and gentle, as if she were ill and he were mindful of her.

175

"I'm all right," she replied, awkwardly taking his hand without rising, hiding her face and the anger that rose in her.

"Yes—yes—," he peered down at the baby, which sucked with distended mouth upon the firm breast. "Yes—yes—" He seemed lost in a dim musing.

Coming to, he shook hands unseeing with the woman.

Presently they all went into the next room, the minister hesitating to help his crippled old deacon.

"I can go by myself, thank yer," testily replied the father. Soon all were seated. Everybody was separate in feeling and isolated at table. High tea was spread in the middle kitchen, a large, ugly room kept for special occasions.

Hilda appeared last, and the clumsy, raw-boned clergyman rose to meet her. He was afraid of this family, the well-to-do old collier and the brutal, self-willed children. But Hilda was the queen among them. She was the clever one, and had been to college. She felt responsible for the keeping up of a high standard of conduct in all the members of the family. There *was* a difference between the Rowbothams and the common collier-folk. Woodbine Cottage was a superior house to most, and was built in pride by the old man. She, Hilda, was a college-trained schoolmistress. She meant to keep up the prestige of her house in spite of blows.

She had put on a dress of green voile for this special occasion. But she was very thin, her neck protruded painfully. The clergyman, however, greeted her almost with reverence, and, with some assumption of dignity, she sat down before the tray. At the far end of the table sat the broken, massive frame of her father. Next to him was the youngest daughter, nursing the restless baby. The minister sat between Hilda and Bertha, hulking his bony frame uncomfortably.

There was a great spread on the table, of tinned fruits and tinned salmon, ham, and cakes. Miss Rowbotham kept a keen eye on everything: she felt the importance of the occasion. The young mother who had given rise to all this solemnity, ate in sulky discomfort, snatching sullen little smiles at her child, smiles which came, in spite of her, when she felt its little limbs stirring vigorously on her lap. Bertha, sharp and abrupt, was chiefly concerned with the baby. She scorned her sister, treated her like dirt. But the infant was a streak of light to her. Miss Rowbotham concerned herself with the function and the conversation. Her hands fluttered, she talked in little volleys, exceedingly nervous.

Towards the end of the meal, there came a pause. The old man wiped his mouth with his red handkerchief, then, his blue eyes going fixed and staring, he began to speak, in a loose, slobbering fashion, charging his words at the clergyman.

"Well Mester—we'n axed you to come here ter christen this childt, an' you'n come, an' I'm sure we're very thankful. I can't see lettin' the poor blessed childt miss baptising, an' they aren't for goin' to church wi' 't"—he seemed to lapse into a muse—"So," he resumed, "we'n axed you to come here to do the job.—I'm not sayin' as it's not 'ard on us, it is. I'm breakin' up, an' mother's gone. I don't like leavin' a girl o' mine in a situation like 'ers is, but what the Lord's done, He's done, an' it's no matter murmurin'.—There's one thing to be thankful for, an' we *are* thankful for it, they never need know the want of bread.—"

Miss Rowbotham, the lady of the family, sat very stiff and pained during this discourse. She was sensitive to so many things, that she was bewildered. She felt her young sister's shame, then a kind of swift protecting love for the baby, a feeling that included the mother; she was at a loss before her father's religious sentiment, and she felt and resented bitterly the mark upon the family, against which the common folk could lift their fingers. Still she winced from the sound of her father's words. It was a painful ordeal.

"It is hard for you," began the clergyman, in his soft, lingering, unworldly voice. "It is hard for you today, but the Lord gives comfort in His time. A man-child is born unto us, therefore let us rejoice and be glad. If sin has entered in among us, let us purify our hearts before the Lord—"

He went on with his discourse. The young mother lifted the whimpering infant, till its face was hid in her loose hair. She was hurt, and a little glowering anger shone in her face. But nevertheless her fingers clasped the body of the child beautifully. She was stupefied with anger against this emotion let loose on her account.

Miss Bertha rose and went to the little kitchen, returning with water in a china bowl. She placed it there among the tea-things.

"Well, we're all ready," said the old man, and the clergyman began to read the service. Miss Bertha was godmother, the two men godfathers. The old man sat with bent head. The scene became impressive. At last Miss Bertha took the child and put it in the arms of the clergyman. He, big and ugly, shone with a kind of unreal love. He had never mixed with life, and women were all unliving, biblical things to him. When he asked for the name, the old man lifted his head, fiercely.

"Joseph William, after me," he said, almost out of breath.

"Joseph William I baptise thee— —" resounded the strange, full, chaunting voice of the clergyman. The baby was quite still.

"Let us pray!"—It came with relief to them all. They knelt before their chairs, all but the young mother, who bent and hid herself over her baby. The clergyman began his hesitating, struggling prayer.

Just then heavy footsteps were heard coming up the path, ceasing at the window. The young mother, glancing up, saw her brother, black in his pit-dirt, grinning in through the panes. His red mouth curved in a sneer, his fair hair shone above his blackened skin. He caught the eye of his sister, and grinned. Then his black face disappeared. He had gone on into the kitchen. The girl with the child sat still and anger filled her heart. She herself hated now the praying clergyman and the whole emotional business; she hated her brother bitterly. In anger and bondage she sat and listened.

Suddenly her father began to pray. His familiar, loud, rambling voice made her shut herself up and become insensitive. Folk said his mind was weakening. She believed it to be true, and kept herself always disconnected from him.

"We ask Thee, Lord," the old man cried, "to look after this childt. Fatherless he is. But what does the earthly father matter before Thee? The childt is Thine, he is Thy childt. Lord, what father has a man but Thee? Lord, when a man says he is a father, he is wrong from the first word. For Thou art the Father, Lord. Lord, take away from us the conceit that our children are ours. Lord, Thou art Father of this childt as is fatherless here. Oh God, Thou bring him up. For I've stood between Thee and my children; I've had *my* way with them, Lord; I've stood between Thee and my children, I've cut 'em off from Thee because they were mine. And they've grown twisted, because of me. Who is their father, Lord, but Thee? But I put myself in the way, they've been plants under a stone, because of me. Lord, if it hadn't been for me, they might ha' been trees in the sunshine. Let me own it, Lord, I've done 'em mischief. It would ha' been better if they'd never known no father. No man is a father, Lord, only Thou art. They can never grow beyond Thee, but I've hampered them. Lift 'em up again, and undo what I've done to my children.—An' let this young childt be like a willow tree beside the waters, with no father but Thee, oh God. Ay, an' I wish it had been so with my children, that they'd had no father but Thee. For I've been like a stone upon them, and they rise up and curse me in their wickedness. But let me go, an' lift Thou them up, Lord—"

The minister, unaware of the feelings of a father, knelt in trouble, hearing without understanding the special language of fatherhood Miss Rowbotham alone felt, and understood a little. Her heart began to flutter, she was in pain. The two younger daughters knelt unhearing, stiffened and impervious. Bertha was thinking of the baby, and the young mother thought of the father of her child, whom she hated. There was a clatter outside in the scullery. There the youngest son spat into the fire, and made as much noise as he could pouring out the water for his wash, muttering in deep anger:

"Blortin', slaverin' old nag—"

And while the praying of his father continued, his heart was burning with rage. He stood frustrated by the noise. On the table was an open paper bag. He picked it up and read "John Berryman—Bread, Pastries etc." Then he grinned with a grimace. The father of the baby was baker's man at Berryman's. The prayer went on in the middle kitchen. Laurie Rowbotham gathered together the mouth of the bag, inflated it, and burst it with his fist. There was a loud report. He grinned to himself. But he writhed at the same time with shame and fear of his father.

The father broke off from his prayer. Awkwardly, the party shuffled to their feet. The young mother went into the scullery.

"What art doin', fool?" she said.

The collier youth tipped the baby under the chin, singing:

> "Pat-a-cake, pat-a-cake baker's man,
> Bake me a cake as fast as you can— —"

The mother snatched the child away.

"Shut thy mouth," she said, the colour coming into her cheek.

> "Prick it and stick it and mark it with P
> An' put it i' th' oven for baby an' me—"

He grinned, showing a grimy, and jeering and unpleasant red mouth and white teeth.

"I s'll gi'e thee a dab ower th' mouth," said the mother of the baby, grimly. He began to sing again, and she struck out at him.

"Now what's to do?" said the father, staggering in.

The youth began to sing again. His sister stood sullen and furious.

"Why does *that* upset you?" asked the eldest Miss Rowbotham, sharply, of Emma the mother. "Good gracious, it hasn't improved your temper."

Miss Bertha came in, and took the bonny baby.

The father sat big and unheeding in his chair, his eyes vacant, his physique wrecked. He let them do as they would, he fell to pieces. And yet some power, involuntary, like a curse, remained in him. The very ruin of him was like a lodestone that held them in its control. The wreck of him still dominated the house, in his dissolution even he compelled their being. They had never lived; his life, his will had always been upon them and contained them. They were only half-individuals.

The day after the christening he staggered in at the doorway declaring, in a loud voice, with joy in life still: "The daisies light up the earth, they clap their hands in multitudes, in praise of the morning." And his daughters shrank, sullen.

# *Odour of Chrysanthemums*

The small locomotive engine, Number 4, came clanking, stumbling down from Selston with seven full waggons. It appeared round the corner with loud threats of speed, but the colt that it startled from among the gorse, which still flickered indistinctly in the raw afternoon, outdistanced it at a canter. A woman, walking up the railway-line to Underwood, drew back into the hedge, held her basket aside, and watched the footplate of the engine advancing. The trucks thumped heavily past, one by one, with slow inevitable movement, as she stood insignificantly trapped between the jolting black waggons and the hedge; then they curved away towards the coppice where the withered oak-leaves dropped noiselessly, while the birds, pulling at the scarlet hips beside the track, made off into the dusk that had already crept into the spinney. In the open, the smoke from the engine sank and cleaved to the rough grass. The fields were dreary and forsaken, and in the marshy strip that led to the whimsey, a reedy pit-pond, the fowls had already abandoned their run among the alders, to roost in the tarred fowl-house. The pit-bank loomed up beyond the pond, flames like red sores licking its ashy sides, in the afternoon's stagnant light. Just beyond rose the tapering chimneys and the clumsy black headstocks of Brinsley Colliery. The two wheels were spinning fast up against the sky, and the winding-engine rapped out its little spasms. The miners were being turned up.

The engine whistled as it came into the wide bay of railway-lines beside the colliery, where rows of trucks stood in harbour. Miners, single, trailing, and in groups, passed like shadows diverging home. At the edge of the ribbed level of sidings squat a low cottage, three steps down from the cinder track. A large, bony vine clutched at the house, as if to claw down the tiled roof. Round the bricked yard grew a few wintry primroses. Beyond, the long garden sloped down to a bush-covered brook-course. There were some twiggy apple trees, winter-crack trees, and ragged cabbages. Beside the path hung dishevelled pink chrysanthemums, like cloths hung on bushes. A

woman came stooping out of the felt-covered fowl-house half-way
down the garden. She closed and padlocked the door, then drew herself
erect, having brushed some bits from her white apron.

She was a tall woman of imperious mien, handsome, with definite
black eyebrows. Her smooth black hair was parted exactly. For a few
moments she stood steadily watching the miners as they passed along
the railway: then she turned towards the brook-course. Her face was
calm and set, her mouth was closed with disillusionment. After a
moment she called:

"John!" There was no answer. She waited, and then said distinctly:
"Where are you?"

"Here!" replied a child's sulky voice from among the bushes. The
woman looked piercingly through the dusk.

"Are you at that brook?" she asked sternly.

For answer the child showed himself before the raspberry-canes that
rose like whips. He was a small, sturdy boy of five. He stood quite
still, defiantly.

"Oh!" said the mother, conciliated. "I thought you were down at
that wet brook—and you remember what I told you——"

The boy did not move or answer.

"Come, come on in," she said more gently, "it's getting dark.
There's your grandfather's engine coming down the line!"

The lad advanced slowly, with resentful, taciturn movement. He was
dressed in trousers and waistcoat of cloth that was too thick and hard
for the size of the garments. They were evidently cut down from a
man's clothes.

As they went slowly towards the house he tore at the ragged wisps
of chrysanthemums and dropped the petals in handfuls along the path.

"Don't do that—it *does* look nasty," said his mother. He refrained,
and she, suddenly pitiful, broke off a twig with three or four wan
flowers and held them against her face. When mother and son reached
the yard her hand hesitated, and instead of laying the flower aside, she
pushed it in her apron band. The mother and son stood at the foot
of the three steps looking across the bay of lines at the passing-home
of the miners. The trundle of the small train was imminent. Suddenly
the engine loomed past the house and came to a stop opposite the
gate.

The engine-driver, a short man with round grey beard, leaned out
of the cab high above the woman.

"Have you got a cup of tea?" he said in a cheery, hearty fashion.

It was her father. She went in, saying she would mash. Directly, she returned.

"I didn't come to see you on Sunday," began the little grey-bearded man.

"I didn't expect you," said his daughter.

The engine-driver winced; then, reassuming his cheery, airy manner, he said:

"Oh, have you heard then? Well—and what do you think——?"

"I think it is soon enough," she replied.

At her brief censure the little man made an impatient gesture, and said coaxingly, yet with dangerous coldness:

"Well, what's a man to do? It's no sort of life for a man of my years, to sit at my own hearth like a stranger. And if I'm going to marry again it may as well be soon as late—what does it matter to anybody?"

The woman did not reply, but turned and went into the house. The man in the engine-cab stood assertive, till she returned with a cup of tea and a piece of bread and butter on a plate. She went up the steps and stood near the footplate of the hissing engine.

"You needn't 'a brought me bread an' butter," said her father. "But a cup of tea"—he sipped appreciatively—"it's very nice." He sipped for a moment or two, then: "I hear as Walter's got another bout on," he said.

"When hasn't he?" said the woman bitterly.

"I heered tell of him in the 'Lord Nelson' braggin' as he was going to spend that b—— afore he went: half a sovereign that was."

"When?" asked the woman.

"A' Sat'day night—I know that's true."

"Very likely," she laughed bitterly. "He gives me twenty-three shillings."

"Ay, it's a nice thing, when a man can do nothing with his money but make a beast of himself!" said the grey-whiskered man. The woman turned her head away. Her father swallowed the last of his tea and handed her the cup.

"Ay," he sighed, wiping his mouth. "It's a settler, it is—"

He put his hand on the lever. The little engine strained and groaned, and the train rumbled towards the crossing. The woman again looked across the metals. Darkness was settling over the spaces of the railway and trucks: the miners, in grey sombre groups, were still passing home. The winding-engine pulsed hurriedly, with brief pauses. Elizabeth

Bates looked at the dreary flow of men, then she went indoors. Her husband did not come.

The kitchen was small and full of firelight; red coals piled glowing up the chimney mouth. All the life of the room seemed in the white warm hearth and the steel fender reflecting the red fire. The cloth was laid for tea; cups glinted in the shadow. At the back, where the lowest stair protruded into the room, the boy sat struggling with a knife and a piece of white wood. He was almost hidden in shadow, only his movement seemed visible. It was half past four. They had but to await the father's coming to begin tea. As the mother watched her son's sullen little struggle with the wood, she saw herself in his silence and pertinacity, she saw the father in her child's indifference to all but himself. She seemed to be occupied by her husband. He had probably gone past his home, slunk past his own door, to drink before he came in, while his dinner spoiled and wasted in waiting. She glanced at the clock, and took the potatoes to strain them in the yard. The garden and the fields beyond the brook were closed in uncertain darkness. When she rose with the saucepan, leaving the drain steaming into the night behind her, she saw the yellow lamps were lit along the highroad that went up the hill away beyond the space of the railway-lines and the field. Then again she watched the men trooping home, fewer now, and fewer.

Indoors the fire was sinking and the room was dark red. The woman put her saucepan on the hob, and set a batter pudding near the mouth of the oven. Then she stood unmoving. Directly, gratefully, came quick young steps to the door. Someone hung on the latch a moment, then a little girl entered, and began pulling off her outdoor things, dragging a mass of curls just ripening from gold to brown over her eyes with her hat.

Her mother chid her for coming late from school, and said she would have to keep her at home the dark winter days.

"Why, mother, it's hardly a bit dark. The lamp's not lighted, and my father's not home yet."

"No, he isn't. But it's a quarter to five! Did you see anything of him?"

The child became serious. She looked at her mother with large, wistful blue eyes.

"No, mother, I've never seen him. Why? Has he come up an' gone past to Old Brinsley? He hasn't, mother, 'cos I never saw him."

"He'd watch that," said the mother bitterly, "he'd take care as you didn't see him. But you may depend upon it, he's seated in the 'Prince o' Wales.' He wouldn't be this late."

The girl looked at her mother piteously.

"Let's have our teas, mother, should we?" said she. The mother called John to table.

She opened the door once more and leaned out to look across the darkness of the lines. All was deserted: she could not hear the winding-engines.

"Perhaps," she said to herself, "he's stopped to get some ripping done."

They sat down to tea. John, at the end of the table near the door, was almost lost in the darkness. Their faces were hidden from each other.

The girl crouched against the fender slowly moving a thick piece of bread before the fire. The lad, his face a dusky mark on the shadow, sat watching her who was transfigured in the hot red glow.

"I do think it's beautiful to look in the fire," said the child.

"Do you?" said her mother. "Why?"

"It's so red, and full of little caves—and it feels so nice, and you can fair smell it."

"It'll want mending directly," replied her mother. "And then if your father comes he'll carry on and say there never is a fire when a man comes home sweating from the pit.—A public house is always warm enough."

There was silence till the boy said complainingly: "Make haste, our Annie."

"Well, I am doing! I can't make the fire do it no faster, can I?"

"She keeps waflin it about so's to make 'er slow," grumbled the boy.

"Don't have such an evil imagination, child," replied the mother.

Soon the room was busy in the darkness with the crisp sound of crunching. The mother ate very little. She drank her tea determinedly, and sat thinking. When she rose her anger was evident in the stern unbending of her head. She looked at the pudding in the fender, and broke out:

"It *is* a scandalous thing as a man can't even come in to his dinner. If it's crozzled up to a cinder I don't see why I should care. Past his very door he goes to get to a public house, and here I sit with his dinner waiting for him——"

She went out. As she dropped piece after piece of coal on the red fire, the shadows fell on the walls, till the room was almost in total darkness.

"I canna see," grumbled the invisible John. In spite of herself, the mother laughed.

"You know the way to your mouth," she said. She set the dustpan outside the door. When she came again like a shadow on the hearth, the lad repeated, complaining sulkily:

"I canna see."

"Good gracious!" cried the mother irritably, "you're as bad as your father if it's a bit dusk!"

Nevertheless she took a paper spill from a sheaf on the mantelpiece and proceeded to light the lamp that hung from the ceiling in the middle of the room. As she reached up her figure displayed itself just rounding with maternity.

"Oh mother——!" exclaimed the girl.

"What?" said the woman, suspended in the act of putting the lamp-glass over the flame. The copper reflector shone handsomely on her, as she stood with uplifted arm, turning her face to her daughter.

"You've got a flower in your apron!" said the child, in a little rapture at this unusual event.

"Goodness me!" exclaimed the woman, relieved. "One would think the house was afire." She replaced the glass and waited a moment before turning up the wick. A pale shadow was seen floating weirdly on the floor.

"Let me smell!" said the child, still rapturously, coming forward and putting her face to her mother's waist.

"Go along, silly!" said the mother, turning up the lamp. The light revealed their suspense, so that the woman felt it almost unbearable. Annie was still bending at her waist. Irritably, the mother took the flowers from out of her apron band.

"Oh mother—don't take them out!" cried Annie, catching her hand, and trying to replace the sprig.

"Such nonsense!" said the mother, turning away. The child put the pale chrysanthemums to her lips, murmuring:

"Don't they smell beautiful!"

Her mother gave a short laugh.

"No," she said. "Not to me. It was chrysanthemums when I married him, and chrysanthemums when you were born, and the first time they ever brought him home drunk he'd got brown chrysanthemums in his button-hole."

She looked at the children. Their eyes and their parted lips were wondering. The mother sat rocking in silence for some time. Then she looked at the clock.

"Twenty minutes to six!" In a tone of fine bitter carelessness she continued: "Eh, he'll not come now till they bring him. There he'll stick! But he needn't come rolling in here in his pit-dirt, for *I* won't wash him. He can lie on the floor——Eh, what a fool I've been, what a fool! And this is what I came here for, to this dirty hole, rats and all, for him to slink past his very door. Twice last week—he's begun now——"

She silenced herself, and rose to clear the table.

While, for an hour or more, the children played subduedly, intent, fertile of invention, united in fear of their mother's wrath and in dread of their father's homecoming, Mrs Bates sat in her rocking-chair making a 'singlet' of thick, cream coloured flannel, which gave a dull wounded sound as she tore off the grey edge. She worked at her sewing with energy, listening to the children, and her anger wearied itself, lay down to rest, opening its eyes from time to time and steadily watching, its ears raised to listen. Sometimes, even her anger quailed and shrank, and the mother suspended her sewing, tracing the footsteps that thudded along the sleepers outside; she would lift her head sharply to bid the children "hush," but she recovered herself in time, and the footsteps went past the gate, and the children were not flung out of their play-world.

But at last Annie sighed, and gave in. She glanced at her waggon of slippers, and loathed the game. She turned plaintively to her mother:

"Mother!—"—but she was inarticulate.

John crept out like a frog from under the sofa. His mother glanced up.

"Yes," she said, "just look at those shirt sleeves."

The boy held them out to survey them, saying nothing. Then somebody called in a hoarse voice away down the line, and suspense bristled in the room, till two people had gone by outside, talking.

"It is time for bed," said the mother.

"My father hasn't come," wailed Annie plaintively.

But her mother was primed with courage:

"Never mind. They'll bring him when he does come—like a log." She meant there would be no scene. "And he may sleep on the floor till he wakes himself. I know he'll not go to work tomorrow after this!"

The children had their hands and faces wiped with the flannel. They were very quiet. When they had put on their nightdresses, they said their prayers, the boy mumbling. The mother looked down at them, at the brown silken bush of intertwining curls in the nape of the girl's neck, at the little black head of the lad, and her heart burst with anger at their father, who caused all three such distress. The children hid their faces in her skirts, for comfort.

When Mrs Bates came down, the room was strangely empty, with a tension of expectancy. She took up her sewing and stitched for some time without raising her head. Meantime her anger was tinged with fear.

## II

The clock struck eight and she rose suddenly, dropping her sewing on her chair. She went to the stairfoot door, opened it, listening. The children were evidently asleep. She went out, locking the door behind her.

Something scuffled down the yard, and she started, though she knew it was only the rats, with which the place was overrun. The night was very dark. In the great bay of railway-lines bulked with trucks there was no trace of light, only away back she could see a few yellow lamps at the pit-top, and the red smear of the burning pit-bank on the night. She hurried along the edge of the track, then, crossing the converging lines, came to the stile by the white gates, whence she emerged on the road. Then the fear which had led her shrank. People were walking up to New Brinsley; she saw the lights in the houses; twenty yards further on were the broad windows of the "Prince of Wales," very warm and bright, and the loud voices of men could be heard distinctly. What a fool she had been to imagine that anything had happened to him! He was merely drinking over there at the "Prince of Wales." She faltered. She had never yet been to fetch him, and she never would go. Yet, while she was out, she must get some satisfaction. So she continued her walk towards the long straggling line of houses standing blank on the highway. She entered a passage between the dwellings.

"Mr Rigley?—Yes! Did you want him? No, he's not in at this minute."

The raw-boned woman leaned forward from her dark scullery and peered at the other, upon whom fell a dim light through the blind of the kitchen window.

"Is it Mrs Bates?" she asked in a tone tinged with respect.

"Yes. I wondered if your Master was at home. Mine hasn't come yet."

"'Asn't 'e! Oh, Jack's been 'ome an 'ad 'is dinner an' gone out. E's just gone for 'alf an 'our afore bed-time. Did you call at th' 'Prince of Wales'?"

"No——"

"No, you didn't like——! It's not very nice." The other woman was indulgent. There was an awkward pause. "Jack never said nothink about—about your Mester," she added.

"No!—I expect he's stuck in there!"

Elizabeth Bates said this bitterly, and with recklessness. She knew that the woman across the yard was standing at her door listening, but she did not care. As she turned away,

"Stop a minute! I'll just go an' ask Jack if 'e knows anythink," said Mrs Rigley.

"Oh, no—I wouldn't like to put——!"

"Yes, I will, if you'll just step inside an' see as th' childer doesn't come downstairs and set theirselves afire."

Elizabeth Bates, murmuring a remonstrance, stepped inside. The other woman apologised for the state of the room.

The kitchen needed apology. There were little frocks and trousers and childish undergarments on the squab and on the floor, and a litter of playthings everywhere. On the black American cloth of the table were pieces of bread and cake, crusts, slops, and a teapot with cold tea.

"Eh, ours is just as bad," said Elizabeth Bates. Mrs Rigley put a shawl over her head and hurried out, saying:

"I shanna be a minute."

The other sat noting with faint disapproval the general untidiness of the room. Then she fell to counting the shoes of various sizes scattered over the floor. There were twelve. She sighed and said to herself, "No wonder!"—glancing at the litter. There came the scratching of two pairs of feet across the yard, and the Rigleys entered. Elizabeth Bates rose. Rigley was a big man, with very large bones. His head looked particularly bony. Across his temple was a blue scar, caused by a wound got in the pit, a wound in which the coal-dust remained blue like tattooing.

"'Asna 'e come whoam yit?" asked the man, without any form of greeting, but with deference and sympathy. "I couldna say wheer he is—'e's non ower theer!"—he jerked his head to signify the "Prince of Wales."

"'E's 'appen gone up to th' 'Yew,'" said Mrs Rigley.

There was another pause. Rigley had evidently something to get off his mind:

"Ah left 'im finishin' a stint," he began. "Loose-a' 'ad bin gone about ten minutes when we com'n away, an' I shouted, 'Are ter comin', Walt?' an' 'e said, 'Go on, Ah shanna be but a'ef a minnit,' so we com'n ter th' bottom, me an' Bower, thinkin' as 'e wor just behint us. Ah'd a ta'en a hoath as 'e wor just behint—an' 'ud come up i' th' next bantle——"

He stood perplexed, as if answering a charge of desertion of his mate. Elizabeth Bates, now again certain of disaster, hastened to reassure him:

"I expect 'e's gone to th' 'Yew Tree,' as you say. It's not the first time.—I've fretted myself into a fever before now. He'll come home when they carry him."

"Ay, isn't it a bit too bad!" deplored the other woman.

"I'll just step up to Dick's an' see if 'e *is* theer," offered the man, afraid of appearing alarmed, afraid of taking liberties.

"Oh, I wouldn't think of bothering you that far," said Elizabeth Bates, with emphasis. But he knew she was glad of his offer.

As they stumbled up the entry, Elizabeth Bates heard Rigley's wife run across the yard and open her neighbour's door. At this suddenly all the blood in her body seemed to switch away from her heart.

"Mind!" warned Rigley. "Ah've said many a time as Ah'd fill up them ruts in this entry, sumb'dy 'll be breakin' their legs yit."

She recovered herself and walked quickly along with the miner.

"I don't like leaving the children in bed, and nobody in the house," she said.

"No, you dunna!" he replied, courteously. They were soon at the gate of the cottage.

"Well, I shanna be many minnits. Dunna you be frettin' now, 'e'll be a' right," said the butty.

"Thank you very much, Mr Rigley," she replied.

"You're welcome!" he stammered, moving away. "I shanna be many minnits."

The house was quiet. Elizabeth Bates took off her hat and shawl, and rolled back the rug. She was in a hurry to tidy the house. Somebody would be coming, she knew. When she had finished, she sat down. It was a few minutes past nine. She was startled by the rapid chuff of the winding-engine at the pit, and the sharp whirr of the brakes on the rope as it descended. Again she felt the painful sweep of her blood, and she put her hand to her side, saying aloud, "Good gracious!—it's only the nine o'clock deputy going down," rebuking herself.

She sat still, listening. Half an hour of this, and she was wearied out.

"What am I working myself up like this for?" she said pitiably to herself, "I s'll only be doing myself some damage."

She took out her sewing again.

At a quarter to ten there were footsteps. One person! She watched for the door to open. It was an elderly woman, in a black bonnet and a black woollen shawl—his mother. She was about sixty years old, pale, with blue eyes, and her face all wrinkled and lamentable. She shut the door and turned to her daughter-in-law peevishly.

"Eh, Lizzie, whatever shall we do, whatever shall we do!" she cried.

Elizabeth drew back a little, sharply.

"What is it, mother?" she said.

The elder woman seated herself on the sofa.

"I don't know, child, I can't tell you!"—she shook her head slowly. Elizabeth sat watching her, anxious and vexed.

"I don't know," replied the grandmother, sighing very deeply. "There's no end to my troubles, there isn't. The things I've gone through, I'm sure it's enough——!" She wept without wiping her eyes, the tears running.

"But mother," interrupted Elizabeth, "what do you mean? What is it?"

The grandmother slowly wiped her eyes. The fountains of her tears were stopped by Elizabeth's directness. She wiped her eyes slowly.

"Poor child! eh, you poor thing!" she moaned. "I don't know what we're going to do, I don't—and you as you are—it's a thing, it is indeed!"

Elizabeth waited.

"Is he dead?" she asked, and at the words her heart swung violently, though she felt a slight flush of shame at the ultimate extravagance of the question. Her words sufficiently frightened the old lady, almost brought her to herself.

"Don't say so, Elizabeth! We'll hope it's not as bad as that; no, may the Lord spare us that, Elizabeth. Jack Rigley came just as I was sittin' down to a glass afore going to bed, an' 'e said, ''Appen you'll go down th' line, Mrs Bates. Walt's had an accident. 'Appen you'll go an' sit wi' 'er till we can get him home.' I hadn't time to ask him a word, afore he was gone. An' I put my bonnet on an' come straight down, Lizzie. I thought to myself, 'Eh, that poor blessed child, if anybody should come an' tell her of a sudden, there's no knowin' what'll 'appen to 'er.' You mustn't let it upset you, Lizzie—or you know what to expect. How long is it, six months—or is it five, Lizzie? Ay!"—the old woman shook her head—"time slips on, it slips on! Ay!"

Elizabeth's thoughts were busy elsewhere. If he was killed—would she be able to manage on the little pension and what she could earn?—she counted up rapidly. If he was hurt—they wouldn't take him to the hospital—how tiresome he would be to nurse!—but perhaps she'd get him away from the drink and his hateful ways. She would—while he was ill. The tears offered to come to her eyes at the picture. But what sentimental luxury was this she was beginning?—She turned to consider the children. At any rate she was absolutely necessary for them. They were her business.

"Ay!" repeated the old woman, "it seems but a week or two since he brought me his first wages. Ay—he was a good lad, Elizabeth, he was, in his way. I don't know why he got to be such a trouble, I don't. He was a happy lad at home, only full of spirits. But there's no mistake he's been a handful o' trouble, a handful o' trouble, he has! I hope the Lord'll spare him to mend his ways, I hope so, I hope so. You've had a sight o' trouble with him, Elizabeth, you have indeed. But he was a jolly enough lad wi' me, he was, I can assure you. I don't know how it is...."

The old woman continued to muse aloud, a monotonous irritating sound, while Elizabeth thought concentratedly, startled once, when she heard the winding-engine chuff quickly and the brakes skirr with a shriek. Then she heard the engine more slowly, and the brakes made no sound. The old woman did not notice. Elizabeth waited in suspense. The mother-in-law talked, with lapses into silence.

"But he wasn't your son, Lizzie—an' it makes a difference. Whatever he was, I remember him when he was little, an' I learned to understand him and to make allowances. You've got to make allowances for them—"

It was half past ten, and the old woman was saying: "But it's trouble from beginning to end; you're never too old for trouble, never too old for that——" when the gate banged back, and there were heavy feet on the steps.

"I'll go, Lizzie, let me go," cried the old woman, rising. But Elizabeth was at the door. It was a man in pit-clothes.

"They're bringin' 'im, Missis," he said. Elizabeth's heart halted a moment. Then it surged on again, almost suffocating her.

"Is he—is it bad?" she asked.

The man turned away, looking at the darkness:

"The doctor says 'e'd been dead hours. 'E saw 'im i' th' lamp cabin."

The old woman, who stood just behind Elizabeth, dropped into a chair, and folded her hands, crying: "Oh, my boy, my boy!"

"Hush!" said Elizabeth, with a sharp twitch of a frown. "Be still, mother, don't waken th' children: I wouldn't have them down for anything!"

The old woman moaned softly, rocking herself. The man was drawing away. Elizabeth took a step forward.

"How was it?" she asked.

"Well, I couldn't say for sure," the man replied, very ill at ease. "'E wor finishin' a stint, an' th' butties 'ad gone, an' a lot o' stuff come down atop 'n 'im."

"And crushed him?" cried the widow, with a shudder.

"No," said the man, "it fell at th' back of 'im. 'E wor under th' face, an' it niver touched 'im. It shut 'im in. It seems 'e wor smothered."

Elizabeth shrank back. She heard the old woman behind her cry: "What?—what did 'e say it was?"

The man replied, more loudly: "'E wor smothered!"

Then the old woman wailed aloud, and this relieved Elizabeth.

"Oh, mother," she said, putting her hand on the old woman, "don't waken th' children, don't waken th' children."

She wept a little, unknowing, while the old mother rocked herself and moaned. Elizabeth remembered that they were bringing him home, and she must be ready. "They'll lay him in the parlour," she said to herself, standing a moment pale and perplexed.

Then she lighted a candle and went into the tiny room. The air was cold and damp, but she could not make a fire, there was no fireplace. She set down the candle and looked round. The candle-light glittered on the lustre-glasses, on the two vases that held some of the pink chrysanthemums, and on the dark mahogany. There was a cold, deathly smell of chrysanthemums in the room. Elizabeth stood looking at the flowers. She turned away, and calculated whether there would be room to lay him on the floor, between the couch and the chiffonier. She pushed the chairs aside. There would be room to lay him down and to step round him. Then she fetched the old red table-cloth, and another old cloth, spreading them down to save her bit of carpet. She shivered on leaving the parlour; so, from the dresser drawer she took a clean shirt and put it at the fire to air. All the time her mother-in-law was rocking herself in the chair and moaning.

"You'll have to move from there, mother," said Elizabeth. "They'll be bringing him in. Come in the rocker."

The old mother rose mechanically, and seated herself by the fire, continuing to lament. Elizabeth went into the pantry for another candle, and there, in the little pent-house under the naked tiles, she heard them coming. She stood still in the pantry doorway, listening. She heard them pass the end of the house, and come awkwardly down the three steps, a jumble of shuffling footsteps and muttering voices. The old woman was silent. The men were in the yard.

Then Elizabeth heard Matthews, the manager of the pit, say: "You go in first, Jim. Mind!"

The door came open, and the two women saw a collier backing into the room, holding one end of a stretcher, on which they could see the nailed pit-boots of the dead man. The two carriers halted, the man at the head stooping to the lintel of the door.

"Wheer will you have him?" asked the manager, a short, white-bearded man.

Elizabeth roused herself and came away from the pantry, carrying the unlighted candle.

"In the parlour," she said.

"In there Jim!" pointed the manager, and the carriers backed round into the tiny room. The coat with which they had covered the body fell off as they awkwardly turned through the two doorways, and the women saw their man, naked to the waist, lying stripped for work. The old woman began to moan in a low voice of horror.

"Lay th' stretcher at th' side," snapped the manager, "an' put '*im* on th' cloths. Mind now, mind! Look you now——!"

One of the men had knocked off a vase of chrysanthemums. He stared awkwardly, then they set down the stretcher. Elizabeth did not look at her husband. As soon as she could get in the room, she went and picked up the broken vase, and the flowers.

"Wait a minute!" she said.

The three men waited in silence while she mopped up the water with a duster.

"Eh, what a job, what a job, to be sure!" the manager was saying, rubbing his brow with trouble and perplexity. "Never knew such a thing in my life, never! He'd no business to ha' been left. I never knew such a thing in my life! Fell over him clean as a whistle, an' shut him in. Not four foot of space, there wasn't—yet it scarce bruised him."

He looked down at the dead man, lying prone, half naked, all grimed with coal-dust.

"''Sphyxiated,' the doctor said. It *is* the most terrible job I've ever known. Seems as if it was done o' purpose. Clean over him, an' shut 'im in, like a mouse-trap"—he made a sharp, descending gesture with his hand.

The colliers standing by jerked aside their heads in hopeless comment.

The horror of the thing bristled upon them all.

Then they heard the girl's voice upstairs calling shrilly: "Mother, mother—who is it? Mother!—who is it?"

Elizabeth hurried to the foot of the stairs and opened the door:

"Go to sleep!" she commanded sharply. "What are you shouting about? Go to sleep at once—there's nothing——"

Then she began to mount the stairs. They could hear her on the boards, and on the plaster floor of the little bedroom. They could hear her distinctly:

"What's the matter now?—what's the matter with you, silly thing?"—her voice was much agitated, with an unreal gentleness.

"I thought it was some men come," said the plaintive voice of the child. "Has he come?"

"Yes, they've brought him. There's nothing to make a fuss about. Go to sleep now, like a good child."

They could hear her voice in the bedroom, they waited whilst she covered the children under the bedclothes.

"Is he drunk?" the girl asked, timidly, faintly.

"No! No—he's not! He—he's asleep."

"Is he asleep downstairs?"

"Yes...and don't make a noise."

There was silence for a moment, then the men heard the frightened child again:

"What's that noise?"

"It's nothing, I tell you, what are you bothering for?"

The noise was the grandmother moaning. She was oblivious of everything, sitting on her chair rocking and moaning. The manager put his hand on her arm and bade her "Sh—sh!!"

The old woman opened her eyes and looked at him. She was shocked by this interruption, and seemed to wonder.

"What time is it?"—the plaintive thin voice of the child, sinking back unhappily into sleep, asked this last question.

"Ten o'clock," answered the mother more softly. Then she must have bent down and kissed the children.

Matthews beckoned the men to come away. They put on their caps and took up the stretcher. Stepping over the body, they tiptoed out of the house. None of them spoke till they were far from the wakeful children.

When Elizabeth came down she found her mother alone on the parlour floor, leaning over the dead man, the tears dropping on him.

"We must lay him out," the wife said. She put on the kettle, then returned and kneeling at the feet, began to unfasten the knotted leather laces. The room was clammy and dim with only one candle, so that she had to bend her face almost to the floor. At last she got off the heavy boots, and put them away.

"You must help me now," she whispered to the old woman. Together they stripped the man.

When they arose, saw him lying in the naïve dignity of death, the women stood arrested in fear and respect. For a few moments they remained still, looking down, the old mother whimpering. Elizabeth felt countermanded. She saw him, how utterly inviolable he lay in himself. She had nothing to do with him. She could not accept it. Stooping, she laid her hand on him, in claim. He was still warm, for the mine was hot where he had died. His mother had his face between her hands, and was murmuring incoherently. The old tears fell in succession as drops from wet leaves; the mother was not weeping, merely her tears flowed. Elizabeth embraced the body of her husband, with cheek and lips. She seemed to be listening, inquiring, trying to get some connection. But she could not. She was driven away. He was impregnable.

She rose, went into the kitchen, where she poured warm water into a bowl, brought soap and flannel and a soft towel.

"I must wash him," she said. Then the old mother rose stiffly, and watched Elizabeth as she carefully washed his face, carefully brushing the big blonde moustache from his mouth with the flannel. She was afraid with a bottomless fear, so she ministered to him. The old woman, jealous, said:

"Let me wipe him!"—and she kneeled on the other side, slowly drying as Elizabeth washed, her big black bonnet sometimes brushing the dark head of her daughter. They worked thus in silence for a long time. They never forgot it was death, and the touch of the man's dead body gave them strange emotions, different in each of the women; a great dread possessed them both, the mother felt the lie was given to her womb, she was denied; the wife felt the utter isolation of the human soul, the child within her was a weight apart from her.

At last it was finished. He was a man of handsome body, and his face showed no traces of drink. He was blonde, full-fleshed, with fine limbs. But he was dead.

"Bless him," whispered his mother, looking always at his face, and speaking out of sheer terror. "The dear lad—bless him!" She spoke in a faint, sibilant ecstasy of fear and mother love.

Elizabeth sank down again to the floor, and put her face against his neck, and trembled and shuddered. But she had to draw away again. He was dead, and her living flesh had no place against his. A great dread and weariness held her: she was so unavailing. Her life was gone like this.

"White as milk he is, clear as a twelvemonth baby, bless him, the darling!" the old mother murmured to herself. "Not a mark on him, clear and clean and white, as beautiful as ever a child was made," she murmured with pride. Elizabeth kept her face hidden.

"He went peaceful, Lizzie—peaceful as sleep. Isn't he beautiful, the lamb? Ay—he must ha' made his peace, Lizzie. 'Appen he made it all right, Lizzie, shut in there. He'd have time. He wouldn't look like this if he hadn't made his peace. The lamb, the dear lamb. Eh, but he had a hearty laugh. I loved to hear it. He had the heartiest laugh, Lizzie, as a lad——"

Elizabeth looked up. The man's mouth was fallen back, slightly open, under the cover of the moustache. The eyes, half shut, did not show glazed in the obscurity. Life with its smoky burning gone from him had left him apart and utterly alien to her. And she knew what a stranger he was to her. In her womb was ice of fear, because of this separate stranger with whom she had been living as one flesh. Was this what it all meant—utter, intact separateness, obscured by heat of living? In dread she turned her face away. The fact was too deadly.

There had been nothing between them, and yet they had come together, exchanging their nakedness repeatedly. Each time he had taken her, they had been two isolated beings, far apart as now. He was no more responsible than she. The child was like ice in her womb. For as she looked at the dead man, her mind, cold and detached, said clearly: "Who am I? What have I been doing? I have been fighting a husband who did not exist. *He* existed all the time. What wrong have I done? What was that I have been living with? There lies the reality, this man."—And her soul died in her for fear: she knew she had never seen him, he had never seen her, they had met in the dark and had fought in the dark, not knowing whom they met nor whom they fought. And now she saw, and turned silent in seeing. For she had been wrong. She had said he was something he was not; she had felt familiar with him. Whereas he was apart all the while, living as she never lived, feeling as she never felt.

In fear and shame she looked at his naked body, that she had known falsely. And he was the father of her children. Her soul was torn from her body and stood apart. She looked at his naked body and was ashamed, as if she had denied it. After all, it was itself. It seemed awful to her. She looked at his face, and she turned her own face to the wall. For his look was other than hers, his way was not her way. She had denied him what he was—she saw it now. She had refused him as himself.—And this had been her life, and his life.—She was grateful to death, which restored the truth. And she knew she was not dead.

And all the while her heart was bursting with grief and pity for him. What had he suffered? What stretch of horror for this helpless man! She was rigid with agony. She had not been able to help him. He had been cruelly injured, this naked man, this other being, and she could make no reparation. There were the children—but the children belonged to life. This dead man had nothing to do with them. He and she were only channels through which life had flowed to issue in the children. She was a mother—but how awful she knew it now to have been a wife. And he, dead now, how awful he must have felt it to be a husband. She felt that in the next world he would be a stranger to her. If they met there, in the beyond, they would only be ashamed of what had been before. The children had come, for some mysterious reason, out of both of them. But the children did not unite them. Now he was dead, she knew how eternally he was apart from her, how eternally he had nothing more to do with her. She saw this episode of her life closed. They had denied each other in life. Now he had withdrawn. An anguish came over her. It was finished then: it had become hopeless between them long before he died. Yet he had been her husband. But how little!

"Have you got his shirt, 'Lizabeth?"

Elizabeth turned without answering, though she strove to weep and behave as her mother-in-law expected. But she could not, she was silenced. She went into the kitchen and returned with the garment.

"It is aired," she said, grasping the cotton shirt here and there to try. She was almost ashamed to handle him; what right had she or anyone to lay hands on him; but her touch was humble on his body. It was hard work to clothe him. He was so heavy and inert. A terrible dread gripped her all the while: that he could be so heavy and utterly inert, unresponsive, apart. The horror of the distance between them was almost too much for her—it was so infinite a gap she must look across.

At last it was finished. They covered him with a sheet and left him lying, with his face bound. And she fastened the door of the little parlour, lest the children should see what was lying there. Then, with peace sunk heavy on her heart, she went about making tidy the kitchen. She knew she submitted to life, which was her immediate master. But from death, her ultimate master, she winced with fear and shame.

# Appendix I

'Odour of Chrysanthemums' fragment

## *Note on the text*

This manuscript fragment is located at the University of Texas; deletions in the manuscript are here marked ⟨ ⟩; insertions are marked ⌐ ¬.

# 'Odour of Chrysanthemums' fragment

Elizabeth shrank back with a low cry. The old mother inside wailed aloud, and this calmed the other. She turned, and Rigley hurried away.

"They'll have to lay him in the parlour" said Elizabeth, pale, calm, thoughtful. She lighted a candle and went in the other room. It was so small! There ⟨was⟩ ⌜were⌝ just ⟨room for a piano,⟩ a couch, and ⟨an⟩ four chairs, and the room was furnished. Elizabeth cleared away the chairs, and brought the old table cloth the children had played with, and another cloth, and laid them over her bit of a carpet. Then, hesitating, she went and put the ⟨p⟩ kettle on, and got a clean shirt out of the ⟨draw⟩ dresser drawer, and put it to air by the fire. As she was doing this, there was the sound of feet, all jumbled shuffling footsteps. The mother was too terrified to cry. She stood at the open door. They were bringing him on a board, and the board wouldn't come in at the door, it was too ⟨wide⟩ ⌜big⌝. The women had the awful picture of a man trying to back into the ⟨room⟩ ⌜house⌝ with a black board, on which ⟨lay the⟩ ⌜they could see⌝ two heavily shod feet, and the suggestion of a figure. Then the men talked in low voices. They laid the board on the garden—on the double primroses.

"Where will you have him?" they asked quietly.

"Here?"—and she showed the clear space in the parlour. As they carried him in, the coat with which they had covered him slipped off, and they laid him, naked to the waist as he was at work, on the parlour floor.

"E's not marked" said one of the men, who *had* to say something. "The stuff fell behind him, an' shut him in,"—he made a gesture with his hand. Elizabeth felt her body strangling again in the hand of a great terror and horror. Then they heard the girl calling shrilly upstairs:

"Mother—who is it?,—who is it?—Mother!"

Elizabeth caught herself up, and going towards the stairs, she called:

"Go to sleep—it's nothing—go to sleep, and don't be silly"—then she went upstairs:

"⟨Go to sleep.⟩ What are you calling for? It's only your father, and he won't make any noise. Go to sleep now?"

"I thought it was some men come!" wailed the child.

"They only came with your father—and you must go to sleep, he won't make any noise.—He's asleep."

"Is he in bed?"

"Yes. And don't wake him. Go to sleep now."

"What time is it?"—the pitiful thin voice of the half comforted girl, and the plaintive question, were too much for the men downstairs. One by one they got their caps, and stepping over the body, they tip-toed out of the house, hearing the mother answer as they went:

"Ten o'clock!—There, go to sleep now." Her voice too, was dreadful in its tenderness. They knew she kissed the children; ⟨they⟩ and the little ⟨wo⟩ ones sank down again straight to ⟨slumber⟩ ⌜sleep⌝, so was the terror lifted off their hearts.

When Elizabeth came down she found ⟨t⟩ his mother sitting on the floor rocking herself—the tears running down her cheeks.

"We must lay him out" she whispered, and straightway she went and knelt at his feet and began to unfasten the knotted leathern laces. She could hardly see, and had to bend her face quite close to the great boots. At last she got them off, and ⟨the grandmother⟩ ⌜the old woman⌝, rousing herself, helped her to pull off the great pit breeches, and the red and black 'mingled' stockings, with dirty tape garters. When they rose and looked at him lying naked in the grandeur of death, the women experienced suddenly the same feeling: the sense of motherhood. Elizabeth knelt and put her cheek against him and put her arms round him; the mother took his ⟨o⟩ hand ⟨bac⟩ and held it, sobbing, whispering "My son!—Oh my son!" ⟨After a while they calmed themselves, and⟩ Elizabeth kissed him again and again, and touched him with her hands and her face. Then suddenly she saw how dirty he was from the ⟨mine⟩ ⌜pit⌝, and she rose, and poured hot water in a bowl, and brought soap and flannel, and gently washed him, beginning with his face, which she washed gently like a mother does a childs. And the old woman, jealous, took off her ⟨sa⟩ shawl, and with her bonnet on her head, kneeled on the other side and wiped him softly as the other washed. They were a long time, the two women, and they worked lovingly. At last it was finished.

He was a handsomely built man of thirty, even a man with a handsome face, which showed just faint traces of the disfigurement of drink. He was fair, and full fleshed.

"Bless him" whispered his mother "he looks as if he ⟨'d just gone to sleep." She⟩ ⌐was just⌐ waking up. He's smiling a bit, bless him, bless him"—and the tears ran down her face. Elizabeth looked at him proudly, and smoothed his yellow hair from his forehead.

"White as milk, and as clear as a baby—bless him—the darling!" whispered his Mother. "He went peaceful, Lizzie,—and there's not a mark on him:—as clear as a child of twelvemonth, Lizzie, and a skin finer and whiter than yours. Oh, my child, my child!"

Elizabeth bent and kissed him on the smooth, clear ⟨muscles⟩ ripples just below the breasts. She loved him very much, now—and she was content. Her tears were all for the pity of it—and for the pity of him. Ah, the pity of it! But the pity of it was not death. No, death restored him to beauty and grandeur and tenderness. Ah, she loved him, how she loved him now! Think how he might have come home—!—not gently smiling.—But ⟨with⟩ ugly, all befouled and disgusting. She was content, so content, and she loved him. How she had loathed him, loathed him! It was strange. How wise of death to be so silent! If he spoke her anger and scorn would rise like fire. But he would not speak, no, just gently smile, with wide eyes. She was so sorry to have to disturb him to put on the shirt— — but she must. The shirt was aired by now. But it would be terrible hard work to get him into his shirt. Poor dear, he was more helpless than a baby—and so beautiful.

# *Appendix II*


'Two Marriages'

## Note on the text

The manuscript is in the collection of Mr George Lazarus. Its pagination has been indicated, enabling the reader to observe DHL's first stage of revision. Full stops omitted at the ends of sentences, and omitted or misplaced apostrophes, have been supplied or adjusted. Page and section numbers editorially established, and editorial emendations, are marked [ ]. Deletions in MS have not normally been recorded, but deleted page numbers, and a small number of deleted but essential words, have been marked ⟨ ⟩.

# 'Two Marriages'

I.

Miss Louisa loathed her brother-in-law. Most folk were merely pitiful or contemptuous in their attitude towards him, but Miss Louisa knew better. He was not insignificant; rather very significant in her life. She loathed him, with horror. Beneath her habit of religious dutifulness, she was deeply indignant with both her parents for having given Mary to such a little monster.

The Reverend Ronald Lindley and Mrs Lindley appeared, however, to feel no contrition with regard to their eldest daughter. Their lives had become little more than a mannerism, and the marriage was in accord with this mannerism of duty and self-sacrifice.

Mr Lindley was the first vicar of Aldecar, which place, until 1860, had been a tiny agricultural hamlet lying among the last hills of Derbyshire. Fifty years ago, however, a coal-mine was sunk outside the village; then another, two miles north, at Underwood; then at Nethergreen, and at Moorgreen, and at Watnall, a constellation of collieries, crescent shaped, stretching for ten miles. The colliery railway, connecting them ran blithely over a beautiful landscape, now blotched with dwellings, crossing on an embankment over the /1/ monks' ancient meadows at Beauvale, cutting through the oak-glades of Sherwood, by Robin-Hoods well, at Watnall.

Now the people of Aldecar had for centuries attended the old church at Greymede, two or more miles away. There were Church paths cutting clean across the farm lands. But the new colliery population would not trudge two hilly miles to hear a parson. Therefore Aldecar church was built, a quaint little place with two turrets, like a crouching mouse with pricked ears. Occupying the open fields between the two-fold ugliness of Old and New Aldecar, it was almost as conspicuous as some crumbling church stranded in the fens.

Mr Lindley, new from college, became first vicar of Aldecar. His church was scarcely more than a Chapel of Ease from Greymede, his stipend, all told, scarcely more than £120 a year. But he had a large, unwieldy flock to gather in his corner of a large, unwieldy parish. He

209

married the daughter of a Cambridgeshire clergyman. She was a haughty, healthy young lady, with £800 fortune. She expected to queen with arrogance her husband's parishioners, as she had been used to queen the farm-laborers in the fens. She was mistaken: so was her husband. The colliers were ridiculously well-to-do, and insolent beyond belief. They insulted her flagrantly when she passed round to receive /2/ her first homage. Their attitude towards her was one long insult. She held the whole people in aversion. Then poverty came, and further undermined her pride. After the first year, the vicar's lady was never seen outside her vicarage, save on her short transit to Church each Sunday morning, or, very rarely, seated in the trap hired from the 'Robin Hood' to drive her the three miles to the station. Gradually she retired onto an invalid's sofa, her only refuge from overwhelming mortification of poverty, worry, and insult: she had eight children.

The vicar succeeded no better. In his populous, disorganised corner of a parish he was set at nought. The miners' wives were nonconformists, who did not hesitate to tell him what they thought of him; the miners were nothing in the way of religion. Mr Lindley, however, continued to be patronising. His voice was sonorous, his manner pompous, as his father's had been before him. He visited where he might, and wherever he visited, he condescended. Perhaps he loved his flock collectively. Certainly, individual by individual, he hated them almost without exception: those he knew, that is, for the greater part were strangers to him.

He had been nearly twenty years in Aldecar when he went, one Christmas, down to the Durants' on an errand of consolation. John Durant had been the village tailor, and his wife had kept the one haberdashery shop in Old Aldecar, for forty years. /3/ The woman, although she was over sixty, had smooth, nut-brown hair, and a quick interest. She sat in her rocking chair, her hands folded over her apron, musing bitterly. Opposite her, her husband, a very large but not stout old man, sat on the sofa wrapped in a brown blanket, looking lovingly at the fire. He was ten years older than his wife, and the life was dead in his eye.

The Durants were Church of England people, at least, nominally. The vicar tapped at their door, then entered without summons. It was just after eleven o'clock. The room was hot and teeming with plenty. On the table the little lunch was not cleared away. The vicar glanced at the beer jug, the piece of home-made pork-pie: he was too late to be invited to partake. Mrs Durant was starting from her chair:

"Oh, it's you Mr Lindley!" she exclaimed. She had not the vernacular; she came from Nottingham, was a burgess' daughter.

"Goodmorning Mrs Durant—Goodmorning Mr Durant. I am very sorry to hear of your new trouble—that is, in one way—perhaps for your sakes—today—I am sorry; but considering all things, I am glad." He sat down.

"Indeed!" said Mrs Durant, coldly.

"It is true, I presume, that your son Alfred has run away from home and joined the Navy."

"Yes, it is," she replied, tartly.

"Well, as I say, you may feel it as a trouble today. /4/ But in the long run it will prove a very good thing for everyone concerned. He needed to be put under control."

"The Lord above knows what'll happen in the long run—and it seems you do as well. But it's little comfort to me as sits fretting for him back, and thinking what'll happen afore I see him in this room again."

"We must trust that to Higher Hands than ours, Mrs Durant. One thing is certain: your son Alfred will be better in the Navy than your son Walter is in the public house."

"Walter's not happy in his wife. There's a wide difference between Walter and Alfred. Besides"—she suddenly flashed in wrath "—I don't know as I wouldn't rather have my lad sitting drunk in that chair where you are, than dressed in a blue blouse and climbing ropes like a monkey at another man's bidding—and I would!"

"It is an impious wish, Mrs Durant,—I must say—and it seems to me unmotherly."

"Yes and it may do!"—she rocked herself in grief.

"Tha' 'appen thinks as ivrybody's as glad ter get rid o' their children as thee," muttered the inanimate old man, looking slowly, and dully, at the Vicar.

Mr Lindley took no notice, but turned to the wife.

"Your son Walter is a disgrace to Aldecar—he's killing himself with drink: do you like to see that? Your son Jim is going the same way—can you deny it? And this /5/ boy Alfred, with his violent temper and his little respect for authority, would doubtless have started on the same course—"

"How *can* you sit there and say it!" cried Mrs Durant. "Where could you find a steadier lad, and where a better! Just because he's hasty and impulsive, because he fights a man as insults him, his name's to be dragged through the dirt. Let me tell you, he'd more lovingness and consideration in his little finger that *most folk* have in their whole bodies, all their days—." There was a pause—"And to go for a Queen's sailor, to be treated like dirt, like a dog, by any jack-sprat—" she broke off in bitterness.

"I think it will do him a great deal of good," said the Vicar.

"Then if it does," she flashed, "I wish it wouldn't. I'd rather he was bad than that he was a dog for any man's kick."

"I think you mistake yourself—" began the vicar.

"And I'm content to, Mr Lindley," she cried. Her hurt was too new to admit of such consolation.

There was a silence. Mr Lindley drew a large, folded white paper from a bundle he carried. Laying this on the table, he said, in a cold tone of displeasure:

"The new Parish Almanac."

"I hope it's a better one than last year's," replied Mrs Durant.

"That you no doubt will decide for yourself. As it is a gift, you can scarcely expect to order the particulars."

"Well, I don't ask for it," she replied. She reached for /6/ the large square, opened the Almanac, and exclaimed, petulantly: "I *do* like a bit of colour!"

The vicar made no reply—she looked at one picture after another.

"You did well to put 'The Sailor's Homecoming' in!" she said ironically. And as she handed the great sheet to her husband:

"How *is* it?" she asked, "that they can't have a bit of a coloured picture in their almanacs nowadays?"

"If the *people* appreciated and supported the *Church*," he said, "they might be expected to grumble when the almanacs that are *given* to them do not please them."

"Might as well 'ing a newspaper sheet up," muttered the old man.

"And you can take it back, if you're that choice of it," the wife replied to the vicar.

"I have brought it, and have no intention of carrying it away again, Mrs Durant."

"Well, it'll do to hang in the scullery," she said. "You'll see last year's there, if you look."

There was a pause.

"I also wish to say," the vicar began, "that Mr Brentnall has very generously offered the church a new organ, which we have needed many years."

"True, we have," she said. He swallowed.

"It will be necessary to provide a salary for the organist. /7/ I am asking all members if they will contribute a small sum annually for that purpose."

"And who's to be the organist?" she asked pertinently.

"Miss Louisa," he replied, very coldly.

"And does she need to have a salary for that bit of a job?" asked Mrs Durant. She knew the vicar was in debt to Mr Smeaton, the butcher, to Dakes, the grocer—so she rubbed it in. The vicar was righteously incensed.

"It is not a question of her need, it is a question of an organist's salary," he replied, very haughtily.

"And must two old people be asked to pay for her?" she sneered.

"Two old people, living in the lap of luxury—"

"My Sirs!—the lap of luxury!" she exclaimed.

"Ought," he continued, "to be only too glad to contribute a little to help the Church work, before they are called to their account."

"I'm quite ready to meet *all* my accounts, Mr Lindley, both in heaven and down here. That's more than *everybody* can say. I'd rather face my Maker in my shoes than in yours."

"Mrs Durant, if I have had your answer, I will take my leave," he answered. "Another Judge than I will decide your acts."

"For which I'm very thankful, Mr Lindley. But I haven't said I wouldn't help Miss Louisa—" /8/

"It was the organist's salary I spoke of, Mrs Durant. You mistake yourself."

"I don't mistake you, I think, Mr Lindley," she said. Then, closing her eyes ironically—"But I am ready to help with the organist's salary. Miss Louisa was always as nice a young woman as ever stepped in shoe-leather—"

Mr Lindley went away shaking with mortification—and with five shillings of the old woman's money in his pocket. It was no wonder he loathed his flock individually. /9/

---

## 2.

He had a large family, six girls and two boys. Mary, the eldest, a fine girl with a haughty clear brow, was a peripatetic governess, who gave lessons to the tradesmen's daughters. Louisa also was at home. She was house keeper, and peripatetic music teacher, giving lessons on the piano to all but miners' daughters. Frances was a missionary in China. Ronald was a bank clerk in Nottingham. Muriel was married to a poor curate in Newcastle. Rachel, newly home from school, was hanging about, getting on everybody's nerves. Luther would shortly be coming home: Hilda had two more years at the school for clergymen's daughters. It was an accumulation enough to worry any man into the grave. Mrs Lindley's resource was to become an invalid.

It happened, when Miss Mary was twenty seven years old, her father broke his leg. The son of one of Mrs Lindley's cousins offered to come and officiate for the time being. His coming was much looked forward to. Who was there in Aldecar the girls might marry? No one, absolutely: only colliers, petty tradesmen who despised the parson's poverty—and no one else. Miss Louisa and Miss Mary /⟨5⟩10/ were public figures. No one gave them any other name than Miss Mary, Miss Louisa. They were respected for their quietness and dignity, but Miss Mary was called haughty, Miss Louisa sulky. No wonder that the coming of an eligible and very distant relative was keenly anticipated, though little was said. The Lindleys, in their home, were silent, almost sullen people.

The Reverend Edward Massey arrived. It was a great shock to the women. He was a Cambridge man, thirty years old, Master of Arts in Roman Law, about to be preferred to a five hundred a year living in South Notts: to a tiny little place in the heart of agriculture. What could sound better to Miss Louisa and to Miss Mary. But he came. He looked like nothing in the world but an abortion, a foetus of a man. He was very little, meagre to the last degree, silent, very nervous, looked about him in a vacant, goggling way from behind his spectacles, was apparently an idiot: he had the stoop and the rambling gestures and the vacant expression of one. Yet one soon felt he had an indomitable little 'ego'. His silence became terrible when it would be followed by some venomous little sneer, or by his giggling little laugh of irony. Instantly the girls heard that, they were afraid of him. He was unremittingly shy, kind, and thoughtful as he could be: what he sneered at was stupidity, illogical reasoning. He would put himself to endless trouble to help anyone who asked for help, but was so agonisingly shy, that to proffer assistance was too much for him. He would sit up /⟨6⟩11/ with Mr Lindley if the pain were bad, would ⟨take⟩ great pains with the official regulations, spent diligent hour after hour in putting in order all the accounts and papers of his sick brother, thought out a plan for getting a younger son to Cambridge in a decent manner, undertook to carry it out—and so forth.

But in human relations he was intolerable. Quite unable to converse, he padded silently round the house, sat in the dining-room looking nervously from side to side, never joining in the family talk, but occasionally making some ironic remark, which would often be followed by a little, sneering giggle. No one else ever laughed. He was a man who always giggled alone over his own gibe.

Mary, in her queenly, patrician way, tried to be hospitable.

"You would perhaps like to take a walk?" she asked, raising her dark head from her sewing, and allowing her clear grey eyes to rest womanly upon him. This needed an effort, but she was schooled in self control.

The little man writhed with nervousness. He was painfully frail and thin. It was some time before he could answer, in rapid, fluttered tones:

"I may not walk far, thank you—thank you very much."

"You have not been well?" she asked, in her kind, dignified way.

"I have something wrong—internal," he replied.

He was not aware how this made her shudder inwardly. /12/

There was silence, whilst she, bowed over her sewing, recovered her composure.

"I am sorry to hear that," she murmured.

There was a long space of silence. At length it became intolerable.

"You will excuse me," she said. "I have to pay a sick visit."

He looked up, agog.

"I will do that," he said.

"No—it is rather far, and the roads are bad. I will go."

"I will go," he said, and he padded out of the room, fixedly keeping his idea. It never occurred to him to try to persuade anyone, and he never was persuaded. He seemed not to hear, he *did* not hear, persuasion.

Presently he returned wearing a cap, and buttoned up to the chin in a black overcoat. He was bent-shouldered. From behind he looked a sickly lad of thirteen. Mary pitied him, but she felt some aversion.

She was twenty-two years old, of handsome figure, tall and with beautiful repose of demeanour. Her clothes were poor. She wore a silk scarf round her neck because she had no furs. As the people saw her walking down hill to Old Aldecar, her tall and proud, beside the feeble little man, they turned and gazed after her dumbfounded.

"My Sirs alive, Miss Mary's got a catch there! Did ever you see such a badly little gudgeon?"

Miss Mary knew well enough what they thought, but she held /13/ her head only the proudlier. She pitied the little creature beside her.

They were going to see old Mr Durant, who was struck down with paralysis. Mrs Durant admitted them, and they went upstairs.

"How is Mr Durant this morning?" asked Mary.

"He seems no different to me—but there, how should he!"

The little man had not spoken. The three stood for some time looking on the form of the large old man stretched prostrate. The grey beard spread over the sheet.

"It is very dreadful," said Mary.

"It's how I always thought he would die," replied the wife, quietly. Mary looked at her, rather shocked.

The two women were uneasy, waiting for Mr Massey to say something. He had not spoken since he entered the house. At last, with a great effort, he said, blinking:

"It is a paralytic stroke?"

"Yes—the doctor gives him not more than three days now."

"Can he—can he understand?"

"Sometimes, a very little."

"Not—not—there is nothing I can do?"

"No thank you."

They stood again in silence. The sick man looked round vacantly. Except for his eyes, he was as one dead. To Mary this waiting was intolerable. What did Mr Massey want? She dared not turn to take leave, feeling that he had not finished. /14/

As they stood in suspense, they heard a man's footsteps, and then a man's voice called softly:

"Are yer upstairs, mother?"

Mrs Durant started. She was much agitated. She moved towards the stairs, but already the heavy tread sounded on the boards. The mother was at the top of the stairs, looking down. The son, running up quickly, said:

"He's not gone, mother? They let me off—"

Then he put his arms round her and kissed her. He was a young man in sailor's clothes. Mary stood much moved. Mr Massey blinked nervously: he seemed not to understand: the general emotion excluded him. They felt him there a witness, nervous, shrinking, but dispassionate. The mother and son conquered their emotion, entered the room. The sailor's boots clicked on the plaster floor. He was very ruddy, and he bowed his head with dignity. Miss Mary knew Alfred. She was ashamed to be there at the moment.

"The doctor gives him three days at most," said the mother.

Alfred, looking at the impassive form of his father, at the dead face and the great grey beard of the sick man, and at the wandering eyes, turned very pale. He bit his lip, and his breast began to heave.

"Oh, my son!" came a little cry from the mother. She had borne and hidden as much as she could bear, now she lifted her hands to him.

"Mother!" he said, and he hid his face on her shoulder. She /15/ wept a few, fierce sobs on his breast. She was a small woman, did not reach above his breast. Mary saw his form shake, but he made no sound. She and Mr Massey stood on one side of the bed, mother and son on the other. Between them was spread the dying man.

The young woman turned away, bitterly shamed to intrude. Mr Massey stood blinking. Mary knew he did not understand, neither the awfulness of death, nor the bitterness of grief, nor the keen pain of love. He was too small to contain the greater emotions. She felt a flash of hatred towards him.

"Shall I offer a prayer?" he said, gently, timidly, but in a voice devoid of understanding. The mother knelt down, hiding her face; the son knelt beside her. Mary and Mr Massey knelt on the other side the bed. The grey-bearded old man stretched between them.

Mary, grieved in her proud spirit, kept her head erect, and was open-eyed during the prayer. She saw the thin, brown hair of the mother, with its straight parting, close beside the dark head of the son, whose hair, thick and crisp with vitality, allowed no parting. She noticed the thin, white, grooved nape of the mother's neck, with its wisps of hair, and the flat broad strength of the son's. They knelt close together, as if they were lonely. Mary's heart stirred.

And all the time Mr Massey was praying nervously. His thin voice had a certain decision in it that forbade scorn. Mary heard whilst she watched. She noted the honesty of the prayer, its genuine kindliness, its almost scientific fittingness, and she respected Mr Massey. But there was a lack of reverence, a lack of the sense /16/ of the greatness of sorrow and of love, which made her ashamed to be there obtruding upon these people's natural nobility.

She talked about it to Louisa that night. She and Louisa were exceedingly dear to one another.

"Yes," said Louisa, "I often go and see Mrs Durant. There is a sense of honour about her."

Miss Louisa hungered for this, after the life at the vicarage.

"But he seems," said Mary, of Mr Massey, "he seems not to have more than a part of human nature."

"He's an imbecile, I think," said Miss Louisa.

"No he's not—oh no, not by any means! He seems to me like a —a seven month's child—or a six month's. Can you remember that—" She could not get any further.

"No but," she resumed, "he seems to have been born before his time—the spirit didn't fill into him. He's got all the sense—but not the understanding. That's why I shudder to be near him."

Nevertheless, in a year's time she was married to him. And never, in their courtship and marriage, did he kiss her. The religious ideal is self-sacrifice; her parents would have Mary sacrifice herself. In doing so, she practically cut herself off from the rest of the world. People looked at her /17/ husband, looked at her, and were shocked. This isolated her, as the little man was isolated. It would need a pathologist to study his mind, hers we can understand.

---

### 3

She went away with him to the tiny village. There, as everywhere, the men looked in contempt on him, the women in horror. Mrs Massey led a terrible year. Then her first baby was born. It was a healthy lad, bonny and fine. Her husband, in a kind of pleased amazement, entered the service of his child. His wife he tyrannised over, never harshly, and perhaps unconsciously. Yet he succeeded in tyrannising over her, first because of his abstracity, his unconsciousness of her, which made his mind use her as an insensate instrument, secondly because, once she revolted, even in a small thing, there would spring the irreparable breach between them—for she would have definitely to say to him: "No Edward, I do not wish to, and I will not do this," whereupon he would look at her in amazement and anger, not understanding anything but her thwarting of his just design: then probably there would be definite hostility between them, and she was afraid of it, so she submitted.—Once she revolted, the horror would be too great, the marriage would be smashed. She could go on in self-abnegation. But, of necessity, she must accept no sympathy. That would be to begin the revolt. This put barriers between her and her beloved. It put an unconquerable breach between her and Louisa. The two sisters loved each other devotedly, they continued to love each other all their lives long, yet after Mary's marriage there was a great, unspanned distance between them. They were never other than reserved and conventional one with the other, though /⟨8⟩18/ their souls were full of profound love.

This hardened the individuality of both women. Louisa, in face of such gross trespass, set up her own judgment. She had been brought up to submission, self-subordination, she had been trained never to judge save by the given canons, never to be independent, never to move save on authority. But now the woman in her rose and judged. "My father and mother did this to Mary: they would do the same to me. Is this love? I would die rather than be disposed of in such [a] way."

She *said* nothing, she *did* nothing: but her parents bore themselves deferentially towards her.

The one definite emotion she would allow herself to show was her loathing of her brother in law. On no occasion would she speak to him, or appear to notice him. This did not much matter, as he never addressed anyone save his wife.

Mary had another baby, a girl, when her boy was three years old. That year her husband's health was worse than usual, and he was always extremely delicate. Mary felt she could not endure to stay in her rectory this Christmas, it would drive her mad.

"I should like to go home for Christmas, Edward," she said. The little man looked at her for a minute or two, blinking, absorbing the idea.

"We should have to take baby by train," he replied.

"Baby is ten months old," she said.

"It is too cold," he said. /⟨9⟩19/

"It is not too cold, Edward. Whatever I suggest, you thrust 'Baby' in the way. It is enough to make me detest the child."

He cast up the balance of this. It seemed to him that it would never do to have hostility in the mother's feeling.

They went. When they were in the train, it began to snow. From the window of his first class carriage the little man vacantly watched the almost solid whirl of snow across the open country. The storm seemed worse owing to the race of the train.

"Sit right back in this corner," he commanded his wife, "and hold baby close back. We had better—we had better—." He tailed off, thinking in front of his words, or considering them not worth saying.

"Cross to this side, Jack, sit on this side, out of the draught," he commanded his young son.

"Look, mother, look!," cried the child, ignoring him. "They fly at my face—." He meant the snowflakes.

"Take this seat, Jack," the father repeated. "You're in a draught there." But in vain his command. He had not the slightest authority over the child.

"Tell him to come on this side," the little man ordered his wife.

"Jack, father wants you to come to this window," Mrs Massey said quietly.—"Come along," she added.

The boy slid over to her.

When they got to the vicarage at [Aldecar] it was half past two. They had not had dinner. /⟨10⟩20/

"How are you Edward?" said Mr Lindley in his most patronising tone. The vicar was pale and thin, with a worried, haughty look, and he gave one the impression of being coldly angry with the whole world.

"How are you Edward?" said Mrs Lindley. "You'll excuse me if I do not rise. What a dear baby!"

She was a stout woman with a heavy sulky jaw. Her voice was almost snarling. What she seemed to want was a passive existence of indifference. Everyone who spoke to her intruded upon her and made her angry.

"I did not want to bring the baby—I am afraid she has taken cold" was all Edward's reply.

"Nonsense Edward," said Mrs Massey, in wifely tones.

Louisa was looking at the baby, whom she had never seen.

"Ah, you poor little beauty," she cried. The baby was strong and healthy as the boy.

Edward glanced furtively at Louisa. She took no notice of him.

"Will you put baby into a hot bath, Mary?," the little man said.

"I think there is no need Edward," Mary replied.

"Don't you? I will go and bring down her flannels," he said, and he went upstairs to unpack the bag.

"I can give her a bath in the kitchen," said Mary, quietly.

"The girl is scrubbing there," said Louisa, very cold and displeased.

Louisa brought in the bath, and put it on the hearth rug.

The dining room was very gloomy and threadbare. The large window looked onto a scrap of lawn, hardly bigger than a white /⟨11⟩21/ pocket-handkerchief as it shone in the snow, and round the lawn was a barrier of black, high shrubs. Mrs Lindley was exclusive.

The pictures were black, their heavy gilt frames all dull. There were only ponderous dark ornaments of Victorian age, and the chandelier was so black and so barbarous looking, it should have hung in a vault.

In the warmth of the fire they laid the bath. Mrs Massey quietly undressed the child. The little man held the flannels to warm, and then the towel. The boy was hanging on the door knob to get out.

"Come away from the door, Jack," said his father.

Jack tugged harder at the door. Mr Massey blinked round like a naked owl shrinking up.

"Tell him to come away from the door, Mary. There will be a draught if he opens it."

"Jack, come away from the door. Go and tell Auntie Louie what you saw in the train."

Auntie Louie loved Jack, but she had eyes only for the domestic scene. Mr Massey stood with much solemnity holding the towel in readiness to receive the baby.

"Put me on this seat," cried Jack.

"Louie, do you mind lifting Jack," asked Mary. The father was not strong enough to do it.

When baby was flannelled, Mr Massey went upstairs, returning with four pillows, which he heaped before the fire to warm whilst the child was being fed. Again he stood waiting, watching /⟨12⟩22/ the mother and baby like a critical plucked owl that had a monomania.

Meanwhile Louisa, seething with rebellion, was preparing a meal for her sister and brother-in-law. The parents went upstairs, father carrying pillows, mother the baby. After a while Mr Massey came down.

"What is Mary doing?," asked Mrs Lindley.

Mr Massey started, and began to flutter.

"She is staying with baby till she goes to sleep. I may not stay upstairs in the cold because of my illness. Mary will ask the girl to put a fire in the room," the little man answered, rapidly and nervously.

"—But Mary has had no lunch at all," said Louisa, with hostility.

"I will take her something—what can I take?" he nervously asked.

No one said anything: because, through Mary, came nearly a hundred a year to help with the Aldecar vicarage.

"I would die rather than eat that little creature's bread," thought Louisa. Not because Mr Massey was mean, but because he had married her sister. Mr Massey was very generous to her father. Louisa went upstairs. Her sister sat there in the cold, silent and impassive.

"Your eggs are getting cold, Mary," she said.

"Baby will soon be asleep," Mary replied, in very quiet tones. It was the resignation that hurt Louisa most. She went downstairs.

"I have to go out," she said to her father. "I may not be home to tea."

---

### 4

No one remarked on her exit. She put on her fur hat, /⟨13⟩23/ that the village people knew so well, and the norfolk jacket that they said was immortal. Louisa was short, plump, and plain. She had her mother's heavy jaw, her father's proud brow, and her own grey, brooding eyes that were very beautiful when she smiled. It was true, as the people said: she looked sulky. Her one attraction, according to them, was her glistening, heavy, deep-blonde hair, which shone and gleamed with a warmth, a splendour that looked foreign to her.

"Where shall I go?" she said to herself, when she got outside in the snow. She did not hesitate, however, but, by mechanical walking, found herself descending the hill towards Old Aldecar. In the valley that was black with trees the colliery breathed in stertorous pants, sending out high conical columns of steam that stood upright, white as the snow on the hills. Louisa did not know in the least where she was going till she came to the railway crossing. Then the bunches of snow in the twigs of the old apple tree that leaned towards the fence told her she wanted to see Mrs Durant. The tree was in Mrs Durant's garden. /14[24]/

The old man had been dead some years. Alfred now kept his mother, and they two lived together in the old house that stood down in an ancient quarry bed, where the Durants had lived for a hundred years. From the highway hedge, by the railroad crossing, the garden sheered down steeply, like the side of a hole, then dropped straight in a wall. In this depth was the house, its chimneys just level with the road. Miss Louisa descended the stone stairs, and stood in the little back yard, the wall and the garden bank rising high behind her, the house sheer in front, while big boughs of the fruit trees bent overhead. It was a quaint, secret dwelling, down in that pit.

Louisa felt snug and secure from the world down there. She knocked at the open door, then looked round. The tongue of garden narrowing in from the quarry bed was white with snow: she thought of the thick fringes of snowdrops it would show beneath the currant bushes in a month's time. The ragged fringe of pinks hanging over from the garden brim behind her was whitened now with snow-flakes, that in summer held white blossom to Louisa's face. It was pleasant, she thought, to gather flowers that stooped to one's face.

She knocked again. Peeping in, she saw the scarlet glow of the kitchen, red firelight falling on the brick floor and on the bright chintz cushions. It was alive and magic as a peepshow. She crossed the scullery, where still /24[25]/ an almanac hung. Mrs Durant was nowhere about.

"Mrs Durant," called Louisa softly. "Mrs Durant!"

She went up the brick step into [the] front room, that still had its little shop counter and its bundles of goods, and called from the stairfoot. Then she knew Mrs Durant was out.

She went into the yard, to follow the old woman's footsteps up the garden path. Passing between the currant bushes, she went by the pigsty, that was dug out of the bank like a prehistoric dwelling, and where the pigs nosed towards her squealing. Then the wall ended, and the land shelved down to the path, the bright brown raspberry canes flourishing over her head, patches of snow between. She emerged from the bushes and canes. There lay the whole quarry bed, a great garden white and dimmed, lying half submerged. On the left, overhead, the little colliery train rumbled. Right away at the back was a mass of willow trees.

Louisa followed the open path, looking from right to left, and then she gave a cry of concern. /25[26]/ The old woman was sitting rocking slightly among the ragged snowy cabbages. Louisa ran to her, found her whimpering with little, involuntary cries.

"Whatever have you done?," cried Louisa, kneeling in the snow.

"I've—I've—I was pulling—a brussel-sprout stalk—and— Oh—h!—something tore inside me. I've had a pain—" the old woman wept from shock and suffering, gasping between her whimpers—"I've had a pain there—a long time—and now—Oh—Oh!" She panted, pressed her hand on her side, leaned as if she would faint as she sat, looking yellow white against the snow. She was turned seventy. Louisa supported her.

"Do you think you could walk now," she asked.

"Yes," gasped the old woman.

Louisa helped her to her feet. /⟨16⟩26[27]/

"Get the cabbage—I want it for Alfred's dinner," panted Mrs Durant. Louisa picked up the stalk of brussel sprouts, and with difficulty got the old woman indoors. She gave her brandy, laid her on the couch, saying:

"I'm going to send for a doctor—wait just a minute."

The young woman ran up the steps to the public house a few yards away. The landlady was astonished to see Miss Louisa.

"Will you send for the doctor at once to Mrs Durant," she said, with some of her father in her commanding tone.

"Is somethink the matter—?," fluttered the landlady in concern. Louisa, glancing out up the road, saw the grocer's cart driving to Eastwood. She ran out and stopped the man.

"Will you tell Dr Forman to come to old Mrs Durant at once. Dr Forman—old Mrs Durant—at once—say *I* sent you," Miss Louisa repeated as the man looked vacant.

"Is there—?" the man began.

"Be quick," commanded Louisa. And he went.

Mrs Durant lay on the sofa, her face turned away to hide its distortion from suffering.

"I'd better put you to bed," Louisa said. Mrs Durant did not resist.

Louisa knew the ways of the working people. In the bottom drawer of the dresser she found dusters and flannels. With the old pitflannel she snatched out the oven shelves, wrapped them up, ran and put them in the bed. From the son's bed she took a /17[28]/ blanket, and, running down, set it before the fire. Having undressed the little old woman, Louisa carried her upstairs.

"You'll drop me, you'll drop me," cried Mrs Durant.

Louisa did not answer, but bore her burden quickly to bed.

She could not light a fire, because there was no fireplace in the bedroom. And the floor was plaster. So she fetched the lamp, and stood it lighted in one corner.

"It will air the room," she said.

"Yes," moaned the old woman.

Louisa ran with more hot flannels, replacing those from the oven shelves. Then she made a bran bag, and laid it on the woman's side. There was a big lump on the side of the abdomen.

"I've felt it coming a long time," moaned the old lady, when the pain was easier, "but I've not said anything; I didn't want to upset our Alfred."

Louisa felt bitterly towards 'our Alfred.'

"What time is it?" came the plaintive voice.

"A quarter to four."

"Oh!," wailed the old lady, "our Alfred'll be here in half an hour, and not a *bit* of dinner ready for him."

"What shall I do?" asked Louisa.

"There's that cabbage—and you'll find the potatoes and the meat in the pantry—and there's an apple pie you can hot up. But *don't you* do it—!"

"Who will do it then?" asked Louisa. /18[29]/

"I don't know," moaned the sick woman, unable to consider.

Louisa did it.

The doctor came and gave serious examination. He looked very grave.

"What is it doctor?," asked the old lady, looking up at him with old, pathetic eyes in which already hope was dead.

"I think you've torn a bit of skin a tumour hangs in," he replied. "You've not *done* anything very serious."

"Ay!," she murmured, and she turned away.

"You see, she may die any minute—and it *may* be swealed away," said the old doctor to Louisa.

The young woman went upstairs again.

"He says the lump may be swealed away, and you may get quite well again," she said.

"Ay!," murmured the old lady. It did not deceive her. Presently she asked—

"Is there a good fire?"

"I think so," answered Louisa.

"Alfred'll want a good fire, coming home from the pit," the old mother said plaintively. Louisa attended to it.

Since the death of Durant, the widow had come to church occasionally with Alfred. And between Mrs Durant, in her age and sorrow and the young woman in her deep trouble, there had sprung a friendship. Mrs Durant had been fairly /19[30]/ well educated. She was still very active and energetic. With her, experience counted for something, and it was for this fruit of experience that Louisa came to her. Mrs Durant had had six sons and one daughter. The daughter had died a few years back, at the age of forty. Of the sons, one was killed in the pit, one was killed with drinking, another was killing himself in the same way, two were well-to-do miners, and Alfred, her youngest and her darling, was at home with her now.

As a boy, Alfred had been spoiled: him alone of all her children she spoiled. He was gentle, and somehow, full of native honour. On the other hand, he had grown ungovernably passionate, and unconsciously selfish. Like the other boys, he had wilfully insisted on going into the pit as soon as he left school. This had been a trouble to her. He had never drunk, however, and had never liked women's society, preferring his own company on the whole. The garden had occupied him when he was not in the pit, and besides this he was fond of swimming, and played cricket with the Church team.

Then he had run away and served seven years in the Navy. This had cured him of his spoiling. His love for his mother, rid of overgrowth, became the strongest force in his life, which life had remained remarkably pure. Now for four years Alfred had kept his mother at home. He was thirty one /20[31]/ years old, and had never had a sweetheart: not because he was timid or a ninny, but because he had never turned his thoughts to a girl, being never in a position to marry whilst his mother needed and monopolised him. He was very erect, very healthy, buoyant in his spirit. The Navy training had left him with a keen sense of his own person, so that he still did the physical exercises, bathed, and was carefully barbered. For the rest, he was naïve as a lad of fourteen, and played the flute very well. Miss Louisa had accompanied him at various concerts, so they knew each other, and were friendly. She did not concern herself seriously with him, because he seemed such a lad, amiable, and clean, but innocent of the dark and bitter side of life, which was her important side.

## 4[5]

It was not often Durant was impatient for the time to pass so that he could get away from pit. As a rule, he worked away vigorously in the stall with his mates. There were three butties and two day men in the stall. No one was worked harder than Durant, although, whilst they did a thing, most of the men did it lustily. Then they would sit and chat. Endless talk and gossip goes through the pit. Naked to the waist, hot and sweaty with labour, they would squat on their heels for a few minutes and talk, seeing each other dimly by the light of the safety lamps, while the black coal rose and jutted round them, and the props of wood stood like little pillars in a low, black, very dark temple. Then the pony came, and /21[32]/ the gang-lad would generally have some order, or a message from Number 7, or a bottle of water from the horse trough for a man particularly thirsty, or some news of the world above. The day passed pleasantly enough. There is, or was, an ease, a go as you please about a collier's day, and a delightful intimate camaradie of men shut off alone from the rest of the world, in a dangerous place, and a variety of labour, holing, loading, timbering, and a glamour of mystery in the atmosphere, that makes the pit very attractive to men who have thoroughly got used to it.

This day, however, Durant wearied of the afternoon. There was not a great deal to do: he did not want to talk. He never did talk much, and never about the Navy, which he had hated. He was sick of the pit that afternoon; by five minutes to four he was dressed and ready to depart.

"Loose-all," came the word. Durant would not quit the stall, as some of the men did, at a quarter to four, so that, after he had walked his mile underground, crawling out into the black bye way, pushing open with his shoulder the solid draught doors that the wind pressed hard, calling to the men swinging their lanterns, unrecognisable, along the underground main road, whose sleepers stand bolt out of the thick silted dust, and make the walking very heavy—standing in the hollows in the coal face as a little train rumbled by, hearing the drub drub of miners' feet echoing from the sleepers in the tunnel /22[33]/ he came at last to the white-washed coal walls of the underground office, and felt the warm, stifling presence of the stables. Round the bottom of the stack, down which black, heavy drops of water fell 'plop!' into the sump, sat dozens of miners, lighted by the electric lights and by the faint glare down the shaft. They had blown out their lamps.

"It's been snowin', Sorry!" exclaimed one of the men as Durant came up.

"Tha niver says!" ejaculated the young man.

"Ah bu' though, it has: four inch thick."

"Ne'er mind: ma'e us a' feel cosier when we get whoam."

"Tha mun well talk," said another, "as 'asna no farther than th' gates to go. If tha had ter lug up to Eastwood—"

"I sh'd 'appen get stuck 'a'ef way," said Durant.

"Ay ay!!" exclaimed a chorus of men heartily.

"Yes an' I'll wager tha would," said the man. "Tha'd want a drop o' summat ter get thee up ter th' top."

"I reckon my own legs 'ud be enough," said Durant.

"Tha'rt a big handy feller—what *dost* do wi' thysen? Tha'rt non married, tha'rt a teetotaller—"

"'E keeps rabbits," twitted another man.—Everybody laughed.

"But that's a rare house o' yourn. Tha might let me ha'e it when thy mother's gone. Why, you could put one leg out o' bed an' be down pit, and put t'other out on th'opposite side into th' New Inn." /[34]/

"Tha'd oftenest put thy left leg out," said Durant.

"'E would that!" and there was a shout of laughter. The thought of snow made the men merry.

The cage came down, a dozen men lined on. Durant noticed tufts of snow on the perforated dome, and on the bars. It pleased him, with its hint of white freshness, at the bottom of the pit.

"Yes, Sorry!" said an old man, as the chair rose, and the feet of twelve men vanished upwards. "Thy mother's non goin' ter last for ever. *Then* we'll see what'll happen, when an emp'y house turns thee out."

"I'm not goin' ter fret my fat about it yet," said Durant irritably.

"'Appen tha'rt not, 'appen tha'll ha'e to. 'Er's been lookin' poorly of late. Th'd better be castin' round thee for a 'ousekeeper o' *some* sort, ter take 'er place. Owd wimmen doesn't live for ever."

"Who said they did!" exclaimed Durant.

"Well, tha nedna get thy shirt in a knot. I'm nobbut tellin' thee. Tha'll be a bit more pal-ly, I'm tellin' thee, when 'er 's gone."

"Tha nedna din it in," said the young man.

"No—I'm not dinnin' it in. It on'y just struck me, tha'd ha'e ter ma'e pals o' some on us, when th' hearthstun wor emp'y."

The cage came down. Durant wrathfully watched the elder being whirled to realms above.

"It 'ud be a long time afore I made pals o' such as thaïgh," he muttered. The legs of the elder swiftly vanished.

Presently it was Durant's turn. /[35]/

The upper world came almost like a flash: the snow glimmered so. Hurrying along the bank, and giving his lamp in at the office, Durant came out into the open. Up the hills on either hand the snow went pallid and blue in the dusk. Along the railway the fall was mottled, but it stretched far off to the dark cave of the spinney, before which all was blue and smooth. To the west there was a pinkness in the sky, amongst which a star glimmered. Already the lights of the pit came out crisp and yellow, while the lights of Old Aldecar twinkled in a row in the bluish, raw twilight. /[36]/

Durant quickly swung down the line, among the dragging groups of miners. *They* were many of them bowed or twisted, had most of them the right shoulder higher than the left, but he was very straight and robust. He felt angry with the man for suggesting his mother might die.

## 5[6]

By the great, white gate of the railway, in the fence, was a little latch gate that he kept locked. As he unlocked this wicket, he noticed the kitchen window shone duskily onto the bushes and the snow outside.

"She's burning a candle till the night's fair set in," said he, smiling at her little economy. He slid down the steep path to the level below, and came through the bushes to the house. The mother, lying in bed, listening, exclaimed to herself, in panic:

"There he is!," as she heard his great boots ring on the scraper.

"I had better go and tell him," said Miss Louisa.

While she was running downstairs she heard him say, from the doorway:

"How much worth of oil do you reckon you save by that candle, mother?"

He had just put down his bottle and snap bag, and was hanging his coat behind the scullery door, when Miss Louisa came upon him. He was smiling. He ⟨had⟩ small, white teeth with spaces between them, and his /25[37]/ scarlet lips shone in his black face.

"Good evening!," said Miss Louisa.

He started round. Immediately his subconscious fear leaped up.

"Your mother's had a little accident," she said. His face went blank.

"How!," he exclaimed.

"In the garden," she answered.

He seemed quite dumbfounded.

"And where is she?," he asked.

"She's in bed," said Miss Louisa, who found it hard to deceive him. He was silent waiting for her to tell more: she did not know where to begin. He went into the kitchen, sat down heavily in his father's old chair, and began to pull off his boots. His head was small, rather finely chiselled. His dark hair, close and crisp, seemed too full of vitality. Having taken off his coat, his arms were bare to above the elbow. He wore a black waistcoat and the heavy, moleskin trousers that have just the stale, exhausted scent of the pit. Women hate the miners' cumbrous moleskins. He put on his slippers.

"What is it?," he asked.

"Something internal," she replied.

He went heavily upstairs. His mother was terrified at his coming. Louisa felt his tread /26[38]/ shake the plaster floor of the bedroom.

"What have you done?" he asked.

"It's nothing, my lad," said the old woman soothingly. "It's nothing. You needn't fret, my boy, it's nothing more the matter with me than I had yesterday or last week. The doctor said I'd done nothing serious."

"What was you doing?" asked her son.

"I was pulling up a cabbage, and I suppose I pulled too hard; for oh—there was such a pain—."

The son looked at her quickly. She laughed at him.

"But who doesn't have a sudden pain sometimes, my boy. We all do— — —."

"And what's it done?."

"*I* don't know," she said, making mock of her own hurt roguishly. "*I* don't know! Nothing, to my thinking. *I* don't know why they're keeping me in bed, I'm sure."

The big lamp in the corner was screened with a dark green screen, so that he could scarcely see her face. He shivered with apprehension, and with many emotions. All found vent in a burst of something like anger.

"What did you want to go pulling your inside out at cabbages for?" he said loudly. "I've told you times and enough not to do them things. Why couldn't you leave it for me to do? What the Hanover did you want to go dragging at cabbage at all for, in the snow, and /27[39]/ the ground frozen! Wasn't there no potatoes in the house."

"And *don't* you look down your nose if it's potatoes and cold meat," she teased him.

"No I don't, I never say a word."

"There's no need to *say*, your look is enough."

She had guided him safely away, and was smiling to herself. Miss Louisa, who could hear him plainly downstairs, thought he was [a] bully, and she was angry with everybody.

"But are you sure it's nothing much, mother?," he asked, plaintively, after a silence.

"Yes, my lad, yes," smiled the old woman.

"I don't want you to—to—to be badly—you know."

"I'm not badly," she mocked, and her heart wept with anguish, for she knew she was going to die: moreover the pain was torture just then. "They're only cossetting me up a bit because I'm an old woman. Miss Louisa's *very* good. I couldn't have thought anybody in the world could be so kind.—And she'll have got your dinner ready, my lad, and you must go and eat it, or else I s'll have to get up and look after you—and they say I mustn't, for a day or two at any rate— — —"

He felt very strangely choked, as if he could scarcely breathe: why did he feel so miserable, if she was going to be up in a day or two—and he believed her, that she would. He put his hard, black hand on hers for a moment: he was as black as a negro with coal-dust; then, /28[40]/ feeling a little bit relieved, he went downstairs.

He had resumed the old habit of his brothers of eating his dinner before he washed himself. Down the mine, he must eat his food amid stale air and coal-dust, and with black hands. What difference did his hands make at home!—Miss Louisa served him his dinner. She loved doing it, it was so living, so different from the hateful barrenness at home. It was so personal, to live in this way with people: it seemed to satisfy her. She watched him as he sat for a few moments turned away from his food, looking in the fire, thinking, and he seemed pleasant to her eyes. His black face and arms were strange, his red mouth under the small, trimmed, but very coarse-fibred moustache, that looked like cocoanut fibre, only of a lighter brown, startled her. But in its dirt his face had a kind of nobility, now he was sad and thinking. His coarseness was not repulsive to her, because it would wash off, and for the rest, he was so natural.

She ran upstairs, presently coming down with the flannels and the bran bag, to heat them, because the pain was on again.

"What's that?," he asked. He was half way through his dinner. His appetite vanished.

"To soothe the wrench," she replied.

He half rose.

"No," she said, "you mustn't go upstairs now." /29[41]/

He understood from her tone, and he sat down again. She went upstairs. The poor old woman was in a white, cold sweat of pain. Louisa wept silently to herself as she went about to relieve her, as she sat afterwards and waited. After a time, Mrs Durant said faintly:

"Alfred's washing himself—he'll—he'll want his back washing."

Louisa thought she was rambling, and did not reply.

"He says—he can't sleep if his back isn't washed—for the coal dust—," the old woman gasped. Louisa rose, wiped the cold sweat from her brow, and kissed her, murmuring:

"Must I go and do it?"

"If you will," murmured the sick woman.

Louisa waited till she saw her patient grow easier, then she ran downstairs. She scarcely considered what she was going to do. Like a nurse, everything was duty, nothing was personal.

Alfred was kneeling on the hearthrug, stripped to the waist, washing himself in a very large panchion of red, thick earthenware. It is so common for the men to wash themselves thus before the fire, that no one notices it, any more than if they merely were washing their hands. Even in [the] presence of strangers, it seems as natural to a miner as it seems to some folk to dip their fingers in a finger-bowl after dinner. /30[42]/

Alfred had just lathered his head thick with soap, and was rubbing the white cap of suds vigorously, doing the back of his neck repeatedly at the same time. Louisa watched him. It seemed a strange adventure to her, that she should wash the shoulders of a young man. When he had soused his head free of soap, and pressed the water out of his eyes, she said:

"Your mother said I was to wash your back."

He ducked his face round, looking up at her in a very comical way.

"How funny he looks with his face upside down," she thought. But she appeared so calm and official, that he merely groped in the black water, fished out the soap and flannel, and handed them backwards to her without a word. Then he remained with his two arms thrust straight in the panchion, supporting the weight of his shoulders. His skin was beautifully white and unblemished, of an opaque, solid whiteness. Miss Louisa flushed to the roots of her hair as she sponged him and saw that his neck and ears had grown flaming red. He was glad, however because he knew he was so perfectly developed, and in such good condition. She knew nothing either about development or condition, only that he had a beautiful skin. They were neither of them sorry when /31[43]/ the washing was done. She put down the flannel and fled upstairs, flushing furiously.

The pain was easier. Mrs Durant looked at the young woman and smiled.

"I'd forgotten you weren't used to the colliers," she said.

Miss Louisa did not answer, save to ask after the pain. Mrs Durant mused a while, then she said plaintively:

"I suppose you wouldn't marry a collier, Miss Louisa."

"I'd marry any man I loved," replied Louisa.

"Ah, we only love where we know it's any use, or else where we get encouraged to love, don't we?" said the old woman. Louisa experienced a great wave of revolt against her parents, and their outlook.

"Often!," she said, hotly.

Mrs Durant wondered a little at her. Then in a pain-weary voice she said:

"I'd leave him to you, if you'd have him."

"He hasn't asked me," quickly replied Louisa.

"If you let him—he will do," said the faint, monotonous, impersonal voice, that now sounded so tired and hopeless. Louisa was silent.

"And," the faint voice resumed, "if he's left with nobody, he'll go wrong. And after all my prayers for him, after all the prayers I've said for him, he mustn't go wrong. He must live here, for the garden—and—." /⟨32⟩31[44]/ She panted a little. Louisa kissed her, saying:

"You're tired—try to rest now."

She sat with the old woman's hand in hers, till Mrs Durant said, from out of a half-sleep of pain—

"Have you sent word to the vicarage?"

"No!"

"Oh, you must. You say you *will* stay. Send them word by Alfred," the plaintive singsong voice protested.

"I will write," said Louisa softly.

The young woman put Mrs Durant's worn old hand under the bed clothes, then went downstairs.

Alfred was sitting with his arms on his knees, his head dropped. He glanced up quickly. There was still in his face some of the red which the sea and the wind had beaten into it when he was a sailor. The skin on his cheeks was slightly irregular, as if it had been burnt. That was how it had suffered from exposure, because it was delicate. He put up his brown, crisp eyebrows in a question to Louisa.

"I want to write a note to the Vicarage—will you give me some paper?"

He looked at her very keenly. She noticed his eyes were golden brown, with a very small pupil.

"He is very keen sighted, he can see a long way," said Louisa, looking full at his eyes. "But he can't see into things, he's not introspective. Ah well!" /33[45]/ A certain look of misery about him told her that he felt, unconsciously, rather hopeless.

"Yes," she said aloud, "I am staying all night with your mother—just for company for her—and I wish to."

Quietly, with an accurate precision in his movements, and a certain unyielding carriage of the head, both due to his training, he supplied her with writing materials. It seemed to her very strange, and at the same time intimate and delightful, to have a man going about the house in his shirt sleeves, his waistcoat unbuttoned, his throat bare, waiting on her. He moved gracefully, with a vigour of limb.

As she sat writing, he placed another candle near her. Their rather dense light fell in two places on the rich overfolding of her hair till it glistened like a heavy live thing, like a dense golden plumage folded up. Then the nape of her neck was very white, with fine down and pointed wisps of gold. He grew warm. Suddenly, he realised that she was far above him, she was beyond him in education, in thought as well. Yes, she was beautiful. She had beautiful white plump hands— which had washed him an hour ago. He grew very hot. How beautiful she was—and how desirable. She must have a great store of inner riches. He longed for her keenly.

The candles glistened on her hair, and seemed to fascinate him. He felt a little awe of her. Till he got out of the house. Then suddenly he began to pant with sobs, because the snow and the stars made him feel that he was in the midst of sorrow, and of an immense, dark unknown. /34[46]/

---

### 6[7]

His heart was wrung with anguish. He ran up the road in an agony, not knowing what it was all about, but feeling as if red hot iron were gripped round his chest. He shook two or three tears onto the snow. Yet he vowed to himself he did not believe his mother would die. As he sat in the hall of the Vicarage, waiting whilst Mary put things for Louisa into a bag, he wondered why he had been so upset. He felt abashed and humbled by the big house, he felt again as if he were one of the common, cheap rank and file. When Miss Mary spoke to him, he almost saluted.

"An honest man," thought Mary patronisingly. But the patronage was only applied as salve to her own great sickness. She was rich, so she *could* patronise: it was almost all that was left to her.

Again, as Alfred came to the latch gate, he felt his grief come on him. He stood a moment looking northward to the Plough clambering up heaven, and at the far glimmer of snow in distant fields. Then his grief came on again like physical pain. He clung to the gate, gasping and panting 'Mother!' It was a fierce, cutting, *physical* fever of grief, that came on in bouts, as his mother's pain came on in bouts, and was so acute he could scarcely stand. The great emotions, love and grief, are beyond our knowledge and control. The real drama goes on beneath our knowledge. /35[47]/ The whole great tide of our soul, as it gathers hugely towards grief or love and death, we are not aware of, it is too big, too comprehensive, it carries all the fritter of life, all the fritter of emotions, all consciousness on its surface, as a boat loose on the dark sea knows the waves and ripples, but not the tide.

When the young man had regained control, he went indoors, and there he was almost gay. It seemed to him fun, adventure to have Miss Louisa staying in the house. He felt in high spirits: he was almost winsome in his little quips of jest. He sat on one side of his mother's bed, Louisa on the other, and all three were really gay. It was reaction.

Alfred kissed his mother and went to bed. When he was half undressed, the thought came upon him, his mother was ill, the knowledge came upon him that she was suffering dreadfully and was going to die, and he lay on the bed tight screwed up in agony. It lasted so long, and exhausted him so much, that he fell asleep, awaking after midnight to find himself stone cold. He undressed and got into bed, and was soon asleep again.

At a quarter to six he woke. Instantly he remembered. /36[48]/Having half dressed and lighted a candle, he went into his mother's room. He put his hand before the candle-flame so that no light fell on the bed.

"Mother!" he whispered.

"Yes," was the soft reply.

"Should I not go to work—I don't want to."

"I think I'd go, my lad."

"Are you sure you want me to, mother?"

He let his hand down from the candle flame. The light fell on the bed. There he saw Louisa lying looking up at him. She quickly shut her eyes and half buried her face in the pillow, her back turned to him. He saw the rough hair like vapour about her round head, and the two splendid plaits flung coiled among the bedclothes. It gave him a shock, and a peculiar flame passed over him. Louisa cowered down. He looked, and met his mother's eyes. He was bewildered.

"Yes, go to work, my boy," said the mother.

"All right," he replied, kissing her.

As he was going away he glanced again at Miss Louisa.

"Alfred!," cried his mother faintly.

He came back, with beating heart.

"What mother?"

"You'll always do what's right, Alfred?" the mother asked plaintively.

He was too terrified and bewildered to know what /37[49]/ she meant.

"Yes mother," he said.

She put up her mouth to him. He kissed her, then hurried away, from very terror. He went to work.

---

## 7[8]

By mid day his mother was dead.

The word met him at the pit-mouth. As he had known, inwardly, it was not a shock to him, only a ratification. He went home calmly, feeling only heavy in his breathing.

Miss Louisa was still at the house. She had seen to everything possible. Very succinctly, she informed him of what he needed to know. But there was one point of anxiety.

"You *did* half expect it—it's not come as a blow to you?," she asked, looking up at him anxiously. Her eyes were dark and calm and tender, with a certain assurance in their sorrow.

"No," he said. "I knew all along."

He looked aside, unable to endure her eyes on him.

"I could not bear to think I might have deceived you," she said.

"No, I'd gathered," he muttered.

Occasionally, he glanced at her furtively. He felt it a great strain to have her near him at this time. He wanted to be alone. As soon as the relatives began to arrive, Louisa departed, and came no more. While everything was arranging, and a crowd was in the house, whilst he had business to settle, he went well enough, with only those fearful private paroxysms of grief. Before the rest, he was whimsical, /38[50]/ almost gay. By himself, he endured the fierce, almost insane bursts of grief which make a man wonder what and where he is. They detach life from its normal station, and leave the sufferer bewildered in chaotic places, beyond the sphere of ordinary rational consciousness.

When all the people had gone from the Quarry Cottage, leaving the young man alone with an elderly housekeeper, then the real trial began. The snow had thawed and frozen, a fresh fall had whitened the grey, this then began to thaw. The world was an impossible place of livid grey slosh. Alfred had nothing to do in the evenings. He was a man whose life had been filled up with small activities: in summer the garden, swimming, cycling; in winter shoe-mending, soldering, making canny little contrivances for the household, and then smoking and reading for an hour or two, or practising for an hour on the flute, or playing a game of cards with his mother. The pivot and main-spring of his life had been his mother, as a woman usually is, knowingly or unknowingly, the main-spring and centre of a man's life. Even now, when the old housekeeper had gone home, he might still have gone on in his old way. But the force and balance of his life was gone. He was like a watch with the main-spring broken. He sat pretending to read, all the time holding his fists clenched and holding himself in, enduring he did not know what. He walked the black and soddened miles of field paths, till he was tired out: but all this was only running away from whence he must /39[51]/ return. At work he was all right: if it had been summer he might have escaped by working in the garden till bed-time. But now, there was no escape, no relief, no help. Man, perhaps, is made for action rather than for understanding; for doing rather than for being. Let him be shocked out of his activities, and the very life that supported him, suffocates him: as a whale that should suddenly forget how to swim.

For a week, Durant had the force to endure this suffocation and floundering, then he began to get exhausted, and knew he must come out. The instinct of self preservation became strongest. But then was the vital question: where was he to go? Either someone must come to him, and set him to his stroke again, or he must drink, to obliterate himself. These were the alternatives. He had longed like a sick man or a baby for Louisa to come to his aid: but she was again 'Miss Louisa.' On the Sunday after the funeral, when all the Durant people had attended church, Alfred had seen Miss Louisa, sulky and reserved, sitting with Miss Mary, haughty and very distant, and with the other Lindleys, who in their /40[52]/ poverty and pride seemed people removed, living in another pale world than the world of the miners. Alfred knew he could never cross over to this 'superior' world of theirs. Miss Louisa was beyond him. She could stoop to succour, as any great lady might, but she could not descend to give herself away. After service she had come to him, and shaken hands.

"My sister would like you to come and play the flute one evening, if you would be so good."

He looked at Miss Mary, who bowed. Out of kindness, Mary had proposed this to Louisa, although, strictly, she did not approve of Durant. In fact, she was slightly jealous.

"Well," said Durant awkwardly. "I'll come if you want me."

To himself he said "She feels sorry for me." And he was offended.

"You will come tomorrow evening then, about half past six." He went: he played his flute well enough. But Miss Mary, calling all her haughtiness to order, disapproved of him in the drawing room. He disapproved of himself. They had him stay to dinner, a paltry but genteel meal. They were all very nice. Mrs Lindley called him 'young man.'

"Will you sit here, young man?"

Mr Lindley kept a special tone for him, different from that he used to anyone else, even the maid: a kind of brother-in-Christ but er—you know your place, don't you! Durant was humiliated and angry. He was /41[53]/ perfectly self contained. Floundering as he was in the deeps of life, struggling under the surface of it all, such mere grimacing and antic roused his contempt. Yet he felt that these people had had their heads shoved under, knew what life was: but their knowledge was not allowed to extend to sympathy.

He left them in contempt. Miss Louisa felt this, and flushed to the very soul of her. They were all very quiet about him.

---

## 7[9]

Next evening Miss Louisa tapped at the door of the Quarry Cottage at half past six. He had finished dinner, the woman had washed up and gone away, but still he sat in his pit dirt. He was considering the question of the 'New Inn.' He would begin and go there—what else was there to do! It seemed a paltry thing to do. A public house was all right, a self respecting man need never drink too much: yet, at the bottom of his soul, he knew that to resort to alcohol, and to the public house, as an abiding resource, was only to clamber out of the water onto the mud that is more stable but far more deadly in its final suffocation. His own pristine honesty scorned the public house: go in, and watch the men, and see if they are not half sunk in contemptible mud. Nevertheless, he must go. He could endure himself no longer and he could think of nothing else.

He was in his pit dirt when he opened the door.

"I have been debating with myself whether to call—but I thought I would," she said, and she settled herself in his mother's low round-staved arm-chair. He often felt like pitching the /42[54]/ housekeeper out of that same chair, and now was relieved to see it restored to dignity.

"I ought to have been washed by now," he said, glancing at the clock, which was adorned with butterflies and cherries, and the proud name of "T. Brooks, Mansfield." He laid his black hands along his mottled dirty arms. Louisa looked keenly at him. There was a reserve, and a simplicity, which she respected in him.

"I am afraid," she said. "That I wasn't kind in asking you to dinner yesterday."

"Oh that's all right, don't you bother about that," he said, smiling with his mouth, showing the red lips and the small, interspaced white teeth. His eyes, however, were heavy and serious.

"I am not *bothering*," she smiled. Her repose was exquisite, and her dark grey eyes rich with understanding. He loved her violently. With this they left the subject.

"How do you get on alone?" she asked.

He glanced at her very quickly.

"He begins to read at the back of words," she thought to herself.

"Pretty bad," he answered, smiling.

Her face flew to a seriousness, as if she would weep.

"How close it is in this room. You have such immense fires. I will really take off my coat, if I may."

He watched her take off her hat and coat. She wore a cream cashmere blouse embroidered with gold silk. It seemed to him a very exquisite garment, fitting her throat and wrists so close. /43[55]/ He felt she was very lady-like.

"What were you thinking about that you didn't get washed?," she asked, gently. Again he glanced at her swiftly and furtively. The whites of his eyes showed very distinct in his black face. He laughed.

"Oh," he said. "I was just thinking what I should do."

"And what will you do?," she asked.

He shook his head quickly, and smiled.

"I can't tell you," he said.

"Why not?"

"I don't know myself."

"What were you *thinking* of doing?," she persisted.

"I don't know."

She left the question very abruptly. He would not confide.

"Your mother told me," she said, and the tears came to her eyes, "that if I had nothing else, I was to have that big flat brooch, with the pebble—that she always wore. I want it for her sake."

He started up in his chair.

239

"Our Fred took it. They all had their pick. They took everything.—
But I'll ask him for it back," he said.

"No—oh no—no, not for the world. I am sorry now that I
mentioned it. Don't think of it again please."

He was leaning forward on the arms of his chair, watching her
closely. Her face was crisped with keen emotion. She fought back her
/44[56]/ disappointment, which for some reason or other was very
bitter. Her face was pale and averted, her hair shone richer as she grew
white. She seemed herself so strong in her loneliness, that he knew
she must be accustomed to grief. He felt himself stifled. He bent his
face for a moment or two out of sight.

"I wish I'd ha' known," he said, in a low voice.

But by now she had recovered her composure.

"Oh, it's quite nothing. I only fancied it as a keepsake: and I had
harped on wearing it, you see, to keep me company. But it's gone now,
and it's quite nothing."

Which made him feel very hopeless again.

She reached for her hat. He cursed himself, hated himself: he didn't
know what for. Why is it that the climax of an emotion so rarely carries
the action with it, but either slips away as an opportunity, or else drags
the actual crisis clumsily some distance behind. She was pinning on
her hat. At any rate, he would tell her what he had been thinking. She
might— —.

"I was thinking," he said, answering her now distant question, that
he had balked before. "I was thinking there was nothing else to do,
so I'd just go across to the 'New Inn'."

She took her hatpin from her mouth.

"You remember your mother's last words," she said.

He stirred uneasily.

"But there's no harm in that," he said.

"And it isn't going wrong, even the least shade?," she asked.
/45[57]/

"Not with a man as knows how to restrain himself," he replied. She
did not suggest that this was open to question in his case, but:

"And can you think of *nothing* better to do?," she cried.

"I can't—can you? I've thought till I've felt as if I should burst
with thinking."

"*Nothing*?," she repeated, insistently.

"No nothing," he said stubbornly. "And there's no harm in it."

She quietly went on pinning her hat. The subdued finality of her movement terrified him. Feeling it was all over, he was trembling violently, and labouring with his breathing. She was buttoning the belt of her jacket.

"I will call occasionally, for your mother's sake," she said, very quietly, and distant. She was Miss Louisa now, with a vengeance.

"Can *you* think of anything else for me to do?," he cried, in a little frenzy of anger and grief.

"Not if you can think of nothing yourself," she said gravely.

"What's the good of thinking; I don't get no nearer."

She would not say anything.

"I could get married," he floundered.

"Get married, then," she said, with grave sternness.

"Who to?," he said, almost insolently.

She shook her head.

"That is your affair," she replied cruelly. She was angry with him.

"You've got to marry somebody," he protested.

This made her smile: what a child he was, after all his experience. /46[58]/ Still, perhaps he only meant to say, that he didn't know of anyone he wanted to marry. 'You've got to marry somebody—.'

"It is true," she smiled in answer to him.

"Well—!." He was at the end of his tether, and he could not give a jump and break it. His masculine modesty was worse than any maidenly.

She was angry with him, very angry. Should she leave him, the jibbing, shying child. She was piqued almost to that extent. But she was generous.

"Do you *want* to marry?," she asked, firmly.

He looked full at her, and trembled. "Oh these men!," she sighed.

"Do you *definitely* want to marry?," she persisted, with an effort. She managed to look up at him. She was startled, almost shocked. He was biting his lip with his white teeth, and from his eyes the tears were just running over. His face was quite distorted. Then she was very sorry. Her own tears sprang to her eyes.

"I will come if you want me," she managed to say, and as her voice broke, she crossed involuntarily to him, took his head on her bosom. He sobbed there a little while, painfully. It was not much he had ever cried, and it hurt. Her own tears fell fast on his hair.

In the end, when they were more quiet, she lifted his face, and kissed his forehead and his cheeks, tasting them of tears and coal-dust.

"I've been so upset with my mother an' one thing an' another," he mumbled, /47[59]/ very much ashamed of himself. She stooped and kissed him fervently. Then he closed his arms round her, and the dangerous light rose into his eyes as he looked at her. It was her turn to hide her eyes. She pressed her face on his bosom, which smelt so strangely of coal dust and perspiration and life.

An hour afterwards, when she stood disengaged again, he looked at her, and said laughingly:

"Your face is as black as a tinker's."

"And yours is piebald," she laughed.

"You're not going?," he said.

"I am already late for dinner," she replied.

"Stop here," he said. "You'll like it better than up there."

"That is a dishonorable suggestion," she laughed. "You have not proposed to me yet."

"I suppose it's not right to get married straight away?" he said.

"Does it seem right to you—when you think of your mother?" she asked him, seriously.

"Yes—she'd want me to—I know she would," he replied, almost with bitterness.

"Ay," she smiled, sadly.

There was a pause of silence.

"Did she say anything?" he asked.

Louisa nodded slightly. He seemed grateful as a child, and he held his breath to keep the tears back.

"I must go," said Louisa.

"If I was washed I'd come up the hill with you," he suggested.

"I'll wait five minutes. Wash your hands and face quickly."

/48[60]/

### 7.[10]

As they went up the hill, the night seemed dense with the unknown. They kept close together, feeling as if the darkness were alive and full of knowledge, all around them. In silence they walked up the hill. At first the street lamps went their way. Several people passed them. He was more shy than she, and would have let her go had she loosened in the least. But she held firm.

Then they came into the true darkness, between the fields. They did not want to speak, feeling closer together in silence. So they arrived at the vicarage gate. They stood under the naked horse chestnut tree.

"I wish you didn't have to go," he said.

She laughed a quick little laugh, mostly joy, but part sorrow of pity.

"Come tomorrow," she said in a low tone, "and ask father."

She felt his hand close like iron on hers. He took a deep breath.

"All right," he said at length.

She gave the same sorrowful little laugh of pity. Then she kissed him, sending him home.

At home, the old grief came on in another paroxysm, obliterating Louisa, obliterating even his mother for whom the grief was, raging like a burst of fever in a wound. So it was for a long time, these paroxysm[s] came on him.

## 8.[11]

The next evening he dressed to go to the vicarage, feeling as if he were going to be put to public shame and torture. He loathed to go. /49[61]/ They ushered him into the little study, which was fireless. By and by the vicar came in. His voice was cold and hostile as he said:

"What can I do for you, young man?"

"He suspects, and is angry," thought Durant, and for his own part he felt his antagonism revive. This vicar was so stuck up, and mean minded. Alfred rose, nervously gripping his cap.

"I think," he began, and then he felt himself growing doubtful. Very likely she would not have him after all—it seemed, /49[62]/ in the hateful atmosphere of the vicarage, a monstrous impertinence to have asked her. He hated the whole vicarage bitterly: it robbed him so of his natural value and manliness. He knew that there he showed common, cheap, vulgar—he almost felt so.

"You think—," said the vicar, sneeringly.

Durant broke into a cold sweat, but answered with perfect calmness.

"I asked Miss Louisa if she would come and live with me—"

"You asked Miss Louisa if she would marry you—yes—," corrected the Vicar. Durant reflected he hadn't asked her this:

"'If she would marry me'—and, I came to *tell* you."

"And perhaps you will inform me of Miss Louisa's answer."

"I couldn't tell you exactly," said Durant. He stood very erect, though he was white and sweating.

"Will you come this way," said the Vicar.

He led into the dining room, where were Mary, Louisa and Mrs Lindley. Mr Massey had returned home.

"I think this young man has asked you a question Louisa," said Mr Lindley.

"He has," said Louisa, her eyes on Durant, who stood erect, in discipline.

"And your answer?," asked the vicar in white wrath.

"I will marry him," said Louisa.

Mary bowed her head.

"Are you a collier?," cried Mrs Lindley, at Durant. He bowed.

"Yes madam." /50[63]/

"Then what impudence to think of it—" began the incensed mother.

"Hush mother, that is for Louisa to say," said Mary, with quiet bitterness.

"What means have you to support a wife?," haughtily demanded the vicar.

"My earnings average £120 a year: I have seventy pounds in the bank: the home is mine: and the lease of the house is to be transferred to me," answered Durant, like a sailor.

The vicar could not say "And what is this to support my daughter?," because it was well known he had little more himself. He did not know what to say. He was in a boiling rage.

"You do not consent, Ronald," prompted stout Mrs Lindley, who was roused to a great pitch of wrath. No child of hers should marry a *collier*, if she could help it.

"Certainly I will *not* consent, it is not right," snarled the vicar.

There was a tense silence in the room. Then Mary rose, pale, agitated with much bitterness. She was tall and well-dressed.

"Father, you will re-consider," she said, with a ring of very bitter command in her quietness. "And mother, please do not counter-command," she said. She leaned gracefully as she spoke. It was not apparent how violently she trembled.

Her parents went exceedingly pale. Mrs Lindley collapsed into her invalid condition. Mary watched her father. He cleared his throat several times.

"If Louisa—kh, kh!—if Louisa has accepted—kh!—then it is no use with holding my consent." Everyone waited. /51[64]/

"That is so, Hannah?," he turned to his wife for confirmation.

"I suppose so," said the mother, with sneering bitterness.

Mary sat down again slowly, sank her head, and beat her fingers lightly against her dress.

"Thank you father—thank you mother," said Louisa, in clear voice.

"Thank you sir, and madam." Durant bowed. "And you will marry us, Sir?" he asked.

The vicar hesitated: the vicar's lady shifted on her couch. The vicar looked at Mary. That daughter sat with head bowed right down, her face out of sight. He saw her fingers rapidly flying and beating the black voile of her dress.

"I will marry you, Sir," he replied.

"Thank you. And we will put in the banns—?", he glanced at Louisa. She pitied him the effort it was costing him.

"Now, if you will—," said Louisa.

"Will you take our banns, Sir, to be asked next Sunday, the Sunday after that, and the Sunday after that."

"No," cried the vicar.

"No, in this place, never," cried the vicar's wife.

Mary lifted her face. They were all afraid of her.

"I was married from this house, at your church, father, and so ought Louisa to be. There should be no difference for her."

The vicar stood and shook. He was dry lipped.

"I suppose it should be so and for her sake, I will—" he fetched the book. /52[65]/

As he was going, Durant shook hands with the Vicar, with Mrs Lindley, and with Mary. He kept himself in discipline to do so. Mary gave him her hand coldly, without looking at him.

As the sisters had never discussed the first bridegroom, so they did not mention this. Louisa did not even ask: "You agree with me, don't you, Mary?"—and Mary did not felicitate Louisa. There was a wider distance than ever between the two sisters. They were their husbands' women. They loved each other deeply, yet they went henceforward separate, scarcely holding any communication one with another. And neither ever stayed at the other's house.

Durant was infinitely glad of his wife. He served her his life long. But he had sufficient reserve, so that she never wearied of him.

She found a good deal of humiliation in her life: she was, socially, neither fish, flesh, nor good red herring, as she laughingly said to her husband. She refused the association of the miners' wives, and elsewhere she was refused. But what woman is not able to live socially alone, if it please her. She lived close and beautifully with her husband.

Alfred was quiet, and usually busy. Occasionally, after their marriage, he would sit and fall into an intense brooding. If she spoke to him, she would see his eyes draw away from her with a heavy, haunted look. Then she /53[66]/ knew she would have to leave him alone. At first, it was bitter to her. And at first, when she heard him in his sleep talking inarticulately, and evidently suffering again a little delirium of grief, she was tempted to wake him, to comfort him. But she did not. Then, when perhaps he seemed coarse to her, she remembered these things, and she readjusted her outlook.

He had a passion for the house and the garden, working at them unremittingly, scheming, planning, carrying out little improvement after improvement, little convenience[s] for his wife, making one thing after another please her taste. Soon, wherever she looked about the house or garden, she saw his spirit: she was always using things he had contrived to be handy to her, or taking pleasure in things he had planted for her.

"The house is fairly clothed round with his work," she said to herself once as she sat waiting for him to come from pit. Then suddenly she saw that their home was a fabric made out of his energy of tenderness: he had woven it out of his spirit. She sat still and worshipped in reverence. And she thought of the vicarage, where she had lived. Her children would be born into a real home, whose very stuff would have in it some of their father's spirit—and their mother's—and of their forefathers' and foremothers'. It would be nearly like a living thing, of their own blood. It was indeed a home. She dreamed of the boy, like Alfred, who would have the home when she left it. He would be like Alfred, but she would educate him.

She had several children, and was not disappointed. /54[67]/

# Explanatory Notes

## The Prussian Officer

1:1–2 **The Prussian Officer [Honour and Arms]** Written in June 1913, 'Honour and Arms' appeared in heavily cut form in the *English Review* in August 1914 and in *Metropolitan* in November 1914. DHL restored the cuts and made some minor revisions in 1914 for the first edition. 'Honour and Arms' is a quotation from G. F. Handel's oratorio, *Samson* (1743), where the giant, Harapha, taunts the blinded Samson: 'Honour and Arms scorn such a Foe,/Tho' I cou'd end thee at a Blow.' For this story DHL drew on his observations of the Bavarian infantry regiments and on the landscape of the Isar and Loisach valleys during his two sojourns in Bavaria in June–August 1912 and April–June 1913.

4:32 **Herr Hauptmann** Captain (German).

5:10 **cast** Squint.

7:26 **Schöner** Literally 'handsome' (German).

7:37 **dithering** Confusing.

11:36 **hook** Crook (dial.).

11:38 **the shepherd** Is DHL thinking of Christ comparing himself to 'the good shepherd' who 'giveth his life for the sheep' (John x. 11)?

## The Thorn in the Flesh

22:1 **The Thorn in the Flesh** Written in June 1913 as 'Vin Ordinaire', this very different version of the story was published in cut form by the *English Review* in June 1914. It is set in Metz, on the outskirts of which Frieda's father, Baron Friedrich von Richthofen, lived in a French grange similar to that described in the story; Alsace-Lorraine was under German occupation (1871–1918). The Baron, like his fictional namesake, had been wounded in the right hand (37:23–4). Revised extensively in July and October 1914, it was retitled in reference to St Paul in 2 Corinthians xii. 7: 'there was given to me a thorn in the flesh, the messenger of Satan to buffet me, lest I should be exalted above measure.'

28:29 **Fräulein** Miss (German).

29:39 **the frontier** Metz was less than eight miles from the French border.

30:15 **Sacred Heart ... *prie-Dieu*** In Roman Catholicism devotion to the Sacred Heart of Jesus originated from a vision experienced by a French nun, Marguerite M. Alacoque (1647–90). *Prie-dieu*: prayer-stool (French).

31:39 **the Reichshalle** Official state building (German); town or city hall.

33:29 **"Wenn ich ... Mutter seh' ..."** 'When I go to my child / I see his mother in his eye' (German), from the ballad opera *Die Zillerthaler* (1848) by J. F. Nesmüller.

36:31–2 **In this ... her being** Cf. 'For in him we live, and move, and have our being' (Acts xvii. 28).

37:26 **Ober-leutnant** [Army] lieutenant (German).

# *Daughters of the Vicar*

40:1 **Daughters of the Vicar** First written as 'Two Marriages' in July 1911 and revised that autumn for the American *Century* magazine, which rejected it, this story was rewritten in July 1913 when DHL gave it its present title. After further rejections he heavily revised it in July and October 1914. The Lindleys are partly modelled on the family of the Rev. Percival Page, 4th vicar of Brinsley (cf. Aldecross), north of Eastwood, from 1881 to 1918. In 1906 Mabel, his eldest daughter, married the Rev. Albert C. Hooper, who had helped in Brinsley parish in 1905. The Durants occupy the cottage at Brinsley crossing lived in first by DHL's grandparents, then by his uncle George. However, it was DHL's brother George who joined the King's Own Scottish Borderers in 1895 to the vexation of his mother.

41:3 **throng** Pressed for time (dial.).

41:4 **we're chapel** Nonconformist, as opposed to Church of England; by implication, working class rather than middle class.

42:26 **wideawake** Soft felt hat with broad brim and low crown.

43:4 **tundish** Funnel (dial.).

48:25 **chétif** Weak, sickly (French).

65:19 **a bran bag** A flannel bag filled with bran and warmed up in the oven.

66:1 **swaled away** Wasted or consumed (dial.).

68:6 **Fabians** Members of the socialist Fabian Society, founded 1884.

69:1 **"Loose-all"** Whistle signalling end of shift (dial.).

69:11 **"A green Christmas, a fat churchyard"** Old superstition that the infirm die more readily when cold weather follows Christmas.

70:9 **snap-bag** Bag containing miner's meal to be eaten during a shift.

87:30 **Barford** I.e. the nearest registry office where they can be married; Barford is based on Basford, a suburb of Nottingham.

## A Fragment of Stained Glass

88:1 **A Fragment of Stained Glass** First called 'A Page from the Annals of Gresleia', then 'Ruby-Glass', this early version of the story was submitted as a competition entry in the *Nottinghamshire Guardian* in 1907. When DHL rewrote it in 1911 a new title, 'The Hole in the Window', was erased in favour of the present title. This revision was published in the *English Review* for September 1911. It was lightly revised in 1914 for Duckworth. Beauvale is based on Greasley, east of Eastwood, and its vicar on the Rev. Rodolph, Baron von Hube, vicar of Greasley from 1866 to 1907. DHL was indebted for historical details in the story to von Hube's antiquarian *Grisleia in Snotinghscrire* (Nottingham: Nottingham Book Co., 1901).

88:28 **a Laocoön** A classical statue of the Greek priest Laocoön and his two sons being squeezed to death by sea serpents.

89:13 **wrathed** Angered (arch.).

95:1 **rose-berry** Berry of the wild rose.

95:20 **stems** Makes headway (dial.).

## The Shades of Spring

98:1 **The Shades of Spring** DHL first wrote a story on this theme (called 'A Modern Lover') early in 1910 after reviving his love affair with Jessie Chambers during a visit home at Christmas. In December 1911 he wrote a second story on the same theme first called 'The Harassed Angel', then 'The Right Thing to Do / The Only Thing to be Done'. Revised in March 1912 with a new title ('A Soiled Rose'), it was published in the American *Forum* in March 1913 and in the *Blue Review* in May 1913. Heavily revised in July 1914 under the title 'The Dead Rose', it was further revised in October 1914 when it received its present title. Willey-water Farm is based on the Haggs Farm north of Eastwood, where the Chambers family lived. Hilda is loosely modelled on Jessie Chambers, and Syson on DHL.

102:7 **pippin** Pipkin or cooking pot (dial.).

104:10 **"What a ballad of dead ladies!"** Cf. 'Ballade des Dames du Temps Jadis' by François Villon (b. 1431), tr. by Dante Gabriel Rossetti (1828–32).

104:32 **a sycock** A mistle-thrush (dial.).

105:15 **a throstle's or a blackie's** A song-thrush's or a blackbird's (dial.).

105:31 **Arcady** Arcadia, an ideal region of rural felicity in classical literature.

110:3 **'Qu'il était ... l'espoir'** 'How blue was the sky, and high the hope', lines 13–14 of Paul Verlaine's 'Colloque sentimental' published in *Fêtes Galantes* (1869).

110:8 **his Botticelli angel**  Cf. *Sons and Lovers*, where Miriam (also based on Jessie Chambers) 'always reminded Paul of some sad Botticelli angel' (chap. VII).

110:11–12 **Dante to some Beatrice**  Dante Alighieri (1265–1321) wrote the *Vita Nuova* about his youthful love for Beatrice.

110:30 **the poem of William Morris**  William Morris's 'The Chapel in Lyoness' (1856) was collected in *The Defence of Guenevere* (1858).

## Second–Best

113:1 **Second–Best**  Written in August 1911, this story was published in the *English Review* in February 1912. It was extensively revised in July and October 1914 for book publication.

114:15 **Ollerton Feast**  Ollerton, 17 miles north of Nottingham, had a fair or feast day on Mayday.

114:32 **fret her fat**  Wear away her fat through worry (dial.).

115:15 **joie de vivre**  Joy in life (French).

119:1 **moudiwarp**  Mouldywarp or mole (dial.); literally 'earth-thrower'.

119:3 **got your rag out**  Made you angry (dial.).

## The Shadow in the Rose Garden

121:1 **The Shadow in the Rose Garden**  Written in autumn 1907, the story was probably revised in August 1911; it was published in the American *Smart Set* in March 1914. In July 1914 DHL revised it, rewriting the end completely, and only lightly corrected the proofs in October 1914. DHL, his family and Jessie Chambers went on holiday to Robin Hood's Bay in Yorkshire in August 1907 and this provides the setting for the story.

121:9 **"The Stag at Bay"**  Famous, much reproduced painting (1846) by Sir Edwin Landseer, RA (1802–73).

125:21 **standard bushes**  Roses whose stem is supported by a 'standard' or stick.

126:37 **John Cotton**  Popular brand of tobacco.

132:11 **the whole hogger**  'All the way' (sexual slang): this passage provides the earliest example in *A Supplement to the OED* (ed. Burchfield).

## Goose Fair

133:1 **Goose Fair**  First written by DHL's fiancée, Louie Burrows, in 1909, it was revised by him in October 1909 and published in the *English*

*Review* in February 1910. In July 1914 DHL heavily revised this version for the Duckworth first edition. Nottingham's Goose Fair occurs early in October. DHL set his story in the 1870s during a period of industrial unrest. Lois and Will are modelled on two of DHL's fellow students at University College, Nottingham.

133:20 **passing through ... white lace** Lace-drawing, removing the connecting threads between the strings of machine-made lace.

134:2 **stockingers** Weavers of stockings.

134:9–10 **war with the Prussians** The Franco-Prussian War, July 1870–February 1871.

135:2 **Man proposes – the devil disposes** Deliberate misquotation of Thomas à Kempis's saying, 'Man proposes but God disposes', in *De Imitatio Christi* (1418).

135:7 **the Lambs** The Nottingham Lambs were men paid during the 1860s to create disturbances at Parliamentary elections.

136:9–10 *Sesame and Lilies* Book of lectures by John Ruskin published in 1871; its second section is concerned with the 'queenly power' and responsibilities of women.

141:10 **tanger** Tang means to pierce or sting. Hence a sharp, stinging person (dial.).

141:16 **squirts an' teasers** Water-squirting syringes and whips.

141:17 **off their dots** Off their heads (slang).

## The White Stocking

143:1 **The White Stocking** First written in 1907 as an entry for the Christmas competition in the *Nottinghamshire Guardian*, this version was based on an incident in DHL's mother's youth when she attended a ball at the Castle in Nottingham (see 150:7). Twice revised in January 1910 and April 1911, it was rejected by the *English Review* and further revised in August 1913 for publication in the American *Smart Set* in October 1914. DHL rewrote the story in July 1914 and heavily revised it in October for the first Duckworth edition.

143:5 **"What the Hanover's ..."** Euphemism for 'what the hell', derived from the unpopularity of the first two Hanoverian kings, George I and II.

143:18–19 **"Rise up ... shine forth"** Cf. 'Arise, shine; for thy light is come, and the glory of the Lord is risen upon thee' (Isaiah lx. 1).

143:28 **seven and sixpenny house** I.e. with a rent of seven shillings and sixpence a week.

145:40 **a comic** I.e. a comic valentine card.

146:18–20 **"Doctor Wyer ... puff!"** Nursery rhyme turned into a popular music hall song in the nineteenth century.

149:3–4 **like chickens . . . to roost**   Proverb: 'Curses, like chickens, come home to roost', i.e. rebound on the head of the curser.

150:29 **an *amourette***   Cupid: a 'passing affair' in French.

160:5 **backfire**   I.e. put on the back of the fire.

160:26 **trolley**   Trollop, sexually promiscuous woman (slang).

## A Sick Collier

165:1 **A Sick Collier**   Written in March 1912 and revised in July 1913, the story, set in Eastwood, was published in the *New Statesman* on 13 September 1913. It was further revised in July 1914 for the Duckworth edition.

165:22 **gaffer**   Master (dial.).

166:8 **clommaxed**   Clumped (dial.).

166:14 **snap-bag**   See note on 70:9.

166:17 **clammed**   Famished (dial.).

167:27 **hawkse**   Haul (dial.).

167:31 **sleck**   Slack; small coal (dial.).

168:8 **the national strike**   26 February–11 April 1912.

168:37–9 **skinchin' . . . blood-alley**   Being mean . . . bright red marble (dial.).

171:2 **gorping . . . clat-fartin'**   Staring . . . gossiping (dial.).

## The Christening

172:1 **The Christening**   Written in June 1912 as 'A Bag of Cakes', then as 'Pat-a-Cake, Pat-a-Cake, Baker's Man' before being retitled 'The Christening', revised in July 1913, this story was published with four short cuts by the American *Smart Set* in February 1914. In July and October 1914 DHL revised and rewrote the ending for its book publication. DHL based this story on the actual Eastwood home and family of Joseph Winterbottom, an ex-miner, his three daughters (two of them schoolmistresses) and one son.

175:33 **hub**   Hob.

177:25 **A man-child . . . unto us**   Cf. 'A man child is born unto thee' (Jeremiah xx. 15).

179:13 **Blortin'**   Bellowing nonsense (dial.).

179:27–32 **"Pat-a-cake . . . baby an' me –"**   Traditional children's song. 'A bun in the oven' is slang for a baby in the womb.

180:14 **they clap . . . the morning**   Cf. 'all the trees of the field shall clap their hands' (Isaiah lv. 12).

## Odour of Chrysanthemums

181:1 **Odour of Chrysanthemums**  Written in 1909, this story was revised for the *English Review* in March 1910, again that summer, and in
April 1911 for its publication in the June 1911 issue. In July and October
1914 DHL made extensive revisions including rewriting the ending on
both occasions prior to its appearance in the first edition. The story is
partly based on DHL's uncle, James Lawrence, a miner, who was killed
by a fall of coal in Brinsley Colliery in 1880. He and his wife lived in the
cottage described in the story. They had three children including one
born after the father's death. However, DHL also drew on his own
parents' marital relations for some of the story.

181:17 **the whimsey**  Pool of water near the pithead originally used for the
steam winding engines ('whims' or 'whimseys').

181:33 **winter-crack trees**  Late-ripening plum trees.

183:1 **mash**  Make tea (coll.).

183:35 **settler**  A conclusive argument (dial.).

185:9 **ripping**  Cutting away from the roof of the stall being worked.

185:28 **waflin**  Waving (dial.).

190:6 **Loose-a'**  See note on 69:1.

190:11 **bantle**  Batch, group of men (dial.).

190:34 **butty**  Middleman or contractor who agrees to raise coal at so much
a ton.

198:24 **not dead**  The page proofs for *The Prussian Officer* read 'dead'.
There is no knowing if the alteration was DHL's or a presumptuous
printer's.

199:21 **she winced ... and shame**  The page proofs for *The Prussian
Officer* continue beyond this enigmatic ending with: 'For in death she
would have no life, for she had never loved. She had life on earth with her
children, that was all.'

## 'Odour of Chrysanthemums' fragment

205:12 **Ah, the pity of it!**  Cf. *Othello* IV. i. 205–6: 'O! Iago, the pity of it,
Iago!'

## 'Two Marriages'

*Note*  These notes supplement those on 'Daughters of the Vicar' where new
material requires them.

212:31 **that choice of it**  Think that highly of it (dial.).

216:2 **a badly little gudgeon**    Poor-looking simpleton (dial.).
228:18 **nedna get thy shirt in a knot**    Needn't get upset (dial.).

## POUNDS, SHILLINGS AND PENCE

Prior to Britain's decimalization of its currency in 1971, the pound sterling (£) was divided into 20 shillings (20/- or 20s). A shilling was itself worth 12 pence or pennies (12d).

A price, therefore, could consist of three elements: pounds, shillings and pence (£, s, d). Thus it might be written as £2 4s 6d or £2/4/6, which was spoken as 'two pounds, four and six(pence)' or 'forty-four and six'. Prices below a pound were written as 19s 11d or 19/11, and spoken as 'nineteen and eleven(pence)'. The penny was itself divided into two half-pennies or four farthings.

The guinea was £1 1s and was used by professional men such as doctors as the unit with which to charge fees. Four guineas meant £4 4s and half a guinea was 10s 6d. The coins in use in DHL's time were the sovereign (£1) or 'quid', the half-sovereign (10s), the half-crown (2s 6d), the florin (2s), the shilling (1s) or 'bob', the sixpenny bit (6d) or 'tanner', the threepenny bit (3d), the penny (1d) or 'copper', the half-pence or ha'penny (1/2d), and the farthing (1/4d).

Since 1971 the pound has consisted of 100 pence distinguished from the old pennies by the use of 'p' instead of 'd'.

# Further Reading

For a listing of the numerous articles about the stories collected in *The Prussian Officer and Other Stories*, see the bibliography at the back of Janice Harris's book, listed below. This should be supplemented for works later than 1983 by the MLA Bibliography on disc.

Black, Michael, *D. H. Lawrence: The Early Fiction*, Macmillan, 1986. (*Concentrates on patterns of imagery.*)

Cushman, Keith, *D. H. Lawrence at Work. The Emergence of the* Prussian Officer *Stories*, University Press of Virginia, 1978. (*Traces the evolution of six of the stories.*)

Ford, George, *Double Measure: A Study of the Novels and Stories of D. H. Lawrence*, Holt, Rinehart & Winston, 1965.

Garcia, Reloy and Karabatsos, James, eds., *A Concordance to the Short Fiction of D. H. Lawrence*, University of Nebraska Press, 1972.

Harris, Janice H., *The Short Fiction of D. H. Lawrence*, Rutgers University Press, 1984. (*The most reliable book devoted exclusively to DHL's short fiction.*)

Hough, Graham, *The Dark Sun: A Study of D. H. Lawrence*, Duckworth, 1956.

Leavis, F. R., *D. H. Lawrence: Novelist*, Chatto & Windus, 1955. (*Devotes an entire chapter to 'Daughters of the Vicar'.*)

Moynahan, Julian, *The Deed of Life: The Novels and Tales of D. H. Lawrence*, Princeton University Press, 1963. (*One of the most perceptive treatments of DHL's short fiction.*)

Sagar, Keith, ed., *A D. H. Lawrence Handbook*, Barnes & Noble, 1982.

Spilka, Mark, *The Love Ethic of D. H. Lawrence*, Indiana University Press, 1955.

Thornton, Weldon, *D. H. Lawrence: A Study of the Short Fiction*, Twayne Press, 1993. (*Contains criticism of selected stories by author and other critics.*)

Vivas, Eliseo, *D. H. Lawrence: The Failure and Triumph of Art*, Northwestern University Press, 1960.

Widmer, Kingsley, *The Art of Perversity: D. H. Lawrence's Shorter Fictions*, University of Washington Press, 1962. (*Concentrates on DHL's perverse, self-annihilating modes of experience.*)

## Further Reading

Worthen, John, ed., *The Prussian Officer and Other Stories* by D. H. Lawrence, Cambridge University Press, 1983. (*The authoritative edition on which this text is based with informative introduction, notes and textual apparatus.*)

# READ MORE IN PENGUIN

In every corner of the world, on every subject under the sun, Penguin represents quality and variety – the very best in publishing today.

For complete information about books available from Penguin – including Puffins, Penguin Classics and Arkana – and how to order them, write to us at the appropriate address below. Please note that for copyright reasons the selection of books varies from country to country.

**In the United Kingdom**: Please write to *Dept. JC, Penguin Books Ltd, FREEPOST, West Drayton, Middlesex UB7 0BR*

If you have any difficulty in obtaining a title, please send your order with the correct money, plus ten per cent for postage and packaging, to *PO Box No. 11, West Drayton, Middlesex UB7 0BR*

**In the United States**: Please write to *Penguin USA Inc., 375 Hudson Street, New York, NY 10014*

**In Canada**: Please write to *Penguin Books Canada Ltd, 10 Alcorn Avenue, Suite 300, Toronto, Ontario M4V 3B2*

**In Australia**: Please write to *Penguin Books Australia Ltd, 487 Maroondah Highway, Ringwood, Victoria 3134*

**In New Zealand**: Please write to *Penguin Books (NZ) Ltd, 182 190 Wairau Road, Private Bag, Takapuna, Auckland 9*

**In India**: Please write to *Penguin Books India Pvt Ltd, 706 Eros Apartments, 56 Nehru Place, New Delhi 110 019*

**In the Netherlands**: Please write to *Penguin Books Netherlands B.V., Keizersgracht 231 NL–1016 DV Amsterdam*

**In Germany**: Please write to *Penguin Books Deutschland GmbH, Friedrichstrasse 10–12, W–6000 Frankfurt/Main 1*

**In Spain**: Please write to *Penguin Books S. A., C. San Bernardo 117-6° E–28015 Madrid*

**In Italy**: Please write to *Penguin Italia s.r.l., Via Felice Casati 20, I 20124 Milano*

**In France**: Please write to *Penguin France S. A., 17 rue Lejeune, F–31000 Toulouse*

**In Japan**: Please write to *Penguin Books Japan, Ishikiribashi Building, 2–5–4, Suido, Bunkyo-ku, Tokyo 112*

**In Greece**: Please write to *Penguin Hellas Ltd, Dimocritou 3, GR–106 71 Athens*

**In South Africa**: Please write to *Longman Penguin Southern Africa (Pty) Ltd, Private Bag X08, Bertsham 2013*

# READ MORE IN PENGUIN

Penguin Twentieth-Century Classics offer a selection of the finest works of literature published this century. Spanning the globe from Argentina to America, from France to India, the masters of prose and poetry are represented by the Penguin.

If you would like a catalogue of the Twentieth-Century Classics library, please write to:

Penguin Marketing, 27 Wrights Lane, London W8 5TZ

(Available while stocks last)

# READ MORE IN PENGUIN

## A CHOICE OF TWENTIETH - CENTURY CLASSICS

**Ulysses**   James Joyce

*Ulysses* is unquestionably one of the supreme masterpieces, in any artistic form, of the twentieth century. A modernist classic, its ceaseless verbal inventiveness and astonishingly wide-ranging allusions confirm its standing as an imperishable monument to the human condition. 'It is the book to which we are all indebted and from which none of us can escape' – T. S. Eliot

**The End of the Affair**   Graham Greene

'One of the most personal and most interesting of Greene's stories, containing not only his mature thoughts on the literary life and the dubious fame it brings, but also on the nature of an adulterous love affair, the joy and guilt it generates in roughly equal proportions' – Anthony Curtis in the *Financial Times*

**Tigers are Better-Looking**   Jean Rhys

Jean Rhys wrote about women – society's victims – with all the passion and despair of a loser. Set in Paris, London and the Caribbean, her bitter-sweet, tantalizingly evocative stories conjure up the loneliness of a rented room, the regrets of a failed love affair and the temporary oblivion of alcohol with astonishing power and poignancy.

**Babbitt**   Sinclair Lewis

In chronicling the follies, ambitions and fantasies of Babbitt, Sinclair Lewis captures with superb realism and biting satire the small-town mentality of America in the twenties. 'One of the greatest novels I have read for a long time' – H. G. Wells

**The End of the Chapter**   John Galsworthy

Here Galsworthy writes about the lives and loves of the Cherrells, cousins of the Forsytes. Galsworthy's grasp of political and social change and its effect on a family, as well as his incisive sense of character, make this a fine trilogy with which to end The Forsyte Saga.

# READ MORE IN PENGUIN

## A CHOICE OF TWENTIETH - CENTURY CLASSICS

### Between the Acts   Virginia Woolf

'Her posthumous novel ... suggests several new directions ... Its weave of past and present, quotidian reality and imminent catastrophe, the thin line between civilization and barbarism, its erotic overtones and continual humour make a powerful and prophetic statement' – *The Times*

### Gentlemen Prefer Blondes   Anita Loos

*Gentlemen Prefer Blondes* had its first acclaimed appearance in *Harpers Bazaar* and was later made famous on stage and screen. In this brilliant satire of the Jazz Age Anita Loos has created the funniest Bad Blonde in American literature.

### The Living and the Dead   Patrick White

To hesitate on the edge of life or to plunge in and risk change – this is the dilemma explored in *The Living and the Dead*. 'Scene after scene is worked out with an exactness and subtlety which no second-string novelist can scent, far less nail to paper' – *Time*. 'He is, in the finest sense, a world novelist' – *Guardian*

### Go Tell It on the Mountain   James Baldwin

'*Mountain* is the book I had to write if I was ever going to write anything else. I had to deal with what hurt me most. I had to deal with my father' – James Baldwin. 'Passionately eloquent' – *The Times*

### Memories of a Catholic Girlhood   Mary McCarthy

Blending memories and family myths, Mary McCarthy takes us back to the twenties, when she was orphaned in a world of relations as colourful, potent and mysterious as the Catholic religion. 'Superb ... so heartbreaking that in comparison Jane Eyre seems to have got off lightly' – Anita Brookner

# READ MORE IN PENGUIN

## A CHOICE OF TWENTIETH -CENTURY CLASSICS

**The Grand Babylon Hotel**  Arnold Bennett

Focusing on Theodore Racksole's discovery of the world inside the luxury hotel he purchased on a whim, Arnold Bennett's witty and grandiose serial records the mysterious comings and goings of the eccentric aristocrats, stealthy conspirators and great nobles who grace the corridors of the Grand Babylon.

**Mrs Dalloway**  Virginia Woolf

Into *Mrs Dalloway* Virginia Woolf poured all her passionate sense of how other people live, remember and love as well as hate, and in prose of astonishing beauty she struggled to catch, impression by impression and minute by minute, the feel of life itself.

**The Counterfeiters**  André Gide

'It's only after our death that we shall really be able to hear'. From puberty through adolescence to death, *The Counterfeiters* is a rare encyclopedia of human disorder, weakness and despair.

**The Great Wall of China and Other Short Works**  Franz Kafka

This volume contains the major short works left by Kafka, including *Blumfeld, An Elderly Bachelor*, *The Great Wall of China* and *Investigations of a Dog*, together with *The Collected Aphorisms* and *He: Aphorisms from the 1920 Diary*.

**The Guide**  R. K. Narayan

'There is something almost Irish in the humour, buzz and blarney of Narayan's world which seems continents removed from the anguished India of most fiction, and the rope trick of irony, fun and feeling is beautifully adroit' – *Observer*

**The Fight**  Norman Mailer

In 1975, at the World Heavyweight Boxing Championship in Kinshasa, Zaïre, an ageing Muhammad Ali met George Foreman in the ring. Mesmeric and profound, *The Fight* covers the tense weeks of preparation and the fight itself.

# READ MORE IN PENGUIN

## D. H. LAWRENCE

NOVELS

Aaron's Rod
The Lost Girl
The Rainbow
The Trespasser
Women in Love
The First Lady Chatterley
The Boy in the Bush
(with M. L. Skinner)

Lady Chatterley's Lover
The Plumed Serpent
Sons and Lovers
The White Peacock
Kangaroo
John Thomas and Lady Jane

SHORT STORIES

Three Novellas: The Fox/
  The Ladybird/The Captain's
  Doll
St Mawr *and* The Virgin and
  the Gipsy
Selected Short Stories
The Complete Short Novels

The Prussian Officer
Love Among the Haystacks
The Princess
England, My England
The Woman Who Rode
  Away
The Mortal Coil

TRAVEL BOOKS AND OTHER WORKS

Mornings in Mexico
Studies in Classic
  American Literature
Apocalypse
Selected Essays

Fantasia of the Unconscious
  *and* Psychoanalysis and the
  Unconscious
D. H. Lawrence and Italy

POETRY

D. H. Lawrence: Selected Poetry
Edited and Introduced by Keith Sagar
Complete Poems

PLAYS

Three Plays

Penguin are now publishing the Cambridge editions of D. H. Lawrence's texts. These are as close as can now be determined to those he would have intended.